TITAN
RACE

TITAN RACE

Book One of the MANU SERIES

Edentu D. Oroso

ISBN : 978-1-989524-02-2

Melodicrose Publishing

www.melodicrosepublishing.com

Published by Melodicrose Publishing Montreal

PRAISE FOR TITAN RACE

"Edentu's writing is so layered with sensory descriptions. I'm in awe at how he describes a landscape, a skyline, a car approaching a place...and how he leaves the reader with something so tangible, so visual to experience. Edentu's words carry you in and out of scenes with real-time fluidity. Masterful prose!"

Maribeth Parot Juraska, Ed.D., author and retired Professor of English.

"Titan Race is a compelling original story with a strong narrative voice, a captivating adventure, full of intrigue that will leave readers voracious for more."

Mopelola Adeniyi, author of A Rough Diamond.

"A classic in the making: this highly imaginative story written like the old masters, will transport your mind into another spectrum. With the superb use of the English language, and cleverly interwoven with modern day romance, this well-crafted TITAN RACE is the ultimate for Science Fiction/Fantasy lovers."

Charles Ayling, author of Sunrise at Noon and the forthcoming Borneo Experience.

For Weriepere . . . .

Whose care was boundless.

ACKNOWLEDGEMENTS

I owe a debt of gratitude to the following for fine-tuning the manuscript to what it is:

Andrew Ame-Odindi Abah, I can't thank you enough for your edits, recourse to details and patience.

Camellia Morris, you're such a rare breed and friend. I treasure your support.

Mar Marburg, I'm glad our paths crossed. Thanks for being a great friend and beta reader. Domo arigato mi Amiga always.

Dahna Schaublin, I'll always remember your insightful beta reading.

Sam Ogabidu, I'm honoured by your enduring friendship; for always nudging me on, believing and over-hyping this story.

Aditya Deshmukh, you're an amazing and talented friend and editor who saw lapses where others didn't.

Corrie Lavina Knight, Mick Rose, Benoit Chartier, Ayo Gutierrez, and a host of other talented writers too numerous to mention, thank you so much for your invaluable feedback on the first few pages of this book.

Mark Ogbuabo, Gloria Chima and James Shinyi, I'm grateful for your wonderful typesetting of the first draft of the manuscript and friendship.

THE TITANS ARE COMING!

When the day dims and the golden glimmer of an age
Wears no more the hood of its proud beginnings,
The gardeners will once more prune their fields:
The Titans are ploughing!

When all else is noise, and the fury of the ascent
Robs the light of day and enthrones dusk at dawn,
The silver skies will once more split with meaning:
The Titans are sowing!

When the stars starkly sing of their toil
To keep us abreast of the sea to which we plunge,
Know the big bell of time has tolled:
The Titans are reaping!

When even breath is fouled by earth's own dust
And the sun and the moon are no longer in concert
And the earth cringes to its own resonance:
The Titans are here.

Table of Contents

Part One

NEWLAND, RIAGENA

Newland, Riagena. January 10, 1996......................3

Wisdom Hall, Disk Center, Blackhole................... 13

Sagol Sea, Newland, Riagena. 23

PlayToy, Xamuder, Mars.. 37

Newland, Riagena. January 14, 1996. 51

Part Two

ATLANTIS

SONGHAI, ATLANTIS. Twenty-five thousand
years ago. 133

Disk Center, Blackhole... 162

Disk Center, Blackhole. 248

Fini blanched. 266

Part Three

NEWLAND, RIAGENA

Newland, Riagena. January 16, 1996. 301

Part Four

BLACKHOLE

Disk Center, Blackhole. 2023. .... *399*

Part Five

NEWLAND, RIAGENA

Part One

NEWLAND, RIAGENA

MODERN DAY

Chapter One

Newland, Riagena. January 10, 1996

The old wooden armchair creaked as Netu Deo steadied himself on it. His gaze fixed on the blanket of darkness beyond broken panes in the bedroom window. The creepy cry of an owl was answered by the high-pitched chant of crickets. Like a sad song from a mourning crowd, it sent a chill snaking up his spine.

Netu stood from the armchair and strode to the open window. Parting the cream curtains apart, he let in the musty air. A huge ball of bright light streaked across the dusky evening sky, trailing an explosion of fading colors.

His heart pulsed faster. Something seemed out of place. Balls of light seldom flashed before his eyes, except as triggers of imminent, urgent action.

Netu's dark brown eyes widened in search of the next sign. The brief glimmer of a red star amid the splash of orange-gold in the sky caught his attention. He acknowledged this as the symbol of the Guardians, call to duty.

"Not again! Enough of this Guardian game," Netu

said, scratching his close-cropped black hair. The strands, taking on an extraordinary flair, as they reflected the moon's ribbons of gold. "Got to do it my way."

"Pick up your gauntlet and fight, Netu," ordered an inner voice. "Time to meditate."

Netu turned on his heels, eyes darting around the bedroom. But nothing stirred beyond the pounding of his heart.

He pondered. Why should I pick up my gauntlet and fight?

When no answer came, Netu retraced his steps from the window and went to the left corner of the red rug in the bedroom. There he sat down and began to meditate as commanded.

Soon after, Netu felt the gentle sensation of his soul's upward drift. Now enveloped in bright light, his winged soul rose in degrees out of the apartment. It soared with ease on the soft currents, heading toward the horizon beyond Newland's network of skyscrapers.

A spectacular view panned out in his gaze. On the eastern stretch, a mass of water came into view. He reckoned this as the Sagol Sea, its waves rippling only to break against the sand. A stand of pine trees on the western belt tapered off to the farthest reaches of Newland, Riagena's commercial city. The northern horn held a network of beaches, broken here and there by a couple of mangrove-lined tributaries. The light of the full moon caressed the world softly, like the touch of petals and kept his soul and everything else aglow with streams of orange-gold.

A strong current welled up inside of Netu at that moment, pulling him backwards, as if to re-possess his body - the damp clay he had broken away from moments earlier in the bedroom. This frightened him.

Netu managed to maneuver to a stop in the return flight. He turned sideways in the sky and noticed a sea of flickering light points heading in his direction. They came rather fast, shooting towards him from the direction of the forest of pine trees. At once sensing danger, he built a force-field around himself and waited for the inevitable.

"Damn the Secthwi," Netu cried as he discerned the flickers of light as swords brandished by fierce looking cult members.

Recent confrontations between him and the notorious cult flashed through his mind. They hated his guts, as much as he hated the thought of their evil ways.

"The Secthwi be damned!" he fumed once more, as they assumed a formation around him from a distance of about fifty meters.

They charged at him in unison, cursing. Their swords missed target and clanged instead against each other's.

"Bastard," thundered a Secthwean in a guttural voice. "Get him. Don't let him get away. He deserves to die, get him."

"Come get me, fools," Netu leered, laughing.

"Hit straight and fast," snapped another Secthwean. "Make every blow count."

"Come on, let's do it," ordered Netu's first attacker.

They swooped like a hive of angry bees towards Netu's spot in the sky, lashing out at him from different directions. "Strike hard. Hit him," they chorused.

To their surprise, Netu did not shift from one jot, neither did his poise show any sign of fear or weakness. His eyes blazed instead with an unknown flame. The twenty swords descended on Netu like bullets shot at an armored tank, ricocheting off an invisible shield he had cast.

"Proving to be a tough guy, ehn?" a Secthwean raged, sensing how ineffectual their attack had been.

A triumphant grin reared on Netu's face, as his assailants again charged in a new formation. "Fools! Get the job done, won't you?" Netu mocked.

"The great Secthwi," boomed the one in charge. "The stupid dance of a dog doesn't frighten a lion in the forest. Let's finish our war. Kill the bastard."

"Kill the bastard. Kill the bastard," the entire throng roared.

Netu stretched forth his right hand above his head, reaching for something in the sky. For a giddy moment, his hand remained suspended. By the time he lowered it, he held a flaming sword. A gift from the realm of the Guardians, he thought.

"You want war, right? Then war you'll have," ranted a Secthwean, soaring from the right flank, upon sighting Netu's sword.

"We'll spill your damn blood, bastard," hollered the leader of the group, swinging his sword at Netu.

Netu parried the blow, thrusting his blade into his attacker's midsection. Drawing blood with his sword, he smiled over his feat. "Not as smart as I thought."

The Secthwean lost his balance, screamed in agony and plummeted downwards. This stunned the rest of the assailants. In telepathic accord they regrouped in a V-like formation and charged again at Netu.

With a circular motion of his left palm, Netu cast a huge film of protective white light around himself. Enveloped now in the dazzling bubble, he laughed. "Get the job done, fools."

Netu repelled his attackers arrayed now in an arc formation. A few of those not already in the semi-circle flew towards the rest with flaming swords, to serve as buffers.

Netu had the upper-hand. The serrated blade of his sword impaled a Secthwean's right side who, gurgling and groaning aloud, tumbled headlong.

The front-line of the attack regrouped as a result into two clusters of five each. One band had the leader of the Secthwi in front and the other had its own cluster leader. All set to end a battle that began twenty-five thousand years ago.

Netu's opening prowess might have bloated his ego. But the unrelenting spirit of the horde worked in their favor. Not more than a heartbeat's span, Secthwean swords descended on Netu's protective shield.

Three of them attacked him from behind while four others came at him from the front. Dodging their ferocious blows instinctively as he could, Netu did not notice the two men who sneaked upon him from the left flank with their blazing swords directed towards his nape. Looking askance, he parried both swords and took an offensive pose.

Netu's dare emboldened the invaders who realized they could hold their forte with almost the same stoicism, batting away his swipes and thrusts, but not with his kind of perfection. This came with a measure of respect for Netu.

It was the opportunity he needed. In quick succession, Netu delivered his sabre and drew swathes of flesh and blood spurting from two Secthweans who had underestimated his prowess and commitment to winning the aerial battle.

To Netu's far right, the sword of a solitary invader, morphed into a bow and quiver.

"No escape this time," the attacker mumbled and fired.

The arrow sped through its course without harm against the envelope of white light Netu had conjured against it. The Secthwean realized his best shot could not permeate Netu's ancient power shield. His stunned gaze deterred the rest cult members for a few seconds.

"So you want to use ancient power now?" groaned a Secthwean close to Netu. "Then it is ancient power you'll get in return."

"Bring it on," Netu retorted.

"Spells of fire," another guy barked through their thought-waves. "Aim at his bubble of light. Do it!"

Huge forge balls hurtled from the glistening, fiery eyes

of the Secthweans towards Netu's bubble, somewhat neutralizing his protective spell. Rendered vulnerable for a moment, Netu swiped his sword in defense. A powerful flame oozed from it, deflecting the combined force of the enemies' forge balls skywards as they reached him. They screamed in throes of pain, hit by the flood of flames from Netu's sword ricocheting against theirs.

Capitalizing on their momentary discomfort, Netu lashed out at two of the bodies nearest to him on the right with his sword's cavorting flame. His broad wings flailed out with searing and blinding crimson light. One of them got disoriented by the burst of burning light from Netu's wings.

"Son of a seven-humped toad," the man bellowed. "Power of the Sacred Light. That's what he's using. Power of the ancients. Neutralize him fast," he agonized, plummeting.

"Gadabaa gadabaa datushii," the rest of them chanted in unison. *"Bantaliyaa kumkushii kumkushii."*

Metallic wings sprouted from their shoulders like alloys in a furnace. *"Zuunkalii beyatushii,"* they chorused again. *"Taaduun zuwuyaa kumtubuu kumtubuu."*

Their shapes altered into fierce-looking creatures with human bodies and eagle-like heads. And their swords took on flames like Netu's.

"Idaatushii brigidaa idaatushii," Netu retorted with his transformation into a lion's head with wings flapping and burning so bright. *"Brigidaa mekatanube mekatanube."*

"Taaribatusikayaa," he chanted further, charging at the throng of Secthweans with his wings and flaming sword.

Missing them in his path, he glided sideways. He kicked out with his legs, hoping to stun a few others with the torrent of fire from his mouth, wings, and sword.

They surged forward in defiance and tried to cut off Netu's wing flaps with their metallic wings of fire. He evaded these, soaring above their trajectory.

Not what I thought, Netu cursed, confounded by the Secthweans' resilience. He powered his flaming wings for another attack from a vantage position, but they spewed forth more fire balls from all directions.

Now he almost could not keep track of his bearing. Knowing he could only outwit them with brevity, he enveloped himself in a bubble of fire. "Tired of the chase and flight so soon?" Netu mocked. "C'mon, let me feel your pulse."

In his light globule, Netu reached out to new heights in blighting speed, blocking the Secthweans' weapons with it. When they rushed at him at his new height, he dived low and flew sideways at an odd angle. He returned blow for blow, sword for sword, swing for swing, not the least intimidated by their massive attack.

The risks in the aerial clash were glaring. The warrior in Netu, yet, refused to cringe, no matter the odds. He made a fast detour to safer ground only when his chances of victory in the air seemed slim.

Newland's deserted, broad Sapphire Street provided the next battlefield. The Secthweans were fast in pursuit along the street's sleek pavement. They swelled in number as other members from neighboring alleys who were not part of the aerial battle joined in the fray.

The music of the dance changed with the emergence of the new Secthwi cult members. Netu had a new kind of problem to tackle. Their serrated swords now became pump-action guns. He saw that coming. He knew they could not outsmart him in a game of swords and sorcery being a Guardian. The guns would be it, the last resort. Rather than shoot, they formed a horizontal file. Sneering and daring him to escape as they closed ranks on him on a street lit by the moon's streaking orange-gold.

"The game is over, I guess," jeered a Secthwean from the motley crowd. "As you can see, you're going under."

"You think so?" Netu asked, his eyes flaring like a raging flame.

The Secthwean spat on the ground in mockery, eliciting a peal of laughter from his colleagues. "Want to make a last wish, bastard?"

"Nah! Foul mouth would only lead you to your grave, fool! Your types don't scare me. Not the least. Go on with what you have in mind." Netu never meant what he said, but wanted enough time to manage the crisis on hand.

The Secthweans gained a few more paces, edging closer now to Netu on the silky pavement, aiming their guns at target. His heart pumped faster. A numbing sense of fear reeled up his spine. Flapping his huge wings, he leapt to a free spot on the pavement. This surprised and caused them to give way as he readied himself for the kind of fierce attack he envisioned. By a stroke of luck, he happened to be standing on the pavement's intersection with an alley – the perfect opening he needed to stun them with superior tact.

When Netu leapt again on the offensive, a few paces from the street corner, a Secthwean shrieked with a mixture of surprise and terror. The man's howl as Netu's wings hit him resounded enough to startle others closing up on Netu.

Not spooked enough by Netu's attack, one of the startled men struck back with a gunshot at Netu's ribcage. The hot lead grazed Netu's body without spraying blood. Instead, the lead rebounded and flayed the Secthwean's flesh clean from his bulbous body like a sword. The man growled like a mad bull, attracting the attention of his co-combatants.

The Secthwean leader cursed under his breath, sensing another painful loss. He could not marshal a frontal attack and be everywhere at the same time, the reason they came out in droves. So, honoring his groaning comrade with a baleful, farewell glance, he swung around and sought swift revenge on Netu.

Firing his pump-action gun at the smokescreen spell cast by Netu around his body, the Secthwean had hoped to wreak a prompt and satisfactory vengeance. He fell back instead on the pavement in a pool of his own blood due to the gun's jerking force and the rebound power of Netu's Sacred Light. He stared up in fright at Netu's foreboding sword descending like a menacing guillotine.

With a gibberish war cry and the instinct of a warlord, the Secthwean leader rose and dashed to a safer spot on the pavement near the point in the alley's intersection. This move had its merits for it took him to the middle of the other Secthweans who now interposed themselves between him and Netu. It also gave Netu the breather he needed to re-launch his assault.

Nursing his great wound in the midst of his colleagues, the leader bawled. "Damn, he's got me! Kill the fool! Kill him now!"

His second-in-command, a wiry man of average height with blistering eyes, took a lethal sword swipe at Netu. They heard a deep crunch as if a bird's bone had broken into two as Netu deflected the sword towards a Secthwean on his left hand side. Netu's burning sword sundered the Secthwean's sword, and took with it the poor fellow's foot.

A few seconds later, two guns thundered from the direction of the horde in the vague skylight. Netu repelled the shots with a quick motion of his left hand. He noticed his sword again transforming into a pump-action gun, with which he sprayed deafening rounds of salvos at them. The Secthweans' cries in the crossfire rent the evening's silence. Fate, yet, had a bigger surprise for Netu.

# # #

Wisdom Hall, Disk Center, Blackhole.

Numa paced back and forth close to the Command Module mains in Blackhole's Wisdom Hall, his mind ravaged by deep thoughts. Inflamed by an intuitive disposition, he could not resist the urge to look at the backdrop of the Command Module, where the time screens were situated.

The first time his sweeping glance went in the direction of the screens, the scenes of Riagena flickered into view, appearing normal enough not to worry himself or the other Guardians. It had other images. Some of the various Playhouses of the Guardians across the galaxy were also harmless by his reckoning. However, they did not call him patron of the Blackhole for nothing. A prophetic gift and rare acuity into the past remained a part of the lining of his consciousness. He called forth and dispensed of such foreknowledge, at will. Though he fought the desire to ignore the screens, his intuitive nature, gave him keen insight into the danger regarding the Guardian in Riagena. Thoughts of their PlayToy loomed in his mind.

The monitors drew his attention for the second time, and he thought, *Why such an impulse? Certainly, our Playhouse must be on the boil again.*

The screens converged into a singular screen as his thought waves aligned with the scenes. Netu's soul drifting away from his body and subsequent flight over the expanse of Newland appeared on the main screen. Numa observed Netu's gradual increase in altitude and felt a sense of elation in the manner the athletic thirty-three-calendar old Guardian, whom they called Finia in Blackhole, tried to master the sea of ether. The way Finia manipulated his soul's flight, especially in his new disposition as the PlayToy's Guardian after a faltering start, amused Numa.

Just then, Numa saw the horde of fast-approaching Secthweans from beneath Finia's flying form. How right his intuition had been! Danger! His huge wings stopped their gentle flutter as he became engrossed with the scenes of the Playhouse.

14

Titan Race

The energy-field oozing forth like a film of gas on the vague floor of the Wisdom Hall increased in intensity in consonance with his thoughts. His eyes, sparkling and enchanting like the essence of a Blackhole's radiation, dimmed now as his brow arched in thought. The furrows on his kindly, feline face added layers of age to his otherwise time-defying handsomeness when seen in the light of his close-cropped gray beard, moustache, and flowing white dress.

Numa glowered reckoning with the scheme of things on the PlayToy.

"This must be it. I bet our Guardian is on the scale once more. Let's see how he fares this time."

Meanwhile, Ramune, a towering Guardian, a suave character with an aquiline nose and light-blue eyes, regarded as the witty one of Blackhole's bunch, walked into the Disc Centre along with Hemse, a fellow Guardian.

"Another Guardian on the grille, Father of the Blackhole?" Ramune asked.

Hemse could barely wait for Numa's response; his deep-set, brown eyes flared, probing. Hemse had a way of lurching his broad shoulders upwards to boost his near six feet if worried about a thing. Numa's inference to the Guardian, in Riagena, had pricked his curiosity.

"We got bathed in your thought waves. We thought it wise to check what possibly could be amiss," he said, jerking his shoulder for emphasis.

Numa ignored Hemse. Instead, he pointed at the monitors with his brow kneading. The aerial battle between Netu whom they referred to as Finia in

Blackhole and the Secthwi cult came across as enough evidence of his worries. The three Guardians watched in silence as Finia took on the Secthwi cult, stunting at times so low, and then soaring in desperation so high, all in the bid to escape to safety from their swords and use of the Power of the Sacred Light.

At a point, Finia's victory seemed certain to the Guardians for they felt it too ordinary. Yet, they observed how he made a quick detour to Sapphires Street, Newland, Riagena when the chase became too fierce for his comfort. In spite of it, the Guardians nursed no fears until the Secthweans aimed an array of pump-action guns at Finia. This apparent disadvantage caused by the Secthweans' numerical strength and weapons against Finia made them glance at each other with a faint hint of apprehension.

Hemse's impatience glared in his restless shuffling of legs, which left quaint scars in the cloudy film of gas on the floor of the Disc Centre. "Could this be a floundering of a Guardian or what? Can't find the right words to explain Finia's weakening of spirit."

"It's a question of their numbers and weapons," Ramune said. "I'm not sold on the idea that Finia is scared. Maybe a bit disadvantaged. That's all to it - a fundamental disadvantage."

"He ought to ride on the crest of the storm; turn his situation into an advantage. It demands our support, though."

"Certainly.""And fast too."

"I guess you're right, Hemse."

"There's no alternative, of course. We should intervene before the Secthweans overwhelm him. We won't let them run roughshod over a Guardian, do we?"

"Let's have a moment's silence, both of you," Numa warned.

Numa walked in haste towards the main screen with his translucent and glowing wings fluttering once again behind him. Ramune and Hemse fell into step in silence behind him to the edge of the main screen. By Numa's gesture, they sensed the drama about to unfold. His dark brown eyes were steady and fixed on the time screens.

Just as the gloating Secthweans lifted their guns in unison to shoot, Numa touched Netu's profile on the main screen with an outstretched forefinger. An instant shock-wave passed through Numa's finger's across the vast sea of the constellation to Netu's soul on Sapphires Street, Newland.

Numa withdrew his finger from the main screen of the Command Module with a sense of great assurance, but kept his gaze transfixed. Ramune and Hemse watched in silence, their expectations heightened by Numa's melodrama.

# # #

Netu Deo's sudden awareness of an electrifying power within became acute. He shuddered like a boulder on the verge of a fall, but it fortified him instead, and his confidence returned like a surging sea as he heard the rat-ta-tat firing of the Secthweans' guns.

The bullets from their guns, as Netu noticed, hit a vague protective shield around his body and fell to the ground like a pack of cards. He laughed, taunting at them. An intervention caused by the Guardians had taken place in his favour.

Netu shot his hand forward with renewed confidence and set to projecting a vortex of energy with his bare palms and fingers towards the Secthweans. Incandescent light sped forth from his hands in their direction. Adepts at such matters, one of them close to Netu lifted a marble pillar at the edge of the pavement with the powers of his mind and hurled it at Netu with an unparalleled force. The yanked pillar shuttled towards Netu who, on sighting it, flew away from its path.

Another Secthwean caused a fountain nearby to break into two and teleported the remaining half like a swift missile towards Netu as he touched down on the far side of Sapphire Street. Netu did not see this coming but turned in a blink of an eye. He sent it ricocheting towards the Secthweans.

Aided by an incredible will to survive, Netu's offensives were on target.

With both of his hands stretched forward in a cyclic motion, he projected spirals of light like a thousand laser beams converging on the clusters of the Secthweans on his right side. They countered the blinding light by linking their hands in a phalanx. In a concerted twirl, they reversed the luminescence ascended towards a high-rise building on the left, where it came crashing as if a bomb had been unleashed on the edifice.

A few giddy moments later, Netu got himself into a tight corner in spite of his safety mechanisms. An indescribable force-field projected by the leader of the Secthwi hit him in his right rib cage. It hurled him off his feet like a pebble in flight and sent him crashing into an open window of an adjacent building.

Hurting from the tidal waves of pain all over his body, Netu's breath almost failed him as he choked and coughed. He tried to rise, shaking off a million stars in wild dance in his foggy brain, but found it difficult. Then he heard the noisy advance of the Secthweans cursing and howling some meters away. He had no choice but to get up and fight. It took him quite an effort to get back to his feet. He then went on a daredevil attack causing more destruction to their ranks.

The Secthweans' projectiles hit him a couple of times more, but without much damage. When Netu's strength began to fail him with few of them left in the fray, he rose in languid motion from where he had fallen for the third time and like a whirlwind, disappeared. His disappearing act caught the Secthweans unawares, ending the confrontation.

Meanwhile, with Netu's vanishing, his higher-self reeled back to its body on the red rug at the corner of his bedroom in Newland where he had been meditating, still quaking from the import of the fight in the other realm. His eyes opened micro-swirls later as he re-entered his body and took a deep breath of relief. He became once more aware of his physical environment. In the safety of his bedroom, no Secthwean tormented his soul, and the other sphere of many battles no longer reared.

The night had just drawn its curtain. Netu's meditation reminded him of the struggles ahead. He did not bargain for them, yet they had become part of his manifest destiny as an incarnate Guardian. He wished this aspect would unfold in a different way.

# # #

"Well, not a bad learning experience for Finia, I must say," Numa, Blackhole's ageless patron, theorized to no one in particular. The Guardians had observed Netu's disappearance in the midst of the Secthweans on the main screen of the Command Module in the Blackhole. "It isn't too impressive either."

Though Numa directed his words at no one, Hemse and Ramune knew it meant a kind of signal of an unspecified agenda. Certainly, one they would all help to script and act in accordance with Blackhole's mandate.

"I almost gave up on Finia a moment ago," Ramune began as a way of engaging Numa in his line of thought. "But, I -"

"Really?" interjected Hemse.

"There were moments I thought he wouldn't sail through."

"How do you mean?"

"But he proved quite resilient in his handling of the heady bunch of humans."

"I disagree, Ramune," Hemse said.

Ramune sensed some kind of contradiction in his fellow Guardian's remark. "I don't get your drift."

"When the Secthweans became trigger-hungry, Finia was at his wit's end. Numa's intervention mopped up his apparent mess. He should have fared much better, you know, Ramune."

"What's the meaning of your insinuation, Hemse?"

"You heard me."

"Are you of the opinion he failed the test?"

Hemse shook his head. "Not my line of thought."

"What are you thinking?"

"He has been our eyes in our Playhouse in other aeons."

"I know," Ramune said.

"It presupposes a superior intelligence and conditioning, one meant to withstand the onslaught of the Secthweans or those of similar hue."

"You're probably right, Hemse. But don't forget he is in a new body."

Hemse shot Ramune a shrewd glance. "So?"

"Of course, it means a totally new experience. You know how these things play out, Hemse."

"I don't. Tell me, Ramune."

"Enough of the banter," Numa chided, his eyes flashing with wisdom. "Fellow Guardians, there's ample work for us."

"Okay, Father of the Blackhole," Ramune and Hemse said in unison

"From our observation a moment ago, it's crystal

clear our PlayToy project is still a long shot from its grand finale. We are certain it has just begun. It entails going back to our laboratory right away," Numa explained in earnest.

Ramune's incomprehension glared in his shifty eyes. "What lab now?"

Numa ignored Ramune's question. "Ramune, you will shuttle down to Riagena in a matter of micro-swirls. I expect you'd play games with Finia when you get there."

Numa turned towards Hemse and looked him straight in the eyes. "Your task is rather simple. Hemse, liaise with the Martian Guardian and instil their war instincts in Finia. You'll take him through the *Fiery Furnace*. When he is through, he should be finer than a diamond. I'll keep a tab on both of you while you're gone. I'll join you later if need be. Be gone!"

"Yes, Father of the Blackhole," said Hemse and Ramune.

Chapter Two

Sagol Sea, Newland, Riagena.

Ramune and Hemse where specs compared to the void in Blackhole when they micro-swirled to Riagena. Despite Hemse's experience Ramune was expected to continue Hemse's assignment and for now they considered it better to work as a team.

Netu thought back of the surprise attack when a whoos of wind exploded, a portal where Hemse and Ramune appeared in his bedroom.

Netu's excitement showed in his arched brow. "What a pleasant surprise, fellow Guardians!"

"Finia, we are embarking on a little trip right away," Ramune said.

Netu's higher-self wheezed out of his body and stood watching its grossness with a sense of bewilderment.

"Where are we headed?" Here is Netu Deo, and over there is Finia, he thought.

"You'll know when we get there. Are you ready?" Ramune said, in an urgent but calm tone.

Finia walked to the bedroom door. "Lead the way then."

"This way, Finia," Ramune pointed at the wall opposite Finia's stationary body. "We are going this way. After you."

Finia's gaze slid toward Ramune and then at Hemse, suspicious. He knew just what they meant, in spite of his fugitive mental state.

"After me?"

Sensing Finia's hesitation, Ramune reached for his left hand and held it gently. In telepathic accord, Hemse held Finia's right hand. With part of their wings providing a buffer behind him, the Guardians breezed out of the apartment wall with Finia, the night sky awash with starlight. Finia's body remained in its meditative posture in the bedroom corner, where it had been.

Outside the main gate of the one-story building, they stopped for a moment. Here, they relinquished their hold on Finia and pushed him forward.

Projecting himself skyward in a swoop of wings, Ramune said with great glee, "I guess it's time to be upward bound. Fellow Guardians, to the beach of the Sagol Sea at the eastern edge of Newland we go."

Hemse also projected himself over the air currents like a swift bird. "Right after you. Be airborne, Finia."

"Sure." Finia raised both hands and exerted a slight downward pull on the air currents, feeling a surge of energy released from within. The next moment, he found his higher-self airborne. Though he flew without the aid of wings as the other Guardians, he rode the airwaves with as much ease.

The three Guardians rose in swift bursts above the tapestry of Newland's skyscrapers and kept a steady northern course. Then they veered toward the Sagol Sea. Some micro-swirls after, they saw the great expanse of water roiling and rolling eastwards from the stretch of beach that separated it from the highbrow sections of Newland.

In his usual soul flights, Finia had seen from a vantage point in the sky, the spectacular scenes provided by the sea and its life forms. Yet, he could not help marvelling each time he had the privilege of seeing it all in one stretch of the imagination, the mystery of its many hidden civilisations. The thought that they were probably uncharted or unknown to man, made him smile; and the notion of what more meets the eyes thrilled his heart as he flew over the sea.

With Ramune leading Hemse and Finia, they flew further seaward in silence. After a stretch of about five nautical miles into the sea, Ramune sped ahead of his fellow Guardians and then turned course without warning. Now facing Hemse and Finia headlong, he charged and thrashed out with his wings at them. Hemse who had prior knowledge of the move dodged the blow of Ramune's powerful wings.

Caught unaware in the scheme of the Guardians, Finia lost his balance in the air. He gasped as he plummeted toward the Sagol Sea, trying everything he could in the circumstance to regain control of the flight of his soul.

"Why in the name of Blackhole did you hit me with

your wings?" he cried in-between gasps, trying to recover from the plunge.

Hemse and Ramune, now facing the same direction, in psychic agreement, thrashed out in unison with their wings at Finia, forcing him to plummet further down. Finia tried to counter the effect of their thrashing by building a force-field, preventing his descent into the sea.

"Can somebody explain what this is all about?" Finia's plaintive cry went.

Contrary to Hemse and Ramune's expectations, Finia did not nose-dive into the sea due to his counter-measure. He took instead their subsequent blows with a force of will, determined to defend self if they gave him no plausible reason for the attack.

"I need answers right now, Hemse and Ramune."

When no answer came, and he realized their intent to force him into the sea, Finia flew upwards and tried to strike back at the Guardians - a necessary evil, since he had no clue to why they had attacked him. They left him no other choice.

"Ramune, it's about time," Hemse said, giving Ramune a cryptic look.

Instead of striking out with his wings, Ramune swept his right hand in an arc and a strong energy-field surged forth toward Finia. It hit Finia like a heavy ball of lead and sent him spinning downward.

"Let's do it now!" ordered Ramune.

For a moment Ramune and Hemse were suspended in space; no longer flying or attacking Finia with their wings. An indescribable force-field ensued from their eyes, overwhelming whatever residual defence Finia thought he had. His strength weakened, and he belly flopped listlessly into the Sagol Sea.

When he broke out of the sea surface gasping, the salty taste of sea water blending with the repulsive odour of marine offal assailed his nostrils.

"Gosh, what a crazy thing to do! This Guardian thing sure stinks," he cursed in fury.

The waves of the sea stirred a bit, but he had to dive low in order to escape their successive crushing impact. Finia's rage seemed palpable as he re-emerged after a huge wave.

"Is this another damn script of Blackhole?" His yelp fell on deaf ears.

Ramune and Hemse smiled, watching and mocking Netu's struggles from a considerable altitude from the sea level.

Finia knew that getting angry with the Guardians amounted to a waste of energy. He contemplated what he could do about his situation, while a gnawing fear ran through his spine.

Would he make it to shore as safely as he desired? A great distance lay ahead and he did not know if the sea creatures would permit such a move. What if his strength failed him?

With such thoughts tearing his mind apart, he began to swim towards the shoreline, hoping against hope.

Finia noticed with each stroke of his hands that the

waves of the sea ceased to tower above him. From his reckoning, an unusual calm had returned to the sea.

Above his form, however, Hemse and Ramune kept a keen watch of his antics. When Netu's strokes were no longer forceful enough to get him to the shore, and that he might drown, Ramune descended in haste to sea level to make sure everything went well as planned. Ramune's next move was enshrouded in mystery. He stepped onto the sea surface and walked with confidence as if on solid ground, parallel to Finia.

Finia floated on his back for a while, shocked by Ramune's sense of dominion over the elements. The sudden calm of the once raging sea all around him showed he could make it to the shore if he strove a little.

Ramune's way of walking on the sea appeared the only alternative, but how? Finia lacked the right answer. His exasperation was visible. "Get me out of here! Get me out!" he hollered. 'I can't imagine you doing this to me."

Hemse joined Ramune at the sea level, both walking on its surface and looking out under the light of the night sky for creatures of the sea that could pose a threat to Finia.

"You'll do well to conserve your energy rather than shout," Hemse urged him.

"This is some kind of game to both of you, isn't it?" said Finia in palpable anger. "Well, I don't think I share in the fun. Just get me out."

"In your shoes, I'd keep my mouth shut," Ramune mocked. "Now, get up and walk on the thing that stifles you."

Finia did not quite place Ramune's joke. "On the sea?"

"On what else do you imagine?"

"I suppose you'll also tell me how?" Finia wondered sarcastically. With his head above the waves, he swam a few more meters towards the shore and then stopped to exhale. He felt nauseated due to the scent of fish and salt carried in the blustery wind of the now simmering sea.

"As you can see, I've done it," Ramune said, keeping pace with Finia's form. "So will you, Finia."

"Listen to the sound of your words, Ramune. You're certainly not in my shoes. Remember I'm at the receiving end of the spectrum."

"Meaning?"

"Just get me out."

Ramune's bewildered gaze fell on Hemse. "This is what happens when you get holed up in this retrograde playhouse of ours as its Guardian. The tendency is to forget you ever had higher faculties than most of the species in our numerous playhouses."

Hemse laughed at Ramune's sense of humor. "Not really the fault of any Guardian, though," he said. "It's just the way it is. The grossness of the PlayToy seems to numb whatever consciousness there is. Finia is a good example. Here we are trying to put him through the drill again even as a Guardian."

"Ok. Let's do what we came here to do," Ramune said. "Now, Finia, move your body out of the sea. Be fast about it."

"You haven't told me how?" Finia insisted, taking a couple of breast-strokes toward shore.

"If you can't remember the how, at least, you must remember the where," Hemse said. "If you can't remember the where, then, don't forget who you are."

"I don't understand."

"Why? You're what you seek. Don't look further than you should." Hemse's laughter echoed with a mocking hint, infuriating Finia further.

"Hmmnn. Now I know what this is about."

"Not until you find the answers to the questions you've asked," Ramune corrected him. "On the inside of you, you'll find the right answers. But swimming is a far greater risk, and you know this, Finia."

"But why?"

"Sharks. Whales. Dolphins - all manner of sea creatures – the Merganisa, and the Vazeninas. The sea is certainly not safe for you with these. So, up you go now."

A stream of consciousness coursed through Finia. "I know where I came from: Blackhole."

"Well, a good start!" Hemse glowered. "But it isn't enough. Come to terms with your essence."

"My essence?"

"Blackhole's priming."

"It's rather simple, Ramune," gasped Finia, suppressing a choke from the swallowed salt water. "Light. The source of all life. Got it?"

"Good," Ramune responded, walking on the sea beside Finia's swimming form. "What would you do with the ether in this sea if you could control them with your imagination?"

Finia thought for a while, floating on his back, his form bobbing with the gentle waves. "Everything, I suppose."

"Bring it then to bear in your circumstance."

"Should I?"

"I think we've wasted enough time already. You ought to be out of there by now, Finia." Hemse's furrowed brow betrayed his impatience with Finia. He took a few steps backward, and gave him an enigmatic, warning stare, having sensed danger offshore. "Ramune, the tide's here."

Ramune looked in Hemse's direction and beyond, through the veil of night. He too felt the warning signal. "The choice, I guess, is yours, Finia," he said matter-of-factly. "Join us when you think you're ready."

The sea stirred again. Ramune and Hemse flew back to a considerable height above sea level where they observed the high splash and squealing of a whale less than a hundred meters away from Finia. Then the maneuvering of a shark towards a prey in the opposite direction of the whale drew their attention.

"Finia, look, a shark - on your right flank," Hemse screamed. "It's heading for you."

"A whale and a Merganisa at the opposite end too, Finia," Ramune enjoined mischievously. "What are you going to do now?"

Finia's eyes dilated with fear as he turned in both

directions to gauge his double jeopardy. His gaze to the right coincided with another splash of the dolphin.

"Hey, you can't leave me here! I've got to get out!" Finia called out as a huge wave splashed over him and he resurfaced in the trough, gasping. "Do something."

"Like what?" Ramune said.

"Get me out of this bind," Finia shrieked. By this time, the shark was barely fifty meters away.

Perceiving the ether of the sphere as solid elements he could grasp, Finia desired above all to stay alive. So came the will to explore the unexplored. Although tired now, he stretched forth his hands above the sea waves and clutched at the air currents as if they were solid objects. To his greatest surprise, his grasp held. He forcefully pulled downwards at those vague strings and sensed an upward lift of his body. His heart pumped faster with excitement at the prospect of escape. With his inner power working again, he kept pulling at the space above his head and found his upper body rising out of the sea. The sight of the approaching shark increased the adrenalin surge in his heart. Fear became his companion. Yet he knew he had to live.

The shark dashed at Finia, though he was inundated with fear, the desire to stay alive, outweighed any of the pandemonia that rattled his heart. In one desperate pull at the vague strings he had imagined in the airwaves, Finia managed to rise above the sea before the shark struck in vain at the spot he had been moments before. He heaved a sigh of relief, having achieved the incredible at the nick of time. He felt lucky seeing the shark's restless maneuvers.

He wondered why a shark's attack in a non-material domain, and why it took him such a long time to reckon with what he should have done much earlier. This thought haunted him as the shark swam away southwards.

"Wow! A pretty dicey escape," exclaimed Ramune, grinning.

Finia turned towards Ramune and Hemse, both suspended in the sky. He felt uneasy at Ramune's remark, which he considered rather scornful. "Isn't that what you wanted?"

"There are just no odds which the will cannot surmount," Ramune said.

"Spare me the riddles," Finia replied, angered by the turn of events, especially his escape.

"Riddles? Who's talking about riddles?" probed Hemse.

"Riddles," Finia reiterated.

"Well, Finia, as you know, you proffered your own answers to your own questions," Ramune quipped, laughing.

"What do you mean?"

"I certainly don't know why it took you so much time to get out of trouble zone. But it's to your credit you got out when it really mattered. That's what counts."

"You still haven't explained a damn thing about the rationale for all this, Ramune?" argued Finia for the sake of it.

"You'll find out soon enough," said Hemse. "However,

it would be in your interest to note that you wasted so much time in there for not reckoning with one thing."

Hemse's words kept Finia's curiosity astir. "Which is?"

"The mind travels faster than the body. Do you realise this?" Hemse asked. "The mind is what you refer to as the energy forge. Your feelings represent the energies you need to stir it into positive action. Remember this, Finia."

Hemse's postulate interested Finia. "What exactly are you trying to say?"

"Well, let's look at it this way. A light year of travel with the body is like a micro-swirl of travel with the mind," Hemse explained. "The mind transcends all barriers. You only need to know how to situate it to make it count. Your emotions trigger all manner of outcomes. Some of these are desirable, some are not. To set the matrix in motion is to set your mind right. Period."

"I suppose you're referring to my earlier encounter with the shark?"

"Maybe," Hemse admitted. "Mastery of the spheres entails proper control of the reins of your mind."

"And apply it in whichever direction I choose?"

"Right," Hemse concurred. "Now, we're done with the Sagol Sea. We are moving on - to yet another sphere. To Mars!"

"Not until I'm done with what you've started."

Not the kind of response Ramune expected from Finia. "What are you toying with in your mind?"

"Read my lips instead," Finia said with a triumphant

air. "Time to play the game of suspense to the hilt! You started it. You might as well finish it."

Finia descended to sea level. In the realm of his mind, the fluid surface of the sea became a solid embankment. With positive imagination, he walked with an air of pride on the sea as would someone who had done it a couple of times before.

"What do you all say to this?" Finia said, with a smirk.

He appeared to be enjoying his walk. His strides were inspired by a feeling of conquest. He realised he had unlocked the vaults of time and had availed himself of its hidden treasures. It dawned on him too he would never be afraid of sharks, whales, or other sea creatures such as the Merganisas for whatever reason if he had to confront them again in the future or even at the moment. Besides, he had learned the hard way the lesson the Guardians wanted him to learn through the metaphors of sharks and whales; to be a master of his mind - to control the elements as surely as his breath.

Chapter Three

PlayToy, Xamuder, Mars.

Mikuthi, the Martian warlord, led a select team of Martians to welcome Finia, Hemse, and Ramune as they arrived in Mars after their escapade in the Sagol Sea.

"It's an honour to have you in the PlayToy, fellow Guardians," Mikuthi said, ushering them to the main base, an intricate network of military installations that sprawled in the heart of Mars' second largest city, Xamuder.

"As you can see, this hub is the centre of real Martian action. I presume we are exploring its frontiers right away?"

"Of course," responded Hemse. "The *Fiery Furnace* is our first port of call."

"Consider it my pleasure to lead the way," Mikuthi said, grinning.

PlayToy reminded Finia of an indescribable phantom. The expanse consisted of a huge crystal dome, with skewed peaks, like a mountain range. Each structure appeared like an artistic masterpiece. The designs were linked by a glazy network of space-strips, serving as roads. During previous visits, Finia had gained knowledge about them. The structures represented some of the holding sections of the Martian war fleet.

Beyond the area of the dome, a gigantic spacecraft took up a massive space-strip, near an adjoining structure to the operational base. Its globe-artichoke shape protruded with weird flanks that would frighten an observer from another clime.

Finia had prior knowledge of this Martian chest of flying saucers, the variant of the Guardians' Lightship. He gazed at the metallic grey, against the reddish haze. A thin layer of frost formed around the atmosphere of Mars and he was lost for words. The sharp blend surrounding the spouts became an immaculate portrait, as it reared on both sides of the space-strip. They were approaching the spacecraft, *Lightship-2*.

"This is not just another courier craft in our fleet," Mikuthi said, as the vessel's doors slid open.

They halted beside its huge trunk.

"This is the *Fiery Furnace*, the melting pot of our war instincts."

"Take us to the cache of saucers, Mikuthi," Hemse said.

"Come on board. They are in the belly of the ship," Mikuthi answered, with a sense of duty.

Hemse wore a mercurial expression on his face. He had non-negotiable orders to carry out.

"Prepare one of the saucers for action," he said.

"Will do," Mikuthi replied, as he climbed up *Lightship-2*, followed by Hemse and the rest.

Hidden behind a panel adjacent to the cockpit, the flight of stairs led to the centre of the spaceship. They reached it in a couple of strides through the door. Mikuthi placed his palm on a small identification console and the panel gave way, revealing a spiralling staircase. They descended in single file, with Mikuthi taking the lead.

"Here we are," he grinned, excitement causing him to become short of breath, as they entered the expansive belly of the spaceship.

Over thirty flying saucers of different molds and colours were berthed in specific holdings.

"We are up to date on our fleet."

"Which one is prepped for action?" Hemse asked.

The whir of the side-lights of a saucer on the eastern wing of the spaceship alerted them.

"Over there," Mikuthi said, pointing.

"Keep the simulations ready, Mikuthi," Hemse said, an authoritative edge, creeping into his voice. He walked towards the clam-like saucer with two quaint antennae on both sides.

"Ramune and I are going on board with Finia. The rest of you know what to do."

Finia saw the lower base of the saucer flip into a graduated pad upon which the Guardians climbed up. He followed suit. The lid recoiled to its original position.

The Guardians on the belly of *Lightship-2* looked on with great expectation.

The saucer's design accommodated six people; three at the controls and three for support. It could be used for ballistic purposes without the crew.

"Get on the controls," Hemse said, with a wan smile at Finia. "You're piloting affairs."

"Tell me you don't mean it," Finia said, his heart pounding with apprehension.

"I mean every word of it. Get cracking."

"Everyone's waiting. Don't you understand?" Ramune said.

Finia did not answer. He turned away from them and took his seat in front of the controls.

Ramune took the next one followed by Hemse.

"Now what?" he asked, without expecting a reply.

Hemse volunteered one. "Fly this damn thing, Finia."

Finia considered his next action. He had flown some other versions of Blackhole saucers before but this craft was unfamiliar to him. Yet, the Guardians would not budge until he did their bidding.

His mind reeled, while he heard the hum of the saucer. It gave him a start. Micro-swirls passed and the saucer wobbled. It elevated a few feet about the ground and he realized he did not touch the control panels. The next moment, it meandered past three other saucers, which were stationed in their holdings.

Finia thought the saucer would crash along with them. It got close enough to the wall of the spacecraft and slid through a large door on its own accord. They came out to open space and incurred more speed as they made the ascent. Mikuthi and his crew scurried, into the simulation room in the Lightship, to observe the ensuing drama. Each one taking charge of their designated responsibilities.

The saucer rose away from *Lightship-2* and into the reddish haze of Mars' sphere. Finia did not comprehend the control basics. Other saucers of similar designs, spewed forth from *Lightship-2*. They took strategic positions, besides Finia's saucer. His dilemma began with this realization. How would he avoid colliding with other saucers within his flight path?

The nonchalance of Ramune and Hemse surprised him. He was at their mercy and their silence unnerved him. Another saucer came on a collision course with his. Finia directed the saucer with his mind and it veered in the direction of his thoughts, sparing him from getting into a fatal crash.

"The saucer was thought-driven." Finia smiled at the thought.

He had uncovered an integral piece of the Guardians puzzle.

"The mind is such a funny thing to play tricks with," he joked.

Finia sent his saucer off course, avoiding the oncoming ships.

"These are the possibilities, the energy forge avails for us Guardians," Ramune said. "Our prerogative is to tinker with the mind whichever way it soothes us."

"Little wonder this place is called the PlayToy" Finia said, his face glowing with a juvenile disposition.

"Your feelings are what fuels the energy forge. It's the electricity that ultimately stirs the engines," Hemse cautioned.

"Hey, watch out, another saucer is coming."

Finia mind-controlled his saucer, deflecting it from the left flank in time, only to discover a missile fired by another fast-advancing one. Keeping Hemse's warning in mind, he created another trajectory in his mind for the missile. It veered away almost without hitting his saucer.

Ramune commended Finia. "Fast thinking!"

"There is more to survival instincts than thinking on your feet. This craft should be your PlayToy. Play around with it a bit, Finia."

Finia got the hint. He triggered the control panel with his mind. Missiles belched out from the flanks of his saucer, heading towards the attacking fleet.

"A mind-guided war of saucers," he echoed with a smile. "This is it!"

"Don't be too cocky about it, stay on course," Ramune warned.

"You bet these Martians are in for a treat," boasted Finia. He laughed and rocked his head while stunting with his saucer.

The ensuing crossfire of missiles was mind-guided by the Martians and Finia. They turned the reddish sphere into a crimson furnace and it became sparked by exploding canisters and projectiles. The aerial stunts, especially the mind-aided re-routing of missiles, appeared too real to be mistaken for mere simulations. Only Mikuthi, Hemse, Ramune, and the other Martians knew the script. The other saucers vanished from Finia's view. He heard a command from Hemse over the saucer's console unveil the plan of the Guardians.

"The Furnace is over! Call off the attack, Mikuthi. We are making a detour," Hemse said with emphasis. "Turn the craft homeward, Finia."

"Fine," Finia concurred, with a wry smile.

He realized the import of the order, that it spared him further mind stunts. He steered the saucer with greater ease back to the belly of *Lightship-2*. The unexpected happened as he touched down on the saucer's holding.

The holding caved in and the saucer fell into a vaporized hollow at the base of *Lightship-2*. Finia's heart skipped a couple of beats with the saucer's plunge, his face ashen with fear. Knowing what was at stake, Hemse and Ramune took the rude shock with calmness.

The hollow's size was bigger than the holding. A boiling substance almost filled it to the brim. Thick haze emitted through the air, enveloping the saucer at a high temperature. Intense heat seethed through the alloy of the saucer, trapping Finia and his companions in its lid. Beads of perspiration trickled down their faces.

Finia overcame the initial shock from the plunge. He noticed something sinister about it. The saucer's alloy began to disintegrate, starting from its outer panels. This exposed the Guardians to the stark reality of the reddish liquid substance. The lack of life sustaining gas worsened their plight, almost asphyxiating them.

Ramune and Hemse conjured up protective shields around their bodies, micro-swirls, before the remaining alloy buckled into the heat. Noticing his companions' desperate bid, Finia called forth the same shield from the depths of his being. It encased him, as the liquid broke through to their position by the saucer's control panels. By this time, the saucer remained an empty shell.

The three Guardians floated in the fluid substance, like globules in a raging sea, before noticing the opening atop the hollow's lid. The liquid's level increased until it bore the floating bodies of Finia, Ramune and Hemse close to the brim. Some helmeted Martians in prosthetics lifted them off the liquid surface, onto safer ground on the belly of *Lightship-2*.

"Welcome back from the *Fiery Furnace*," Mikuthi boomed through his helmet.

"Thanks for the tour," Hemse said, diffusing his protective shield in the same mysterious manner he had conjured it.

"It takes some guts to go through this, you know," Ramune bantered.

"You can say that again," Finia said, with a hint of sarcasm. At last, like Ramune, he had undone his shield. "I suppose the saucer is gone?"

Mikuthi shook his head. "No. You may want to take note of what transpired in there. Come with me."

Mikuthi led the way through the tangle of saucers in the holding. They veered to the left of the belly of *Lightship-2* and took a flight of stairs. They entered a room full of monitors, pressed against an arc panel wall.

"Please, take your seats," Mikuthi said, indicating the seats in front of the panel. "Here are the records of the simulations."

He fingered one of the buttons on the lower base of the panel, bringing up the scene of the hollow of liquid substance.

Finia observed the gradual disintegration of the saucer, their floating globules, and the increase in the liquid levels. After their exit from the liquid surface, the dismembered saucer came back together like a jigsaw puzzle.

Finia grinned. The liquid substance disappeared and the hollow transformed into the saucer's initial holding in the belly of *Lightship-2*.

"A wonderful trip into the crypt, no doubt. You came out finer than you went in," Mikuthi said.

"Really?" Finia felt ill-at-ease with the Martian's dry sense of humour.

"Instincts are often defined by the environment. This is a perfect example."

"Mikuthi, riddles rather compound the problem," Finia remonstrated. "Speak to me in plain language."

"We had to trigger your survival instincts, by creating an environment that stifles."

"And?"

"Alter your alchemy by way of our own injections as to what you saw in the liquid substance. You are certainly better than when you went in, Finia."

"Is this all?"

"If you can withstand the heat in there, you can withstand whatever pressure you'd face anywhere."

"I understand," Finia said, realizing he had just been reprimanded.

"Not exactly."

"What do you mean?"

"You believed everything you went through was reality based. These experiences materialized into something that appealed to your senses. Yet they were all illusions. We had to put those simulations in place. It's all a mind game. Illusions!" Mikuthi laughed.

"Mikuthi, are you saying I ought to look at it from a different perspective? Would it be to my advantage, if I perceive the challenges of a Guardian as illusory as the simulations?"

Mikuthi cleared his throat for emphasis.

"Something close to it. When you were caught in the cauldron, you experienced the reddish fluid. A simulation, meant to mimic the atmospheric pressure you would face on the PlayToy. They are only illusions."

"What do you mean?"

"The human mind is capable of contemplating

deep truths. Yet, we often limit our minds, seeing just a fragment of reality. In other words, you only observe things through the lens of your own desire, ignoring what you ought to see."

Finia had no time to ponder this, for Hemse spoke, cutting through his thoughts. "Fellow Guardians, we must take our leave now," he announced, with a nonchalant air.

Hemse rose from his seat and patted Finia on the shoulder.

"It has been one hell of a ride for you. You need to catch up with your body. On our part, we have a shuttle to make - to Blackhole."

"Good work, Mikuthi. We are on our way now," Ramune said.

"Should I arrange for your trip back?" Mikuthi said, with a patronising tone.

"It won't be necessary. We still have enough strength as it is, to cross the void on our own," Ramune said.

"Finia, get moving, your body needs you. We will meet again soon, at the Blackhole meetings," Hemse said.

Finia felt an instant tug from within, returning him to his body. In a few micro-swirls, he crossed the void and stood above his stiff body. He lowered his higher self into it and in the next breath awoke with a start.

The night creatures had begun their noisy chant. The sounds melting into the din of his friend's voices. They sat on the other side of the two bedroom apartment. Netu did not bother to turn on the light. A numb sensation fell across his hands and feet. He flexed them to get the blood circulating through his veins. He had been meditating for two hours.

Netu recalled the lessons of his soul's flight with a sense of duty. The Guardians would not have taken the pain to drill him if they did not think it important; a sort of warning of the opposition he might come against and his capacity to cope. The thought did not frighten him. Rather, it inspired him to answer the call of duty with the doggedness it deserved. He still had a few hours before dawn and continued with his night's meditation. It seemed the only way he could keep a rein on these vile forces.

# # #

"Welcome back to Blackhole," Numa greeted Hemse and Ramune on their arrival at the Wisdom Hall, Blackhole.

"Thank you, Father of the Blackhole," they chorused.

"Finia has not lost much of his instincts," Ramune began. "He needed a little touch to ignite memories of the past. I believe he fared well."

"I believe so too," Hemse said. "But my reservation is whether we did our part well."

"You did fine," Numa said. "Please, take your seats."

"Couldn't we have given him more?" Ramune asked, taking his seat on Numa's right.

"We will, later," Numa said.

"I'm not sure he needs too much prepping."

"I guess you're right, Hemse. But let's concern ourselves with what we should be doing now."

"And what's that?" Ramune probed.

"A little celebration for a job well done. Finia has all it takes to confront the inevitable for now. All our other playhouses are stable. So we deserve a moment of rest, don't you think?"

Hemse liked Numa's suggestion. "Yes."

"Come with me. We are going for a cruise on the Tamed Star. It's time you were rewarded for a job well done." Numa glowered.

Together they walked out of the Wisdom Hall and boarded the Tamed Star, Blackhole's gigantic space vessel of diverse functions; in this particular case, used as a fun cruise through the cosmic sea.

Chapter Four

The loud thud of feet on the granite-strewn driveway was amplified rhythmically towards the main door of the exquisite mansion. Lina Phillip Uwa had heard the semblance of faint drumming from far down the street a moment before her drift into dreamland. Now stirring under her blanket, she listened to the pattern of the sound with a strong presence of mind. The impact of the thud on pieces of granite, she reckoned, could not have come from one man's feet.

Her brow arched with a hint of fear, which overtook her calmness. Not a known tradition, for no stranger would dare to dawdle around the house late at night, with the security team doing alternate duty rounds. She had lived alone for a long time and never heard anything close.

Lina sat up at the edge of her exquisite mahogany bed and threw off her blanket. She tried to understand the meaning of this late-night intrusion in the yard. She peered through the bedroom window and beyond the dark veil of night.

"This is stupid," she decided, knowing she had drawn the blinds, thumbed out the bed lamp and took cover under her blanket before the flurry of feet on the driveway stirred her out of sleep. Groping around her dressing table now, she switched on her bed lamp. Warm light flooded the room.

Lina got up and whisked her fur coat from the dressing table where she had flung it before jumping to bed. She struggled into it with trembling hands. Taking a deep breath to calm her quaking nerves, she headed downstairs to confront the strange intruders.

The first set of stampeding feet had reached the front door by the time she left the bedroom. She heard a slight though persistent bang against the door, a hastened attempt to undo the handle. She hurried down, throwing caution to the wind.

What would Gabriel be looking for so late into the night? she cursed as she clattered down the stairs. Couldn't he wait till dawn to sort out whatever? He must have sold the screws of his stupid head to think he could rob me of my sleep.

"Gabriel!" hollered Lina. "How dare you deprive me of sleep? Don't you have an iota of respect for me? Would you explain the rationale for this intrusion into my house?"

She had reached the last rung of stairs, surprised that no response came from the other end. Had she miscalculated? *No, it must be Gabriel – perhaps, just being mischievous, or trying to infuriate me, or scare me out of my pants.* She quivered.

"Stop ignoring me, Gabriel," she fumed, fumbling with the key to the main door.

"It is me. Please, open the door," said a man in panicky voice.

She braced herself for he didn't sound anything like Gabriel. She quivered the more. "Who are you and what is your business in my house at this hour?"

Perplexed, the man behind the door replied, "Don't you recognize my voice, Lina?" A mixture of fear and anxiety perceptible in his voice.

"No, I don't," she said.

"I'm Netu. Now would you let me in or not?"

"Netu? Netu Deo, you mean?" she enquired eagerly, pressing her ear to the doorframe. She realized how dumb she had been not to have recognized the soft, enthralling voice that was almost part of her life.

"Yes, the same Netu."

"Pardon me, Netu. Honestly, I didn't recognize your voice. You got me anxious, you know."

"Netu, are you okay?" she asked, opening the door. "Is something wrong?"

"I'm okay, I guess," he said, looking over his shoulders. "Please get rid of them."

"You are not alone?" probed Lina, remembering the loud clambering from the driveway before.

She observed him. Nothing ruffled his cool, easy-going mien beyond the presence of two young ladies with glazed-eyes who stood near the edge of the steps to the porch. Their poise hinted Lina of wild animals out for a diabolic feast.

"Who are they?"

Netu's gaze dropped to her feet. "Some friends of mine," he said, somewhat ashamed of them.

Lina screwed her eyes near-shut and studied him, and then, the duo. They hissed and taunted her by their defiant attitude.

"I see." Rage rose within her and she fixed Netu a stern gaze. "Would you now tell me what their business is in my house, Netu?"

Netu scratched his brow instead of a reply. The help he needed from Lina, he knew she would give, but not without explanations. As much as he hated to admit it, he could not shy away from the truth. He needed her shepherding to feel safe. Lina perched on the tree of his life like a mother eagle, ever watchful of the tender eaglet in the nest, daring any creature to come near.

"They sort of stalked me here," Netu explained in a low voice, still afraid to confront Lina's gaze. He sensed he had said the wrong words and was sure he would regret it later.

Lina weighed what he had said as ambiguous. She hunched her weight on the door panel, stood akimbo, tapping the polished tiles with her foot. Friends do not stalk friends, she reasoned. It did not make sense to her. Someone was playing smart.

Lina leered at his unexpected guest. "If they are your friends, how come they stalked you?"

"I think you should ask them."

"Oh no, no! I'm asking you, Netu. These ladies don't

mean anything to me, but you do – the reason you must tell me the simple truth. That's all I'm interested in."

Netu turned half way on his heels and stared at the ladies. "They seem to have this wrong notion I have something of theirs," he said with derision in his voice.

"Really?" pried Lina. She fidgeted with the door panel. "What did they say their possession is that you have?"

Netu shrugged. "I don't know. I'm not a keeper of people's possessions."

Lina's face glistened with surprise. "You say you don't know what it is, yet, they chased you all the way here?"

Netu gave a grave nod. "Yes, correct."

"He's lying," growled one of the ladies, fire burning in her eyes. She had average height, and lithesome, ebony skin. "Tell him to return my gift or else I will unleash the fury of hell."

Lina looked at the vociferous lady and riveted the glance on Netu. "Go on, Romeo! Tell us about her precious gift and why you're keeping it."

Netu gave Lina a 'don't you push me' kind of look. "I said I don't know anything about it," he snapped. "Can I go in now? Or are these vixens the reason you won't let me in?"

Lina held up a hand in warning. "Hold on a minute!" she crooned. "You'd enter as usual when we shall have cleared this mess. Now, I want it all straightened out. Who is fooling who?"

"You know too well he's not telling you the truth," said

the frail lady of ebony skin. She sounded more embittered than before. "How could Netu be so unreasonable? How could he do this to me? He promised me heaven itself and left me hanging, hoping against hope. He made me part with the one thing I cherished with all my life and then vanished. Perfidious, don't you think?"

Her veins rose like high tide on her perspiring face. "I want my gift back right away," she went on. "He must give it or he'll ever regret knowing me. I'll make him pay with his last pint of blood. No one ever cheats me and goes Scot free." Her hands looked gnarled by the force of her clenched fists.

Netu looked at Lina for a brief moment but remained silent. The second lady, sturdier and lighter in skin tone, with deep-set eyes and fleecy curls, edged toward the steps.

"Just imagine a twerp like Netu doing this to Anne!" she said, gritting her teeth. "He must think he's pretty smart. He promised my friend the sun and the moon; marry her, and such stuff. She believed every word of his lies only to discover he's a bad dream not worthy of recall." She clenched her fist and continued. "He had his fun, all right. Now it's our turn to see him fall....I'd love to see him whimper like a hurt urchin."

"Agnes is right," the other lady edged in. "He made me cry without end. He stole my heart to heights I didn't comprehend and tore it into pieces. I want him to suffer." A devious grin played at the corner of Anne's lips, which Lina considered sardonic.

"Is this what the whole goddamn fuss is about?" Lina asked, suppressing her temper. Netu's alleged victim in particular roused her interest.

"Yes," said Anne with derision in her voice. "If I can't have him, I'll have my gift back; or have his neck. The choice is his."

In Netu's mind, Anne's remark splintered a sanguine, perfect world. A world in which he and Anne had built everlasting monoliths of passion, endless streams of wealth, castles of happiness, and a future as stolid as the breadth of the widest mountain range. They would float forever on its blissful wings. Now, though, he saw the various pieces of that world, and knew that it would never be the same again.

A different Anne was now stalking him. The tender and often cajoling lady he had loved, and who had relied much on his spiritual strength and gentle manliness, his forgiving spirit, and high career prospects, had disappeared. Now, Anne looked like a savage from a dense jungle of his passion, thirsty for his blood, sworn to vengeance, and cutting corners to nail his coffin. Netu cleared his eyes with the back of his hand and stared hard at Anne, in disbelief.

"And if he rejects either of your options?" Lina scoffed at the ladies.

"Don't even think about it," Anne shot back with confidence. "He has no choice but to take an option."

Lina turned to Netu. "Did you tell this twat you'd have anything to do with her?"

"Not at all," Netu said. "We were just friends, same way with other people. Nothing extra."

"Good," replied Lina on a strident note, and then turned to the ladies. "You heard the man. He said he didn't promise you a single pin, and that you gave him zilch. Now, if you'd excuse me, get lost."

Lina stepped aside for Netu. "You are free to go inside now," she said. Once again, facing the ladies' direction, she continued. "You'd agree my generosity is quite robust, wouldn't you both? To have allowed you to trespass on my property so long means I'm quite large at heart. I'll be humane enough to let you slip out of here. On the other hand, if you insist on making trouble, be sure you'll have it from me double. Now get lost!"

Netu scurried in, stopping by the stairway. Through the gaping door he peered at Lina and her unwanted guests. The ladies were hesitant, as if to give Lina a fight; but she appeared to be in control. Lina noticed their defiant posturing and ventured with aggression towards them, but they retreated in haste to a safe distance. From there they turned their hate full force on this woman who stood between them and Netu.

Lina never before felt so insulted. Daring her to a fight, the ladies did not reckon with her as the 'Queen' revered by their kind, same Lina to whom they submitted in the spiritual world. What had gone wrong with decorum, she thought. In her world, the law remained the law; and the Queen represented the law. I will string them just where they belonged, she told herself. A malicious smile punctuated her thought.

"I take it by your impudence you don't know me," she said, now less on-guard, "and you're ready for a fight. If you want to get Netu, there's only one way: get me first.

Simple deal, don't you think?"

Lina leapt on Anne, narrowly missing target. Swinging off her assailant's path by instinct, Anne retreated towards the main gate, and stood on a luscious, well-groomed lawn.

"I'm beginning to understand your sudden concern for Netu," she cackled like a savage in a jungle. "You're having it real good with him, not so? It makes you think you can piss me off so easily. If you think you're so good at defending him, why don't you carry your sword and fence around town, defending every man who touches your thighs? What makes you think you're not just one of his many flings? No doubt, a great defender of cheats and liars you are."

Agnes coughed a glob of spittle onto the lawn and stormed across the driveway towards the right flank of the yard, facing Lina's direction. "We have no business with you," she ranted, "but with this smart ass you're shielding. Let him come face the music."

"Then come and get him," Lina roared, signaling to the stairs. "Your prey is right in there. Go have your feast."

Anne started fretting. Netu had been too slippery. On her first date with him, she recognized that she did not know a thing about him. He loved her as no other person had done. So, she thought she had him caged and would conjure his form at will. To her surprise, he slipped out of the box like a slithering serpent. Now she found herself in the cage.

"I should've seen the signs long ago. I was off my mind, I should've known better," Anne whimpered. "Please, fellow woman, don't do this to me. You know what it means to be hurt. Stay clear of this, and you'd ease my pain. We'll settle it on our own terms. If you bungle my mission because of sentiments, how will I gain promotion in my world? Netu knows why he came to you. With you he's sure of protection; but consider the consequences if I fail in this assignment."

Lina winced at Anne's piteous drama. *My heart sure chimes the right impulses all the time and never fails to alert me*, she thought. *A stupid egghead Netu is. Never would listen to advice. His magnified ego wouldn't let him. Just how long do I continue to beat it into his empty head to stay away from women? It is the only hurdle left for him to cross, but he always crashes into it. He needs to learn a lesson or two about life. Perhaps, I should allow these women to have to take their pound of flesh. Netu believes he's just what he is...insulated from people of Anne's deviousness. Now, he will learn.*

Nonetheless, Lina knew she could not afford to see Netu hurt. She was fond of him in a strange way. She had not been able to put words to that emotion, but she knew she cared a lot about him and sometimes tried to show it. It was proper, she thought, to defend someone you cared for. So, she would stand by him at this hour of need.

"What sort of promotion did you say you want?" Lina asked Anne aloud. "I figure you have an overblown ambition and I feel obliged to help you. If what I think is the kind of promotion you desire, you can count on me. I'll be on hand to grant it. If you want to know, I'll tell you where to. I'll promote you to hell!"

Anne and Agnes shuddered from Lina's grave voice.

"But for Netu and people like him who do not listen

to advice," Lina went on barking, "rats, small rats like you, won't dare to encroach on my privacy and insult me like this. For the last time, I tell you, know your limit or you'll forever curse your stars."

Lina paused, turned towards Netu by the door. "Lover boy, Netu," she jeered. "Come hear what your girl is saying. She wants promotion, and your neck would be the prize for getting it."

She looked at the ladies with scorn in her eyes and said, "So what's your choice, life or promotion in hell? If your choice is hell, then wait for me."

Lina dashed into the house. Her brusque movement drew Agnes' suspicion. Should this ruthless woman spring a surprise, would it not be disastrous for both of them? In this circumstance, the best option would be to accept defeat. She scurried to Anne's side and pulled her.

"What are you waiting for?" Agnes whispered hard. "Can't you feel the bull in this woman? She's meaner than we thought. Besides, she's still the Queen. Let's get out of here fast. Let's scram while we still have time on our hands. Hurry!"

On hearing Lina's clattering steps down the stairs, Anne scampered away with Agnes. By the time Lina reappeared at the doorway, they had disappeared into the night.

Lina leaned on the door frame, drawing in a lungful of air. She exhaled the draft with a rasping sound. She felt drained. Thankful for her sheer guts in averting an ugly scene, she allowed the cool breeze to tease her face and rustle her negligée, followed by another stream of fresh air, coursing through her lungs and calming her frazzled nerves. Then she saw a missing piece of the jigsaw puzzle falling into place: Gabriel!

Where had he and the other guards been all the while? Asleep? *I will go fetch these lousy, good-for-nothing oafs before I get on to a real roast of this stubborn, stray-feet Netu*, she thought, stomping down the steps toward the large mansion.

# # #

Lina Phillip Uwa rolled over to her right side of her bed disrupting the flickering reel of the dream. Suppressing a choke, she clutched her bosom to nurse its tingling pain. She then rested her body on the headboard. She tucked a pillow between her and the wall giving her head a snug incline.

So she had been dreaming, she admitted. She wondered at how real it seemed.

Back to real life now, she realized it came as a warning of some sort for Netu. Lina Uwa glanced about her in dismay, somehow derided by the ironical jokes life often played on individuals. Not quite a minute gone, she had found herself swinging in the cloak of a revered Queen, enjoying the accompanying affluence and splendor of a large mansion. It was quite annoying waking up to real life of her haunting plight - a divorcee whose existence hinged on her will to overcome poverty. She gazed at the one room she had managed to maintain for over two years and felt the revulsion. Not the mansion of her spiritual flight but a drab square space clustered with bundles of time-worn clothes and a stack of utensils.

The almost bare room had as tangible furniture, two stools, a cast iron bed, and a medium size bench. She had fabricated the rest of the furnishing in her imagination, hoping someday she would smile at the fruits of her mind's seed.

Where went the trappings of the spiritual affluence in which I lived? Life has not been fair, she thought. She would have loved to live the life of a Queen forever, but reality as she saw it now, came with just one tinted meaning: bit by bit, calculatedly, life meted out its blows and she lacked the resilience to counter it.

Her plight was not her utmost bother; rather, Netu seemed the pain seething through her being, rendering her restless. The way he went about things - such carefree attitude as she had never seen in any man. She knew he would get himself hurt one way or the other, and she could well narrow down the scope of hurt to a single cause: women. Of course, she admired how he had tried to tame his great libido in spite of his teeming female admirers. Quite inspiring for an intelligent, handsome, and well-bred young man. While she did not see him as promiscuous, he always ended up with the wrong company as her dream had shown.

Though a mere dream that she could wish away, from her past experiences, her dreams were almost always accurate prophecies.

In slow motion, Lina rolled up on her pinto bed and gave a heavy sigh. She then sought to still herself with an even heavier breath to feed her strained lungs. She gazed across the room at the taut string above her head, and then at the flaps of old issues of magazines and newspapers hung on it beneath the green bulb in the small room.

Whether Netu Deo would listen to her this time or take it in his strides as he had always done in the past, she would steer him clear of the enemy's hatchet. It would not be easy, she knew, but she would do it even if it meant another scar on her pride. The dream replayed itself to her in harried clarity, and Lina saw in Anne a monster.

The previous evening, Netu had showed up giving flimsy excuses, but she figured he wanted an escape route out of her clutches, to scamper to areas he would ease out his hidden desires. He had said he would be back the next morning, but morning had passed and night had fallen. Still, no sign he would keep his promise. In spite of her feelings, Lina felt confident she would see him soon. And when he did show up, she would let him have it clear and crisp. The bitter truth, and he would have no choice than to face up to it.

Lina uncoiled herself on her bed and tried to go back to sleep by relishing the memories of Netu. She found sleep hard to come as her mind was troubled. She kept gazing at the white ceiling boards for a long time before she was swept off her worries into deep, unobtrusive slumber.

# # #

"Lata, turn the stereo volume down," ordered Netu. "We are not in a discotheque. The stereo noise may stir trouble for us from neighbors. You know how irritated they often are. Just turn the volume down."

Lata grinned, his eyes glinting in his characteristic exuberance. "Neighbors and trouble, you say?" he responded in defense. "Come on, Netu! I don't buy it any more than you do. They play music louder than anyone else in the neighborhood, but no one ever complains." He wheeled to the stereo beat and the overhead light embellished his fair complexion with a slight flare.

"Will you do as I say, Lata?" snapped Netu, worried by the young man's defiance.

Agitated, Lata stared at both Netu and John, an uncle. John urged him with a slight nod to obey Netu's order. Lata was astonished they thought he courted trouble with the blaring stereo speakers, which did not penetrate the four walls of the room. Anyhow, he rose from his couch, switched off the machine and went back to his seat.

"Now what?" he sneered.

"Stop the nonsense," John warned. "Can't you see what Netu said is right? Since when have you become full of air?"

Tall, dark-skinned, oblong-faced, square-shouldered and with piercing eyes, John was in his early twenties. He seemed amazed at the insensitivity of Lata, who took too many things for granted, as if great values and tradition were eroded by the passage of time. He shrugged with disdain seeing that his brother, Lata, exemplified a child lost in the web time made him.

"I'm sorry," Lata apologized coming to terms with the situation. "I didn't intend to be rash. I'm sorry."

"Sounds better," John said, impressed.

Netu felt indifferent. Life had turned him round too often in circles and left him at the mercy of other people to the extent he felt thick-skinned about it. What people thought of him or how they reacted at times to his words no longer counted. Yes, life had jeered at his inability to interpret and understand its rhythms, the reason his ego had suffered without mercy.

The bond between Netu and the two younger men had no tint of blood to it, but a product of a once intense friendship he had enjoyed with their late uncle, Tom. On the crest of OldHill, the middle class residential area on Newland's western fringe, the three-bedroom apartment they lived in stood as one of six apartments in a grand, one-story building. They occupied the third apartment downstairs. Netu had often given his weight to the thought that the apartment came across as Tom's unsigned will for them before his premature transit to the beyond.

Until early in January of 1996 when a sword of fate swung and spilled Tom's blood on the day's bright hue, he had believed he could simply reach out and pull the brilliant strings of his life. He felt this way, knowing he had a friend he could trust. A friend who understood the intrinsic depths of his being, believed in him, and shared the burdens of his aspirations. Since the pillar Netu reclined so much on had been snatched by fate, nothing had been the same again.

Netu also realized that in this world nothing ever remained the same, except for one to constantly adjust to the forms ever altering before one's eyes. One had to adjust even to time itself. This had been his lot in recent times. Netu brushed aside such thoughts. The past remained the past, and his business belonged in the now.

The day had begun on an inspirational note, the reason Netu and John had enjoyed a refreshing chat in the apartment. They had broached on far-ranging issues concerning their lives as each had been entangled with Tom's. Also, they had examined the plight of man on the globe and of the roles they wished they played to reverse the tide of fate with a critical mind. They had also shared the intrigues of a box-office movie. It had all been wonderful, if not for Lata's need for loud music.

Netu smiled to himself on recollecting his own exuberance at twenty. *You just can't figure what one is capable of doing at twenty. The world is like an exquisite toy you want to fiddle with. Often times you want to remold it to your childish fancies; and it hurts your soaring zeal when you realize things don't really work the way you think. Then you are told politely in the dialectics of the time, you must bend so the world can accommodate your rough edges. And how many times had he yielded to this strange cajoling? He had lost count,* Netu admitted.

He thought it rather queer about life. Either one bent as dictated by time or a natural process enforced it. This amused him. Lata appeared to be struggling out of shoes Netu had long out-grown. Even then, the world never stopped pressurizing his frame to bend, especially with the awareness of his predestined role as Light Bearer.

The process by which nature made things bend its way intrigued Netu and the stuff of life he was yet to grasp. He had been responsive to several pressures before. In spite of the mystique surrounding those situations, they came without the kind of manipulation he felt in his relationship with Lina. The earlier pressures could be explained in the light of an economic drought.

Without the gritty realities of a drought of any type, the latest pressure dug deep into his being, stirred wells of emotions, and held his mind captive.

Netu could feel the steel bars of Lina's charm imprisoning his mind again with frightening irresistibility. He did not like it one bit due to its implications. Still, he could not in any way refuse the protection Lina offered. He had never really thought about how he got mixed up with Lina, beyond the awareness that she had a strange pull on his heartstrings. It often made him swing in her direction when the force tugged at him from within. As he thought about her again, he realized how inextricably nestled he was in her care and overbearing protection.

Netu saw Lina last a day or two previously, yet it felt like light years had gone unnoticed. Why did he always feel this way about her? He could not understand how she had managed to have him so strung on her. Not in any way close to the archetypal romantic beauties he had known most of his life, but Lina had something going for her: she melted his heart as would any damsel.

Lina's spirituality often magnetized the steel in him, yet she felt confused just as he when he hinted of the strangeness of the feelings they shared. Nevertheless, he knew she had more at stake in their relationship but kept it secret.

Netu straightened up from the couch where he had been sprawled and made for his bedroom. "I guess I've had enough rest for the day. This sort of idleness too often gets one softened. I've got to get my legs and mind kicking again," he announced with glee. His real intention was the urgent need to see Lina Phillip Uwa.

"Why? The day's still young," John grumbled, stirring on the couch from which Netu had earlier stood up.

"Your sense of time amazes me. It's already four o'clock in the evening and you still think it's early?"

"How long will you be out?" John enquired.

"A few hours," Netu said. "I'll be back soon."

"Anne might be here. What do we tell her?" John called after Netu.

Netu's voice echoed from the half-shut bedroom door. "Tell her to hang around here for me. I won't be long out. Understand?"

"Yes," John said with a hint of cheer.

Netu Deo returned to the living room minutes later, donning a pair of brown cotton trousers topped with an orange-colored polyester shirt, with its uppermost button undone. On his slightly exposed chest a gold pendant dangled from a gold chain wound around his neckline.

Lata thought Netu looked gorgeous in the expensive trousers and shirt. The black sheen of Netu's shoes and black belt gave his figure a gentlemanly air. Lata knew Netu never compromised on his tastes, no matter how high the odds seemed. Since the time Netu came to pass some nights in the house before Tom's sudden death, and even when he later accepted to stay with them due to Tom's insistence, Lata had noticed Netu's passion for the good life. Though it was not quite easy for Netu to live out his dreams due to financial constraints at the time, things had taken new shape after the death of Tom. The new shape of things favored Netu as he could see.

"Hey, in your dress, you look much like the renowned Don Juan!" Lata teased as Netu caught him gazing at his outfit.

"Here you go again with your flattery," Netu said, sounding not too impressed.

"You never ever take me seriously, do you? To be honest, you look real sweet, like a happy moon."

"All right, just this once, Lata, I'll take you for your word."

Netu fetched a couple of Rinai bills, fresh from the mint, from the side pocket of his trousers. "Use this for whatever you guys have in mind for the evening," he said, handing it to Lata. "It will take care of dinner, at least. See you in the evening."

Netu made for the front door, but halted midway. "I'm sure Anne Ofino will buzz in anytime," he added. "Let her ease off steam with you guys till I get back, okay?"

Lata nodded profusely, gazing at the Rinai bills in his hand. They heightened his excitement.

The crispy sound of the bills in Lata's palm aroused John's interest. He however cautioned himself against the cash being spent right away.

"Alright, guys," Netu said. "I'm buzzing off."

John waved back. "Later then, pal."

Netu shut the door and felt his feet light on the vague passageway separating the other two apartments downstairs. His mind was focused on Lina Phillip Uwa as he veered towards the main gate. Once again, he found himself yielding to her force-field of abstract magnet, which he seemed unable to resist. At the gate, he waved down a taxi and called out his destination: Vidya Valley.

# # #

Lina Phillip Uwa had never slept so deeply. She woke up late this morning and it surprised her. Yet, the drowsy, dreamy lure persisted with a sense of unwanted pleasure. She willed herself against a further dose of sleep and sat on the edge of her bed, her breath heavy with the alien haze of spiritual vibrations lingering from the realms she had visited in her sleep.

The radiant morning sun had streaked through the slit line of the only window of the room, forming dancing blotches of orange light in the faint darkness. She admitted the sun's rousing effect with an unusual mental flight. Resisting the urge to turn on the electric light and thrust out nature's gift, she stepped with caution toward the window.

It gave way outward as she pushed its latch. The penetrating glare of the mid-morning sun stung her eyes as she peered. She squinted, inclining from its magnificence. The not too tempered flare gave her momentary solace, except that the room's bright points almost equaled the one from outside.

A soft wind blew through the torn window net and eased its way soothing into the room. Neighbors went about their callings with same clamor, rueful chatter, or occasional glee – the same sounds she had heard every morning since she moved into the house. Unlike other mornings when she felt ill-at-ease with the combination of neighborhood exchanges, Lina Phillip Uwa seemed to be comforted by this morning's sounds. They provided her a kind of insulation against her feelings.

She felt particularly lonely this morning. The idea of living alone did not strike her as a bright one for any woman. Her life as a divorcee began when her husband abandoned their matrimonial home. She had overcome the shock of his sudden exit from her life after a long and agonizing period of bitterness and emptiness. Those were the days of lonely brooding when, being afraid of renewed heartaches, she turned down men who tried to fill the gap left by her husband with diplomacy. For a whole year, she took precaution, never allowing anyone touch her heartstrings. She had decided that love could never succeed with her twice, and in the same manner. She soon realized that her heart once more reined towards someone.

From his refined world, Netu Deo leapt like a brave warrior to her wilderness of loneliness, lifted her off a dreary past with finesse, and placed her with tenderness in the arms of peace, hope, and affection. Like treasure-seeking adventurers in a wild countryside, he had come with his late friend, Tom. They rode to her plain with astounding gallantry in search of psychic counsel. But from the moment her eyes beheld Netu's handsome face, memories of the near past came flooding her mind. She had felt a sweet jolt in her heart she did not discern; like the tease of sweet breeze from nowhere. What could have made her feel this way for this man who belonged to another world quite distinct from hers, a man five months younger than her? His world revolved on immense refinement, class consciousness, and pedantic intellectualism. Hers, to her dismay, showed like an unwanted log in eddies and the gaudy corners of his cultured society. What then caused their bond despite the disparity in their social status? Not his macho ways, height, handsomeness, or a future entwined in his aura. Not even his intellectual edge could overwhelm her spiritual guts. Most times, she had conceded not a single reason but all the reasons thinkable had been responsible for her fondness. Still, it took her a long time to accept that this softness had the colors of love emblazoned in the way she felt.

The mist of thought paved way to a clearer vision. Through the window Lina observed the scenes and movements of the neighbors around the premises. It annoyed her to be indoors while everyone busied themselves outdoors. How long had she been standing by the window without a fixed thought? All the while her dreamed threats to Netu's life had been her recurring flicker of thought. Drawing the window curtain, she switched on the bright light. How she wished the man would come soon! She must warn him of a remote danger, and then it would be up to him to guard his steps.

An hour later, Lina Phillip Uwa had taken her bath and done with an oats meal for brunch. She realized how hungry she had been and ravenously sated her large appetite. After that, she felt her emotions lift up, but did not feel the urge for much work. Yet, she decided she would check her store at Ashi Park on the steep of Vidya Valley. A walk to her store a few minutes from Ashi Park, she believed, would not strain her much. Afterwards, she would cook a nice meal Netu would like, should he show up as promised.

Lina returned from her store two hours later. Business had not been good but she had forced herself to tarry a bit at the store, nursing the hope of a chance miracle of sales. Things are not working out well with a lot of people these days, she thought. Times were in the past when she would have made great sales within two hours, but economic depression was affecting even her second-hand clothes business. She felt content though with the little income the day offered.

Outside, the sunset crawled to oblivion in gold. Lina hastened her dinner preparations. She did not like the idea of Netu calling without a sumptuous meal laid out for him. She had done this only for her ex-husband, but it gladdened her heart that someone else enjoyed what he had rejected for reasons she never got to know.

Lina waited an anxious moment for Netu to make his usual sudden appearances, but when he did not, she ate alone. Hers was the kind of vanquished spirit a jilted lover feels, the food tasting as if this was not the outcome of her exquisite cuisine.

The knock came light in her ears the first time, and she thought it was from the opposite door. The second time she heard it clearly.

"Yes, who is there?"

"Netu here."

Spurred, Lina hurried to the door. "Netu, I've been expecting you all day long," she gasped, ushering him in.

Her sensitivity often amazed Netu. "How did you know I'd be here?"

"Don't you know I always sense some of these things?" She waved him to sit on the bed, which he preferred to the bench or stools. Netu plunked down, flinching at the impact of the small bed.

"But then you can't always know and predict my every mood and move." He wondered, smiling.

Lina studied him, noted his insinuation, with no comment. She sat on the bench adjacent to the bed and continued her intent watching.

"You didn't keep your promise yesterday evening, why?" she demanded in a cool tone.

"I know, Lina," Netu said, his tone apologetic. "I couldn't possibly help it - too much running around."

A red glint shone in Netu's brown eyes, a signal she recognized well. It always preceded his bouts of hunger, but his stubbornness astonished her. Like a heady horse, he never demanded anything from her until she had pressed him. She had often been patient with him, and she would again. After his meal, she would try a war of wits with him on the other areas troubling her mind.

"I just finished dinner. Alone. There's still some fried beans and plantain, it's fresh fish stew. Eat something first, and then, we talk."

"Fresh fish stew. I like the sound of it," Netu enthused, but not unmindful of her coy complaint of eating alone. He had known her long enough to sense she had a game up her sleeve. He, however, lacked insight into the nature of the game she had contrived. He would wait until she unfurled it herself, he assured himself.

Lina ladled the food in cream china and laid it on one of her stools. Netu drew the stool towards him. After a moment of silent prayer, he began to eat. Lina watched him munch the fried beans and plantain, ignoring her stare. It had been her way of caring, and it soothed him.

Netu finished dinner and drank a full glass of water placed next to the china. She offered another fill but he declined politely. He gave Lina a pat of appreciation, cleared his throat, and reclined against the wall by the bed.

Lina cleared the dishes and mopped up with diligence. After laying the china into a large plastic bowl of water on the main table, she took her place on the bench, but she did not pelt him with her worries right away.

Netu did not like her stalking. He wanted the game over with, and yet, he did not want to initiate anything he would regret; so he kept his calm.

The guest belched.

"Easy," Lina exclaimed.

Netu noticed a rather seductive mood about her, though it was not her intent. Food makes one appreciate some negligible aspects of living – like beauty, he mocked himself. He had not seen this side of Lina until he had eaten. Hunger made him plunge into dark oceans of unappreciative brooding, which he did not understand. He had not eaten at home even when he could afford it; for, he wanted to eat Lina's food. Surprisingly, her pretty nature only struck him after he had assuaged the need. Crazy, he thought.

He studied her in an oblique way. The long black and white skirt she wore increased her five feet of height by some illusory inches. Her buxom build stood out particularly now. She wore a white T-shirt, like a nubile virgin in a maternity ward on her dark skin. Her long hair curled around her shoulders, and emeralds stood in as eyes. Lina's aquiline nose accentuated her sexy eyes with a kind of spell on Netu, especially when he fancied the feel of her lips against his.

Lina soon got ready to quiz him. "I had a dream last night," she began, and pouted. "A knotty kind of dream..."

Netu sensed it coming. He had saved his wits for it. He showed interest. "Something good, I suppose?"

Lina shrugged. "I don't think so."

Netu winched. Her indifference spelt omen. "You don't think so?"

She nodded. "I'm afraid, no. Netu, you really have to be careful. I've told you this several times before, but you don't seem to listen. The dream has its harrowing implications..." Lina broke-off in a worried tone, fidgeting.

Netu noticed her hesitation, but refused to be frightened. "Can we get down to the dream bit by bit now?"

Lina heaved a sigh and then continued. "I had problems at first, trying to figure out the motive behind the chase and the fierce look of the two ladies until Anne's confession....I believe the tense atmosphere induced her confession. I'm certain it wasn't voluntary.....I see it as an explosive revenge instinct."

"The lady you referred to as Anne, what did she look like?"

He had a feeling he knew whom she referred to but did not want to hazard a guess without ample clues from Lina.

Lina thought for a while, her brow in a vague knit, and then she said, "She's petite, lithe, dark-skinned, her hair, not extensive..." Then she remembered more. "Yes, she had this piercing look, with her tiny but glazing eyes, and a smallish nose. I reckon she's not more than twenty-five or thirty years.

"Anything else you recall?"

"No." Lina almost saw the flicker of recognition in Netu's eyes. "Know anyone with such a physique?"

"No, I don't," Netu lied. "Never had a friend named Anne before."

He played with the edge of his black safari suit, tracing the lines of gray around the pockets and neck flap, evading her stare. In spite of his lowered gaze, he spied Lina. Her curiosity had been aroused by the guile she gleaned on his face. He knew that she would not be fooled this time by his good looks and pretense.

"You don't sound convincing."

"What, in God's name, would make you think I lied to you?"

"Inkling."

"What inkling? Meaning I know the girl you saw in your dream? C'mon Lina, give me a break!"

"So you don't know any Anne or her friend, Agnes? And no woman gave you any gift she wants returned? Isn't it intriguing the two came after you and not me or some other person?"

"I must admit it appears phony, but just how do you imagine I would've known what they came for when I still can't picture who they are physically?"

"Then let us skip this bit about Anne and Agnes, whoever they are. But you must remember to be wary of the skirts around. Promise?"

Netu conceded. "Promise. No skirts."

"I'm not so sure if I feel relieved now or not."

They were silent for a moment. Netu tried to appraise Anne's ulterior motive in his mind. What had she given him and why did she flare up? If only he could discover the one thing she had given him in Anne's dream, he knew it would not be difficult to get it from her in real life. It would take only a sweet tongue and a little romantic concession.

Lina thought Netu confounded the whole issue with his fervent denial of his knowledge of Anne. With his denial, she had no reason to insist, and get herself upset.

Netu had a different thought. "Did you by any chance discover what the gift Anne allegedly gave me was?" he broke in.

"Not at all," responded Lina. "You forget so easily. I told you the ladies never gave me a chance to find out anything more than I've told you."

"Lina, sorry I ask so many questions. I'm just trying to

get at something."

"I'm not upset, Netu."

"Would you then explain the promotion thing Anne talked about?"

"Just the way I understood it, perhaps you would have to be sacrificed for her to climb higher in her power hierarchy."

Even though shaken on the inside by the revelation, Netu spoke in a smooth manner. "Thanks anyway for the hint. I'll be a lot more careful this time. Can't spare my neck for some mean girls, you know!"

Lina felt a surge of joy that Netu at last saw the danger inherent in her dream. "Don't you worry, we'll fight it together," she assured him, giving his hand a gentle touch.

Netu grinned. "I'm in your debt then?"

"I'm also in your debt." Lina laughed like a temptress. "It makes us two indebted souls!"

Netu could not help but admit their indebtedness to each other, no matter how minor the debts were. He had come to her aid at a dire point in her financial and emotional life. Now, in reciprocation, she had warned him of imminent danger.

Less than an hour later, they boarded a Pen Station-bound bus at Ashi Park on their way to Salvage Road, off Bishi bus stop. Two months on the count, they had been visiting Loyeb Abe an ex-initiate of the Brotherhood together. Lina and Netu went to Loyeb Abe's home every week, fanning in secret the embers of the Brotherhood to which they all once belonged, despite their triangular

80

cultural difference in Riagena, a richly endowed country of diverse pedigrees, the pride of the continent of Carifa.

"I wonder why the Baruyo, the Bogi, and the Sahua ethnic groups won't give the Waji people a chance even when they are the geese that lay the golden eggs?" Loyeb had joked when the issue of the three main blocks that characterized the sovereignty came up during one of their chats at the dawn of their meetings.

"You Baruyo guys from western Riagena are a strong voice. Why not rally to give them the chance they need?" Lina rebuffed him.

"Good question," Loyeb said. "Is it as easy as that? You know the political equation in Riagena. It almost always favors the majority to the dtriment of the minority. The Wajis from southern Riagena are a minority."

Netu's eyes flared in disbelief. "And simply because we are a minority, you guys think it's your right to usurp our resources to our detriment? The Sahuas don't give a damn if our region is developed or not as long as they hold on to the reins of political power. The Bogis from eastern Riagena are a sell-out any day when it comes to power sharing. They don't see beyond their selfish interests. That's the dilemma of the Wajis – a conspiracy between the Baruyo, the Bogi and the Sahua to enslave us perpetually."

Lina's shrewd glance went in the direction of Netu. "You palter with words, Netu. How come the three of us work to together if your insinuation is true? You're a Waji man, Loyeb is a Baruyo, and I'm a Bogi. So tell me, why are we united in spite of our cultural differences?"

Netu dismissed her with a wave of the hand. "A stroke of luck, perhaps."

"I disagree," replied Loyeb. "We are united because we share a common bond, the Brotherhood. That's the ideal lacking in the political situation in Riagena."

They had all laughed at Loyeb's remark for it made a lot of sense considering the reality of the situation in Riagena.

Loyeb Abe had been expecting them since there had not been a prior visit in the week. Loyeb Abe's determination to keep their secret meeting going through an oath of hospitality and a sense of humanity did not waver. On her part, Lina had not seen any deviation so far from their set goals, in spite of her cynical disposition, typical of the Bogis. A warning in her head kept a tiny shred of fear in her heart for things appeared too good to be real. Anyhow, led on by the thrill of adventure, she believed in Loyeb's harmlessness.

The drapes of night over day had been fully drawn by the speed of time as they left Abe's home an hour afterwards. Stars had begun to dazzle the night sky and the moon took its place amid the sparkling starlight.

Lina encouraged Netu to pass the night in her place but he did not feel too excited about it. She had to soft-pedal in order not to incur his wrath. He argued rather in strong terms that he wanted to be home in time to attend to some pressing needs. He had been full of excuses lately, she reasoned. She had nothing to hinge her suspicion on. Netu could not be denied his freedom as a man with a mind of his own. He had the right to do just what pleased him, so she had to let him go even though she knew he ought to be around, cuddling and whispering in her ears.

At Bishi bus stop, Netu Deo gave Lina Phillip Uwa a peck on the cheek and bade her goodnight. She took a bus to Vidya Valley. When that bus left, Netu jumped into another one to Pen Station on his way to OldHill, his mind racing home to Anne Ofino.

# # #

Anne heard Netu walk into the apartment at a quarter past ten. She had been reading a novel, a story of love and hate, in his bedroom with deep concentration. Immersed in its captivating plot, she did not hear the doorbell ring. She became aware of Netu's presence only when John opened the door for him and an exchange of pleasantries ensued between them. Anne out of excitement dropped the novel on the bedside table, hooked the breech of the trousers she had on and the slit of her shirt, and hurried to the living room to meet Netu.

Netu heard the click of his bedroom door and stared curiously, interrupting his pleasantries with John and Lata. He noticed Vivian fast asleep on the rug. Anne smiled at him from the mid-point of the door, an arm on her hip, and the other, hanging loose. She wore his flannel trousers and shirt. Whenever she visited, she had the habit of wearing his clothes, though slightly bigger than her frame. She had a way of tapping into his spiritual energies through his clothes. The way she posed against the edge of the bedroom door, she looked like a temptress out for a kill.

Netu had no description for her beauty. Her supple black skin and wondrous eyes captivated him beyond measure, but her smile often made his heart huff. Anne giggled like a happy child and, in turn, he curtsied, with a smile.

"How are you, my baby?" Anne asked as he approached her.

His mind played funny tricks on him. My God, what a lovely creature!

"Fine. And you?"

"I missed you," Anne Ofino teased.

"Really?"

"Uh hu!"

Netu slid his left arm around her slim waist and pressed her body to his. She smiled, gazing at his face with dreamy eyes. "Where have you been?" she muttered.

"Trying real hard to survive the times, you know," said Netu, smiling. Anne mistook his smile for a move to kiss her, but somehow he held back. She did not mind. He had just returned home and there would be plentiful time to play romance.

Netu led Anne back to the bedroom and shut the door. She helped him unbutton his shirt and fetched his pajamas from the wardrobe. She then stood next to him and with cheer released the hem of the pajamas top caught inside the back of the pants as he slid into it.

"You must be worn out and hungry after a long day. I've got something for you," she indulged him.

"Okay, let's see what magic you've got left!" He would raise a suspicion only if he told her he had eaten.

He pulled an armchair and sat down, watching Anne strut towards the kitchen. The noise of the sitting room television saturated his ears, infringing on his thoughts.

Anne's devotion to Netu puzzled him as much as his confusion about what to believe - Anne's love for him or Lina's theory on Anne and her fury in the narrated dream? He believed Anne, for she had in a unique way drilled the steel of his heart and played her way with finesse into its core. He believed in Lina because of her eagerness to disprove his invincibility. Lina had often warned him of his vulnerability. The Anne of Lina's dream was an example of why Netu ought to be wary of his female friends.

If he must reverse the force of Anne's hand in the tender depths of his being, he would have to elicit the truth from her with tact. A blunt affront would not do the trick. He would learn to pry into her deepest secrets and let her spill all of it on her own accord as the only way to vindicate himself of his suspicions. He smiled on hearing Anne returning to the bedroom. It is time to play chess, he thought.

"I can see you smiling already," Anne remarked, entering with a tray. "I'm certain what I have here will please you."

"I'm pleased all right."

"About what, if I may ask, my dear?" Lina lowered the dinner tray, with bottled chilled water and two glasses, on the bedroom center table. She drew a chair to herself and threw Netu a bemused gaze.

"Ah, pleased about everything: you, me, everything."

Anne smiled. "If so, I'm happy for us."

Anne poured some water into the glasses and lifted the cover of the china, revealing a splash of fried rice, spaghetti, omelet, and slices of cheese.

"I'm eating with you," she said.

"It's Okay by me, dear. I'm glad you volunteered. Can't finish this mound all by myself, anyway."

"I'm also starving," said Anne. "I had to wait for you. Else, my mind wouldn't let me be. Now, I can eat in peace."

"Let's get on with it, then," Netu goaded.

"Delicious!" he beamed with the first spoonful. "The best meal I've had for a while now!"

Anne watched him with admiration. "C'mon, eat," Netu cajoled her. "Simply delicious." His exuberance made her giggle. She had tasted the food several times before serving it, but she was flattered to hear Netu rave so much about it. She obliged him and ate alongside, with a mild wind wafting into the bedroom.

"Been here long?" asked Netu as he took a bite of the cheese.

She grinned. "Not long enough to be worried."

He reached out for a glass of water and took a gulp. "I was sure you'd be here," said Netu, placing back the glass.

Anne was taken aback. "You were?"

"Sure."

"Nice to know."

He laughed like an animated doll. "You sprung up and covered my mind the whole day like a damn shroud—"

"Shroud?" she interjected, with a grimace. "Well, I guess, that would be a good shroud."

"Yes, it's your edge. You won there!"

"Oh, I did?"

Netu stood up full of mirth at the end of the late dinner, slapping his belly as hint that he had overfed himself. Then he leaned over and gave Anne a soft kiss on her brow and scurried to bed. On sighting the novel Anne had been reading before his return, he picked it up.

Anne cleared the dishes, minutes after which she joined him in bed. She snuggled close and wound her arms around Netu, who sensed her quickened breath and fluttering emotion. He dropped the paperback by the bed lamp and turned around to face her. He lowered his head and his seeking mouth found her parted lips, moist and tender. She let out a moan as he returned the tickling probe of her tongue around his.

At the onset, they were engaged in a tender, tongue-coiling play, and then, the intensity increased, and Anne's moaning drowned their rasping heart beats. She clung on to Netu, ecstatic, stroking his nape. With his left hand, he caressed the contour of her spine under the flannel shirt, while tinkling her earlobe with the right. Their kiss lingered with a hint of passion that neither desired a break.

Anne sensed the explosion of her heart with feelings deeper than the depths of her imagination - blissful stars shining within her, making the ugly tint of life bright and beautiful. She puffed at last and released her hold, her eyes glazing with the fire of desire.

Netu peered into her eyes, a furnace of emotion, as she laid back, content. He recognized the inviting spark he had always seen in those tiny balls whenever she wanted him. Her glistening lips were still quivering from the fierce contact with his.

"You taste so sweet," Anne whispered, propping herself on an elbow, to stare at Netu.

Netu responded with a light kiss on the tip of her nose, sought her eager lips, and bathed her face with a splash of kisses. When his hand strayed onto her teats, naked under the shirt, she emitted a shrill, ticklish cry. As he squeezed Anne's taut, clammy breasts, she reached out for his broad chest, moaning and stroking its ridge. Unzipping Netu's pajama's bottom, she pulled him down fully onto her body, unable to care if his weight might crush her. A strong bulge around his groin pressed against her loin, increasing her exhilaration. Netu rolled over and cradled her weight on his trunk. Astride of Netu, Anne felt like an expert rider on a race horse crossing plain upon plain, rocking from side to side. With a lavish kiss, she squirmed to the pressure of the manhood roiling under her.

Anne wanted Netu beyond measure, as if her whole world depended on the union; but she knew he would not go beyond this point. He would permit her to indulge regarding other things, but never to cross the thin line she had always longed for. Though she knew Netu as a knuckle-headed romantic at heart, he could at times become inhibitive for reasons he had explained to her. Anne never doubted Netu's love for her, but she hoped he would someday cross the Rubicon, where she would feel him completely. For, in his amiable ways, Netu remolded her world's many imperfections.

While Anne probed his body, Netu interrogated himself on whether to pry into her secrets or not. He did not intend to hurt her, but the need to know the truth about her role in his life became uppermost in his mind. His immunity lay in whatever he could unearth concerning her. So he would do it and handle her with soft gloves, should she get hurt in the process. She would come to understand that he meant no harm.

Anne rained another round of kisses on Netu, enflaming his feelings with her expext smooching. Netu knew the time for his prying, what he called a chess game, had finally come.

He cupped her firm bust in his hands with tenderness and smiled. "Anne," he whispered. "These financial hills and valleys we always journey through, what do you suppose we could do to eliminate them entirely? I'm getting kind of weary about them."

Anne snapped out of her ecstasy, sensing his dark feeling - a rhetorical hint to his inner uneasiness. "I don't know," she said, adjusting the fine braids of her hair. "I don't know anything anymore. It's all so confusing when you talk about it with such a grim visage, you really mash me into jelly – without guts or hope."

She paused for breath, and added, "I often get inspired by the thought that an improvement is evident in our lives, but the next minute, I see us plunge downhill. I really don't know why life treats us this way."

Netu reached for her right cheek and she inclined her head on his arm. "I don't feel like giving up this fight so soon," Netu said. "But things are pretty messy these days. Up and down, up, down, and up. It's like going round in circles without end, unless, of course, we find a way out. But what way is that?"

Whenever circumstance softened his dogged resolve and made him argue with fate, she felt and shared his pains. Sometimes, she inspired his weary spirit with her vision of how things ought to be and how fate reshapes these aspects for their common good. In spite of it, she had started to sense her own waning resilience as the downhill plunge had become a daily occurrence in their lives, a great omen.

The interspersing moments of financial liberty had been brief, and this financial hill had disturbed her rather brilliant love flight in no small measure daily. Still, she was determined not to let the bleakness of time downplay the rippling sensations in her heart. She would be there for him and together, they would be strong enough to overcome the hurdles he had begun to scale on his own.

"Darling, take no notice of the pressures. They never last forever," said Anne, trying to soft-soap Netu's riled thoughts. She winked. "Remember, Netu, in the vast streams of life, only the tough survive. I know you're tough, tougher than most people I've known. We will overcome if you keep up your toughness of heart and zeal."

She stunned Netu with her philosophical persuasions. He could not help but admire Anne's power of reasoning at times of crisis. When he imagined she had caved in, she would spring up in defiance from an angle he least expected.

"I admire your resourcefulness, your courage and how you stare at the dark points of life without any sense of fear," responded Netu. "But must we go on the tenuous threads of hope and courage forever?"

"There's always a change, surely," Anne remonstrated. "Things have a way of reshaping themselves; and things have not been the same nowadays. We've seen worse times together. Have you forgotten how it used to be a few months back when hope was something we never had? Now, see where we are. You think there's no difference with the past?"

"There's a big difference, of course."

"So hush up. Let's talk only about us - the good moments only, like now," Anne entreated, pulling him closer.

"All right, we'll talk about us. I'll like to begin from a safe point," Netu whispered in her ear as he cradled her for a warm, full kiss. "Anne," he went on after her passionate response, "what do you suppose I could do to gain promotion if I were part of your world spiritually?"

She stiffened, as if a vague serpent had looped itself around her thought. "An odd question, isn't it?" she managed to utter, and then added with boldness, "Promotion to where?"

"You sound dry and look surprised as if you've never for once thought of climbing up the hierarchy. Of course, promotion to higher rungs of power."

"It depends on your ambition."

Netu snorted. "Ambition? Would I be talking of promotion if I weren't ambitious? And would such an ambition include my trampling on others to achieve it?

What I mean is, put yourself in my shoes: what exactly do you have to do to get high up on the ladder of leadership in your world?"

Anne's brow arched upwards, suspiciously. "My world? Is this part of our talk?"

"Somehow, yes, you're on track."

"Are you trying to taunt me?"

"I'm not saying anything you don't know already. I'm just curious, nothing more," said Netu calmly, acknowledging her slight temper.

Anne rolled free of Netu's hold. She recognized the dark hands of spite unsettle a shimmering pond within her. She could feel the new force commanding her whole being to fight the sudden intrusion, Netu. This was the fellow who, seconds before, had been in strange control of her heart, now looming as a dangerous enemy.

"You really think I want to hurt you, don't you?"

Netu chuckled. He had been burning on the inside to banish his fears. Having done his heart's desire, he felt the action did not justify the means. "Far from it," he replied, stretching his arms toward Anne. "You probably didn't get my drift," he explained. "I don't mean....My mind was fixed on–"

"Whatever your mind was fixed on, leave me alone," Anne snapped, jerking herself free of his grip.

Netu knew he had provoked her beyond doubt. Her tone was heavy with venom.

"Be realistic Anne, why would you think I thought you

wanted to hurt me? Is there any sense in what you're saying?"

"Please, Netu, just let me be, will you? You've made up your mind already. You think I want to hurt you..." she trailed off.

Netu felt guilty for triggering the sudden sullenness he saw taking over Anne's hypnotic sensuality. "I'm sorry, Anne," he said in a subdued tone. "I shouldn't have asked you such a dumb question. I didn't intend it to come out like that. In fact, I never saw it as an evil pronouncement on your sweet person. Please, for our sake, just take it as another rash moment of mine. Please."

Netu moved over to her side and held her in his arms.

Anne did not resist the warmth she felt from him. Her sturdy walls of defense dissolved in the heat of his body. Even so, she fought in desperation to hold on to the insulation she derived from those walls by refusing to look at him. His suspicions about her frightened her. Netu had metamorphosed, in her reckoning, from a carefree and overly romantic personality to a man who walked the streets with the notion that friends and foes stalked him. He would snap at every slight opportunity to justify this fear or hunch. She could not blame him much; for, a bird whose precious pinions are garnishing flecks on a ritual table must learn the language of caution in its flamboyant flights. Aware of this, Netu Deo often tried to confide in her about it. They both knew his guided secret as the next in the line of Manus. As such, she knew he had adversaries as countless as a swarm of locusts.

"I don't even know whom to trust anymore," he had told her often. If he suspected her as part of his aches, she would forgive him; for, she had come to appreciate the depth of the rupturing volcano on which he sat as the next in the line of Manus, the Light Bearer.

The warmth of his body and the magic of his dexterous and swift fingers all over Anne melted her resolve. "If you love someone so dearly, you wouldn't even think of hurting such a loved one," she said.

Netu spurned to that scathing remark. "It's okay, my baby. You're not about to hurt me, and nobody's about to hurt anybody. For now, what we have going between us, I figure, matters most. I feel for you from deep within, can't you see?"

Netu drove his fingers like comb through her hair and stroked her with an overruling tenderness. She began to huff, her fire of spite mellowing quickly. She turned and encircled her quaking arms around his neck, and in a half-choking voice, whispered, "I love you so much I don't want to see you hurt. I never ever want to see you hurt; understand?"

Nodding, Netu kissed her, more gently than ever before. She felt gingered back to life again, her darkened mood, lost in the rekindled wave of emotion.

I haven't been able to pry any damn secret out of her, Netu thought. *Did I pull the wrong stunt? From the beginning, she got me feeling guilty with her smart sensitivity. She sure deploys her wiles adeptly, and I'm always the worse for it. I'll let her have the joker for a while; I'll save my laugh for last. After all, I'm mindful of her instinct of vengeance.*

94

The companions spoke little afterwards, the need for words rendered unnecessary by the groundswell of emotion. The magnetism they experienced between them felt stronger after the cajoling he had given her. Words would only have given a superfluous meaning to the lingering silence, since their mutual feeling ruled supreme.

In his characteristic evasiveness, Netu did not mount Anne as she had envisaged. But Anne felt safe entwined with him, believing in the comfort of his strong arms. He meant many things to her and she never doubted the future beauty of her own feelings anchored on his wealth, smile, care, and charisma. She wished both of them could extend the bliss and wanton promise of the moment into the future. She also wished that they could inflame their feelings with mutual care, and let it glimmer like an enchanting eternal light.

Anne closed her wistful-eyes and savored the gift of the moment. The future was still far out in the roiling ocean of time. She would make its call safely if she exercised some patience, she thought. Anne noticed that Netu had dozed off when his grip on her frame slackened. She just could not let go of him; rather she kissed him tenderly and weaned herself to sleep, his sweet breath warming her face next to his on the pillow.

Chapter Five

The morning after, Netu Deo's feelings still centered on his snooping game with Anne Ofino. Against his expectations, he reckoned that, she had outsmarted him, by keeping her secrets intact. The glow of dawn penetrating the bedroom window seemed to re-echo his failure to elicit the truth from her. This frightened him.

His thoughts raced. *Is my vindictive posturing out of tune? Has Anne not proven enough that she cares for me? Didn't I see the spark of her profound love twinkling in her eyes when I gazed down at her and she smiled up like a temptress at me?*

The glaze in her eyes had bewildered him. Perhaps, secrets lurked in them, and he had been caught in their spell. Netu sighed uneasily. A crossfire of thoughts laid claim to his head. Nothing appeared to make sense to him.

He had been awake when she rose from bed quite early in the morning. He knew when she kissed his lips but pretended not to notice. Soon as she had shut the bedroom door his eyes slit open and appraised the speed of time through the window. The sun had risen high and magnificent over paled clouds.

He frisked himself clear of the quilt Anne had pulled over him with care before her quiet exit. Yawning with a throaty noise, he sat on the bed's fringe. He heard Anne's voice as above the din of the living room, with a merry twinge to it. His worry was anchored elsewhere – not their friendly jokes - but on his futile attempt at disentangling from his mind's many clutches. How he would rid his senses of this power which held him to ransom truly worried him. He would take one step at a time, and Anne would be the first step.

Anne sneaked into the bedroom just when Netu rose to flex his weary tendons and tone up his reflexes lulled by sleep. Seeing him awake spurred her.

"What kept you so long in bed?" she asked, full of mirth, swinging to his side. "You didn't even know when I left."

"Even with your kiss on my lips you still think I didn't know?" Netu replied with a hint of humor. He noticed her radiance and sniffed the sweet perfume that hung in the air. "I like the cologne on you!"

"Oh, thanks! If you felt my early morning kiss," Anne chuckled, "how come you didn't say anything?"

"Hmmnn. You could say I was watching you watch me. What a flamboyant peacock you are this morning!"

Anne took the quaint collars of his pajama top in her hands and drew him towards her. "Be drawn to me," she said. "All right, since you've become my watchdog, just stay right here..." She pointed to her heart. "And don't slip away again."

"I won't slip away."

Anne's slender arms encircled Netu's long neck. He was tickled as she stood on her toes to kiss him.

"Did you have a nice rest?"

"I sure did. The best night I ever had."

"What was the noise out there about? Did you win a lottery or something?"

Anne's bewilderment amused him. "You thought I didn't hear you chatting, right?"

"Right. Just catching up on the times, you know."

"As you are catching up on me now I suppose." He laughed as Anne patted his chest.

"Stop the tease."

"I will, provided breakfast is ready."

"Soon. A couple of minutes at most."

Netu smacked her behind mirthfully and eased off her grip. "You sure know how to tease a man! Go and fix us breakfast. I'm starving."

"And you go clean up fast," she said. "No meals until you've freshened up, dear. I don't want you smelling around here."

"I do not smell," he joked.

Anne left, feeling ecstatic.

Netu stood before the mirror and stiffened at his reflection. Stubbles of hair dotted his chin and his brow knitted, no doubt, from mental exhaustion. Though his eyes retained their youthful sparkle, the grim punches of time had created shadows in their corners. His own image staring back at him scared him. It made him feel shy of the obvious - he had stepped higher on the age ladder. In spite of himself and the new meaning age gave to his form and life at thirty-three, his peers envied his youthfulness. They overwhelmed him with nicknames, the most loved one being, Netu, the baby face!

He liked the epithet, for, the spirit of youth kept his burdens light. After all, his countenance reflected the workings of his mind. Netu Deo smiled at the intruding thought. He would promptly take care of the stubbles because they added more years to his age. He preferred the boyish look, which gave him a sense of longevity.

The stark realities of life stared at him. Feeling clammy, he moved away from the mirror and went to shower and shave. Not long after, he walked into the living room, dressed in tennis shorts and shirt, with a pair of flowery slippers. He was ready to share in the jolly chat of Lata, John, and Vivian.

He had observed that Anne did not partake in the din he had heard as she still busied herself with kitchen chores. Vivian, on her usual Thursday off-duty, indulged in it. Most Thursdays, she spent the racing hours at home, except when an urgent social call denied her a deserved rest in the company of loved ones. The rest, not yet gainfully employed, often nestled around the apartment in loud prattle, sometimes to Netu's dismay.

"There's so much excitement here this morning!" Netu said with a humorous edge, plunking onto the living room couch next to Lata. "What is the secret, pal? Fill me in."

"How's the morning like with you?" Lata greeted. "I guess you had a nice sleep. What with your late stirrings?"

"Good, good feelings this morning you may say," Netu replied cockily. "Did you guys sleep at all? It seems you rose with the birds."

John made a humorous defence. "Actually, we crowed before the birds. Those creatures have long shirked their duties. We had to remind them of their duty to creation," he went on, laughing. After some moments, he added, "Hope you slept well? I dare say you were in heaven all night. You simply forgot you still had a place over here."

Netu shrugged. "It would've been nice if I'd been able to remember one jot of fun up there. Heaven, you called it, but I woke up blank. I guess I had a maze of troubling thoughts."

"To me, you don't look at all ruffled," Vivian chipped in. "You're as cute and cool as cucumber."

Vivian's unabashed flatter got Netu grinning. She seldom voiced how she felt about anyone. "Well, you can say I've become an adept in the art of masking inner feelings," he said. "Nowadays, I hardly know the difference between my smiles and frowns."

Vivian's lips toyed with a smile. "With this sweet tongue of yours, you can talk your way through a rock."

Netu noticed that she wore a yellow spaghetti blouse atop blue denim jeans. A mild jerk of her head sent strands of hair flying across her beautiful face. Vivian brushed them aside from blurring her emerald eyes with feminine wile, gazing curiously at Netu.

Netu's frankness amazed Vivian. True, she could not see the difference between his happy and sad moments. To her, they were like two grains: nurtured apart, yet churned in the gentle crucible of his compassion, and sculpted into a genial whole. She had all along seen the whole, but never the opposite grains.

"Really?" Netu enquired with great fascination.

Vivian nodded. "Why not?"

"Breakfast is fixed gentlemen and lady!" Anne broke in with a strident call, as she pranced into the living room with a complacent smile. "I didn't think it would take so much time but it's done all right."

Lata could not contain his excitement. "Okay, sweet sister, let's have it straight on."

"Then come help me with the dishes," Anne called turning back to the kitchen.

"I'm right behind you," Lata said, scurrying after her.

Netu again turned his charm on Vivian. "Now Vivian, perhaps, it's time to revisit your flattery." A wry grin tampered with his attempt to pursue her line of thought. "You really think my words have enough power to disintegrate a rock?"

Vivian stirred, but guarded her station. A thin air of apprehension blew over her high spirit. She could not tell what he had in mind. "In your shoes, I wouldn't over-praise my prowess," she said with a sarcastic edge. "But sure, you're sleek in tongue. Must've caused a hell of trouble for some chaste and well-bred ladies around."

"My God, some wry jokes you make!" said Netu. "Damn the girls. By God, if I ever knew of the power you're humouring me about, they'll all be mine in a flash."

"And get your arse smacked for all the mischief." Vivian's laugh reverberated and Netu joined her.

Moments later, the tantalising aroma of the evening's meal, along with the sweet smell of charred corn flour and spicy chicken stew wafted into the room.

"What do you think it'll be?" John asked Netu, pacing to the dining table.

Netu sniffed the air hard, his brow lifted, with a sagely nod. "Unless the air is treacherous to my senses, I perceive the aroma of roast yam and stew. But, I throw my lot with chicken stew," he boasted, moving to take his seat opposite John.

"Not a score to be proud of. One over two points, Netu," Anne interrupted, clutching a giant tray with a couple of china as she veered from the kitchen. Lata trailed her with another loaded tray.

"Toasted corn bread and chicken stew," she announced.

"Won't you give me thumbs up for guessing right?" Netu demanded.

Anne winked and giggled at him. She served the circle of hungry friends with an officiousness of a seasoned chef in a highbrow hotel. As they ate, Netu told Anne how delicious her food tasted, and she blushed. The decision to serve toasted bread and stew was her singular decision. Since no one complained about the fare, she was delighted. Netu's kind of compliment rarely came her way.

Silence enveloped the atmosphere for some minutes after breakfast. Everyone felt contented and unwilling to take leave of the table. The palatable food aside, the magnificent and bright morning had enlivened their company. The ensuing ambiance called for serene relaxation.

John broke the silence. "Life could be gamely sometimes, you know," he said, rising to his feet, and negotiating clear of the dining table. "At times, especially when one is well-fed and happy, the picture of life one gets in one's head is that of a merry-go-round. One feels that all there is to it is the exciting fear factor and the giddy suspense of the rolling forms." Now hunched over the head of a dining table chair, he paused and glanced at his companions.

"But my dear friends," John continued, "from our individual experiences, somewhere in this rickety journey referred to as life, we've all been pawns in its game. I believe you'll all agree with me without any reservation, that life isn't the roller-coaster ride we often imagine it is."

John's logic, though unpremeditated, stirred his friends' imagination, and got them thinking through a spell of pricking silence.

Netu broke the stillness. "Getting idealistic, eh?"

John's philosophical self-unveiling surprised Netu Deo. Personal traits he had never seen in the young man now came to the fore, such as his spring of wisdom, insight, and a hidden supernatural edge.

"Say that if you will," replied John with indifference. "Life to me is the most complex philosophy. Our daily living is just a concert at understanding its rhythms. We are simply interpreting life's different notes that combine to make the concert meaningful."

"Damn it, I was wrong to think you're naive," Netu exploded, with a smile."

"I don't think John was," Lata remarked. "He is a conservative knowledge bank!"

Laughter pealed around the dining table.

"People with his type of skull are always wise," Vivian said, and then added a physiological angle. "Study the shape of his skull - mid-point between oblong and broad, and with a slight jut to the back, and the curve of his brow – and you'd see an evidence of wisdom!"

"How the hell did you know that?" Lata wondered.

"It's part of our culture," answered Vivian. "We study these traits in our local settings and it enhances our perceptions of our environment and the circumstances."

"Sorry, I'm a city cat!" Lata said shyly. "I don't claim to be wise about such aspects of Riagena culture."

"Then you'd better be close to your roots," Vivian urged.

"Oh, what a morning!" said Netu.

Anne chuckled beside him, her arm about his shoulder. Netu captivated her as the only subject worthy of attention. Not their philosophical or cultural banter.

Soon afterwards, everyone moved away from the dining area to the living room, where the morning prattle continued with intensity. Netu, however, retired straight to his bedroom. Anne's chores at the kitchen kept her away from him for some time. With the increased television sound from the living room, Netu knew his younger companions were hell-bent on sustaining the pleasant mood for as long as it would take.

Two hours sped past, and the morning phased into humid noon. Soon, the weather cooled off in the day's rush towards dusk. Netu and Anne were now alone in the three-bedroom apartment, with Anne having since joined him in his bedroom while the others still chatted in the living room. All of a sudden, silence reigned. When Netu and Anne came out to ascertain what had overtaken the living room noise, he saw the note John had left on the center table. Netu sighed, in relief.

"What's the mystery?" Anne enquired.

"John's note says they've gone out," Netu answered, dropping the piece of paper. "I guess he didn't want to intrude on our privacy."

"Nice guy, John. Well, since we're all alone, and free as the wind, why don't we make the most of it?" Anne coaxed, clinging on to Netu's arms. "I suggest we haul ourselves back to bed and while the hours away."

"Great idea! And what did you say is the best way to while away time?"

"Quite easy," she taunted him back. "Just tag along and you will know how. Any excuse now?"

"Don't say it. I feel it already."

Netu steered Anne back to the bedroom, locking the door, amused as Anne ran across the room, throwing herself on the bed. He caught her wrist in a mock chase, pinning her frame to the mattress. She feigned a wriggle, and then surrendered like a hen to a rooster's fluttering serenade. With their bodies caught in a tango and lips tangled they went gasping as they rocked on in ecstasy.

For many minutes, they lay drained in their silent personal spaces, as the eddies ebbed, exchanging fleeting spying glances.

Anne thought back in time. As a prize, Netu had not come easy. Of course, her robust ambition got stretched to its limit before she won the trophy of love, and on a platter, which amazed even her boldest rival in the multitude of scheming female species.

Each time this memory haunted her and its dart struck at a dreamed future in which Netu straddled their wheel of fate, playing his dignified role as her heart's controller, she managed not to cry. Rather, she would escape into the spirit of self-praise. Besides, few in her league of rivals bore such a scar in their memories. She alone so felt the violent thrust of the secret game which went on among the interested parties. A rivalry that almost claimed her life. Yet, she not only survived it, but also emerged victorious, by sheer inspiration and rugged perseverance. Now, she had every reason to be full of self-praise; at least, this day, Netu was hers.

The war would never be over inasmuch as Netu waited to ascend the throne and bear the spiritual mantle as the Manu long forecasted. In his arms then for the first time, Anne felt overwhelmed by the act of providence:

Anne, the underdog, now victor, and in the arms of one of the most adorable men in Newland. Cheerfully, but at times with a tint of gloom, they had crossed both turbulent and calm seas together. There, the armor of their deep mutual affection and the fragrance of their warmth protected them. Yet, the moment she feared most came. Plotting the intricacies of the battles had been easy, but winning and keeping the prize seemed the real war.

An icy breath stole into Anne's lungs, overwhelming her with fear. Would Netu leave her? Would he betray her trust in him? *Damn all the pressures he had been complaining about of late. Why would the vile forces not hands-off the treasure of her life? Damn all of them. Damn their indignity for striving to ruin her plans.* She had won some fierce battles before and lost them in euphoria. No matter the stakes, she would keep this victory to herself.

Netu too drifted into the realm of thought. He ballooned himself into outer space and remained in the haze of timelessness; an aft state of mind he often liked. This condition gave him access to time's microfilms. A clear way to assuage his mind's torment. His suspicions about Anne necessitated this. By the same degree of mind over-exertion, his rationality suffered as well and rubbed off his otherwise justifiable vindictiveness. Provoked by a similar fright instinct a week before, he had done a swift maneuver with Anne, which she acknowledged as an ingenious gimmick at self-protection, a necessary shield in time of trouble. Slide by slide the intrigue of the past week rewound by the projector of his mind.

Anne had come as usual all the way down to OldHill, from Remwil District of Newland's southern boundary with the Sagol Sea. A place regarded as the oven of integrated cultures, degrading squalor, and vast opulence. She intended to cherish some bliss with Netu. They had been alone in the three-bedroom apartment as they were now and all had gone well with their emotions, until the recurrent bout of fear found foothold in Netu's senses.

If I must give in to her facade of innocence, I must commit her to an oath she cannot revoke, Netu thought. Let her mix her Hemlock with her own hands in case she becomes too clever and perfidious, he reasoned further. Predation seems the ball game in the theatre of life, and survival the only choice. Either I hunt, or I'm hunted. But if my fears are justified, if all I've been told by the Guardians of the Universe in the Blackhole's Disc Centre are equally correct, my peculiar nature would not let me hunt Anne, but I would make her ensnare herself.

The faint blur of the slides of Netu's mind disappeared with amazing sharpness as he remembered in vivid terms how he had out-foxed Anne, while holding her close on the living room settee. The disk player fed their hungry need for each other with a scintillating tune, but as Anne's prey, Netu knew it to be a game he must play well. First, he needed to avoid the race of a scared hare he suspected himself to be, and then to chase with the fury of a hound at the same time.

"Anne, I've been thinking about you and me," he teased.

"Is it?" Anne demanded calmly. She raised her groomed thick eyelashes with sudden interest. "Tell me dear, what's on your mind?" She tucked her right leg under her left thigh on the couch and stared at him, brushing her loose hair backward from obscuring her vision.

"I've been thinking about what you are to me," he said, with a grin.

"Easy to guess," Anne said with pride. "I'm a good friend, your lover!" She touched the ridge of his semi-broad nose, narrowed the slit of her eyes, adding, "And I dare say, your wife!"

Netu laughed dryly. "Not precisely. My would-be wife," he corrected, playfully biting the tip of her retreating forefinger.

Anne squirmed from the tickle of Netu's incisors on her finger and gave him a feeble punch on the chest. "Whatever it is, I'm no meat to chew!"

"You're not, of course, but you're like a mother to me. I've been thinking about this all day." Her flustered look increased his amusement. "You're not only a mother," he continued. "It encompasses the other qualities you mentioned as well: sister, friend, brother, and lover!"

Anne regained her composure. "Pretty romantic way of telling me how you feel, not so?" she drawled.

"Well, yeah, but have you ever seen me as your sister, friend, brother, and lover? What about as your child?"

Anne looked on thoughtfully. "Not often," she confessed, and then in bold defense, added, "I've always seen you as everything to me."

"Everything?" echoed Netu, his forefinger emphasizing the word. "It's still vague, you know what I mean? We are talking in the light of mother and child relationship now. That bond is more enduring than others. Everything as you know it has the tendency of crumbling under a number of wiles."

"So?" Anne goaded.

"Would you take me as your child?"

Anne hesitated. "Uh-hu!" she muttered.

Her brief hesitation and indifferent reply did not fool Netu.

"All right," he said, "as a loving mother, what would you wish your child?"

Anne's brow kneaded. What he fiddled with in his mind she almost could touch in his gaze, yet its texture she could not discern. "Any mother worth her salt would give her child utmost care."

"Wisely said," Netu cheered. "I thought you'd falter around the bend."

"Falter is not the right choice of word. I'm a mother already. Need I tell you about my son, Andy, again? I think I can answer your question from my own experience as a mother."

Damn the circumstance, she did not want her sour romance with an ex-boyfriend recalled while in Netu's embrace but the tricky question he had asked made her mention it. It worried her – not necessarily because of Netu's knowledge of her son and ex-lover, but the fact she loathed remembering giving birth to a son for another man instead of Netu whom she truly loved.

Netu bridged the thin gap between them and kissed her fervently. She gasped and shrugged free in her eagerness to end a move she believed preceded a deeper intrigue.

"We haven't finished the business at hand," she said without pretense. "I'll rather we get done with it first."

"Which is?"

"The thing on your mind, let's lay it bare."

"All right then," he said, pouting. He needed a moment's pause to put his words right. "With the way you carry on, I can tell you know I'm glad with your wish for me as your child. Now as your child, don't forget I'm whining and whimpering in your tender hands. Would you then oblige me the benefit of the sound of your voice in wishing me the things you wish your child?"

Anne tensed up and looked away. She knew it! Damn the fox in Netu. She knew by God he had been beating about the bush to confuse her when she least expected. She admitted she had been stupid to have been so trapped.

"I wish you the thing I wish for my son," Anne said in a defiant tone. Her gaze lowered on the floor as she brooded.

"But you didn't say what you wish your son?" Netu cajoled, trying to win her over. "I'm your son, remember?"

"I've done what you requested. What else do you demand?"

Netu's eyes screwed half-shut with glaring impatience. To calm himself, he scratched his brow, pronged his tongue, and toyed with his thin line of moustache.

"Alright, you've done my bidding, but don't you see

it's partially done? You have not said the words I want to hear. What is it you wish me as your child in your arms? That's what I want to hear you say."

"I wish you everything," Anne said in a voice bereft of the conjuring power of the supernatural.

"Like what?"

Anne did not reply. She sat as a stone-hewed nymph, hoisted in the bulwark of a popular promenade, dead to the enchanted gestures of the throng passing by. Manifold were the implications of what Netu demanded. There were things she could not do with him once she took the oath. It meant too much fun to throw away, another great prize to pay to keep him.

"You're shy, I see," Netu said, inspired by a new idea. "I know the way out. Don't you fret or move now. I'll be back with the answer right away."

Netu rose. He knew he had the trump card and she appeared to be at his mercy. Anne watched him whistle merrily as he wheezed into his bedroom. She bowed her head in contemplation. Must she always give? Would it hurt him if she held back? He asked for something within her powers to give, so why procrastinate or refuse him? Netu's whistling as he returned stopped her train of thought.

Netu dropped a clean piece of paper and a ball point pen next to her on the settee and knelt down on the rug - not in reverence to Anne but an expression of the importance of the issue at hand.

"What the lips can't say the heart can translate to the hand to write," Netu implored. "Here, on this paper, let me see what your heart is saying for me."

Anne laughed, gave Netu a bewitching stare, and then smiled, reaching for the pen and paper. Netu sensed the tinkle of victory in his veins now pulsing with a surge of blood.

Anne scribbled some words on the paper.

Netu craned his head and observed the expressionless mask on her face as she paused intermittently for coherence of thought.

"Have it now, Netu," she said, thrusting the paper into his hand. She eyed his elation dim as he read.

I wish you all I wish my son.

"That's one step forward," he said, not daring to show his excitement. "Step two: don't you wish me care, love, protection, wealth, and all that goes with being your child?"

"I do," Anne said.

"Then put it down on the paper."

Beneath the first line of words, Anne scribbled . . . Protection, care, love and wealth. Then she quizzed him with a knotted brow.

Netu was on cue. "What next, right? Who is making this wish and to whom?"

"From Anne to Netu," she said, no longer tensed up. She had begun to enjoy the joke along with him.

"Excellent! Indicate both names at the appropriate places, and don't forget to add a date."

Anne complied, giving Netu a congratulatory glance. At the top of the lines, she wrote in bold letters *NETU DEO* and underneath, *ANNE OFINO*, dated 7th of January 1996.

Though satisfied with Anne's compliance, Netu reckoned one thing remained undone. "Well done!" he said with a smile. "We are almost through. Read to my hearing what you've scribbled down."

Anne read her wish with a lilting voice and deep feeling, which Netu acknowledged in his heart as a great commitment. Acting on the moment's impulse Netu retrieved the wish from her and wrote his own.

I, Netu Deo by the Grace of the Divine unction, hereby declare on this day, 7th of January 1996, that whatever is meant for Anne Ofino should be given to her without further delay. I call on the Ascended Masters, the Guardians of the Universe, and all the positive forces on the planet to sanction this request with the urgency it demands.

Netu then signed the paper and handed it back to Anne. "I've endorsed mine, you endorse yours," he said.

Anne signed and dated it. "Hope you are not going to use this against me?"

"Why, no. Just watch what I'll do with it right away."

Netu hummed a tune she did not quite comprehend as he hurried away to the kitchen. He returned with a matchbox. "I intend to burn someone's pretty face with it." He laughed and rocked from side to side.

Anne chuckled. "I dare you." She swung to her feet, barricaded Netu's path in a daring, cockeyed poise, and raised a spindly finger to his chest. "Netu, you don't have the hardened nature of a brute here where your heart beats. What's the damn idea you have regarding the match box?"

"Impatience isn't a virtue I'd advise anyone to cultivate or even tolerate," he chided. "Watch me and keep your cool. Can I have the wish one more time?"

Anne ignored his chiding, picked the piece of paper from the settee and handed it over.

"Come with me," he beckoned as he led the way to the kitchen, rolling the piece of paper into a spindle. Anne followed, her heart palpitating with fear.

In the kitchen, Netu threw the paper onto the floor tiles. He struck a matchstick and lit a corner of the spindled paper. The flame caught the edge, crawling in the initial rage up the spindle. It then flared with a faint crack as Netu picked it up and held the untouched end, then its anger spread with bright flames towards his hand. Netu felt the searing of the flame at his fingertips and let go.

Anne brightened at his little prank with the flaming paper. Only then did her heart stop its palpitation. He had not blackmailed her with it; yet, she saw an inexplicable ritual in his antics.

In silence they watched the struggle of the butt of the burning spindle, now consumed, and malformed from its initial whiteness to a mass of black ash on the glittering floor.

Netu sniffed the carbon wafting in the air. Instead of being displeased by the choking smell of carbon, it spurred him. Netu smacked his lips hard and shrugged confidently.

"The gods have heard. It's all over," he said inspired by his newly acquired power.

Anne looked on still stunned by the oddity of his game. If she had any explanation to his intentions, his self-unveiling in his inference with the gods must be it. This seemed a ritual done with the intention of her not detecting its asperity of purpose. But how would the gods, the Guardians of the Universe and all the beings or spirits summoned come to bear the weight he had passed on to them? How would the Guardians come to the knowledge of what they had done in secret, when it exemplified a child's attempt to shoot down a star with a catapult? She admitted Netu remained one damn mystery she never understood. *It hurts me like the blow of a scythe that I don't know this mystery pretty well placed on my tender palms.* She shook her head to steady her mind.

"It's an invocation far beyond your ways," Netu said, as if Anne's mind had relayed her worries to his head. "Clear the ash from the floor and I'll elucidate on this later."

Anne took the ash to the kitchen trash basket while Netu loitered around the kitchen entrance. Once she was through, he held Anne by the arm and led her to the bedroom. He went to the kitchen, opened the refrigerator, grabbed a packet of pineapple juice and two glasses and handed Anne hers.

"This is to us!" he cheered, tinkling his glass against hers. "This is to us!" Anne replied.

After a number of slow sips, Netu said, "What we've

just done looks meaningless to the uninitiated. But you know I wouldn't indulge in something stupid and senseless unless I consider it potent and necessary."

He soothed his vocal chords with another sip, wiped his lips with his tongue, belched, and continued. "It's a funny, little game I play often. This is the third time actually, and it works, my baby! It works in a mysterious way. There is a supernatural allusion to it."

Netu noticed Anne's amusement.

"The other times I tried it," he went on, "the situations were not the same as this. No woman was involved – just I and the creation, the cosmos, the Masters, past and present; and the God of my being. With it, I invoke the whole creation to witness. Sometimes I alter the procedure depending on the need and urgency." He paused to empty his glass.

Anne's respect for Netu towered beyond her measure. He taught her in a number of ways, she reasoned. The feeling that she would learn everything about Netu and yet not know him enough to flaunt it worried Anne. She held up her glass, pretended to sip the juice, and spied him over its rim. A warm feeling rippled within her.

I think I'm truly beginning to love him. His smile always disarms me. By God, his even, sparkling teeth shine like little stars in the night sky. His seductive eyes, with their bushy lashes and bushy brows. His broad lips and small-ridged nose. His crew-cut hair and handsome face, o!

"I've said enough," Netu's voice banished Anne's thoughts. "A man must always endeavor to wield a scepter of mystery which defies a woman's understanding. That way, he keeps her in constant check." Netu's raucous laughter rent the air.

"Anywhere a man goes, he never forgets to display his chauvinist genes, even if he's a spiritual icon," Anne rebuffed him. "First, a man is a man, hence, a chauvinist. Then he's so many other things. Maybe, a spiritual icon," she mocked.

"War of words. Empty war of words."

Anne lowered her glass to the floor, kicked off her slip-on, and slapped him on the shoulder. "Race you to bed," she said, feeling triumphant.

"Let's see who wins this war," Netu joked. "It's your guts against mine."

He went stoically after her. She strove to parry his grasp but he was swifter on the bed. As they crumbled into a bundle, they rained kisses on each other.

Anne took a long drawn breath and steadied her composure when Netu released his hold. "The wish I wrote down for you is the same my ex-boyfriend, Mike, trouble me about," she revealed. "He said he'll do anything for me if only I'll oblige him."

"And, did you?" he snapped, unable to hide his envy.

"If I did I wouldn't have repeated it with you, would I?"

"I would've been damned if you did," Netu said, with a sigh of relief. "Thanks, baby, for saving it all for me! Clever you! I know, from now on, you won't forget I'm your baby."

"A promise remains a promise. It's an obligation that

must be met to its logical conclusion. I've given you my word, and that's it."

"Did your ex-boyfriend tell you why he wanted the request honored?"

"Yes. He explained it would enable him accomplish all his dreams - some kind of magical touch that would seal his future."

"He knows your spiritual station then?"

"He knows a lot about me."

Anne swelled with joy. She could not hold back any secret from him, having allayed her fear. She gazed into his eyes and grinned. "Netu, the difference between you and all the men I've ever known is that you are intelligent," she said, riveting her gaze to the wall to stifle laughter.

Netu felt flattered. "Really?"

"Sure. Smarter than anyone I've known." She fell back into his arms and they lay down together, smiling and smooching, oblivious of the world's cadences.

This happened a week prior, a victory he had celebrated by over-pampering Anne with attention. The assurance they got through their new mother-and-child pact had sustained this victory over Anne.

Strange feelings began to give doubt to their well-knitted love barely a week after. Claws of suspicion fought hard to capture his mind, luring him to a depth he could not understand. In artful self-defense, for the second time in a week, he almost reneged on his vow to never again hurt Anne. He regretted this.

He did not doubt the relationship though, except for some intrusions in their love. Netu termed these as "the ugly hands of evil." He had to save Anne from this rearing evil, or from his doubts, by making sacrifices.

Would Anne perhaps misinterpret my move as a blatant bluff? Would she not imagine I had given her a wild stallion kick just to fulfill my desire? Netu blocked such thoughts from spoiling what had to be done, and done fast.

"A perturbing silence, wouldn't you say?" Anne broke in. Her probing gaze prompted him back to the present. "What were you brooding about? I saw a slight crease on your face."

"Just thinking; darts, here and there," Netu drawled. "Couldn't focus on a single thing. I could tell you were thinking too."

"Yes," responded Anne. "Same vagueness of thought. Nothing to hold onto. A romance with fear, of what I couldn't say. It just hovered around my heart – like I was scared of losing something really special."

Netu got the hint. "Mine wasn't fear as such but the thought of decisions that must be taken without delay."

Anne reclined her head on her palm and propped her elbow between jutting pillows. "What decisions?"

Netu supported his head with an elbow and peered into her face. He saw a mask of concern there. "Decisions in our best interest," he answered in a solemn tone.

Anne feigned ignorance. "Oh, I didn't realize we were that pressed."

"The pressure on us is no longer sublime, as it were,"

Netu said, with a churlish chuckle at the import of his statement. "Some moments ago you felt it too. You said so, if I remember correctly. It's been so with me for some time now. I've tried to kill it in my head, fling it into the deep seas, but it just wouldn't leave. The decisions come at times of confusion, like this moment, because that's the safest way both of us would go unhurt."

A sudden quake rumbled in Anne's belly, along with spasms of fear and disorientation. By God, don't let him say something stupid. She tried to cover her inner trembling with a wry grin. "My ears are eager to hear your judgment, my lord," she said with a forced calmness.

"There are two decisions to be made; no, two choices rather," Netu explained. "Sounds more humane to see them as choices. Embedded in those choices that I would give you are the solutions to an impending disaster. I'm trying to forestall the unavoidable canon fire our emotions would face if we overlook the anxieties that had enslaved us in recent times. We need to make those choices if we must sustain our hopes for better dawns.

He paused, smirked at Anne, and went on. "It's a fact that we're in love with each other. It's also true that we don't want to hurt each other. The only way we can safeguard our mutal feelings and protect our future is to make the right choices."

Anne's mind raced a marathon. She could not tell what he was up to.

Netu observed in Anne's shifty maneuvre on the bed, a weird blend of fear and faked easiness. He could perceive her struggle to resist by sheer will power a wave of anger rising against her senses, yet the betrayal of fear of something unknown glared in her restlessness.

Netu grunted, and then resumed his proposition. "Anne, you must think deeply of these options before you make your choice. It's for the sake of our love. There's a revenge instinct driving its tendrils into our hearts. We can both trace its origin to our past lives - many incarnations and civilisations ago. We have to stop the growth of these dangerous tendrils."

Netu knew his punch line – the options with which he would stun Anne – but he foot-dragged instead. "I've examined and re-examined the choices with care," he said, lowering his gaze, seeking for an inner empowerment to voice the design of his heart. "For our sake you would have to choose between me and what you think I could do to erase the instinct of vengeance in you."

In Anne's mind, the options sounded like clapping thunder, leaving her gaping as if blinded by a strong wind. She tried to rise from the bed but sat instead at its edge. Her head ached in disbelief and confusion. Despised, she felt a desperate need to defend herself.

As far as her blighting thoughts went, she felt trapped like an unyielding parachute, stuck to no fault of hers. "What kind of talk is this?" she muttered almost to herself, with a shrewd glance.

Damn my indiscretion! She cursed. *If I'd not told Netu Deo of our four other incarnations and the chain of intrigues imported to the present, he would not haunt me now with those memories. Damn him for probing and eliciting such cherished secrets from me from time to time! But is Netu aware of those times, and only wanted to confirm what he had already known? Damn, I've told him of the deadly schemes that marred, made, and remade those incarnations even if he knew! And here I am, a fool for it!*

Netu read her fears well and tried to ride the turbulent wave of her incensed emotion. "It's the best thing to do," he said with caution. "Let me explain. In the options, we have individual claim to a great future, though devoid of collective ambition. The first choice offers you the chance to fall in love again. And it's a natural way to erase from your consciousness any lingering impression that I might have left behind. There might be evergreen memories in spite of the new affair but with time, you'd learn to forget me completely. The alternative to this choice, if you view it as too harsh, is to tell me the one vital key that would unlock the vaults of vengeance. This, I believe, will liberate in your being the sweet force of love. The second choice, you'll admit, will unite us and lead to the fulfillment of our collective ambition. As for the other choice, you know where it puts both of us. What do you say to this?"

Anne had never in her life experienced so grave a shock. Her perfect universe was in shambles, thanks to Netu's deadly whim. Had his love song been a ruse? What a height of treachery? How unpardonable his wiles to chop off her heart for sale in the market stalls? Had she been wrong to trust in love, to give her being wholesale to the deft beckon of cupid's hand? To blazes with his options, whatever they mean! There would never be another man that could replace him in her heart with as much relevance. She had loved him boundlessly. No man could command so much of her respect and care as he had done, in spite of her faint awareness of his guilt conscience, what he termed a tempest of vengeance.

Just yesterday, with his sly remarks about promotion, he had incensed her like a fiery hornet, and she had managed to tame the violent wave of suspicion with her own embankments. With the present options, however, Netu had gone ahead to demystify her heart's stronghold, rendering her prone to the torment of the elements.

"If you love someone so deeply, you wouldn't ask such a person to make the kind of choice you ask me to make," Anne stammered. Her voice quivered, masking a strange, wracking pain inside her. Tears squirted and blemished her gorgeous face. "Do you really love me?" she sobbed, as she fought to take hold of her emotion.

The room became hazy. The entire world spun with blighted fury before Netu's eyes. The atmosphere dazed him with uncalled-for images which shocked him into tears, but chivalry restrained him.

No warrior would permit himself to weep in a battlefield; it is the greatest weakness, he argued with himself. He needed all the courage he could summon to end this war, though subtle.

"I love you, Anne," Netu said, in a waning voice. "Perhaps, I've not told you this before, but you know I do. I can't bear to see you hurt. That informs my action; choices, I mean."

"You say you love me?" Anne queried. She still sobbed, hiding her face in her palms.

"Yes, I do." He seldom used the word, love, for those he cared for but he regretted nothing, having said the word she wanted to hear. Balls of insistent tears rolled down his eyes and fell on his T-shirt. Embarrassed by his swelling emotion, he wiped his eyes with his palm. A warrior never cries, he thought.

"Netu, if you love me, why do you do this to me?"

"What I've just asked of you is the sacrifice of love," Netu said. He fought back his splurging tears and tried to take Anne back into his arms.

She stiffened at the force of his words. He did care after all! But did he give his choices on selfish grounds or for mutual interest? Even through the maze of jeering images, she could see the glint of hope in the tumultuous, hazy expanse. By her reckoning, these options belonged to the devil.

Sacrifice of love, he had called it. Should she make the sacrifice? Dreadful thoughts assailed her. She shuddered to consider the reality of such a sacrifice: Netu dashing out of her life like a vagrant shooting star.

Netu wound his arms around her shoulders and weakened her resistance. "Please, Anne, don't make me lose control," he pleaded in a quivering voice. "Stop sobbing, if not, I too will break down. Please, calm down." He suppressed a choke in his throat, swallowing hard.

Anne turned in his clasp and stared at him with bleary tear-rimmed eyes. When she noticed the squirting tears in his eyes, her heart exploded with feelings.

"*Sacrifice of love!*" A husky sob accompanied her echo as she threw herself onto Netu's shoulder. "*Sacrifice of love!*" she repeated once more, bathing Netu's shoulders with tears.

"It is okay, my baby," Netu coaxed on, stroking her

back. "It's okay. I love you, calm down. You still have me. Hush, now. I'm here with you."

She pulled away and smiled. Her charming face carried not the faintest trace of anxiety, anger or despair. The gloom of her sobs surrendered to a mood of wild delight. Perplexed, Netu eyed her with curious excitement.

Anne smiled even more broadly. "Netu, the choices you gave me were in line," she said. "We'd better be done with them then." She paused, rearranged her braids to a neat knot behind her earlobe, and retraced her thought. "The first option excites me more; a lasting antidote I must say, since we won't have to come back to face our weights all over again. So, I'd go for the first option." She glowered. "I remember your words all too clearly: *sacrifice of love!* Let's make that sacrifice for our sake."

Netu knew Anne's ingenuity had taken him to his wit's end. He conceded this fact. If he gave Anne Ofino a hard shove, she would find her way back into his heart with an uncanny relevance. He had thought she would go for the second choice, fearing the consequence of the first; but she had tried to outsmart him in his own game, denying him the code to her heart's tempest of vengeance.

"If that's your choice, well, all right," Netu said, knowing she could not have meant it. "But I would most certainly subscribe to the second option. It soothes us more. With it, we can have ourselves caring and sharing for eternity."

"Do you really believe I like the idea of leaving you for someone else?" Anne asked, pressing her bosom against his chest and imprisoning his neck with her slim arms. Her nipples hardened under her shirt. Yet, it did not arouse Netu. Instead he fixed his mind on the sour mood he had been trying to alter to mirth. "I don't ever wish to leave you; not even for a second, no matter what happens between us," she spluttered, the tears oozing out. "I am scared of losing you, Netu. Please, don't ever leave me."

Anne Ofino sobbed. Her earlier resolve, melted away, and she relapsed into a listless state of anguish and despair.

Netu held her close, cajoling her with sweet words, rocking her to a lullaby. "Let's forget all about options," he said. "No one ever said anything about options and none of us must remember anything of the sort. The issue is buried. Let's not exhume it. Just remember: nothing has been said and nothing will anymore be said about our future. We have each other and that's the best we could ever have! Promise, you'll forget about it."

Anne gave a weary nod, her sobbing staunched by his words.

"Fine," Netu continued. "You and I together we'll reach the highest peak, and there, we'll know our paradise! How about that?"

"Whatever you say," Anne said.

Silence hung over the pensive mood. The combined charge of their entangled bodies dissolved the stubborn knots of fear and tears.

When at last the orange-gold luminescence of the imperious sun fell over the precarious western edge of Newland's expanse, enthroning a round moon on the eastern horizon and the silvery shawls of a bright night, Anne got ready to leave. She had spent two days at Netu's place. Her joy was such that even he could not help but admire her shock-absorbing spirit. She took the day's arguments and the pressures of the past week in her strides as if nothing had transpired. They resolved after the argument on his options to be a strong team. They would work out their destinies together as a team, and allow no fear or suspicion to threaten their deserved peace.

Netu Deo escorted Anne Ofino to OldHill's bus stop and dallied around until she boarded. "I'll see you at the weekend," she half-shouted to Netu as she sat down. In the same breath, she added cheerfully, "Netu, don't do what I wouldn't do."

"I won't," Netu replied, smiling. The bus zoomed off towards Diosh Park, where Anne would disembark for another bus to Remwil District. She waved him, smiling, while Netu reciprocated. He turned and walked down the slope of OldHill back to the apartment. His fast softening heart intrigued him. Would it ever stop huffing especially for Anne Ofino?

Part Two

ATLANTIS

THE PAST

Chapter Six

SONGHAI, ATLANTIS. Twenty-five thousand years ago.

Tonka Manu drew open the drapes of the nearest window in the large oval penthouse. A sudden surge of emotion took over his mind - a prickly sense of premonition in the depths of his heart. While his right forefinger traced the edges of the drapes, his heart reeled in the grip of an intense revelation he could not place. It had a lot to do with Atlantis. This worried him. He knew not what it meant or how it could be overcome.

His dark-brown eyes were first fixed on the outside of the penthouse's window. His gaze then rose beyond the Divine Theatre, the lush expanse of the intervening gardens and arching tapestry of Manu Square's tangling mansions. He beheld the northern horn of civilization. In the view, great riches and architectural masterpieces spread all around him like the magnificent bloom of a Lotus flower. In Tonka's eyes, the skyline was awash with glimmering sapphires of triangular, dome-shaped structures. They reflected the hazel glare of the lazily hovering sun. Beneath them, varied economic trees spread their foliage like royal canopies along a plush-green avenue. Under the shades, gold-plated, eight-lane carriageways schemed into side streets, sparkling amidst the enchanting surroundings. On the streets of Songhai, aerophibian cars and buses, their wings idly tucked to their sides, vied with a variety of posh automobiles. The automobiles moved with ease and emitted no poisonous exhaust. In the steps of the many Atlanteans prowling the busy streets of Songhai, the essence of the divine glared from Tonka Manu's assessment. This aspect had fed the initial phase of the civilization and inspired the humans to heightened accomplishments in later phases. A reckless attitude, however, had crept into their joy. In spite of the consequences of their misplaced priorities and spiritual stead, Tonka Manu thought Atlanteans might steer clear of the dangerous cliff and spare him the bouts of anxiety.

A maroon colored Hansa convertible pierced into view through pockets of hazel clouds in its flight. The customized aerophibian car skirted the northern skyline and nose-dived into the fields to the east beyond Manu Square.

Ahead of the Divine Theatre, men and women strolled on the promenades. Some made swift turns into intersecting streets while others strode leisurely into nearby alleys. These movements were inspired by how grande Atlantis was, especially with the aura these folks radiated. The men wore small caps that took up portions of their heads. They looked pristine in cassock-like silk garbs, almost like hollow tendrils stretching below their knees. These covered the better part of their ankle-length trousers, an obvious inelegance when seen in light of the surrounding splendor.

Titan Race

Whorls of large siphons and blouses reflected the women's sense of chastity. Their scarves and shawls covered their hair but exposed their radiant faces, like over-dressed dolls. Young men on trendy bicycles and motorbikes breezed past the pedestrians walking on the bulwarks.

An eagle's antics in the hazel sky also drew Tonka Manu's attention from the vantage point of his penthouse window. It crested the cool currents of the coastal wind, soaring with elegance between trees, above high towers and robust buildings that blended into the beautiful vastness of Atlantis. Soaring on fully spread wings, its tail swayed to the west-bound currents. It did not reckon with the fascination of the Atlantean who observed its tricks from the window of a penthouse in a cluster of mansions that formed an arc round the Divine Theatre in the holy hub of Manu Square, Songhai.

Tonka watched the eagle lift up on the benevolent wind till it crossed the broad reaches of Manu Square. It then skewed skyward and careened to the right in the fierce blast of an opposing east wind. Its wings came flapping down with immense power, and then up, with the force of will in its westward course. In a daring stunt, it broke through the burst of an infringing east wind. It then plunged low and swung back up to the initial height. The next moment, as it gained height, the wind's force sent it askew once more.

The king bird forced a headway through the blasting wind with several maneuvres but it advanced a little only beyond its initial point. Again off-balance in its brisk ascent, the eagle spread its wings and surrendered to the superior force of the counter-wind. With zest it wheeled anti-clockwise and soared along with the opposing wind towards the eastern expanse, done with daring, westward aerobatics.

Tonka Manu, the patriarch of Atlantis, enjoyed the bird's canny sense of surrender to nature's whim. *Humans often lack this ideal. Man's innate stubbornness often makes him an uncooperative creature in the complex mold of creation. In self-deluding belief, borne of a misguided intelligence in which he assumes his whimsies would always prevail against insurmountable odds or upon nature's own renewal processes, man often attempts to take on meaningless challenges,* Tonka mused.

He thought further. *If man had the privilege of a role reversal and assumes the role of the beautiful eagle in the sky, rather than surrender to nature's whim in the opposing wind, man's choice would be to continue with the flight even if ill-fated. A bird, however, understands the mysterious pulse of the wind and the elements and would fly no further without interpreting the rhythms in the air.*

The core of the experience of mortals takes its sterner stuff from such ironical conflicts, Tonka reasoned. *This aspect puts a hole in the main mast of man's ship and often takes the wind out of his sail. This aspect, often times, lurches man's ship of fate ashore. The wrecks, as a result, find pathways into the vast fields of human mind and are smashed on the jagged and treacherous rocks of aspiration.*

Why is man's delight always hinged on playing the fool in paradise, forever satisfied a pawn in the vortex of his being? Tonka Manu asked himself as he observed the eagle in deep thought by the window.

Titan Race

Tonka straightened up by the window and sighed. The penthouse gave him quite a perspective of Songhai, the capital city of Atlantis. The more he looked at its milieu of civilization, the more its perverse tranquillity registered on his mind. A disquieting notion of failure glared through the calm ambience. In his consciousness, the whole idea of progress drummed a gong of an inevitable end. He hated to be at the penthouse end at moments like this because it sparked in him dark emotions regarding Atlantis – an omen he preferred to avoid.

The feeling once again clawed at his heart, striking him with stark images of the Atlanteans' folly. He turned away from the view of the horizon and focused on the plush interior of the penthouse. He cursed his fate for having roped him into laundering the smear on the conscience of Atlanteans. He did not understand why the guilt of Atlanteans was his lot to cleanse. Why did the Guardians assign such a task to him? The height of the Atlanteans' fumble annoyed him the most. His thoughts came to a sad conclusion.

Man could not as yet repent of the sin which mortality embodies. But must the Atlanteans advance to such a peak of civilization only to be blown away by the wind of self-destruction?

Tonka Manu shuffled his feet on the floor and wrestled with the weight about to stifle his mind. He then humped his shoulders and plodded around the palatial confines of the crystal penthouse. Out of instinct, he dodged exquisite brass furniture, sparkling antiques, and a variety of blooming potted flowers, blaming both the Guardians of the Universe and the Atlanteans for the shift in consciousness and the new reality of Atlantis.

The Guardians, he reasoned, had entrusted too much power to the Atlanteans and condoned a high degree of laxity among them. They had dizzied them drunk with a hefty dose of their competencies, making them bankrupt in the spirit to the point of no return. The Atlanteans themselves were to blame. Through Tonka Manu's effort, they had a high awareness of divine tenets. Still, his persistent warnings against their ego trips were useless. They paid him no heed beyond the budding phase of the civilization. They arrogated the Manu station to themselves. With their steady spiritual advancement, they forgot to heed the handwriting on the wall. In a swift rebound, this mistake now haunted the fabric of Atlantis and edged its civilization toward crisis.

Tonka's thoughtful pacing around the penthouse terminated at the right flank of a crescent glass desk. The desk's brass rims gleamed under intricate chandeliers. Raising a leg over the desk's edge, he heaved himself to a half-perch on a free spot, and let his mind wander some more.

He had captained the ship of Atlantis upwards of twenty calendars, yet it dawned on him as if yesterday's reel of events still unfolded in the moment. A fair spiritual weather and the Atlanteans' desire to discover their latent potential seemed the wonderful gale that steered his ship smoothly over divine waters. Atlanteans were quick to learn under his tutelage and developed their innate powers. They wasted no time in harnessing nature's bounties to their advantage. Before relinquishing his baton as patriarch of Atlantis, Tonka Manu's great-grandfather, Waadua, fought to stabilize their ship's wobbling through raging spiritual storms. So when Tonka came on board as Manu, he did not find it too difficult to steer the ship of Atlantis from where his great-grandfather had stopped.

No doubt Waadua's shoes were extra-large for a younger Manu. At the age of thirty calendars, Tonka strove with determination to captain the ship of Atlantis, mindful of the dark indicators Waadua had stressed were likely processions to an anti-climax. Nearly twenty-five calendars after, his great-grandfather had real vindication. The warnings now resounded with potent misgivings in his mind.

Manu Waadua was right, Tonka conceded with hindsight. The anti-climax his great-grandfather foresaw now came with such impunity it shook the whole structure of Atlantis. The Atlanteans having harnessed the bounties to the best of their abilities turned complacent. With the lapse of time, they threw away the tenets of divine love which fertilized the womb of Atlantis into advanced science and technology. The emergent crave for temporary satisfaction in the symphony of the material systems they had put together, a deviation from the normal, shifted their focus away from the divine.

Tonka Manu viewed it in no other light. In his perception as Manu, their notion of progress equated a frightening, retrogressive step.

He rose from the desk's edge, went behind the tinted glass crescent and slumped onto a bronze-glossed swivel chair cushioned with black leather. Tonka Manu huffed and mind-triggered a button on the viewfinder of the short-circuit monitor on the desktop. He then reclined and watched the brightening screen. The magnificent

Divine Theatre in the centre of Manu Square filled the screen like a phantom. It looked like a mountain of sapphire jutting out of the Deemen Sea. Fascinated by the grand aesthetic display of Manu Square, Tonka Manu ascribed to the Divine Theatre the climax of technological mastery, despite the glitzy atmosphere of his sixteen-bedroom mansion. He could not compare it with any edifice he had seen in Songhai or other cities of Atlantis.

A universe of crystals blended well with intricate marble in the five-floor magnificence. Tonka found the greatest amazement in the angular side-flaps stretching towards two gaping saucers which, in turn, merged in opposite directions with a hat-like crystal dome. The Divine Theatre and the neighboring mansions embellished the ingenious traits of the Atlanteans.

He could make out a stream of Atlanteans in solemn motion toward the main entrance, a huge heart made of pure gold. Self-activated slide doors hinged on it and on the inner and outer frames were rims of smallish star lights. The people daily walked in and out of this gold-hewed heart for their morning devotions.

Tonka could also see the motorcade of Belani Ziaku, the Consul-General of Atlantis, along with few other prominent Atlanteans, meandering through the driveway to the Divine Theatre. The array of Aerophibians in the Consul-General's convoy was quite a sight. Their morning rites done, a few others also eased out of the inner chambers of the Divine Theatre.

In their silent stead, those inward bound awakened feelings of an expedient duty in Tonka Manu. His obligation as the Manu, the spiritual patriarch, besides honing of their aspirations, included routine morning shuttles to the Divine Theatre to rekindle the flame of divinity for Atlanteans who sought his guidance. There had been times he had shirked this responsibility without any regret. But, this dawn, the silent beckoning of the throng heading into the Divine Theatre commanded his attention. Yet, he felt he should defy the impulse. Though the urgency of this morning duty required his presence in the Theatre's main auditorium, some thoughts worried him. Would the Atlanteans heed his warnings and safeguard the already endangered ship from the cataracts along the spawn of sail? They were faring badly regarding the sail and his warnings had assumed a rhetorical blandness in the minds of the now proud humanity.

Belani Ziaku, the Consul-General had also developed a false air. Unmindful of the patriarch's support and guidance, he had become too proud of his status as the political rallying point in Atlantis. Tonka could do little or nothing to avert the danger looming offshore. Atlanteans were foolish enough not to recognize this as the sad result of their deviation from the right path. Nevertheless, it remained his duty to caution them till they got to their tether's end and the plugs got pulled off Atlantis.

The viewfinder provided Tonka Manu with a range of options around Manu Square. His mind punched another button on it and the Divine Theatre's main auditorium came into view. Inner-circle members decorated the auditorium in frenzy with fresh flowers as he had noticed back in time. Expectant Atlanteans from Songhai and the neighboring cities filled the row of seats on the tiered floor. The gallery was also filled to capacity. The fast-changing scenes shifted Tonka's attention from the screen.

The skilful blend of gold, glass fibers and mosaic tiles cast a spell on the guests' minds. Large effigies of Manu Waadua took up niches at designated spots throughout the auditorium. Silhouettes of Tonka Manu flickered on the backdrop of the stage, a ship-like marble elevation on which a great crystal star was emblazoned. In it the golden throne of the Manu glimmered. The array of lights dovetailing into the crystal star and refracting around the entire stage mystified the entire scenery. This wondrous work of art fixated Tonka.

Tonka Manu's heart huffed that this splendid display had all been done in his honor. However, in his frequent analysis of the Atlanteans' prowess, self-indictment glared. In the rituals of living, he had no figment of doubt that the end and not the means matter the most.

The urge to enter the Divine Theatre stirred once more in Tonka Manu's heart. He whisked the edge of the crescent glass desk, wheeled himself on the swivel chair to the left, almost to the fringe of the desk, and then thumbed an ebony button on a small console. A screen concealed on the top left corner of the wall flashed into life. Tonka watched the profile of a young man of twenty-six calendars appear on it.

Tonka Manu addressed him. "Daya, how long will it take the theatre to be ready for this morning's devotion?"

On hearing the voice from the console, the young man snapped to attention. "A couple of swirls, I suppose.

Couldn't be more," Daya replied in a sultry voice from the adjoining mansion through the monitor. "I've just checked the theatre. They're cleaning up the auditorium in time for this morning's function."

"I observed that from the monitor. Anyway, get along and inform your colleagues to hasten up. Then get in touch with me in about twenty swirls. Okay?"

"Sure, Manu," Daya acquiesced, bowing. "And where would you be when I call back?"

"The penthouse."

"All right, Manu."

"Blessings of the Manu!"

Tonka Manu mind-punched another button on the console and the screen receded into its original concealed position. He heaved his athletic frame onto his feet. Steering free of the desk and chair, he made a hasty exit from the luxurious penthouse to his bedroom through the nearest door.

# # #

Belani Ziaku grew, a stout man of average height. His glazed brown eyes looked like polished tile, and with a temperament like the undercurrent of a placid river. Most observers consigned his life to the backwoods of history because of his poor background.

By the high standards of Dhusa State, without the financial wherewithal and the political will to live above board, a life's worth equalled a grain in the sands of time. Therefore, nobody thought Belani could become great. In his psyche, however, poverty could never stunt the height a man would attain in life, not when he had foresight and great optimism. Belani lacked neither when, against the grain of popular advice, he opted for politics at twenty-five calendars.

Belani's semi-literate father, Ziaku Kebbia, desired to see at least the eldest of his five children change the direction of their chequered lives. So, he set Belani's step on the threshold of this dream.

Ziaku, like most people who grew up in the suburbs of cosmopolitan Dhusa and Songhai, had known a life of drudgery. Haunted by his circumstance, he had vowed even as a child to spare his children the ridicule of a worthless life, the kind a poor background bequeathes. While he lacked the means to actualize this, the determination to steer them towards the world of academics remained undying in him.

Ziaku Kebbia toiled part time in Dhusa's hovercraft factory in the mornings, and assisted his wife Tummai in her pastry business in the evenings. The shift between the factory and the family business everyday tasked him at first, but over time he got used to it and earned enough to send his children to school, starting with Belani the first-born.

In junior school, Belani's brilliance showed. He excelled and with doggedness kept alive his father's hope of a brighter future for the family. Nonetheless, his truancy worried his teachers as well as parents. His teachers threatened to tame his exuberance, but he always creamed the results at the end of each session.

This gladdened their hearts and provided him an escape route from punishment. From junior through middle school, Belani's remarkable performances in the sciences portrayed him as someone destined for higher things. This culminated in the Atlantis Citadel, Sondibo, where he graduated with distinction in aerophibian engineering.

Afterwards, contrary to all expectations, Belani's career path veered from the sciences to politics. Belani admired the lives of politicians. The magnitude of their powers over the multitude of Atlanteans often amazed him. Only Tonka Manu's role as spiritual patriarch fell beyond the influence of Atlantis' political bigwigs. He desired to wield that kind of power and influence. Something wealth alone could not give to him.

"Son, I don't think this is a wise choice," Ziaku Kebbia entreated when Belani broached the issue. "You have a brilliant career ahead of you as an aerophibian engineer. That's where your nest of fortune lies."

"Nest of fortune? What better nest is there than service to the people?"

"You're moving too fast."

"I appreciate your concern father, but have faith in me. I'll be fine even in political waters."

"That's what you think, son. But you're better off being an aerophibian engineer. Political waters in Dhusa are murky."

"Now, don't fret father. I'll learn to swim in it."

"No matter how good your intentions are, you don't have the right fins to swim in murky waters."

Belani looked at his father and laughed. "I'll make good use of the opportunity to contribute my quota towards building a progressive Atlantis, starting with the Zelibe District."

"No doubt you will," replied Kebbia. "But you know we don't have the political clout in Dhusa or elsewhere. That means you'd be a small fish in troubled waters."

"It's not exactly the way you paint it, father," Belani enthused. "All it requires is the application of my engineering skills to the political turf. It's as simple as that. In due time you'll see that I was right."

Tummia, Belani's mother, who had been silent while the exchange lasted, cleared her throat. "There's absolutely nothing we haven't seen," she said. "Haven't we seen enough of the hypocrisy that goes on daily in the name of 'service to the people?' No, my son, you don't belong to the band of heady fools who think they can steal our birthrights and deceive us all the time with their sweet talk. You're cut out for greater things."

"What things, mother?"

"Like taming the air with aerophibians or hovercrafts," Kebbia chipped in.

"Ah, father," Belani exclaimed, amused by his father's logic or the lack of it.

"Like creating value out of the abundant resources in the bowels of Atlantis," Tummia pressed on. "Don't you think it is a better contribution to humanity than this faceless service every fool talks about?"

"Hnn-hnn," Kebbia intoned. "Your mother is right. I

don't find this idea of politics funny at all, considering where we are coming from."

"Yes, considering where we're coming from," Tummia added. "Do we have the impetus to fly? Can we go beyond our boundary?"

Belani Ziaku's eyebrows creased when he noticed his mother's uneasiness. A hood of apprehension overshadowed the usual sparkle in her eyes. She tried to adjust her beige gown and the cream scarf over her long braids, but in vain.

Why she also tows my father's line of thought beats me, Belani wondered. At fifty she has seen quite a lot, but she has no cause to fret over my political ambition.

"Permit me to use your words, mother," Belani said, with shoulders raised. "I don't fault your judgment. But considering 'where we're coming from,' who would've thought we had 'the impetus to fly?'"

"My point exactly!" beamed Tummia. "Who would've thought an ordinary family like ours could ever produce a son with distinction in engineering from the Citadel?"

"It can be explained," Ziaku Kebbia argued. He looked unconvinced. "Luck and hard work sometimes exalts a man. I'm sure of this. All the same, luck seldom comes to one person in the same dimension twice in one life."

A faint glow in Belani's eyes gave away his line of thought. "Beside luck, a man almost always chooses the path he treads, right?"

"Maybe," Kebbia answered.

"How would you explain my academic success? Luck,

or hard work, or destiny? I really would like to know."

"I think a combination of all," Tummia reassured her son. "Luck, hard work, and destiny. They all had it wrapped up, I should say."

Belani sensed triumph in the air. "The answer to all this, as I see it, is simple."

"Spill it then," Kebbia urged.

"Never underestimate the power of an underdog," Belani said, exuding confidence. "In my vast imagination only possibilities exist. That's the reason I want to try a career in politics. All I ask from you is your support."

"I'm afraid your imagination is quite robust," his mother retorted, "but you're not likely to have our support unless you assure us of your safety. We don't want you making silly mistakes when it matters most. As a family you are our hope. We look up to you. Don't you ever forget."

"I assure you there won't be any mistake if we plot our graph well," Belani said.

"Where will you find the means to plot that graph, Belani?" Kebbia queried with doubt creasing his face.

Belani smiled. "My biggest investments, I would say, are my circle of friends! "While in Atlantis Citadel, I cultivated friendship across board. My friends will be my strength in times of need. With their goodwill and my right frame of mind, certainly the eagle will soar."

Ziaku Kebbia sighed in relief. "Son, your sweet logic beats me hollow. Your never-say-die attitude reminds me of my own stubborn spirit. I wait to see the eagle soar."

"You bet it will, soon enough."

His initial foray into politics met with no real opposition as he pursued his lofty dream with the keenness of an engineer, gauging every move with precision and perfecting the foundations of his creations with each stroke of imagination.

He rode on the crest of the goodwill his parents enjoyed even as ordinary members of the Zelibe community in Dhusa. Coupled with his political strategies, Belani got elected by an overwhelming majority of Zelibeans as one of its thirty members mandated to legislate for the District. He scored this historic political victory at his birth place as a young man approaching twenty-five calendars. It signalled the end of poverty in the Ziaku Kebbia lineage and the beginning of the Belani Ziaku phenomenon in Atlantis.

After a superlative legislative stint which spanned four cycles in the Zelibe District Assembly, Belani felt time had come to stretch his luck and imagination further afield. This time he fixed his eyes on no less echelon than the Dhusa State Assembly. He got elected almost without hassles, as if other eligible contestants did not matter. His meritorious performance in the District Assembly helped to paint a towering profile of Belani which led to his upliftment into the higher assembly. From there, only time stood between him and the unleashing of the Belani Ziaku persona on the sensibilities of Atlanteans, like an unstoppable hovercraft.

Within the first fifteen calendars of his political career, he built for himself a formidable network of friends, mostly power brokers in the Atlantean equation. He also became the Consul of Dhusa State through dint of hard work and tact – a rare achievement, in view of his humble beginnings.

What Belani lacked in political sagacity he made up for in his attitude towards the plight of the common man - in his philanthropy, and discharge of his legislative duties in both houses. When the chips were down this track record oiled his climb up the ladder of power. Belani's young age also favoured him. At forty calendars he became one of the youngest Consuls in Atlantean history and a proactive one too.

Belani's upward mobility, youthfulness, and remarkable sense of commitment to sustainable development and the ideals of goodness as Consul in Dhusa State, drew Tonka Manu's attention at the onset. Tonka's fondness for the upcoming star grew over time.

To the patriarch, Belani reflected the ideals of Atlantis among well-meaning Atlanteans. For this reason, Tonka took particular interest in Belani's political career but kept his distance, feigning neutrality so as not to appear as favoring one citizen over another. The distance soon bridged at the instance of Tonka.

At the end of the tenure of Wanya Powa, the incumbent Consul-General of Atlantis, the elders of Manu Square as a tradition nominated seven eligible contestants for the seat. Tonka Manu had the decisive vote, which sealed the political destiny of Atlantis for another four cycles. Belani happened to be one of the seven contestants. This made Tonka's duty a lot more difficult, knowing how kindly disposed he was to Belani. The electoral polls did not favor Belani Ziaku, an obvious underdog among the six Consuls from other states of Atlantis. Nevertheless, the wheel of destiny rolled towards him, to the consternation of his opponents.

In Tonka Manu's estimation, Belani's amiable disposition, history of proactive engagement, and enviable philanthropy as Consul of Dhusa State, took the shine off the other contestants, notwithstanding their great political pedigree.

"Elders of Manu Square, elders of Atlantis, as part of my duties as patriarch, I hereby cast my vote and place my seal today on Belani Ziaku as our next Consul-General," Tonka Manu declared in the media, sealing Atlantis' political fortune for another four cycles.

The elders of Manu Square and other citizens watched and cheered the ascendancy of the unexpected Belani Ziaku via satellite throughout the cities of Atlantis.

In all critical decisions regarding the governance of Atlantis, Belani sought Tonka Manu's counsel. He ensured that his allegiance to the patriarch and spiritual leader did not waver. This he demonstrated by including his erstwhile opponents in his cabinet's inner caucus, an outcome of Tonka Manu's advice. The decision resulted in cohesion and sense of purpose in the affairs of Atlantis.

The first four cycles of the new Consul-General witnessed a harmonious and robust relationship between him and Tonka. Or so it seemed. The bond cracked towards the end of the first cycle when, to Belani's utter dismay, the notions of a successor was bandied in some quarters. Some top-notch Atlantean politicians hinted Belani on the Manu's intention to replace him. This rumor of a successor being groomed by Tonka Manu, despite Belani's unflinching loyalty to the patriarch and record of achievements as Consul-General, beclouded Belani's sense of judgment.

If the rumor proved true, then Belani felt Tonka Manu had stabbed him on the back at a time he nursed the ambition to re-run as Consul-General. Even as the report had not yet been confirmed, it had sent out a signal that something fishy was in the offing. Belani desired to brooch the matter with the Manu but he feared that the bad blood stirred up in him would hamper such a possibility.

Belani knew that when the ambitions of men stand the risk of failure, their responses to such stimuli are always the same, being products of similar natures. So, he sought the advice of his wife, Melin, whom he married at the age of twenty-eight before the end of his tenure in Dhusa District Assembly.

"A mere rumour shouldn't be cause for concern, Belie," Melin said with caution as the couple relaxed beside their swimming pool.

"Rumours are not mere fabrications in the sky," Belani said. "There's an element of truth in every rumour. Imagine how dumb I'd been with my loyalty for Tonka Manu. If only I'd known it would come to this."

Melin had been married to Belani upwards of twelve calendars. She never thought all the while anything could so upset her husband to the point of the utter regret. It seemed, to her, a dangerous trend.

"Belie, I'm not sure your fears are justified," Melin

chanced again. "I'm afraid you're over-reacting. I believe Tonka Manu means well."

"Everybody thinks I've gone nuts. I'm not surprised you think so too. But mark my words, Melin, unless I act fast, our days in power are numbered."

"I beg to differ on this one, Belie," Melin argued. "Without being hypocritical, I'd say Tonka Manu's vote got us this far. I hope you did not forget this? Of course, he's given you all the moral and spiritual support you've needed as Consul-General. Certainly, he believes in you and will do nothing to the contrary. Please, Belie, forget the rumour. There are better things you should be thinking about right now. I believe those feeding you with such garbage don't mean well. Don't upturn your cart with your own hands."

"Come to think of it, as Consul-General," Belani said, somewhat peeved. "I'm no more than a sitting duck. I do nothing other than Tonka Manu's bidding. I wield a sceptre I can't use. Real power lies in Tonka's palms. He can do whatever he desires and I'm obliged to tag along because he's patriarch. Just fancy that! Why can't I be my own man?"

"Ah, Belie, what an outrageous thing to say of Tonka," Melin almost screamed. She paused, and then continued, lowering her voice. "You're fast becoming unpredictable, Belie. Who would've thought power would change your good sense of judgement so soon. My dear husband, be careful else you'll plot your own downfall."

At thirty-two, with a radiant face and almost six feet tall, Melin looked more like a beauty queen of twenty calendars. Belanie could never ignore her place in his heart, no matter how queasy he felt about her words. The course of his career had been shaped by her prophetic powers in many sublime ways. But when he hinted of the source of real power, she took her off-guard. He reasoned that her reaction could have been one of her usual visions about their lives. In spite of this gnawing thought, he made up his mind not give up on his re-election bid.

One path led to that reality: to be his own boss and never the lame duck of another Atlantean who called the shots from Manu Square, patriarch or not.

# # #

The sweet signature tune from the Holy Realm Band in the Divine Theatre rent the tranquil air of the sixty thousand capacity main auditorium, heralding the entry of the Manu. The Atlantean audience braced up.

"Brethren of Atlantis, the Tonka Manu!" a baritone voice announced, cutting off the signature tune. "All arise and welcome the Tonka Manu to the Divine Theatre!"

A phalanx of Atlanteans on all the floors rose and cheered, "Long live the Manu, Long live Tonka!"

They stood still as Tonka emerged from the right flank and stepped up a few steep steps to the crystal star on the marble ship. On the higher tiers, some of the Atlanteans watched the spectacle on mounted screens. Some preferred the direct import of the glittering furnace of gold, crystal, and hypnotic light. Beams of colored light converged on Tonka's regal form, enhancing his movements with mystique.

Titan Race

"Long live the Manu! Long live Tonka!" the audience's standing ovation reverberated through the large hall.

Tonka's smile lingered, spurring the Atlanteans on. He waved a golden scepter in response, moved around two lush shoots of nurtured palms by the star's periphery and headed toward his golden throne.

From the point of view of the audience, the shimmering light on Tonka Manu's cherubic, scoop-neck dress of gold chain-mails and breastplate, trailed him like a beautiful tendril. His crown sparkled and spread backwards to his neck like the posterior of the Divine Theatre - a spiking blend of emeralds, sapphire, and gold. His ebony skin looked like the hazel sun over Songhaian shades or over the sleek gray of a Hansa in descent. He wore sandals of equal luster. Unlike his great-grandfather, Waadua, who had cultivated a bushy beard, Tonka only permitted a wispy moustache.

Tonka Manu bowed after he had observed seconds of silence on the throne. "Denizens of Atlantis, I convey the blessings of the Most High to you!" he intoned, smiling. Hidden stage microphones picked up his sweet voice and echoed it across the hall.

"Long live the Manu! Long live Tonka!" the audience chorused in ecstasy.

"Please, be seated," Tonka said.

The excited phalanx of Atlanteans complied.

"Denizens of Atlantis, I admire your patience," Tonka said as they settled down. "You tarried so long to see me come out this morning. There's no gainsaying that, as a result, there's a delay already in today's programme.

Some inescapable facts stared at me this morning; facts about us as a people which I had to digest. And I must say here, the issues are grim at best. When I stirred from meditation early in the day, I went to the penthouse's window - the marvellous mansion you built for me. I tried to erase my mind's worries with the panorama of Songhai via the window.

"I pulled the window drapes back and saw a great splendor indeed. On the fertile tree Atlantis represents, I saw three sturdy branches. On each of these branches or aspects of our civilization, were clear evaluations of the height of our advancement as a human stock. These, without a doubt, drew my attention. Our scientific and technological accomplishments hung on one branch. On the other branch hung the seed of divinity, the gem responsible for our great splendor. On the third branch, I saw the huge claws of a hideous and fiery monster. The third branch sought to encircle and maim the other branches without anyone detecting. This was the picture of Atlantis from the vantage point of my window.

"Though the third branch appeared normal, the first two branches overshadowed it. If I hadn't looked with discerning eyes, I would have thought that all is well. To tell you the truth, the claw on the branch in view frightens me. It is the claw of inexorable ego, the fangs of mischief. I saw a trend which would soon afflict us unless, of course, we realize in time that out of stupidity we are removing the protective carpet beneath our own feet."

Tonka Manu paused. He dug a hand into the side pocket of his robe and fetched a handkerchief. Dabbing imaginary sweat beads off his face, he gauged the reactions of his audience. Most of them stared in bewilderment.

"What I'm pointing at is not the newest thing on your minds," he resumed. "My predecessor, Manu Waadua, spoke about it before he left the scene. And I've repeated it in this Divine Theatre in Songhai and in other cities of Atlantis many times over. I'm bothered that we seem not to take our bearing from the divine compass given to us long ago.

"Perhaps, because of the immense blessings upon us, we have allowed ourselves to be led astray by a deceptive air of contentment. It's an irony really. It is also disheartening to note that the plunge to the lowest ebb of our spiritual and material splendor came from the height of our greatness. I've often wondered at man's inexcusable fall after attaining great heights.

"I don't understand why man must climb up such great heights of spiritual awareness with determination and even conquer the world of gross matter through his effort, and then let go the same motivation that took him there in the first place. Why must man falter and endanger his entire existence in one irrevocable descent? Why must he fall back to his starting point? Why can't he keep on with his ascent forever?"

Tonka stole some seconds to appraise how well the audience assimilated his message. Apart from the sultry echo of his last words, he noticed a pensive mood in the auditorium as silence lingered.

The Manu pouted and then broke the silence. "Just look at this beautiful civilization we have here. What would anyone want that you can't find right here? Have you ever stopped for a moment to wonder about the impeccability of our transportation, communication, and industrial systems? Look at the Hansas, the aerophibian buses, and hovercrafts. They strike the imagination with notions of unequivocal mastery.

"Out of grace we've been able to tame the airwaves in unique ways. The communication systems that we've put in place have turned our land into a global village. Never before has man attained such heights. All these mammoth achievements would have come to a berating naught if we hadn't the spiritual zeal to cushion it all. I'm proud to say that it's an area we've been really blessed. But again, in what manner are we now harnessing the blessings? There are a number of traits at our height of greatness that haunts us all as a disabling force. These are the steps that would lead us to obvious extinction.

"That's what bothers me this morning, my beloved denizens of Atlantis," Tonka Manu continued, his eyes again panning over the audience. "I remember the strident warnings of the esteemed Waadua. He used to say that if care is not exercised in our growth process, if we don't watch our crave for the things that we have manifested, which seem to imprison our senses, if we don't continue to fan the flame of our spirituality and place it uppermost in our daily wrestle with life, then we should brace up for a dangerous plunge into a bottomless pit.

"Of course, you know what it means. Either we heed the warnings, or destroy the exquisite sculpture we have made with our own hands. Inconsistency in our divine consciousness has brought us to this point. Whom shall we blame? None other than our selves.

"If we hadn't known any advancement at all as a human

kind, it would've been much better for us. Because the magnitude of our collective fall, the guilt burnished by the so-called flashy things of this civilization, wouldn't be so obvious. One would not have to wonder why there's so much spiritual filth around, and even have the chance to regret presiding over its inevitable end."

Tonka noticed their minds' agitation in their grimaces, which carried forlorn stamps. He also observed from their silence that despite the inevitability of death, an uncanny and mortifying power exists in its foreknowledge. He wondered why even minds enlightened in the art of its mystery, like the Atlanteans, shied away from embracing its foreknowledge.

The Manu's hint on perdition had frightened the Atlanteans. But his referrence to situations that could stop the manifestation of their doomed future seemed to allay their fears. They realized imminent danger could be averted depending on their indulgences or their willingness to stick to the divine order of things. Still, in spite of their claims to spirituality, Tonka knew they lacked the basic understanding of how to stop their glide towards the precipice.

"And I see all kinds of misdirected snares from some of you," Tonka Manu went on. "What's the meaning of all these clandestine moves some of you are making? What are they up to really? As you might have noticed, power isn't a wrong thing to desire if it's of the divine. But if you don't know the purpose for which you desire power, then it becomes dangerous even to you, the possessor. There are some amongst us who have weird and over-exaggerated aspirations, and that is putting it mildly. When put in proper perspective, these aspirations speak volumes of a warped spirituality. Such intentions encourage hatred, irreverence for constituted authority, and debauchery.

"What is the scheming about?" Tonka Manu demanded again, swivelling around on his throne. "None of you knows how Atlantis came to be the great expanse of civilization which is our pride this day. And none of you has the faintest idea of how things would be as we sail this divine boat into the next dawn. Even if you have the right glimpse into the fragile future of our civilization, you'd still be too ill-equipped to predict the timing of coming events.

"This being so, why don't we just hang our gloves and call off this war of attrition? Do they think – I mean those in the league of schemers – do they really think that things will always be manipulated to their advantage? How about divine intervention? *We often kid ourselves with our perfidy, not realizing that divine intervention puts our silly whims where they belong. The amazing aspect of man's gumption is his folly of not acknowledging apparent limits. I'm here, not because I chose to be, but because there's a reason. We're all gathered here for a transcendental cause. I'm here to ensure continuity in this human experiment, whether we decide to blow ourselves up one day.* My duty here as a spiritual patriarch transcends human limits and no drive of ambition can tinker with it."

Tonka's voice rose again. "Take it or leave it, there'll always be someone to continue with what has been laid down, should this civilization flop suddenly. But I really can't vouch for any of you schemers. I just can't say whether you'd be blessed to cross this bridge into the new world. The way I see it, the new world is here already. But it saddens me that these people who think they are the smartest of the bunch just might not see it happen."

Tonka paused and smiled as if he had not dazed the audience with the force of his words. "We've spent a worthwhile half-hour," he began to conclude. "You made my day with your presence here. We carry with us profound blessings and lessons that will endure the test of time. I'm honored by your presence and I'm tempted to indulge you a bit. Why shouldn't we stay on, with nothing on our minds except the great joy of being alive? Yes, you know, let's enjoy this bliss we experience forever. Let's bathe ourselves in it. Let's put on the cloak of spiritual freedom. I believe the Holy Realm Band is prepared to give us blissful tunes. Manu Square has enough rooms, food, and fruits drinks for us all to feast for whatever length of time we want. Everyone would be catered for because you've already provided the means."

A solitary applause reverberated from the auditorium's main floor, prompting others to cheer too. The Atlanteans knew Tonka had a delightful character, but could not interpret his sudden sway of mood. His manner of speech showed that something roiled in his mind, which he only knew, and which he had tried to prise off his chest for what it implied: their doomed future.

"I feel much better seeing the smiles back on your faces," Tonka warmed up. "This is the mood I often want to see on you. Now, you'd excuse me for some privacy. I'll leave for the penthouse any moment from now. My brief absence in your midst shouldn't disrupt your peace or fun. Have a wonderful time. As I take my leave, I want you to think this over: you're the potter of your future.

Mold that unique clay. Do everything you can to protect the model of your mind and greatness from the storm of time. See you again, and soon!"

Tonka bowed as he rounded up his mixed bag of pep talk, recrimination, admonition, and nostalgic flights. The audience bowed in return, applauding. The Holy Realm Band struck up a recessional number that drowned the cacophony of "Long live Tonka! Long live the Manu!"

Tonka Manu rose from the throne, nimble like a kite, and stepped down the stern of his marble ship. The massive audience sang and danced even with his exit, unaware of the twisted wheel of fate hovering overhead, threatening to stampede them few swirls away.

# # #

Disk Center, Blackhole

The screens of the Disc Center's Command Module first displayed an indescribable blur. It then brightened out, revealing the apparent emptiness above Atlantis' orbit. The focus of the Command Module's lenses went beyond Atlantis to encompass the other planets and its immediate galaxy, roaming still farther away to distant celestial structures in the Milky Way.

The occupants of the Disk Center observed with keen interest these scenes as common sights in Atlantis and their other playToys. One of them, however, saw the slides flickering out before him as out of place in their scheme. Of all the Manus sent to the PlayToy from the Disc Center in the past eon, Finia's burden weighed the most. His task: to nurture the seeds of the new humanity envisaged by the Guardians. Never the type to get angry over a tasking situation, Finia had tackled the obstacles against the mandate with great success.

Ramune knew this much, to his chagrin. The source of his worry was not Tonka's anger as seen earlier on the Command Module screens. The privilege of foreknowledge, however, warned him of an impending unilateral decision from Tonka. Ramune believed that giving Tonka a free rein might disrupt their plans for Atlantis.

"What would you call that, a Swan song?" Ramune demanded of Hemse, his companion who had riveted his attention to other flickering screens on the Command Module. Ramune half-turned away from the screen with a queer grimace, glancing at Hemse. "We might just be heading for a crisis down there on that globe. All is not right on Atlantis. I figure Tonka, our Finia in Blackhole, has had it to the hilt."

Hemse grunted. "What's it you say?"

"There's fire beneath Finia's seat and he's getting worried by the look of it," Ramune stressed.

"Oh, that! He's been under the hammer for quite some time, say some eons of Atlantis' time and I haven't seen him get riled up. That doesn't translate to a crisis to me," Hemse replied.

This is unlike a Blackhole member, Ramune thought. Isn't our preoccupation the kneading of the strands of the universe into a harmonious web?

"Don't humor me on a topical issue like this one, Hemse," Ramune snapped. "See the heat on the smiling face of Finia and read the conspicuous writing on his mind sheet. You'd know the fire beneath is burning him real hard. Do you still tell me there's no crisis?"

"Our red print for planetary intercession and realignment confirms the contrary," Hemse responded with a wry smile. He rose from his seat and approached Ramune at the other end of the Command Module. "I believe Finia has enough Blackhole sanction to want to unduly exercise his prerogative," Hemse explained as he perched on the arm of chair next to Ramune. "Why do you suppose we've got a turbulent sea in our little tea cup, Ramune?"

"Roll back the last thirty swirls of the slides on the main screen," said Ramune. "Listen to the Swan and its song of passage and you'll get a pretty good idea of what bothers me."

How interesting the joke has become, Hemse thought. He abandoned the chair and walked to the center of the Command Module and thought-punched a few keys among a myriad. The main screen blipped and a still slide came on.

"Here you are!" Hemse beamed. Going back or ahead in time on the Command Module, excites him like a hen tingled by soft wind. The Disk Center's monitors unravelled the cosmic system like a chessboard. He loved the idea of tossing the pawns of the cosmic drama back and forth on the time screens. Here is another hill to climb, he thought. "What's the next move on the board?" Hemse asked.

"Get the slides moving," Ramune ordered, coming to terms with Hemse's joke.

"Sure." Hemse thought-thumbed another key and the screen came alive. Let's toss the pawns of this game backwards this time, he hummed under breath, grinning.

"And do listen to Finia's valediction and the change of mood," Ramune goaded.

"Understood."

The marble ship of the Divine Theatre zoomed into clear view with its enchanting star top. Finia sat on the throne addressing a large audience as they had earlier seen. Both his voice and temper were aflame.

The companions heard Tonka loud and clear: "We often kid ourselves with our perfidy, not realizing that divine intervention puts our silly whims where they belong. The amazing aspect of man's gumption is his folly of not acknowledging apparent limits. I'm here, not because I chose to be, but because there's a reason. We're all gathered here for a transcendental cause. I'm here to ensure continuity in this human experiment, whether we decide to blow ourselves up one day."

Hemse now acknowledged Ramune's reference point. He concentrated more on the screen and the aural import. Ramune eyed and quizzed him in silence.

"My duty here as a spiritual patriarch transcends human limits and no drive of ambition can tinker with it," Finia resumed, his voice rising. *"Take it or leave it, there'll always be someone to continue with what has been laid down, should this civilization flop suddenly. But I really can't vouch for any of you schemers. I just can't say whether you'd be blessed to cross this bridge into the new world. The way I see it, the new world is here already. But it saddens me that these people*

who think they are the smartest of the bunch just might not see it happen." Tonka Manu paused.

"Cut the slide right there," Ramune said.

Hemse obeyed, glancing at Ramune who was now standing beside him, with his hand on Hemse's shoulder

"Any strange clue to the little puzzle?"

"I get what you mean," Hemse said searching into Ramune's eyes. A sign of concern creased his forehead. "I'd glossed over it somehow. Do you really believe he would pull the plugs soon, even against our sanction?"

"Likely not. But even if he does as we perceive already, there's not much gagging we can give him. Remember he is part of the Blackhole. He's got some latitudes of operation. Our interference is minimal. We would have no choice but to bring him back to order only if he goes out of control."

"How soon do you think that'll be?"

"It depends on the twist of his mind," Ramune replied in a low, husky tone. "You know that the Blackhole and Atlantis are two different institutions, though interrelated. One is the source while the other is a servicing point. And each phase of the experience exerts its own kind of parallax. It's much denser at the level of Atlantis. So, you can't be too sure of his reactions down there as compared to when he is in the Blackhole. But our sanctions work because as gardeners in this big terrain, we know just the right prune on our pretty flowers, and the right shades and water cultures to put in place."

Ramune laughed at his own reel of humor, patting the

other Guardian. He was not the Father of the Blackhole but he knew enough to impress the other Guardians whenever they challenged his wisdom.

The pawns on the chessboard you often push around will garner enough power to give you more trouble than you possibly can handle, Hemse thought. "What must the Guardians do now that the storm is brewing?"

"Well, let him take his gambits and let's take ours. We will checkmate him whenever his moves get too fast."

"Which means?"

"Be keen on the watch."

What conflict of ideas? Hemse wondered. *Seconds past, Ramune was worried because he had sniffed chaos afar on Atlantis. Now he turns into the vanguard of patience saying, we should do nothing other than keep a keen watch. I simply can't understand the Guardians - capricious beings!*

"*Watch! Watch!* is all I hear around here," Hemse lamented.

"That's the best antidote. Guides against fatal impulse," Ramune joked.

"Fatal impulse you say? It might serve as a stitch in time, most especially, if the storm upsets the kind of patience you advocate."

Ramune threw Hemse a brief, shrewd glance and smiled. "You shirk your responsibilities too soon, and that's not in our character as Guardians."

"You drift too far, fellow Guardian," Hemse bantered.

"Then do remember, in articulating the tiny and

intricate threads of the cosmic web, we have just one flashcard called patience. Else, we might soon make smithereens even of our own Blackhole." Ramune paused and then continued. "Every Blackhole member should be wizened by the pains and eons it took them to quicken the little globe into existence. Well, for later generations of Guardians, this knowledge is beyond them because they were not part of its making. But you should know this, Hemse. Maybe, not directly, but taking cue from your involvement in the past eon."

"You remember well," Hemse conceded. "No less than six billion swirls," he recalled with pride. "It took the Guardians six billion swirls to construct our little playhouse. The manipulation of Blackhole radiation wasn't easy to condense to the form we see as the globe down there. It entailed diligent planning and execution with every atom of wisdom and gadget at our disposal. Every Guardian who witnessed the bombardment of ether upon ether at different temperatures - products of sun-stars split across the great sea and redistributed in gravitational cool-offs - would know that it has not been a game of billiards. Of course, the final phase of our plan shaped the energy fields on the globe of that moderate galaxy amongst an avalanche of galaxies. The streams of light became embodied in the forms of life we see there."

Hemse added as an afterthought, "Though it took place in an eon past mine, it is common knowledge from the archives of the Disk Center. Any Guardian who has the time can tinker with our creations forward and backward for a true glimpse of the intricate strands of our universe."

Hemse eyed Ramune, triumph shone from his eyes. He enjoyed playing the fool at times as it made him come out stronger and wiser.

Ramune admired Hemse's recount of the convoluted pathway of life on Atlantis but pursued his line of thought with more concern.

"Time," Ramune said with a comic undertone. "That's the watchword. The time to evaluate the boiling sea down there; the time to tame spurious impulses; the kind of time that gives the patience to watch keenly.

"And don't forget," Ramune went on, leering at Hemse, "the Guardians are not bothered by the barriers of time and space. We are time itself and it gives us all the edge to reappraise our playhouse, taking nothing for granted."

At that moment, humming and mysterious like the inchoate beginning of the Blackhole, a translucent fiber door opened from the extreme right of the Disk Center's spatial confines. Guardian Numa walked in.

Ramune and Hemse sprang to their feet and bowed with reverence. The new entrant also bowed in return and went round a range of complex glass partitions that hedged the far left of the Disk Center. He concluded his brief tour by the Command Module, next to Ramune and Hemse.

"What's new on our puzzle play?" Numa asked. "Any jigsaw to fit in? Any strange meaning to all the fuzz about time and space I heard from afar?"

"Not much of a puzzle," Ramune replied. "It's something that has been with us for a long time. Our Manu in Atlantis seems to have embarked on an uphill ride again. From the look of things, he's getting worked up and impatient."

Ramune eyed Hemse as if pleading for some discreet

understanding and then continued with his elucidation. "As to the issue of time and space you heard, Hemse thinks the Guardians are bunches of slow-witted ducks that watch things go out of hand. He believes our actions must be swift, decisive, and firm. I was just about straightening the little twist he saw in our obligations as Guardians. I wanted him to know, as a matter of fact, we tinkle the bell of time, so we can vacillate between its extremes. Of course, we are not boxed-up in space either."

"Either as slow-witted Guardians, or as decisive controllers of the cosmic paradise," Numa said, "we are doing our duties the way it ought to be. Neither of you are wrong. The species across the constellation are such that sometimes we have to exert our control over their fate, and at other times, simply watch their slow awakening like ducks learning to swim."

Hemse envied the wisdom of the Guardian standing next to them. No wonder he is the Father of the Blackhole! The younger Guardians have a lot still to learn from this being whose existence defies our knowledge of the beginning itself, Hemse thought.

Whenever Numa – as all Guardians called him - appeared before them, he rendered the Command Module ineffectual by manipulating the events interlocking in the strands of the cosmic system. Fellow Guardians marvelled at him for this.

Ramune smiled in his inner recesses. Despite that he had been around for eons and had worked in consonance with the Father of the Blackhole, he still found Numa outstanding and mysterious. Ramune eyed Numa's broad, shiny wings fluttering behind his huge frame. A streaming cherubic robe, a gray shock of hair under a miniature golden cap, a thick, gray beard, and a ridge of salt-and-pepper moustache accentuated his handsomeness. The pretty golden sheen of Numa's skin was deceptive, for he had witnessed innumerable eons.

Ramune noticed a slight stoop to Numa's gait, which was far from senile, with a sort of smokescreen trailing his every step. The winged Guardians looked much alike. Ramune, however, did not remember his or Hemse's fluttering wings until his gaze fell on Numa's that vanished and reappeared with consistency.

"If we let Tonka execute his plans, chances are he might stretch us all too far. And if we streamline his field of action, we may as well be retarding the speed of the wheel we've put in motion for the new order in the life of the galaxy from which Atlantis derives its force. We must tow the line between action and inaction. To the best of our interest, it would mean cautioning Finia," Numa said.

"But, Father of the Blackhole, haven't we done this several times before?" Hemse protested. "And what do they always do, these Atlanteans? They task us all the time with emergencies. Like now."

"There's no mistake about that," Numa conceded. "But don't you see their defiance is the extension of the chessboard of this beautiful paradise? You can't rule out deviations every now and then. However, the end point has always been the sum of the inputs that had gone in at the beginning of the scheming. Nothing is lost, nothing is gained; it's just a continuous process of renewal of forms."

Numa pried on their thoughts and then added, "This point impresses your young minds as somewhat strange. Why do we worry about what happens in our playhouses if at the end there's no gain or loss? You see, my dear Guardians, it's like this: in Atlantis a human being would plant maize seeds and nurture them till they blossom and fruit. Once the cobs mature, the cycle of the maize seeds expires. A human being can eat it as nourishing food or replant the seed to see the process repeat itself. He derives joy from the growth and bloom of the maize seeds and finds nourishment in the eating. If all the species on our various playhouses and in the entire universe were maize seeds as in Atlantis, our joy would be in planting and replanting the seeds. We are excited when they bloom with creative intelligence and realize their place in the cosmic game. Nevertheless, we frown when they wither in ego flights or over-ambition. That's when we replant them."

Ramune's eyes and Hemse's locked in wonderment. Hemse grinned, wondering, *Finia would be the hand that would select the good grains for replanting, I don't envy him one bit. I'd rather be where I am in the Blackhole, viewing all the madness beneath and around.*

"Ramune," Numa burst into the moment's silence. "Call Finia on the Command Module mains! Inform all Guardians and the entire planetary hierarchies, there'll be an emergency Blackhole meeting.

"Hemse, come with me," Numa said, turning. "Before the Tamed Star returns, we'll make a short shuttle to the hundredth galaxy."

Chapter Seven

Two days after the meeting in the Disk Center, Blackhole, Tonka Manu still could not erase from his mind the agitation caused by the Guardians' deliberations. He maintained a calm exterior and exerted needed control as the patriarch of Atlantis, but writhed within. He tried to shelve the nagging feeling, but it bounced back like a ball and hit him straight.

Though the Guardians had clipped his wings in the Blackhole, Tonka understood this to mean routine evaluation of his role as a Guardian in Atlantis. All the same, between Blackhole's sanctions and the Atlanteans' scheming and folly, he had been denied a berth.

Tonka Manu felt insulted by the snobbery of Belani Ziaku whom he had helped to enthrone as Consul-General in Atlantis. Belani's offense was in believing, without ascertaining the truth, the rumor that Tonka would replace him as Consul-General. Tonka, therefore, decided that he would stamp his authority as the patriarch, or his worth would not be more than the pawn Atlanteans were beginning to paint of him.

The notion that he hung between two variables caused Tonka uneasiness. While he could understand the Guardians as a variable, the magnified folly of the Atlanteans' surprised him. Even as a spiritually conscious clan of humans, the Atlanteans still could not differentiate their left from their right. In Tonka's view, their scientific and technological progress headed toward disaster.

He saw a tempest in the making, with him right in its middle. The faintest idea of how to prevent it eluded him. Worse still, those marked for destruction had chosen to scheme against him. He felt the need to turn the table on the scheming humanity, having identified the chief culprits as Vatima Hansi and her clique. An encounter with them the preceding night had reinforced this feeling.

Does she ever exhaust her ploys, he thought. She'll need a little dose of the Guardians' gagging. I won't be the only one to toss them around. And I'll nick her right in the socks.

Tonka's lips parted in a grin, like a cracked rock's face. His eyes, bleary from the night's trance flights, focused hazily at his Lotus posture while his mind sped far ahead. He unlocked his feet under his thighs and thrust them forward, rustling the calm currents of the room.

After a moment of stretching and twisting, he rose from the large oval stud, with a groan of satisfaction. I'll rush through a shower, have a cup of fruit juice and then put the requisite punctuation mark in Vatima Hansi's dreary sentence. So he thought, as he left the room for his devotional rites.

Afterwards, Tonka Manu asked Daya to convene an urgent meeting at the reception lounge overlooking the northern reaches of Manu Square. Those to attend were selected members of the inner circle, some custodians of Manu Square, Vatima Hansi, and Tonka in person. Having taken care of his uppermost concern, he switched his monitor from local broadcast to other cities of Atlantis. The cities flipped by, each a great lesson in aesthetics. Some impressed him while others did not.

Tonka Manu saw the normal clamoring of Atlanteans along busy streets. Squalid conditions in the midst of grandeur showed in the less prominent communities. The sight of idle children on side streets sneering and teasing each other irritated him. He reckoned too with the gentle flame peculiar to the Atlantean spirit slowly blending with the wild traits of its new humanity.

Bored with the broadcasts, he shut off the monitor and turned on Twilight Waves, the radio link of Songhai. The signals came through. Tonka recognized the chatty exuberance of Takuma Siani on the airwaves. The young presenter had just gone over news tit-bits on contemporary Songhai on the "Songhai flash." Tonka tuned in as the presenter increased the tempo with a fast rhythm from Miitay Reboh, the scintillating singer from Sakiraa, south of Sondibo. The fine music wooed his ears. A consistent blip on his miniature console and the charges from its speakers distracted his mind.

"Tonka Manu speaking," he said, thumbing the return key. The call came from Sudura the chief custodian of the Manu Square in neighboring Sondibo town. "How are you, Sudura?"

"Fine, thank you, Manu," Sudura replied through the voice module.

Tonka struck a key on the console and Sudura's smiling profile, clean and debonair, emerged on the wall screen. "What's it like in Sondibo? Any complain there you think I should know about?"

"Nothing we can't handle ourselves."

"The biggest relief I've had in days."

"We are flattered. But Manu–"

"Yes, what is it?"

"Yesterday, the elders came here with Kanuji, regarding your proposed visit," Sudura said. "Kanuji and his clique are hell-bent on maintaining their new thinking in the system. But the elders think such radical fervor is at variance with the ideal our forefathers struggled to put in place. The masses are divided by the power of persuasion from the opposing camps, but I believe the elders still have great influence."

"What did you tell them?"

"I told them we got this far as a civilization by adjusting and readjusting to the unique processes of change," Sudura replied. "I explained that while we cherish practical and meaningful change, it cannot be on the altar of degenerate culture. That, we cannot afford to sacrifice our spirituality to radical thoughts or ego trips."

"Well said, Sudura."

"Thank you, Manu."

"When did they say they would be back?"

"This evening."

"Good. Get two members of the inner circle you can rely on. Talk to the elders and the Kanuji faction when they come. Let them see reason, especially Kanuji, why the people should go for only the grain and not the chaff of his radical philosophy. You must be as diplomatic as you can while trying to make him see reason. Remember, he's our child and the onus is upon us to educate him. Is this understood?"

"Yes, Manu," Sudura said, spurred.

"Okay, get back to your other duties. I have a meeting in a short while. I'll call you in the morning. I hope by then you'd have seen to this Kanuji drama."

Sudura nodded."Certainly."

"Bye for now."

"Long live Tonka! Long live the Manu!"

Just then another call came through.

Daya appeared on the monitor, smiled with obsequy and said, "Manu, they have all been summoned. They await your arrival in the reception lounge."

"Is Vatima Hansi there too?"

"She was the first to arrive."

"All right, make them feel at home. I'll join you soon."

"Yes, Manu." The monitor blanked out. Tonka wheezed, grabbed his golden scepter which sat near the crescent glass desk, and headed to the venue of meeting.

The reception lounge, a crystal arc protrusion at the foot of the great mansion, skirted the rows of exotic gardens at the eastern wing of the mansion. Beyond muffled chatter, the plush interior was tranquil. On the outside, birds twittered around the gardens. The hum of the throng of Songhaians on the fringe of Manu Square filtered through but did not drown the peace within.

In a world of their own and much at ease in the lounge with light refreshments, the invitees looked delighted to be in the Manu's great mansion. The harmonious mood of the lounge remained unbroken until Tonka Manu walked in, accompanied by Daya and Tullami. The phalanx of selected inner circle members, custodians of Manu Square, and Vatima Hansi rose to salute Tonka, dignified and calm as always.

Tonka's gave a demure response. He strode instead toward the eastern row of vases with blooming flowers placed alongside tables and settees. Tonka then lowered his frail body onto his royal seat and observed a moment of silence. As a tradition, the pool of Atlanteans followed his example.

"Privileged members of the inner circle, our revered custodians of the Manu Square, the heartbeat of this civilization, and our dear sister, Vatima Hansi, I greet you," the convener greeted with florish. "I appreciate your coming, in spite of the short notice. It's a sign of our respect for tradition, a sign of growth, and of our collective maturity."

They acknowledged his opening remark with gentle nods.

"If I read your minds well enough, your curiosity centers on why you were summoned here of a sudden," Tonka continued. "It's easy to tell by the austere nature of your reception. We came here not for frivolity, but to try as much as possible to bring back sanity into our notions of life and living, with particular emphasis on our deviant attitudes."

Tonka noticed a wind of unease sweep through the lounge. Gripped by fear, some guests' feet made clumsy shuffles on the marble floor. "Let me clarify right away that some of you are here as mere observers or witnesses of what will transpire," he explained.

Half of the audience relaxed, though nobody could yet tell who was an observer and who was indicted.

"I'll like to inform you about recent events and how some of us are part of the unholy situations," Tonka pressed on. "For a proper understanding of the intrigues we want to expose, fix your mind only on the spiritual sphere, the launching pad for any human aspiration. If this is understood, then we'll proceed." He paused for effect.

"A little over forteen days ago, I had reason to address our dear sister, Vatima Hansi."

Vatima grimaced, worried at the mention of her name.

"We met in my office because of her involvement in renegade spiritual groups. These are groups poised to upturn our sacred values. I'm yet to acknowledge even in a vague sense the existence of such dissenters owing to their triviality. Still, I did not hesitate to caution her then. This rebellious tendency, if allowed to sprout, will endanger her and the whole structure of Atlantis. As alleged, Vatima and her group swore to clog our wheel of progress in the hope of avenging their loss in the hands of Manu Waadua. They want a counter-culture in place of our divinity, with adverse consequences on my tenure as Manu. In the long run, it'll also affect the next Manu's tenure and many more to come. These revelations came, courtesy of some of our respected elders and inner circle members. When I confronted Vatima, she swore she had no hand in any spiritual group. From my point of view, there are elements of truth in it. I gave her the benefit of doubt because you can't treat subjective and objective issues on the same scale. We can only guide an individual and hope their goodwill supersedes. I'm afraid our dear sister didn't learn any lesson from the meeting. The exposures are recurring at an alarming pace."

Tonka had painted Vatima in an awful light, which frightened her. The last time she experienced Tonka's tongue, it took an unknown will and the right propitiation to overcome his accusations. She had sensed the same paralysing wind drifting into her soul a few minutes into this meeting. This time, she knew not the sacrifice the ritual would demand. She only knew she lacked the will to face the facts. Still, she listened, quaking witihin.

Tonka's voice intercepted her thought and grounded her awareness. "We came not to pass judgment on Vatima or anyone," he emphasized. "We are here as concerned Atlanteans. As a family of humans concerned about the plight of our sister, we will only guide and help her, just as many of us here need help in other areas of life. I want us all to understand the obvious. No one is beyond mistakes or reproach. Therefore, do not cast aspersions on impulse, so you don't regret your words afterwards."

Tonka looked at Vatima. "Having said all this, let me go straight to the point," he continued. "Vatima Hansi, is there any aspect of your spiritual life you don't understand, which reflects daily on your actions?"

Vatima quivered. "Just as I said last time, I don't really have a grasp on what's happening to me in the spiritual realm," she stuttered after some hesitation. "Would I know the things bandied about concerning me, and yet keep pretending?"

Tonka reckoned with her response as faultless, yet he treated her with indifference. He had drawn a line a long time ago between spurious mental attitudes and spiritual truths, which seldom waver. That a person who looked naive on the physical could be spiritually gullible and dangerous no longer puzzled him.

"Okay, you don't know any more than we do, but why does your face often attract the absurd?" Tonka quizzed further. "Why are you such a regular character in bizarre spiritual games? It's a puzzle, wouldn't you say? For once, someone else could've been mentioned in all this, but your name keeps popping up. I'm unable to understand your conflict of values. Why have your sterling traits become synonymous with mischief? Do you imagine there's vendetta against you, perhaps, by some unscrupulous Atlanteans? Are we to believe this is just a smear campaign?"

Vatima tried to calm the sickening feeling on the inside of her by running her fingers through the frills of the silky shawl on her head. In the absence of words, her throat ached. She almost choked as bile gushed through her being and overwhelmed her with spite and disgust.

"Who am I to–?" Vatima stammered and broke-off, teardrops blurring her sight.

"Judge anyone?" Tonka cut in. His gaze was without guile. "No, you won't be passing judgment on your accusers if you confirm it is vendetta. You'd be making it easier for us all if you think it is. Give us a reason to believe that you're innocent."

Tonka saw Vatima Hansi fidget on her seat. Then she shuddered and started sobbing.

"In the presence of the Manu, no one cries," Tonka cautioned. "I'm sure you remember this. Besides, there's no reason to cry. Brethren, isn't that so?" Tonka glanced at the other Atlanteans, expecting a response that would please Vatima.

"So true, Manu," they chorused and recoiled into their shells.

Vatima fought her tears with rasping breaths, dabbed her eyes with a handkerchief and sat upright, stiff and daring.

"Last night I had a conviction that rubbed salt into this wound of conscience," Tonka Manu said with a cold edge to his voice. "It is true many have said funny things about Vatima, one time or the other. But that's not the reason for my conviction. As a matter of fact, I had a dirty face-off with this particular clique during my spiritual surveillance last night. Encounters of this kind are uncountable every day. What is worrisome about this unwarranted rebellion is Vatima's role in it.

"Vatima was at the centre stage during the rehearsal of their evil plan," he continued. "And if you'd seen the derision in Vatima's eyes and the guts of the other members of the group in their weird dance of vengeance,

182

you'd understand that human beings are like double-edged swords."

Vatima squirmed with fear as she heard Tonka's words. She knew she had been caught in Tonka's web without the means of escape.

"Even now, the whole scenario rewinds in my mind," Tonka said. "I can see the actors and actresses acting out their tacky roles again."

Tonka shut his eyes and flashed them open the next moment.

# # #

"Yes," he began the long but vivid recollection. "It was on the bed of those quaint hills behind Sondibo town, somewhere near those marvellous valleys. I can still see a notorious spiritual clique, an assembly of the Locci, comprising over a hundred people, mostly women, clustered along the hill's bed. They had chairs, exquisite canopies, exotic lighting, and a high table. Vatima took sat amongst seven other women and two men on the high table. By their positions, the men looked like stooges.

"I recall they had a heated debate over an issue I didn't quite understand till I got close enough to eavesdrop through my aerial surveillance. Vatima's loud command gave her away as one of the leaders in the circle. The theme of their deliberation centered on "Clipped wings". I hung high above the Locci assembly wondering whose wings they wanted clipped. They never saw me or suspected any intrusion. I'd transformed myself into a cluster of pale cloud above the gathering, listening to them. Silence fell over the assembly after Vatima's chiding. Then she addressed the Locci with incensed authority.

"The great Locci is worried because our flight has been unduly hampered," Vatima said, rising to her feet. "At the moment, we are merely clipped wings. It hurts to know that some of us are not bothered one bit that we can't fly as we desire. All we do well is to argue over trivia. Enough of the contentions! We must have a consensus if we want to succeed in our mission. A wise man must recognize the urgency that every mission demands."

The Locci warmed up to her remarks, clapping.

"Our mission needs no further annunciation," Vatima asserted as the applause ended. "We are here to free our hampered wings!" The Locci cheered again. She paused for calm, and then took an ambitious turn.

"We are not about to sit here for eternity, hoping for a tide of events to alter the impossible in our favor. Nor are we going to engage in open confrontation as a means of unclipping our wings. My colleagues of the Locci, we have just one option," Vatima emphasized, again pausing to read the faces of her rapt audience. She continued. "The only way is to clip the wings of the person who clipped ours."

"Free our wings! Free our wings! Free our wings!" chorused the Locci.

"But how?" a strident voice broke-in.

"Hold your peace. I'm coming to that," Vatima bellowed. "We've got to go back to the beginning to understand the Locci's present and possible future. This is not negotiable since our rearmament is coming after a fatal defeat. Don't tell me you don't know who I'm talking about. I mean our defeat in the hands of Manu Waadua, Tonka's predecessor. The Locci's onward success depends on the lessons inherent in our past failures. This is a fact. We failed then for two reasons. First, we underestimated the potential of Waadua.

"The second reason; we handled our key schemes with negligence and tactlessness. Many of our female decoys simply decamped or got trapped into exposing our plans to the enemy. The stupid whims of the Manu and his close disciples caused this because we underestimated him. A grave mistake on our part. We must mend our shattered egos now and forge ahead. We must never allow our past mistakes tie us down forever, or even allow a repeat of those haunting times. Without mincing words, this means, we must plan, and plan well.

"In Waadua we saw a Manu who outsmarted us with his civility. Don't expect the same from Tonka. He might appear a docile, younger horse, and inexperienced, but the Tonka we've seen so far seems more dangerous, more ambitious than his great grandfather. He has all the finesse we lack. I think, and a lot of you would admit this, that Tonka is a bigger problem for us than Waadua was," Vatima concluded.

The pale cloud over the Locci assembly descended to about a hundred metres. Disguised in it, Tonka floated overhead, assessing the assembly's motives and counter-motives. Their gumption amazed him.

"We have to study Tonka's programmes well," Vatima said, exuding an air of accomplishment. "We must come up with strategies that outsmart his one-to-one. In case we are incapable of stopping him, we can at least stall his progress. This is no idle talk and shouldn't be seen as such. Diligence in the highest sense is required of us and we must exercise the finest of tact. Our deception has to be unbeatable to be able to make any impact on Tonka. This is the center piece of our deliberations tonight. I rest my case," Vatima concluded, and sat back, with her head held high, and grinning to the effusive applause of the Locci.

A tall woman spotting a broad-brimmed red hat atop a cream blouse with sequined black skirt, arose at the high table. Tonka looked down from the cloud above them and recognized the woman's face: Feyai Kame, a lady of the Tebi household in Ditara, southwest of Sondibo. He remembered the pretty, ageless and elegant woman. She'd sought his counsel when the affluent but younger Tebi descendants disagreed over the choice of family head. Considering what he had done for her family by resolving the impasse, he could not imagine why a woman of her intellectual and financial stature would belong in a tacky group like the Locci. He looked on, surprised.

"Vatima, thank you for the wonderful speech!" Feyai Kame began. "We are inspired. The great Locci, there's no figment of doubt that Loccien Vatima has spoken our minds. We concede that we suffered defeat during Waadua's tenure. It's up to us to learn and make use of the lessons therein. Furthermore, we've been too tolerant of defecting members. That has to stop. We can no longer condone acts of treachery or cross-carpeting. It's either you're in or you're out. Let me warn that the Locci will not hesitate to deal decisively with those found wanting in any area of duty. The consequences of defection are grave. We are bound by the oath of membership to protect the Locci. If it means being extra-tough on ourselves to bring forth the best qualities into the cause, then we just have to do it without compromise."

Feyai Kame glanced around the Locci high table with the mien of a lioness. Her fellow conspirators signalled her with vague nods, and she leaped back into action.

"What we've dabbled into is a war - a silent war. A war to claim what is rightly ours. A battleground is no place for a frightened rat, neither is it a place for the squeamish. Let it sink into your heads; no idling around a war zone. Our weapons are our minds. Victory is ours when there's a united front, but a bizarre loss we'll incur if we become divisive, incoherent, or argumentative. Set your minds to a goal and strive to accomplish it, no matter what it takes. The Locci lost once, there won't be a repeat," Feyai Kame thundered. "Tonka must be stopped. If we can't achieve this objective, then we must learn to beat a drum he would dance. Once we control his mind, we control Atlantis, hence, our destiny."

"Yes, you're on track," some mebers of the Locci chanted.

"Let's make him dance," another group shrilled.

"Yes," Feyai intoned. "But we can't control his mind unless we control his food, his shelter, clothing, and every other thing around him. Our own people need to infiltrate those sensitive areas of his life. And because there's no man that cannot fall to the wiles of women, we have to co-opt pretty ladies in great numbers to unleash carnal pressures on him. In the long run we hope his puritan stance will give in to our smart strategies."

Feyai raised a finger as a caution. "All the same, we have to tread with care. I have a feeling we are dealing with a cobra. He might strike when we least expect. In this case, should our female agents fail, we would need other areas of leverage through which we can stop the wheel of progress in Atlantis. This also means we need some clout in every facet of the Atlantean superstructure. It's easier to stifle a system from the top downwards. Ladies and gentlemen of the Locci, this is my humble submission."

The Locci applauded as Feyai Kame sat down. Biazi, one of the two men on the high table, rose to his feet and humped his shoulders like a colossus acknowledging the presence of dwarfs. His studied effort for attention, however, proved less effective than the first two female speakers.

Biazi's handsome features shone forth with a broad smile. "Our able ladies of the roundtable have done us real proud with their heart-warming speeches," he declared in a voice under perfect control. "Nothing so warms a man's heart than the knowledge that he has intelligent and committed women toiling to realize a dream he identifies with.

"I'm impressed by their eloquent analysis of the burden on the Locci. I ascribe to almost all the issues they have raised. I'm also of Vatima's line of reasoning. Unlike Waadua's predictable diplomacy which ironically floored us all, Tonka is of finer stuff and would heed the advice of Waadua with whom he still maintains contact in the spiritual realm. This includes the entire chain of Manus."

Biazi paused, knowing he had said the right words up to this point. Nonetheless, a queasy feeling still hunted his innermost thoughts.

"We talk of niceties, of infiltration and stuff," he resumed. "It makes some sense. However, we haven't given thought to the kind of devices at the disposal of the enemy, which could frustrate our plans."

Murmurs of agreemet from the larger assembly as well as muffled appraisals from the high table reached Biazi.

"The task before us is enormous," he pressed on. "We can't pretend we're going to have a work-over. It would be self-deluding to think so. Look at our agents that infiltrated into the top echelon of power. They were as ineffective as our agents in Manu Square. What did we get instead? A horde of men and women who got so intoxicated with the enemy's liquor. They became our undoing. The sheer thought of the enemy's ploys caught them pants down. So we lost out. Infiltration is part of the fun, but what sort do we rely upon? We have it on record there'll soon be a shift in the axis of Atlantis. It says more than we can ever imagine. Our civilization appears to be on the thin edge of the cliff. From what we know about the shifting axis, violence of any kind will be to our disadvantage. We've all agreed there must be action, but we must recognize the obvious, that, there's a difference between mere words and action. What makes the difference is taking the right steps in the right direction. Fellow members of the Locci, this is my submission. It's not by any means perfect. Still, I implore you all to think about it. Thank you for your attention," Biazi concluded, pleased that he had made an impact, which most of the audience seemed not to have expected at the onset of his speech.

The audience's brief applause was more significant than any other. They knew Biazi had poked at a festering wound on their body politic. Only such an act could remind them of their enemy and prepare them for vengeance.

Vatima Hansi did not wait for the applause to subside before she rose to her feet and gestured for calm. Swallowing hard, she said with great emotion, "The mighty Locci has arrived! Yes, the Locci is here to stay. If there's any word that best describes the wave our emotions today, it must be the pride or dignity that we belong. This wave has kept us awash with strength and hope. We are proud to have amongst us people of Biazi's kind; minds that have seen change and endured; minds that find comfort in the new hope each dawn offers; minds that work in tough conditions – the garden where hope is nursed. Everyone here has a unique quality. These rare qualities acted as the magnetic field for the great Locci. This explains why we've seen change and endured its caprice. I wouldn't be mincing words if I say that we believe in tomorrow's promise. It's the reason we reckon with today's dreams. Yet, I'm also expressing a belief that has its paradoxes." Vatima broke off with a derisive smile.

"Why are we such great minds if we're going to be rendered impotent by a paradox such as this?" Vatima continued in a louder, berating tone. "We do believe in what tomorrow offers, but our fear of the enemy's power seems stronger. Nonetheless, it's an unreal fear. It's is a figment of our imaginations. We are frightened over a self-created mystique."

Vatima took a breather to let her assertion sink well. "There is no enemy," she bawled, picking her words one by one. "We are our own enemy. Conquer your fears and the enemy is gone, forever. We created the incubus. Therefore, we can and must, get rid of it."

Vatima's boldness amazed the Locci. "The enemy is coy, no doubt. We need to respect his intelligence, but we must not be frightened by the notion of an enemy who thrives only in our minds."

Biazi winced. He avoided Vatima's fire-spitting eyes the best way he could. Vatima contradicted her initial assertion that a wise person must recognize the urgency of every mission with her new stance. Why she resorted to attacking this viewpoint, which he had tried to explain to the people in a different way, surprised him.

"This time, we're not going to let myths of heroes and villains cripple us," Vatima urged the gathering. "We have to advance into the war zone. Go for your weapons of war. Apply tact and let's advance into the frontiers of war. Don't let fear undo your resolve to fight. Atlantis is ours for the taking," she beamed chivalrously. "Thank you for your time gentlemen and ladies of the Locci!"

Biazi observed that Vatima Hansi's variant perspective of the Locci's mission, though in line with other areas of their plan, gave rise to dissention among the cheering Locci. While a few favored her militant approach, the majority murmured against it.

Biazi also noticed how the grayish pocket of cloud dashing over the crimson moon sank across the skyline with the light of dawn, which bathed the whole place with a kind of enchanting luminosity.

The Locci assembly were rattled by a loud cackle from within the pale cloud overhead. Jolted to their feet by the voice, the Locciens gazed at each other like morons.

A huge dove emerged from the cloud, flapping its beautiful wings as it descended towards the Locci high table. The dove perched in front of Vatima, cooing as if leering at her. Lema, the second male on the table, in a swift, calculated move, lunged toward the dove, but it sprang over their heads and landed on the far right on the high table. There, a lady attempted to grab it but the bird's reflexes were sharper than hers. It twittered away to another position mid-point on the giant table.

"Get that thing fast!" Vatima hollered at the Locciens close to the table, pointing to the strange, elusive bird.

"Easy with the chase. We want that thing alive," cried Feyai Kame at other members of the Locci who had converged around the table bidding to trap down the dove.

They stumbled on each other and cursed between breaths as the dove flew skywards. In triumph it capered and then dived low toward the free end of the table.

The dove's features metamorphosed on landing on the table into the radiant profile of Tonka Manu, who stood smiling and jeering at the Locci.

"Tonka!" the Locci chorused, mesmerized.

"Tonka, no doubt," Tonka affirmed, with a sneer. "And what a beautiful little party you have here!" He glanced at Vatima and other high-ranking members of the Locci who riveted their heads in shame. "Permit me to join in the fun," Tonka taunted them once more. "I want to belong to a conquering team like the Locci. I'm glad to note that Atlantis is ours for the taking. It's high time we struck. So, brethren, where are your weapons?"

No one spoke. They watched Tonka like a pack of petrified rats, wondering how he got wind of their secret rendezvous.

"Well, since none of you could muster the courage to advance to the war zone as agreed, I'll like to take the initiative," Tonka said and brandished a glittering sword from a hidden scabbard. "Here's my sword. Who is ready to fight the fight of warriors?"

The Locci stampeded in all directions, with most of them dashing towards the range of rocks beyond the hills. Their idea of an escape route ended in a cul-de-sac. Tonka let out a prolonged guffaw on seeing their lead quartet of Vatima, Biazi, Lema and Feyai scurrying off their seats to a dead end.

How could these champions and zealous plotters against divine order so abandon their mission in shame? How fragile human gumption can be in the face of a little test, Tonka thought.

He reckoned the Locci's hurried retreat was temporary. Though they would soon reorganize and strike back in secret, he knew a bigger shock awaited them.

Several meters away from the scene, the embattled Locci remembered some of their inherent powers: even in this confusion they still could levitate or dematerialize. They chose the former. One after the other they leaped into the sky with outstretched hands. They gained propulsion that lifted them off from the grossness of Atlantis into the sky. The once alive assembly ground became a desolate bed of fine rock near high hills. Only the cluster of upturned tables, chairs, and canopies reminded Tonka of the place of rebellion of the Locci.

The sword in Tonka's hand vanished in the same manner it had emerged. No alone, not in the least disturbed by the spookiness of the range of hills, he took one last look around the hills, the bird-like flight of the Locciens and chuckled at the ridiculousness of the whole drama.

# # #

"I returned to my body after the incidence," Tonka recalled.

All eyes in the reception lounge of Tonka's mansion riveted on Vatima with spite, alienating her as the scum amidst the innocent.

Tonka looked at their angry faces and then focused on Vatima Hansi.

"Do I need to explain any further why I called the face-off a tacky one from the start?' he asked. "No, it's a great revelation. Vatima is implicated beyond doubt. At this point, we must diagnose her ailment and, of course, prescribe as necessary. A call for rebellion is a germ that needs to be done away with. We'll be kind enough to pardon its bearer, but the germ itself must be eliminated."

Tonka's narrative confused Vatima, yet she calmed her nerves and said nothing.

"My dear daughter, Vatima Hansi," Tonka cajoled in a lilting tone. "Where do you fit into all this? Now, we want to help you determine the root of the problem, but you have to help us understand its nature. Are you willing to submit yourself for scrutiny and accept the verdict?"

Vatima gave a weary nod.

"Good," Tonka said, addressing the select Atlanteans in the lounge. "Feel free to speak if you have anything to say about our sister Vatima."

Vatima shivered at the thought of gallows, the obvious verdict to which Tonka's accusation pointed. She saw spite etched on the faces of those in the lounge like a spectrum of weird strokes. She did not need the wisdom of a sage to know that Tonka had convicted her of the crime, though he avoided passing a direct judgment. She also knew that witnesses to the event would love to see her ridiculed. Absorbing their blows without Tonka's soft touch seemed a grave pain to inflict on oneself. In spite of it, she waited for the inevitable.

The men entrusted with the noose over her head were cautious to step onto the platform and be done with their hangmen's duty. They had a reason to be guarded. Tonka had warned earlier against prejudice, emphasizing that it could be anybody's turn the next dawn. So, they were careful not to incur his wrath.

"Speak out if you've got something to say," Tonka urged them. "This silence won't help Vatima or any of us."

Aloft on guard at the fringe of the lounge's connecting door, Tullami, a gorgeous male of the inner circle, braced himself from his rather cool watch of the unfolding drama. "I crave your indulgence, Manu," he began.

If hangmen were needed to knot the noose around Vatima's neck, Tonka would use the discerning rod of his station to decide who, not me. I'll speak the truth as I know it – a balm on my conscience, Tullami thought.

"Speak," Tonka said when he noticed Tullami's hesitation.

"I'd kept this experience to myself," Tullami said, heaving a sigh of relief, "for a fairly long time. I'd considered it run-of-the-mill kind of...spiritual adventure. But from what you told us and the rumors making the rounds, I'll like to comment on the issue at stake. I made up my mind to speak because my conscience pricks me. I don't know what it will sound like but there's no shying away from this matter. After all, it ought to have been said a fortnight ago. That's the precise timing of the experience I'm about to share. Perhaps, if I had said it earlier, the Manu would've curbed the insurgence of the Locci before it got to this stage. My heart bleeds knowing what wrong the delay has caused."

Tullami bowed and clasped his hands to his chest in contemplation. When he gained the needed confidence, he raised his face and said in a tremulous voice, "I recall it was a gathering of some past Manus. I was lucky to be in their midst, as I didn't, of course, belong among those great souls. They called me into their circle as witness because they felt it necessary to intimate me with the rebellious side of things in this civilization. They mentioned three names as the problem with our great society. Em...em...em...Vatima and the Locci were mentioned as rebels to watch. The two other names in the list are also leaders of other rival subversive groups."

With an audience too willing to jump at the sound of his voice, Tullami threw caution to the wind now.

"As the Manus explained, these three names, each representing a rebel faction, are perhaps the only obstacles to Atlantis' stable growth. They said more baffling things than these," Tullami said and then stalled for a moment to impact on his audience.

Tonka lips parted into a brief smile, a sign that the speaker's revelations pleased him.

Vatima trembled on the inside with a hazy, crest-fallen stare as she listened to Tullami.

"The Manus said Atlantis is gliding down the cliff because of groups such as the Locci," Tullami said. "I figure the Manus were displeased that we're encouraging the growth of these rebellious instincts in uncountable ways. They said this cankerworm must be uprooted with utmost dispatch." Tullami's lips now creased into a pout. "The Manus showed me a special film. I believe you'd want to know its details," he continued. It had a plot similar to the encounter Tonka Manu narrated a while ago. Vatima played a lead role in the film. The props were of the same weird nature and you wouldn't miss out the actors and actresses as the same people we're talking about here."

If Vatima Hansi thought she had a chance to appeal for a fair trial in the Manu's court, she got it wrong. Tullami had just confirmed the verdict: she was guilty. This heightened her confusion.

Are the gods so thirsty they need to spill innocent

blood to propitiate their altars? Lord, plead my cause. Don't let me walk this tight rope anymore!

"I'd better not drag this experience farther than this, Manu," Tullami said, cutting the reel of Vatima's thoughts. "We've put the frames in place already, it's easy to fix in the right pictures. Long live Tonka! Long live the Manu!"

Tullami's head tipped forward, a calculated bow, a subtle prompt Tonka acknowledged in a less banal sense.

"It's good you spoke about the revelation, Tullami," Tonka said. "It seems to me you've used a sponge on Vatima and she's getting cleaner and cleaner by the hour."

The situation demanded a firm stand, but Tonka felt he had to wait till the end. In the interim, the carrot and stick diplomacy sufficed. Let Vatima go for the carrot then he would use the stick when necessary.

Vatima lost control of herself, sprang to her feet, and charged in delirium towards Tonka. Daya who, in the nick of time, saw the fury afoot made to block her but she dodged him and moved toward her target. Tullami dashed at her out of instinct but failed short of a grip.

"Leave her alone, both of you!" Tonka barked, holding up a hand. Tullami and Daya froze at the order.

Vatima reached Tonka's side howling, like a wounded vixen. Anger, bitterness, and the pain of humiliation seared through her as she stood gasping. She would reclaim her lost esteem at whatever cost. In spite of her rage, she could still distinguish between the opposing paths all humans must choose, either by fate or circumstance – the path of winners or the path of losers. Losing was one thing, a gallant loser was yet another. She would rather be the latter.

"What's the matter with you now, Vatima?" Tonka asked, sensing an omen in the air. "What has come over you? Please, get hold of yourself."

Like a shamed child, Vatima buried her head in her palms. Strange bouts of spasms wrestled with her resolve to be calm and coherent. She managed to stammer a reply. "All I know – all I know is that I'm sick and tired of all the mudslinging…"

Moved, Daya stepped forward to steady her, but Tonka stuck out his golden sceptre. "Don't touch her." Daya recoiled. "Let her be. I smell danger offshore."

"I can't hold on any longer," Vatima snarled, trembling. I'm tired, simply tired." By sleight of hand she found the neckline of her blouse and pulled at the fine silk. With a crisp, shrill, hissing, the blouse tore in two, revealing turgid breasts held in place by a black brassiere.

The lounge resonated with gasps of astonishment. This did not deter Vatima. She rather tugged at the torn halves of the blouse and they came off like plucked wings, fluttering on her quaking body. Tonka looked away from her daring, repulsive act. Inertia swept through the lounge as no one seemed poised to stop Vatima's maniacal theatrics. Indeed, none could stop her now. She had reached the pinnacle of her revolt.

In another deft move, Vatima pulled at both the torn blouse and brassiere, peeling them over her shoulder. Gibbering, she hurled the shreds onto the floor.

Tullami and Daya arose like activated twin robots and advanced toward her. To watch this woman swing their fate to a point of endless reprisal without requisite action would be unpardonable. Next, Vatima tore off her loin cloth and underwear before the duo got near. The men stopped dead on their tracks when they saw Vatima stark naked in front of Tonka Manu. A sacrilege never before witnessed in the history of Atlantis.

Tonka uttered no word. He looked demure on his seat, doodling invisible forms on the table cover with his scepter. This in itself was an omen. Now, everything came to a standstill. Vatima also stopped her yammering. The gaping men and women in the lounge could almost hear one another's heartbeats in the tense and surreal atmosphere, which did not last long. Soon enough, some people began to stir.

Tonka walked quietly out of the reception lounge. Daya and Tullami hurried after him in the obsequious way of inner circle members, but he waved them aside.

"Go and attend to Vatima and the others," he instructed under his breath and swung through the door leading to his private chambers.

Daya, Tullami, and the others were aware that the conscience of Atlantis had been tainted and a sinister web had entrapped their kind. Just then, Tullami recalled what the previous Manus told him in a chance spiritual meeting. A time like this would come, Tullami had learnt, which would herald a new era. Though not privy to the details of the prophecy of the Manus, he was certain of one fact: that Vatima had rocked the great ship of Atlantis with her sacrilege.

# # #

Titan Race

Tonka Manu hopped up the main staircase in suppressed fury to the penthouse. He would have preferred the patio between the horizontal, heart-like structure at the southern end of the mansion to the rare view of the northern end in normal situations. In his present mood, the ideal place was the penthouse, a vintage for admiring the elegance of northern Songhai. He needed the spectacular panorama to begin to ward off Vatima's intolerable show of shame. Even then, he did not underrate the harm the occurrence had wreaked on Atlantis.

The whole encounter he had with the Locci in his trance flight presaged nothing but doom. Atlanteans drifted toward the absurd in their ego trips. The situation had drawn them now to the end of a long tether. Tonka allowed himself to acknowledge this aspect of things as he veered in a sharp turn onto the left on the landing of the second floor of the mansion. In a weird sense he felt delighted. The plugs of the civilization were on his palms to pull, perhaps, right away.

A door along the passage swung open to the near right of Tonka. A trolley screeched to a stop and rolled out of the door. Behind it was Pullama, a young, exuberant lad with curious brown eyes. Half-blind from his upset, Tonka would have bumped in it but for the lad's skilfulness.

Pullama adroitly wheeled the trolley back to a corner. "Long live Tonka! Long live the Manu!" he hailed, with an apologetic bow. "Forgive my impudence. I didn't mean to startle you."

Tonka plodded on, indignant, responding to Pullama's salutation with a slight nod. Though salutary, the gesture sent some chill into Pullama who shrugged in disbelief. He had never seen the ever-cautious and courteous Tonka Manu so indifferent. Tonka must have been in a strange, unusual state of mind, Pullama reasoned.

A resident of the mansion and one of the few privileged inner-circle members permitted in that core, Pullama had enjoyed absolute peace there, but recognized the diverse shades of trouble whenever he saw one. He pushed the trolley back on course, pondered what could be troubling the Manu so early in the day. He glanced at the receding figure, shrugged again, and wheeled the trolley forward consoled by the fact that Daya and Tullami would soon reveal to him what had taken place in the reception lounge.

Tonka's sense of urgency as to what step to take made him impatient even with the gliding sleek glass door of the penthouse. It barely parted before he hauled himself in, as if at this moment contemptuous of the enchanting luxury within. He had left the lounge to the penthouse for a mission, but now within its tranquil and posh confines, the exact idea of what he would do eluded him.

I must act, no matter what. Otherwise, it would appear a sign of weakness. Now I'll have to show that the center's strength had never been weakened.

Tonka stood in deep thought close to the door. He had many decisions to take. This affair with the Atlanteans was an experimental idea of the Guardians. He sighed wistfully. The Guardians cannot always have all the fun watching his failure or success from those intangible realms while anxiety made a mess of him in Atlantis. They had better anticipate his move, a return of the burden they had placed on his shoulders.

After a pensive moment, Tonka rushed to the penthouse window, his favorite observation spot in the mansion. This time, the usual scenic sights looked grim. Atlantis vanished from his gaze, leaving an empty space where exotic Songhai once featured.

I've been groomed all these years to oversee this emptiness, the debris of a civilization. So be it, then.

Tonka drew back the drapes, turned from the window, and hastened to his sanctuary to envision what would come upon Atlantis after he had pulled the last of the plugs.

# # #

Hemse often thought the vista of the cosmos on the Disk Center's monitors conformed to the logic of orderliness. To him, it was a ceaseless motion of expansion and condensation of specks of energy jostling for creative relevance in a turbulent vastness. These interwoven strands of creation, to someone unfamiliar to the Blackhole, showed on the Command Module screens as a remarkable work of perfection, despite their chaotic display.

As a Guardian, Hemse was accustomed enough to the intrigues of creation not to be moved beyond a casual viewing of the screens. The recurrent explosion and cooling of photons, the tangled webs of light points, the colossal dissolution of stars as well as the re-bonding of energies, were cheerless cosmic scenes to Hemse. He would have loved instead an excursion on the Tamed Star around the galaxies, which often soothed his ego and stirred his sense of adventure.

On his first galactic trip with Numa, they had visited Starealm, the farthest galaxy, with a stopover at Shiru, the twentieth. His experience of life had been less boring outside the Blackhole. He did not always feel the ennui of being glued to all those screens and the dreariness of the whole galactic chaos. He often looked forward to a shuttle in the Tamed Star or Blackhole saucers around the cosmic sea. Just when he began to yearn for another opportunity to soon leave the Blackhole a male voice echoed with urgency on the Command Module.

"Starealm calling Blackhole, Starealm to Blackhole. Over." Hemse dithered, almost to the point of altogether ignoring it. "Starealm calling Blackhole." The voice came over again more firmly. "Come in, Blackhole. Over."

A strident hint to the voice cut short Hemse's daydream. He acknowledged the name Starealm with exhilaration. The voice had to be a Guardian's.

"Blackhole to Starealm. Over."

"Guardian Urnsa from Starealm. Over."

"I know," Hemse said. "Hemse. Disk Centre, Blackhole. Over."

"The flight of the Tamed Star is due Blackhole in less than five swirls," Urnsa replied. "Father of Blackhole, Numa, on board."

"Copied." Hemse studied the handsome figure of the Guardian from Starealm on the Command Module. He envied the Guardian's mental calmness. "Is that all?"

"No. A meeting of Guardians is necessary."

"Really? Why this proposition?"

"Numa's idea," Urnsa said, exonerating himself of blame. "You are in a better position to know. I thought you–"

"You are right, of course," Hemse interjected, conceding without grasping Urnsa's insinuation. "That's if I know what you mean."

Urnsa's fine face creased in disbelief. Hemse must be a joker. "You don't see what's going on down there?"

"Cut out the riddles. Where?"

"There's a whole new ball game in Atlantis," Urnsa explained. "I suppose you are aware of the details of how Tonka is pulling the reins and not–"

"What about it?" Hemse protested. "We are on guard, I should say. Over."

On guard, indeed. Urnsa knew more than that. Hemse could not have meant what he had said else he would not have asked all those questions. "I suppose then you know Tonka's last resort is to apply his hidden rod on stubborn Atlanteans?"

"Hold on. Let me put fellow Guardians on alert," Hemse said, as a way of evading his usual flight of mind, which often cast him as indolent. He transmitted the arrival time of the Tamed Star on the Command Module, wasted time on trifle details, and turned his attention to Urnsa. "When is this urgent meeting scheduled to take place?"

"Soon as Father Numa arrives," Urnsa replied.

"All right, we'll be ready. I'll relay accordingly. All parties to converge, pronto. Over."

"I'm right on the track of the Tamed Star. Over."

"Till then. Over." Hemse transmitted the call-up signal to the Guardians in the various galaxies.

I'll get acquainted with what Urnsa had discerned that I had not, he told himself.

He rested half his weight on the edge of the Command Module panel for a close-up view of Atlantis on some select screens. The ominous beat of his heart laced with an excitement. Could this be a sort of danger for Atlantis?

# # #

Tonka Manu paced into his sanctuary, delighted by the seeming graveyard silence in the large room of sparse décor. He experienced an unusual peace due to the decision he had taken – more of a final contact with his destiny. This new feeling erased his prior anxiety resulting from Vatima's sordid act.

At last he was face-to-face with the moment he had waited for all his life, to oversee the end of a heightened civilization. Once he had made up his mind on what to do, in spite of anger, he needed no preamble to bring it to fruition.

Tonka approached his wool-laid seat placed on a square rug, a seat that appealed to him as an obedient mule, ready to service his whim.

Titan Race

Tonka's eyes sparkled with wanton brilliance and strange excitement as he sat on the seat. Pre-empting an invocation, he screwed shut his eyes and with a deep breath and inward gaze, propelled his soul out of his body.

Tonka's mind flowed in line with his intention: control the streaming force of the sun upon Atlantis, the invaluable power of the supporting stars and the presence of the moon...eliminate the thin envelope of air and stop the steady ooze of water in the depths and on the Atlantis' surface wrought by the magnetic streak of sun-stars; and eliminate the innocuous power of fire in thunder by tilting the giant ball a little out of orbit upwards or downwards....What would be left of Atlantis? An endangered globe in the cosmic scheme due to the abrupt displacement...

Tonka knew this well: if the moving wheel of Atlantis were to be pulled with less pressure and the forces in random play were to even slightly impact on the globe, the outcome would be the depolarization of Atlantis' axis, or the extinction of life in the displaced parts. Other parts of the landmass would, however, survive the sharp tectonic jolt and still bear the seed of new vegetation, animals, and the human species. This knowledge pleased him.

His mission in Atlantis could not be confused with the role of the mind behind creation, but he had the less exercised prerogative of being an incarnate Guardian of the Universe. Now he had been forced to exercise it, by choosing the option of depolarization.

Spare the globe, re-channel the scam on its surface, and let life again awaken to a new dance - an option long taken by the Guardians. He saw in himself a vicarious interpreter of their script.

Tonka Manu, therefore, began to invoke the forces governing creation at the faint border between the spiritual and the physical worlds.

# # #

The first forecast of changing weather came over Radio Ditara. The brief broadcast warned of fast-roving storm clouds on a diagonal sweep across Atlantis. It was reported as a strong front built up in the raging currents of the Deemen Sea. It made a steady incursion inland two nautical miles east of the sea port of Ditara. The forecast placed the storm high on the Songhaian scales as herald to a hurricane expected to trounce the easternmost bounds of Ditara during the third hour in the second phase of the day. Atlanteans were advised to secure their homes within the shortest possible time. DitaraTel, the television arm of Ditara Broadcasting Centre (DBC), captured the fierce front of the sweeping clouds in their garnered palls and vicious whistling drift inland. A tentative curfew imposed on air, land and sea traffic exempted a few deserving cases on land.

Tonka heard the broadcast over Radio Ditara at the patio while trying to catch a glimpse of the initial flickers of what he had invoked at the sanctuary twenty minutes earlier. He backed away from the banisters and sought the arc of mosaic slab at a corner of the patio with stacks of monitors.

He got there just as the DitaraTel featured the hurricane. Both news items inflated his pride in Atlantis as the melting pot of science and technology. Its progress in this regard enchanted him as would any mortal. A few swirls and the news would spread all over Atlantis, with intensive counter-measures being put in place.

The telecommunication networks were reliable and well prepared against natural disasters of this magnitude, though unprecedented. This storm, Tonka conceded, was different from the whirlpools detected in the past. A queer grin panned out on his lips. This was not even the main scenario expected. He would have the last laugh.

Chapter Eight

All radio and television networks in Atlantis reported the encroaching gale at intervals of three to five swirls. The Songhai Waves made its last broadcast sixty swirls short of the main incursion on the borders of Ditara. Atlanteans could not fathom the extent of the havoc.

Meteorological computations at the Ecology Evaluation Centre had shown that the gale could be managed and would not cause much structural damage. But the frightening television coverage of the storm stunned Atlanteans. This uncommon dance of nature left them trembling indoors.

From the timing of the storm, they had just about sixty swirls of peace before it would unleash its force. From behind closed doors, Atlanteans watched the televised scenes of the intrusive howling wind. The unpredictable storm enforced its own kind of curfew, and the wide, glamorous streets were deserted, the airspace cleared of traffic.

Not quite thirty swirls afterwards, the storm swept towards Ditara, devouring all it touched. Tullami and Daya watched the fierce battering of Ditara, the political base of Atlantis. They had been busy in the communication room at the basement of Tonka's mansion, monitoring the storm for upwards of eighty swirls. The ferocious display of nature's prowess surprised them, for it was unlike anything they had seen.

"It came first as a dream that would phase out soon," a DitaraTel anchor-man reported, his words dripping with emotion. "But now we are stuck with it. The earlier storm which trampled the front east of Ditara, sixty-two nautical miles from here, has overwhelmed our city. The storm heralds a hurricane, and if it doesn't subside soon, Atlantis will be shaken to its core. So far, thankfully, there has been no recorded casualty or property damage. There is persistent blinding dust and debris in the storm's wake. But it is safe, provided people do not leave their homes. We will now go over to the frontiers of the storm to show you what is going on." The reporter paused.

The cameras zoomed in on the storm as it gurgled inland. A bust of thick dust and debris flew in varied swirls, splattering against buildings and with haze that impaired vision. Trees, luxuriant gardens, and poles bowed to the swift wind. Even buildings were forced into a dizzy infernal dance, testing the resilience of Atlantean engineering.

The scene light flicked and the reporter reappeared. "The worst phase of the storm is yet to come, but it is believed it won't cause more damage. Stay tuned and we will bring you the swirl-by-swirl onslaught. I'm Tinko Jalu, reporting for DitaraTel News."

Tullami turned to Daya, seeking something inspiring and brighter than the harrowing scenes. "Do you suppose Tonka Manu is doing anything positive about this storm?" he whispered, afraid that other inner circle members might hear his words and ascribe different meanings to them.

Daya shook his head. "I'm just as curious as you are," he whispered back. "We have to find out quickly."

"Yeah. This phenomenon I reckon is an uncanny invocation. Don't ask me whose."

Daya got the hint. "It's as if you peeped into my mind. Do you think the reception lounge situation has anything to do with this?"

Tullami hesitated. "Maybe. It doesn't seem like a coincidence. My experience tells me there's more to this."

"We are on the same page," Daya said, nodding. "I'll go check up with the Manu before this thing reaches Songhai and everywhere else."

"I'll hang around here to keep tab on the screens till you return," Tullami volunteered, riveting to the screens.

Daya hurried out of the communication room and climbed up the flight of stairs in search of Tonka.

# # #

Five swirls on the dot, all the Guardians summoned for the Blackhole meeting had gathered in the outer chamber of the Disk Center's Wisdom Hall with the exception of Finia. The Guardians rose, ushering Numa,

Blackhole's bright-eyed enigma and patron, ageless in spite of his thick forest of gray beard, hoary hair and stooping stead.

The Wisdom Hall was dazzling and timeless in its grandeur. The Guardians' abstract attire and illusory wings reflected its ivory texture, with the flaming shades of their hair and skin color speckling the cream décor.

The Guardians watched Numa wade through a snow-like drift of ankle-deep gas till he got to the front of a crescent formation of seats. He stopped by his stellar throne before the circle of Guardians.

Contrary to expectations, Numa did not occupy it. Instead, with one hand he held its backrest, and, with the other, balanced his frail physique with a firm clutch of his scepter. When he noticed the Guardians standing, he signalled them to sit. He then paced along the front row of the guests, brooding over the coming calamity.

Numa knew displacing any component of the cosmos would exact a rebound on the entire system. However, this game of restructuring Atlantis, their PlayToy, took after the Guardians' own model in spite of what Finia had caused at the moment. He knew too that the plan had to be modified in the interest of the Guardians.

Numa stopped his prancing near his seat, and broke his deep silence. "Guardians, we proceed with our planetary intercession and realignment scheme right away," he announced. "If we wait a swirl longer, be sure we will be dealing with chaos as robust as the cosmic tree. We have an incarnate Guardian in Atlantis whose anger, evoked by the timid wiles of man, brings us close to an unscheduled action. Of course, we have no other

214

duty than to contain him and the amplifying chaos as it affects the globe and the entire universe. Atlantis is broiling at this moment. Keen observers would tell of the turbulence there. What you'd call the signals of a violent end has been stirred by our Atlantis Guardian. Though our human stock with all their wit, least suspect his intentions and what catastrophe lies ahead."

Numa took guarded but bold steps away from his seat, still clutching his scepter. "Vacillation is over," he went on in a mellow tone. "We must go back to the drawing board to review Atlantis, the interrelating planets in the galaxy, and all the cosmic strands. From our observations of the prevailing conditions, we haven't got much time. Our maneuvre begins without delay after we've heard from the hierarchies of the sister planets in the galaxy. We will precede this with a trip to Atlantis via the Command Module."

Numa backed off a few steps leading to a small platform, with a screen backdrop sprawled across the wall.

"Here's a situation report of the tempest in Atlantis," he said, pointing his scepter at the screen activated by thought waves. "I presume you are all aware of the steps the Atlantis Guardian has taken."

The orbital loop of nine planets around the sun amidst a sea of stars appeared on the screen. The Guardians shifted their focus from the stars to the spherical mass of condensed energy known as Atlantis, and closer still, till the coarse dust of Atlantis and its load of civilization surfaced.

"This is Atlantis, our playhouse. There you see the stock of beings we've carefully nurtured for some eons. On focus is a renowned human city. Look over here," Numa said, pointing his scepter at a cluster of edifices covering half the screen – architecture, magnificent beyond human ingenuity.

"This whole area, called Dhusa, is a typical Atlantis city. Most Atlantean inventions originate here. In Atlantean parlance, Songhai lie one thousand five hundred phantoms southwest of Dhusa. Songhai is the spiritual haven of our Guardian. Right now there's a wild storm, a hurricane front, sweeping over Atlantis. It has rocked half of Atlantis but is yet to reach Songhai – just over here." The screen flicked and Songhai emerged.

"The windstorm which is a few phantoms beyond Sondibo and the adjoining commercial town of Tulla–" the bizarre front of the storm came on focus – "is only a child play of our Guardian's havoc. We lay no blame on him though. You know too well why this is so. He belongs here in the Blackhole. He's one string we've pulled to redirect the rolling cart of Atlantis. He seems to be doing a solo dance nevertheless, deaf to our sanction and blind to our schedule. We think his unilateral action is out of order. Anyway, we'll see to this in due course."

Numa left the flashing screen and walked down the platform. "So much has gone into the making of this playhouse and everything else we see," he flaunted on, halting behind his chair. "Our efforts will come to naught if we procrastinate in pruning our wild seeds and upgrade their intelligence in their ascent up the ladder of consciousness."

"Guardians," he continued, with a more assertive edge to his voice, "I mean seeds that exhibit sterling traits, gem seeds. These must be given the chance to live again in finer conditions than what prevails on this little globe called Atlantis." He waved toward the backdrop. "They must be replanted according to our plan because by the time the real picture of the chaos in Atlantis emerges - just a flash of calm after the hurricane – there'll be nothing left to save or re-culture. There'll be no PlayToy to task our sensibilities other than this disturbing warp, an emptiness we will have to put back in variant shapes someday. We need few humans. We will prepare a few humans from the lot of Atlantis to start a new race.

"I don't need to goad you on the roles each of you has to play to bring our scheme to fruition. Still, it is normal to refresh our minds with details of our individual tasks. I'll restate in broad terms the nature of the operation and leave trifle details to the appropriate departments to handle as the meeting progresses.

"If the hierarchies of Atlantis' sister planets are present, we would like to know from them the prevailing trend with their stock of beings and the general ecology. That would be our yardstick for selecting the species, human and otherwise, which we'll use to repopulate Atlantis in the nascent dispensation along with the few survivors from moribund Atlantis. Those, we will displace, willy-nilly. Their souls will be given a place to hibernate and live out their mistakes till a desired maturity is attained. Perhaps then we can cloak them in finer bodies and see how well they fare. More of this later. Now who speaks first?"

#

Tonka Manu soon became bored with his watch of the flickering screens at the patio's arc of marble slab where he monitored the windstorm. An impulse to head to his sanctuary after the telecast of the raging windstorm on DitaraTel had the better of him. The significance, however, of his glimpses of the far horizon, the evil import of the burst of wind, was something he could not just take his mind away from. It blew too much weight on the mind to bear. Nonetheless, he moved away from the circle of the noisy monitors and the gadgetry contrivances on the slab to the more serene poolside.

He rested his bulk on a marble pillar, one of several mosaic marvels that formed a ring around the entire patio. They held the load of chandeliers on the engraved, gleaming ceiling boards of the wonderful dome-like canopy. Time sped by. Nature continued with its fiery rebellion. Tonka knew only an inconceivable flash of time remained before this song of destruction climaxed and took Atlantis with its ending notes. Yet he stood waiting for the caress of the inevitable.

A brisk movement behind him caught his attention.

"Long live the Manu!" Daya curtsied as Tonka turned to acknowledge the stealthy intruder.

Tonka nodded, replying discernibly, "Daya, your mind is troubled. Are you here because of the garnering force of the elements, the avenging wind?" He moved away from the edge of the patio.

"Yes, Manu," Daya responded in a cool, diffident tone, trailing behind Tonka. They came to a halt by the hedge of marble linking the ring of pillars.

"What worries you?" Tonka asked, focusing on the gathering dark clouds in the horizon.

Daya hesitated somewhat. "I was wondering if the Manu is doing anything about it....It appears violent, so out of order and...." Something clinked in Daya's heart and sounded on a note he thought was irreverent. He could not say if he had not provoked the Manu with his question.

Tonka observed Daya with a hidden admiration. The young man's concern touched a soft spot in him. "It's a good thing you found time to ask me about it. I'll always remember that. And to assuage your curiosity, you'd be pleased to know I'm not in any sense unconcerned about the windstorm."

Daya spurred. "I feel flattered, Manu. This news has taken some burden off my heart. I wasn't the only one that was worried though. Your answer has cleared our doubts. I think I better leave you to quiet contemplation. I'm sorry to have disturbed you in the first place."

"Daya, wait," Tonka called out.

Daya stiffened between strides as if the breath of his life had been denied him.

"I meant something else when I said I'm not unconcerned about the windstorm."

Daya regained his confidence from the confusion the Manu's call and dual meaning of words gave him.

"I see," he said.

Tonka walked up to Daya and placed a hand on his shoulder sensing the youngman's incomprehension.

"Daya, look at all that our civilization has gone through perceptively and you'll feel the level of despoliation," Tonka said. "No doubt Atlantis has been despoiled beyond redemption. The guardian forces of Atlantis are angry. What we are witnessing at the moment is their swift move to put the stable in order."

Daya's brow kneaded. "You mean the storm is a divine will?" he demanded daring to lock eyes with the Manu's probing gaze.

"Whatever allusion you arrive at would fit the situation just fine."

"Then it doesn't seem too grim after all."

"Not as you think. There's nothing anyone can do now to stop the tide of events to come."

Tonka retrieved his hand from Daya's shoulder and went to the pool side.

Daya recognized Tonka's manner as foreboding.

Tonka halted, turning, he glanced at the frightened crease on Daya's face. "It's too late now. Just too late. Atlantis is now on an irreversible course of renewal."

These words, to the best of Daya's understanding, dealt fate's unwelcome blows. In the flurry of uppercuts, however, he had ample chance to decide which way he would dangle the little speck of his life in the fast paced pendulum of fate. And yet he lacked the faintest idea where the vital anchor should be. The rhetoric of the past, the beauty and absurdity of the present, and the mystique of the future stared at him like one hazy picture. His helplessness in the face of imminent danger frightened him.

"Remember one thing, the journey of your life from now onwards, remains inward," Tonka goaded. "This I'd tried for so many years to emphasize. Well, time has come for us to apply what we've learnt all along. Daya, always listen to your inner-self from this moment onwards. Whatever guidance you think you need to scale the heights of the change imminent, you'll always get inwards. Don't listen to the appeal of the chaos on the outside, it's deceptive and leads to self-destruction. Listen to your inner-self - there you'll find a new destiny should Atlantis go berserk. Now hurry and inform every member of the inner circle to go and meditate without delay in the sanctuary for residents. This is a priority. It's the only chance left if souls are to be planted for a new civilization. Hurry, go and meditate. The tide is high!"

Daya, emboldened, rushed out of the patio. Tonka took a baleful breath, waited till Daya was out of sight, and then hushed himself away from the pool side, heading to his sanctuary. Time to select new seeds for replanting," he thought.

# # #

Nemhi, the malleable Guardian of Uranus with a dimpled smile, spoke last amongst the planetary hierarchies in the Blackhole meeting.

"Father of the Blackhole, fellow Guardians, there's not much to be said here regarding Uranus for the planet is in good shape. Her inhabitants have not shown any aberrant attitude. Their intelligence has remained desirable, except for an inconsequential fraction. If the intelligence density on Uranus and the other planets were to be compared, even those who are still far behind are reasonably of a higher intelligence than those on some of our sister planets," Nemhi said. "Uranus, I believe, is ready for the change we came here to address. Thank you fellow Guardians."

Nemhi's impatience glared in his speech - he wanted the impending change over with. Unlike other Guardians who broached on every little detail affecting their planets, his speech was brief and the most inspiring.

"We now have a fair idea of where we stand with our PlayToys," Numa said rising up from his seat. "And that equips us enough, information wise, to commence the reconstruction we scheduled long ago."

Numa advanced toward the crescent of raptly listening Guardians and halted at the fringe. "A whole lot is at stake here," he stressed on. "The reconstruction will touch on every single thread in the universe. All departments of this cosmic factory must do their best. There is no room for errors or loopholes, for we seek a perfect world.

"For some, this operation is just another boring routine in the series of changes the universe has undergone since it came into being few eons ago. For others, it would come as their first real experience of the convoluted knitting of the cosmic threads. It is for this group of Guardians that I elucidate on the nature of our reconstruction.

"The operation is in three phases. Phase one is tagged

Realignment. Phase two is Chaffing - a period of selective replanting. The third and final phase is Rehabilitation. Each phase will involve the hierarchies of the various planets in the zone with the base command coming from Blackhole's Disc Center. Is it clear?"

The Guardians concurred, nodding. Numa paused, wading through a pool of billowy gas on the floor and up the steps that flared to the platform on which the gigantic screen hinged. It flickered into a clear visual of a giant globe in languid rotation around the sun.

"In Realignment, we will cause Atlantis to lose its roundness by some fractions. We will achieve this through careful displacement of the Atlantis' tectonic plates in certain intrinsic areas. This invariably will lift the landmass of the areas not displaced and submerge the affected areas. This is because of the over-flooding of those areas by the run-off waters from the higher lands. The rifts so created in turn would form continental blocks. The interspersing gullies would become rivers, oceans, seas and lakes in defined areas due to the concentration of escaping waters. The globe after this envisioned seismic pull-out will lose its bulge a bit at the poles and would take a spherical cast instead of its present shape.

"If the ongoing windstorm or hurricane is to be taken seriously, Finia - they call him Tonka - the incarnate Guardian in Atlantis, has preceded us with the depolarization process. So we would have little or no trouble in channelling the cataclysmic reality of his cause to our advantage. All relevant changes stated here will be done within the spectrum of life in Atlantis. Our Solar Dispenser will magnetize Blackhole energy and radiate

223

it to Atlantis on a less intense basis. Firstly, to cause the pull-out of continents from the whole. Secondly, to sustain the equilibrium of the new shape and the fundamental elements required for new life. The Solar Dispenser like other vessels will find tentative anchor outside Atlantis' space to avoid intense radiation from tampering with our globe. All three phases will take place almost simultaneously.

"Remember we are not inspired to destroy Atlantis, rather we intend to subject the current breed of humans to a state of perpetual coma, at least, for some time. During the displacement of landmass and emergence of new continents, the whole chunk of the landmass we know as Atlantis would have been overrun with water. Atlanteans stand to lose their bodies - the grain of their pride and deceit - but they would continue to exist in hibernation beneath the emergent seas. Few Atlanteans, however, must be picked alive and hosted for debriefing in the Lightship, the bigger version of the Tamed Star, before the surge of water.

"We have to select the chaff from the grains, mark you. We need the grains to keep the embers of Atlantis alive in a re-ordered dispensation. The chaff we will stow away somewhere till we find use for them, or till they reach their circle of maturity. Of course, no death as such is involved in the Chaffing phase. You may say there'll be a sudden change in their state of consciousness.

"And the spared humans, what would happen to them? They'll be rehabilitated no doubt. Of course, not in Atlantis, for it would have been long buried in the wake of the tectonic shift and violent splurge of water. Our able architects, engineers, gardeners, biologists, and so forth, will come in at this point to map out a new environment conducive for human and extra-terrestrial beings to cohabitate. Such a place will be chosen on a fine bed on any of the split continental blocks, preferably on a little retention of Atlantis - a chip out of the submerged berg. The survivors will be dropped on this plain as sprouts of the new civilization. Subsequently, there'll be a redistribution of the stock of humans all over. Their intelligence will be enhanced as they'd be crossbred with the extra-terrestrial beings from Mars, Venus, Uranus, Moon and Jupiter.

"In the new environment, which will include certain replications of Atlantis-like structures, plant and animal life, the new Atlantis beings will be exposed to varied climatic conditions. The honing they would have received in the Chaffing phase in the hands of seasoned Guardians in the Lightship will aid them to move through Atlantis to rediscover their selves and their past. This knowledge will help them to harness the available resources and reach out to claim the future.

"This is another important experiment for Guardians. It'll be asking too much to expect all the human seeds we will sow to spring forth with equal vigor and intelligence at the same time. The individual constitution of body and environmental influence will not permit this. But one thing is certain, rest-assured of consistent evolution in all spheres of nurture. We will keenly watch the ramifications of this experiment for twenty-five thousand calendars as they say in Atlantis. Then, they would have reached their creative peak and the spread of the stock of humans would have reached an appreciable level. And if traits exist which negates the ideal of the new civilization, then we will have no choice but to embark on a higher experiment. We will do it all over again, and again, till Atlantis knows some level of stability."

Numa huffed, on a tinge of mirth. His heart leapt with joy having rolled out Blackhole's blueprint of planetary intercession and realignment, the lengthiest speech he had made in a long while.

"I'll entertain few questions now."

"Yes, Father of Blackhole," said Tamis, the debonair Guardian of Venus who rose with an air of humility. She had enchanting eyes, an unblemished beauty, a broad smile that stood out among the Guardians.

Numa gestured good-naturedly to her to take her seat.

"Please, sit down and ask your question," he said, standing close to the screen on the platform, his wings fluttering.

"The selected beings from Venus, Mars, Uranus, Jupiter and the Moon are to cohabitate Atlantis after the deluge for specific reasons you said, but the reasons are yet to be clarified. Could you enlighten us more on this?" Tamis probed.

Numa grinned. "A pertinent question, I must say. What our crossbreeding tends to achieve is an issue that would interest the hierarchies of the participating planets. How do we crossbreed without the feminine stock? Except by direct projection. I don't think we want that higher means of self-creation at this stage. The ratio of females among the total number of survivors will cause obvious scramble over time amongst the male specie except the ratio is amended to an extent. Venus, for instance, inhabited by beings of the feminine gender, supplies our need for the new Atlantis in terms of the ratio and new feminine intelligence. In the case of the Moon, there's a marriage of ideals. If we consider Atlantis as the father in spite of the Sun's placing, the Moon naturally usurps the maternal role. Therefore, females from the Moon will complete the stock of the new Atlantis family."

"That singles out the male extra-terrestrials," Tamis pointed out.

"Definitely not," Numa replied. "They are not precluded in the Atlantis family."

"Besides procreative processes, what other roles will they play?" Sujes chipped in. The broad-shouldered, handsome Guardian of Jupiter seemed to pre-empt the Guardians of Mars and Uranus.

"I was just going to ask that question myself," Nemhi said.

"Me too," seconded Mikuthi of Mars, grinning.

"Well, let me explain this the best way you can understand it," Numa said. "It's quite clear that in the deluge or change, we are stripping Atlantis of every single atom of perverted knowledge. The submerged humanity may continue in those ways if they choose to - but the family that emerges out of the mess and restructure will be given back every ounce of knowledge lost in the womb of Atlantis, although slowly. How is this possible? Well, through the Martians, Uranians and Jupiterians. Mars is in advanced stages of nuclear technology - the warlords permit me to say, though the planet is still within order.

The infusion of Martian blood in the new Atlanteans will illumine the path of privileged ones of the family. They will draw directly from that resource and do amazing things that would lead to a climax at the tail end of the span of twenty-five thousand calendars. We don't envisage any trouble from the use of this knowledge. But if they do eventually as we have seen in recent civilizations, we will intervene and arrest the situation through our projected plan of change.

"The Uranians and Jupiterians will supply the other basic scientific skills requisite for such a big experiment. They might not know why they are there or even know their origin per se except they are awakened to this gilded secret by the efforts of the presiding Guardian. Our PlayToy won't be under any threat for a long time and we would have all the breathing space there is to do other things," Numa expatiated.

"This criss-cross construct, does it affect Mars in the same degree? Do we expect something similar or peculiar?" Mikuthi asked, somewhat disturbed about the prospect of such a change in Mars.

Numa looked at the Martian, sensed his apprehension and nodded. "Yes, but on a subtler level." His left hand flailed towards the screen. "Look at the universe at a glance - it's a tight web of tangling, intricate strands. You can't take one single strand out of the loom without interrupting the speed of the spin."

The Guardians saw on the screen an an ensemble of minute balls kneaded across a void of indescribable depth, casting luminous reflections and refractions, which defined the void as a seeming sea of light.

"As desolate or distant as the specks in the universe appear between each form, a magnetic flux binds and permeates even the greatest gulf. A shift on Atlantis, no matter how subtle, is an infringement on the magnetic field holding all the varied forms together. So Mars and the rest planets are affected in some ways as neighbouring planets to Atlantis, but not violently.

"And there's another salient factor in the effect this mission will have on the galaxy, indeed the entire universe - the relationship of the stars to human life. Every human being, low or high on the spiritual plane, is an incarnation of a star.

"Now, back to the point. Yes, all human beings exist in other forms beside their physical bodies. They sparkle as stars too in the cosmic void. To displace human life by any margin is to displace the position of the stars. You'd now understand why this operation is so sensitive."

The Guardians weighed Numa's words as he paused. "I'll take three more questions and we'll bring the meeting to a close," he said afterwards.

Pata stirred from the right of the crescent of Guardians. "Will our fleet of spaceships and saucers just descend on Atlantis and carry out the rescue operation without stampeding the humans with alien presence? Won't there be some sort of precautionary maoeuvres on our part?"

"We won't be that daft for sure," Numa reassured them. "The Solar Dispenser and the Lightship, as I said, will station at reasonable distances from the surface of Atlantis, about thirty to fifty thousand feet above sea level depending on the need of the operation. The other smaller vessels and saucers will also hover within the range. If landing is necessary, it will be in the Chaffing phase. The saucers from the Lightship and the Tamed Star will be the ones to make the needed landing and it will be brief. These saucers cannot be seen by human eye so there'll be no stampede as such. The next question please."

"Is there a criterion for the selection of the humans to be spared in the Chaffing phase or are they to be picked at random?" Fatien's sonorous voice broke through from the periphery of Guardians on the left.

Numa half-turned in the direction of the Guardian of the Red Stars. "The same procedure as the last operation. Analysis of each Atlantean's activity as recorded on daily basis within the span of life will be computed in the Disk Center. If the volition of a human is positive, he or she stands a chance to be among our chosen few."

"I'll like to ask the last question," said Gaam, female Guardian of the Moon who sat close to Numa at the outer fringe. Gaam adjusted her stead. "The primary objective, I figure, for all these alterations and intercessory actions in the two eons gone have been a furtherance of the advancement of the human species. On a broader scale, it implies the perpetuation of universal spiritual idyll. Besides these fundamental reasons for our endless tinkering of the forms that be, what personal satisfaction is there for a Guardian? I mean what do we hope to achieve as Guardians? First, we are delighted in creating so mammoth a vineyard. Then we try to collapse same ingenious work of fantasy. Is it just for the sole purpose of picking a few components of a once beautiful picture?" she demanded shrewdly. "Are there no better ways of maintaining stability in the system? This is not thought inspired by self-conceit, but it seems an irony I'm yet to grasp fully."

Gaam became a cynosure of probing eyes. The Guardians could not just understand Gaam's innuendo. She appeared to be blazing a trail way out of line. The question had its merit in spite of its sting.

Numa read the impressions well. "Don't be stunned by a question such as this," Numa assuaged. "It should be expected once in a while. What satisfaction does a mother derive from nursing her off-springs?" he said directing his words to Gaam. "Is it not to see them grow from whimpering babies into adulthood of profound achievements? Does that portray a senseless adventure in the revered institution of motherhood? I really don't think so. My dear Guardian Gaam, as a mother figure, has there never been a time when you experienced exhilaration by watching the progress and triumph of any of our kind in the universe?"

"I have," conceded Gaam.

"Good. I'll explain. In picking components of a once whole picture time after time, we reconstruct the whole. And it is in this manner some present Guardians made the right leap, the right spiritual ascent that got them into the rung of the Blackhole," Numa explained.

"If this is clear, then we will tidy up this meeting and get down to serious business. We have just about three swirls to get our departments briefed. Three swirls more to be ready for action. At seven swirls from now, the operation begins. All departments must wait for Blackhole's signal. No unilateral actions would be tolerated. Don't forget we will reconvene to assess our operation and the progress of each phase if need be. Meanwhile, I declare this meeting closed. Guardians, thank you for your cooperation. Go in peace!"

The Guardians rose with a subtle fluff of wings, cutting varied scars on the film of oozing gas on the floor. They dispersed in muffled chatter as Numa walked down the platform. He reciprocated their bow and picked up his scepter by the arm of his chair and made a glorious exit through the left flank of the Wisdom Hall's outer chamber. Seven swirls on the countdown.

# # #

The front of the windstorm, now a fully-fledged hurricane, spewed its venom on Songhai thirty swirls after a vicious incursion on Ditara. Because of the violent winds, debris and sand hurtling under the hood of darkness, nothing could be seen.

Yet, as Tonka observed, trees and buildings had fallen, and Atlanteans stampeded by the force of windstorm in other cities. The storm in Songhai, however, seemed to howl like crazy bull on a vengeance mission.

On the third floor of the Divine Theatre, within the large sanctuary, over a hundred inner circle members clustered in deep meditation. The blinding darkness and howling wind outside magnified the fears of Atlanteans. The inner circle members, however, could not afford to watch the impact of the hurricane on their city due to Tonka's order. Those in the sanctuary not yet in trance-flights despite their closed eyes shuddered from the resonance of the violence caused by the hurricane.

Titan Race

The loud crash of an object against a window on the adjacent mansion woke Daya from his meditation. He reclined his back on the wall next to the tinted glass window in the middle of the sanctuary with his eyes still closed, afraid of contravening Tonka's orders.

In spite of the fright caused by the hurricane all around him, even amongst his colleagues in their meditative postures and in the far corners of the city, Tonka Manu had told him the journey to safety lies within. Therefore, Daya focused inwards and sought some inspiration in Tonka's words.

Two hundred poles away, alone in his sanctuary, Tonka Manu sat on his meditation seat as usual and began to observe. So unruffled in the midst of nature's overthrow of man's strongholds, Tonka succeeded in painting an ironical picture of the whole drama as if no evil lurked in the hurricane and no sad end awaited Atlantis. Of course, he had witnessed the heavy shroud of darkness over Songhai and the gradual shift across Atlantis to that point. Nevertheless, what bothered him anchored on how few amongst them would overcome the end of Atlantis.

While Tonka prepared himself for meditation at his sanctuary, Daya had given him the one call he waited for. All the inner circle members had complied with the directive to look inwards and never to open their eyes despite the destruction on the outside. Now he was certain, chaos or not, some Atlanteans would scale the last hurdle.

Chapter Nine

A troubled look lingered on Vatima Hansi's face. Her magnetic eyes dimmed in the crease of her sleek facial features as if she had aged. Her youngest son on the opposite couch, keenly watching the television reports of the hurricane and prattling about it with elder sister and brother, took notice of her sudden ageing. He had also noticed on her return from Manu Square how she had been smug, lacking in the motherly warmth she often exuded.

He crossed over to her couch, tugged at her side, distracting her from her blank stare.

"Mama, are you bothered in any way?" he probed. His eyes glared with deep concern. "Mama, I know the damn hurricane is distressing, yet it seems something else is on your mind. Tell me Mama, what's the matter?"

Vatima blanched; a bit embarrassed her son discerned her darkened mood. She extended a quivering hand and encircled his plumb body, masking her feelings somewhat, gazing into his curious eyes with affection.

"Nothing is bothering me, Hansi Jnr," she said in a

husky voice, drawing him close. "How could I be worried with your cute little face and your radiant smiles around me?" Her lips formed a wry smile, but could not fool the boy with her antics.

Mama is not telling me the truth, Hansi Jnr thought. She must think I'm too naive to notice her lingering brooding. Of course, she's in some kind of pain she finds hard to express. She had never been this weary in spirit before.

Her apparent weakness emboldened his adventurous spirit. He firmed his grip around her trim waistline, a form of strength he thought his arm could avail for her.

"Mama, are you telling me the truth?"

Drawn by the cosy exchange, Manta and Pram, her two other children stopped their prattle. Pram lowered the television's volume by remote sensor.

Vatima leaned forward, almost breathing down on Hansi Jnr, invoking the presence of wilted courage. She touched the tip of his nose with her forefinger.

"You bet it's the truth," she lied, her tone cajoling.

Hansi Jnr tickled, gasped and broke free from her hold, suspicion glaring still in his eyes.

Damn. I'm lying to my own son, Vatima thought. I have to shield him from the bitter truth though. I love my children. They are still tender, highly vulnerable. To expose them to the cruel aspects of the meeting with Tonka is to endanger their aspirations and engender their souls toward the absurd. I'll spare them the ordeal.

"So how come you've been frowning all day, behaving

funny and causing all those lines of stress on your face?" Hansi Jnr probed. Her sudden geniality did nothing to reassure him.

Manta, her eldest son chuckled on the opposite couch. "I didn't quite understand Mama's mood myself. So distant she'd been from us. I thought perhaps it was just the bad weather that affected her."

Pram giggled and gave a girlish assent. "Mama looked like a fiery cloud about to burst when she came home before the windstorm."

"Now, no, no!" Vatima's protest went. "Stop exaggerating, Pram. Maybe, just a gentle frown you saw, not this," dramatizing with a deep tone, "fiery cloud you talk about!"

The children pealed with laughter, amused by their mother's defensive charade. None of them believed her acting though.

"This is a concession I believe?" Hansi Jnr fawned. "A gentle frown," he imitated her, "means I guessed right. You were troubled no doubt."

Vatima looked at Hansi Jnr and saw the handsome copy of his father with the way he acted - huge, exuberant, stubborn at times like a straying mule, but quick in displaying endearing tenderness, which had won a vast crop of hearts.

She peered at his gleaming brown eyes: precocious little things in not too wide sockets, welling with intense inspiration and wisdom at barely ten calendars. They seem to mock her of her own inept handling of life's tender strings at thirty-four.

"It is hard sometimes to conceal even a simple frown," Vatima said truthfully, bringing her hands to a prim placing on her lap. "Some things are better not said. We are subject to trifle individual worries once in a while, but you should be thinking about many exciting things about life and not a transient frown of mine."

The children squirmed and laughed, leering, tempting their mother out of her self-contrived shell.

"Say Mama -" Pram began in a soft tone, raising her crystalline clear eyes in a tease. She heaved her well-shaped body of thirteen on the couch. "Is it wrong to worry about you when you worry about us all the time?"

"Of course, no. That's why we are a family."

"The beauty of a family...is it not the sharing of joys and pains? Is it not what you've always taught us, Mama?"

"Yes, it is."

"Do you mind then if we share your pains?"

"No, I don't mind."

"So what are those things...?" Pram broke-off.

"What are those things better not said?" Manta enjoined, trying to exercise the unfolding wit of his growth process inspired by Pram's mention of a family. In the absence of his father, he played the role of the man of the house at fifteen.

Vatima sat pleasantly stunned for a moment unable to imagine and fathom the depth of her children's wit. Their wisdom bellied their age. She shrugged in amazement. An alien light seemed to streak into her heart's stunned corners, overwhelming her dark feelings with pride - the pride of chatting with adults and not little children who were far from the perilous fringes of reality.

Vatima chewed a corner of her broad lips and her eyes blazed with admiration as she said, "Those things better not said have been said in an oblique sense. Well, I was out to the Manu Square on Tonka's invitation and wasn't too pleased with some happenings there. I didn't know I carried those moments like a damn plague with me back home. Sorry I got you all worried stiff." And as a diversion she added, "We should be worried instead about the threat of the hurricane raging on outside."

The children turned in unison to the television screen not able to pry through the drawn drapes of the windows. Vatima stole a deep breath as they gazed away.

Hansi Jnr could not be dissuaded so easily. He riveted his gaze from the screen to his mother and implored, "Would you at least brief us about the invitation later?"

"After the hurricane, yes," she promised.

"The hurricane had better hush off," Hansi Jnr said.

Vatima could see he anticipated the one story she knew she would never tell. The allure of the television, however, overshadowed his curiosity at the moment.

Vatima never longed for a life more meaningful than this: caring kids by her side, a loving husband too willing to share even the last artery of his heart to please her; the comfort of a dream house, warm and grand, with a rare exotic view and furnishing. And to cap it all, the confidence and security huge fortune brings.

Their mansion, situated on a beautiful knoll at the green belt bordering the sprawling towers of Dawn City, the elitist haven of Songhai, delighted her as an attraction in the plush neighborhood. Every time she had looked at it from a distance, her sense of imagination found derision in the artistry of the beige colored mansion. Eight calendars of toiling with her husband Hansi Snr brought them to this peak of contentment. It had been a journey of faint hardship but now it pleased her to note they could afford such a magnificent house. It came two long years after Hansi Jnr's birth, but worth every dime put into it.

When they moved in from Dhusa, her children were happy. Manta, seven calendars old then, in his childish fascination had shrieked with joy, "This must be another Manu Square.! It's so grand and beautiful!"

Pram, barely five, though shy, threw a hand to her throat in wonder saying, "Mama, I'll be delighted to fly a Hansa and land it flush on this roof someday. It's amazing!"

They had hobbled up the stairs together and danced round every room till they were drained of strength. Then they had joined their parents in the living room and had chatted about their findings. Life had been fun ever since.

The children had grown over the years. Their investments too had yielded dividends and the mansion had seen a number of vital changes. It looked even grander now with spruce gardens flanking both sides of the driveway. The intervening lawns, swimming pool and the fountains looked even more florid than when they moved in. An assortment of rose flowers florished in vases in the living room. They added a natural freshness to the crimson sparkle of baroque-like niches and gold-toned paintings.

Vatima often imagined her home as a mini-paradise. The floor, a mirror of polished terrazzo, reflected the shimmering dance of the overhead chandeliers and made a floating mirage of the two sets of ash-tinted purple couches and golden-legged round glass tables. Draped in thick orange laces with white silk overlays, the windows were impressive in huge crescents and triangular shapes. A massive brass closet on the immediate left held the stash of electronic appliances and the thirty-five inch wide plasma television, while a Gothic-like crystal bar took up the extreme right.

This was her own home, a paradise free from intrusion. And she had lived out the fantasies of a self-professed queen in it, hoping still for more out of life. Yet right in it, she had heard the displeasing knell of her hopes.

Tonka Manu.

Not until a few swirls ago, the name Tonka Manu conjured the jitters in her. Like other Atlanteans she was subject to his spiritual counsel as patriarch of Atlantis. The part of her being which cringed timidly, or perhaps in awe of Tonka's aura, had suffered an abrupt and violent death in the meeting at his exotic mansion.

For a moment, she sensed her spleen vent with hatred. Her right fist gnarled with pain as she clenched it, while her teeth kept gritting like the shrill, offensive grind of stone upon stone.

Forget the meeting at the reception lounge, it never happened, she urged herself. Can't you see it was a sham? A morbid stage rolled out for you to exhibit your naiveté and carry Tonka's brand of ineptitude? Come on, live in the present! Hack out and dump the sticky chords or memories of yesterday that tie you to Tonka or the meeting. You have a life to live now. Be smart.

Vatima, however, knew the harder she tried to wipe out the encounter from her subconscious, the harder the guilt spasms that overwhelmed her.

She jerked her head with vigor and tried to resist by the force of an unknown will the memories of the meeting, but plunged deeper instead into its frightening depth.

Vatima unclenched her fist, adjusted her gown and sat in a manner that drew no attention. Why she charged at Tonka Manu before such a select audience of Atlanteans at the reception lounge she did not quite recollect, but remembered a rupture of anger, an ill-inspired move for vengeance. No doubt Tonka's own brew.

The microfilm of her mind wound backwards revealing in its starkness her nudity in front of Tonka. She shuddered on her seat as she recalled the past. The harrowing events flickered in chain: the awe-struck gaping of Tullami and Daya halted in mid-chase by Tonka; the stunned, speechless stare of Tonka and the select Atlanteans; Tonka Manu's unceremonious exit after she became nude; Daya and Tullami's scurry after him, and his snob. Piece by piece the fragments of her momentous insanity fell back in whole, routing wells of tears in her bleary eyes. She stood firm against tiding emotion and forced the hurried flow of tears backwards. Something remained to be remembered, she told herself.

She recalled standing there like harried weather in the lounge after Tonka's exit. Shivers of guilt and shame paralyzed her body and mind while time made its swift and gloomy strides. She recalled too how scared the select Atlanteans who watched her actions or dirty dance before Tonka were and how they feared to touch her.

Vatima also remembered with a gush of self-pity that it was Tullami who fetched clean white underwear, a tortoise-shell long sleeve shirt and brown chasuble for her as emergency wear. Assisted by Daya, they had draped the clothes in haste over her and frisked her semi-naked form to another room near the reception lounge where she rested and dressed up. Afterwards she was consigned to the care of an elderly Songhaian female present in the meeting who drove her home in her posh convertible Hansa. She had barely entered her mansion in Dawn City when the windstorm started its ferret at the outskirts of Ditara.

"Mama, look, the hurricane is subsiding," Hansi Jnr shrieked in trepidation, tapping Vatima lightly and interfering in her reminiscence of the events at the lounge.

"What is it Junior?" Vatima demanded in a gesture of incomprehension and seeming exasperation.

Her disinterest astonished him. "The hurricane – it is clearing out as the report goes," he explained, indicating the direction of the television.

"It is what you wanted," Vatima replied, her attitude brusque.

Hansi Jnr did not respond. Although her voice had a gentle edge to it, he thought it sounded more like a swipe. He looked away loathing any sign of disaffection.

The reporter's excited chirp on the television and the vestiges of the receding hurricane caught Vatima's attention.

She heard the reporter say, "It would have been worst but Atlantis has not fared too badly. The furious onslaught of the hurricane is over. The shawl of darkness has hurried its ferocious dance away to a horizon beyond Atlantis and we may not see it again. The normal hazel clouds we have known for long have ushered back in the sky."

The children cheered. Vatima grinned, happy the threat of nature had waned. She could not allude to any contrary thought beside that it was nature's own vehemence.

"It is not easy to ascertain the extent of the havoc done at this early stage of recession but there are possibilities of partial damage on vegetation and houses. No human life seems to be in danger yet from an aerial view via our satellites. We hope to bring you detailed report of the hurricane's trail all over Atlantis in a short while.

"The Emergency Unit of the Ecology Evaluation Center confirmed through satellite a while ago that rescue workers have been dispatched in all of Atlantis to visit sites ravaged by the hurricane and see to it no life is lost or endangered in any way. We believe there is not much to fear. For now, happy viewing on Songhai Waves!" the reporter concluded, fading out of focus.

Hansi Jnr jumped sprightly to his feet. "I'm going to have a drink. Anyone celebrating with me? Orange juice to the toast," he exclaimed, twirling toward the kitchen.

"Host me, I'm coming," Pram declared, scurrying behind Jnr.

"I'll appreciate a glass of juice both of you," Manta called after them.

"Even if you want a whole jug, you'll get it," joked Hansi Jnr by the kitchen door. "We deserve a celebration."

"Then make it snappy."

"Sure, big brother."

Hansi Jnr and Pram returned with a giant pitcher of orange juice and three glasses. Pram filed the glasses and gave one to Manta. They began to sip with glee.

The phone rang at that moment and startled Vatima. Hansi Snr calling from Dhusa, she thought. Hell, she almost forgot about him as if he was not the quintessential speck of her whole existence. To think she did not miss his ebullient, loving and caring presence next to her even in the hellish fury of the hurricane due to random thought, said a lot about her state of mind.

Have I become so callous of a sudden? Some kind of crazy wife he must think I am. Pray I'm able to propitiate his fury, she thought as she picked up the receiver.

"Hello?" Vatima said, after a long drawn breath.

"Hansi's residence?" the feminine voice on the line

asked.

Vatima recognized the tingling voice. Almat Bou. Her long-time friend who lived in Straw Avenue down town.

"Almat, are you celebrating too?"

A startled hesitation from the other end, and then recognition came.

"Vatima dear! I would've sworn your voice had lost its seductive edge...a tone huskier you may say...the drawl is not peculiar you know," Almat said intoned. "What's this celebration thing you talk about?"

Vatima made an eye. "My children figure the best way to bade farewell to a receding hurricane is a great celebration," she said without meaning the words. "They are doing it in grand style - and guess what, with orange juice."

"Oh," Almat enjoined. "Did you not see the mayhem the thing called Hurri - what? - Hurricane created around here? Girl, tell you the truth, give me some wings and I'll soar. It's great to be alive after all the noise of wind and blighting thunder, you know." Laughing, she added, "Any dalliance with him?"

Vatima blushed and chided her friend, "Almat, you're impossible."

"Why? There's nothing wrong with that," Almat joked.

"I know," Vatima said brushing her fleecy dark hair at the scarf's end. "Just don't feel like it right now. Besides..."

"Oh, I see. He's off again on his usual business trips, eh?"

"Right. He's in Dhusa but..."

"Ah, ha! I know my dear, same worries again - they never end you know," Almat interjected. "What's it this time? My girl, if you have some time to burn, why don't you come over with the children and let's have a big celebration. My husband, Bou, is back home, the windstorm is gone, curfew on land traffic lifted, the roads are free, the wind outside smells good with hope and.... How about it? A little chat might just do the trick. Don't you think so?"

"If you insist."

"I insist."

"Expect us in about thirty swirls then."

"That's my girl," Almat said and hung up.

Vatima straightened up and announced, "Say you want to celebrate?"

The children stirred with joy, replying, "Yes!"

"Then hurry and change to something sleeker. Aunt Almat is hosting us in half an hour from now."

"Wow, just what I wanted," Hansi Jnr said.

"Mama, I'll be ready in a flash," Pram said.

"Not bad an idea," Manta drawled.

"Fifteen minutes and we'll be gone. So get dreesed quickly," Vatima ordered and made for her bedroom upstairs. The children scurried to their rooms on the heels of their mother to prepare for the outing in Almat's place.

# # #

Disk Center, Blackhole.

Numa tapped the Red Alert button on the Command Module mains and the signal filtered in micro-swirls through vast electromagnetic field and across the great constellation. Hovering vessels above Atlantis' space acknowledged the whirring blip of twin rainbows on their monitors. Blackhole's green light. Six swirls gone in the countdown already.

"All vessels acknowledge position. One swirl more to go," Numa boomed on the console, peering with interest at the flotilla of space ships of various shapes hovering over Atlantis on the screens of the Command Module.

"Solar Dispenser to Blackhole. Signal acknowledged. Guardian Djenemi, Captain on board speaking on behalf of the entire fleet. The Solar Dispenser is on a safe anchor at thirty thousand feet above sea level. The Lightship is on a thirty-two thousand feet range. Over to Blackhole for further instruction."

Poised for action at the left flank of the Disk Center, Numa leaned toward Hemse calling his attention. "Zoom on the Solar Dispenser and compute the reliability of its capacitors."

Hemse struck a combination of buttons on the Command Module and beamed with satisfaction as the Solar Dispenser glared on the main screen. "The capacitors are in prime shape and bolstered by the energy modifiers."

"Meaning the Solar Dispenser can absorb the amount

of energy we want to radiate through it?" Numa asked.

Another brief combination on the Command Module and Hemse proffered an answer. "Positive. No qualms whatsoever."

Numa nodded, impressed. He appraised the Solar Dispenser on the screen. It was a gray metallic wanton, much like the bloom of a globe-artichoke in the middle, with big whorls on each side pronging out in the rear and in front, plus four tripod-like little extensions at the bottom for soft landing. It looked too big to be so swift through this cosmic sea, Numa thought. Nonetheless, the Guardians were proud of the Solar Dispenser.

Back to the console, Numa said, "Blackhole to Solar Dispenser...all departments, your positions are well in order. A check on the Solar Dispenser's capacity confirmed it is in prime shape and would soon be put to use. Do listen carefully to this instruction. Guardian Djenemi, reverse the Solar Dispenser to a height of thirty-five thousand feet, the exact spot where the other vessels are. They are to take your initial anchor at thirty thousand feet. After the reversal of positions, swing your receptors in place ninety degrees towards Blackhole and wait for instruction. Over."

"Instructions taken. Solar Dispenser to Blackhole. Over."

Numa observed the fleet of smaller spaceships swoop down as the Solar Dispenser swapped position to the new point of berth. Within micro-swirls a neat re-order of anchor had been effected and the space above Atlantis remained a calm sea of waiting spaceships.

Numa gave a nod of satisfaction when the huge cone-shaped receptors loomed like weird husks out of the Solar Dispenser's upper posterior, and the radiators, cones of wondrous casts, reared from the anterior.

"Solar Dispenser to Blackhole. Receptors in place. Over."

"Acknowledged. Blackhole," Numa said. He turned to Ramune, occupied with other trifle details of the operation on the right flank of the Disk Center. "Ramune, give us the exact picture of Tonka's indulgence. Just how far has he gone with his causation?"

Ramune swung to action. He came up with a clear report of the hurricane on his side of the many screens. Ramune's eyes glowered with surprise.

"Atlantis has narrowly escaped the blight," he gasped. "It's receding now. Nothing to suggest any harm has befallen the civilization - just few scars here and there as far as the eyes can see."

Numa mocked Ramune with a chuckle. "It's a hoax, Ramune! We all know this, don't we?"

Hemse stirred, confused. "I'm not one for riddles."

"Neither are we." Numa swung his arm in an arc, pointing out over a dozen Guardians in the Disk Center who were busy with various kinds of computation as the swirls sped by. "We just have one on our hands though. The deed is done by Tonka of course. Unless we aid him to bring the job to a neat end, it'll be a disaster for Atlantis."

"Hemse, send the list of our computation on the few humans to be spared to the Lightship. Tell Guardian

Ganua to get ready with a couple of saucers to descend to Atlantis fifteen micro-swirls after the Solar Dispenser's second manoeuvre....The saucers are to fetch the lucky humans alive. No precautionary measure must be over-looked; and remember, they descend before the pull-out of the envisioned blocks.

"Thikaa, get the Tamed Star's Captain astir. They are to contact all the vessels from Mars, Moon, Uranus and Jupiter. Our choice beings from those planets should be transferred without infringing on their state of consciousness to the Tamed Star and acculturated by the Guardians there for the experiment.

"Semmas, find on the monitors our chosen spots for the tectonic shift and rehabilitation and let the engineers, biologists, architects, gardeners, start their part of the operation right away. The other Guardians in the Disk Center, those less occupied with the operation will assist you in this regard. Let each Guardian co-ordinate the operation of a department, it makes the whole game watertight. It is important the departments seek direction whenever there is an unclear course of action or a mist of indecision. And all aspects of this operation must synchronize with the timing of the pendulum we've swung in motion. Get along fast, Semmas.

"Ramune and Hemse, you are working with me here on the main console. We are about to dispense some energy to the Solar Dispenser for onward transmission to Atlantis. The Realignment phase, remember? Good! If we allow intense, direct radiation from Blackhole to bathe that globe, it'll go up in smithereens before you know it. So we will need the Solar Dispenser to modulate the vibration of the landmass, increasing it bit by bit.

This will cause the crust of Atlantis to bloat owing to one principle - the perpetual motion every speck in the universe is subject to. Then it will be easy to shift any region or tectonic plate apart whichever way we desire. And the demise of Atlantis would be as certain as the existence of Blackhole.

"The universe is perpetually a unique vibration as I've explained. What this implies is that we will only accelerate the speed of the vibration of the landmass through the Solar Dispenser's radiation. We'll then re-condense its frames and form in the random twirl of energies. Ingenious, isn't it?" Numa said, beaming with confidence.

Ramune and Hemse nodded, admiring Numa's boundless wisdom. They realized the obvious: as fragile and convoluted as the operation appeared to be, Numa trivialized it as nothing more than a perfunctory tap on any of the numerous knobs and keys on the Command Module. He did not feel the feverish bouts of apprehension making silent rounds in their hearts. Great the responsibilities on their hands, greater still the courage, confidence and calm they must exude to see it come to fruition despite undying memories and archival reminders of past realignments. Frivolous moments were gone. Time for concerted effort to salvage Atlantis' wreck had come.

"Numa, just say the word, we are ready," Hemse ventured, inundated by responsibility.

Numa eyed him. "All right, here we go!" he said, seven swirls on the dot. "Ramune, simulate our beam heads and train them on same frequency with the Solar Dispenser's receptors and let me know when you've got a clear line of anchor."

Ramune got to work. Sprouts from the fringe of the Blackhole, four reflective disks of a radius of about two metres, appeared. He lowered the discs in fractions in the direction of the Solar Dispenser by manipulating some knobs and keys on the Command Module.

Done with the intricate maneuvre, Ramune looked at Numa and smiled, "The beam heads are out of fold and we've got a clear line of anchor."

"Very good! Now, Hemse, find Guardian Urnsa in Starealm, the farthest galaxy. He should liaise with Fatien, the Guardian of the Red Stars and maintain a steady motion in line with the new simulation of our beam heads throughout the galaxies," Numa said.

Hemse complied. Starealm flicked to view on the close-up.

Urnsa responded to the signal sent. "Starealm to Blackhole. Signal acknowledged and action taken. Over."

Numa swirled around on his seat and called on a swarthy Guardian who monitored a set of abstract screens with five other Guardians at the center of the Wisdom Hall.

"Hemmas, you heard my instruction to Starealm's Urnsa and the maintenance of the galactic sway? Make sure you fix your mind and monitors on this. It's up to you to ensure it sticks. A slight lapse and the whole operation would grind to a halt. I'm talking about disequilibrium in the vibration of the galaxy."

Hemmas nodded on the affirmative.

Once again, Numa thumbed the Red Alert button on the Command Module and said, "Blackhole to Solar Dispenser and all departments. Operation begins. Solar Dispenser, switch on receptors. Over."

"Solar Dispenser here. Receptors are on. Over."

Numa's fingers made brisk movements on the Command Module. Three quick combinations and the commands were sent. A smaller screen displayed the mystery of his combination - the streaking haze of intense light to the reflective disks from the Blackhole. Happy at his causation, Numa grinned at Hemse and Ramune who pried on him, anxious and impatient.

"Blackhole to Solar Dispenser. Receive radiation. Ensure retention and extreme care. Over," Numa said releasing on the Command Module a downward streak of crimson light from the reflective disks to the Solar Dispenser.

"Action taken. Solar Dispenser. Over."

For an uneasy, anxious moment, the Disk Center remained a silent circle of rigid stares. The tension perceptible lingered till Numa shut off the streak from the reflective disks half-a-swirl later and spoke on the console.

"Blackhole to Solar Dispenser. Transmission is over. Switch off receptors now. Begin the next maneuvre within the next swirl. You need that much time to return to your former altitude at thirty thousand feet. Action. Over."

The anxious faces of Guardians around Numa gave way to smiles.

"Action effected. Solar Dispenser. Over."

The Solar Dispenser withdrew the bullhorn-like receptors on its large posterior to their respective compartments. It hummed as it descended to the given altitude. The other vessels made swift reversal of positions as Solar Dispenser nose-dived to thirty thousand feet.

When the Solar Dispenser reached the right altitude, Numa said, "Listen, all departments. We start Realignment in less than a swirl. Hone your acts. Hang on. Congratulations!"

Numa huffed and looked around, his heart gladdened by the easy maneuvres. The Guardians grinned in return. The first intrinsic part of the operation had come and gone almost without much hassle and they were pleased.

# # #

Songhai. Five and a half swirls into the second phase of the day.

At the balcony of the mansion on the knoll, Vatima stared at the symphony of nature's rhythm and human color spread all around her, astonished that no vestige of the hurricane's dark umbrella remained in the sky. Now overtaken by a yellow-ringed golden sun, Songhai brightened up like sparks of raw gold in a furnace with the sun's setting rays.

Even the green of the vegetation, scathed in some

parts, glowed with the impeccable beauty of the setting sun. Vatima noticed the people had begun to stir outdoors. Along the streets, cars were streaming all over the town. Aerophibian buses and Hansas skirted the sky as hungry seagulls over a fishpond.

Vatima Hansi could not help but smile fascinated by the feeling of newness from the raging womb of nature. The hurricane had not done much to dim the lustre behind the splendour of Songhai.

In fact, Vatima saw a lovelier Songhai, more revealing in the sun's tones of tinctured gold pouring down from the perspective of the knoll in relation to Dawn City and the environs. Though the rains had not begun their perennial downpour which lasted a month or two in the middle of each calendar, the lush fields in the distance inspired her.

She looked at her garage. The glimmer of her light-brown Hansa, a beautiful aerophibian convertible, parked alongside three other exquisite sports cars and a mini-bus in the open garage, enchanted her. She could not wait any longer to glide it out on the shimmering highways of Songhai and feel the wonder of computerized luxury. If only Hansi Snr would oblige to teach her how to pilot it, she would have loved to fly it all over Atlantis. Hansi Snr, however, drew the line there and she had to be content with a drive around town, and often to the envy of many a people.

Vatima checked the timepiece on her left wrist and her face lightened. Fifteen swirls remained in her proposed fun trip to Almat Bou's place. What had she been doing at the balcony instead of proceeding to Straw Avenue to see Almat? Then she recalled her mind had wandered in introspection. Could she trust Almat enough to divulge the haunting scene at Tonka's reception lounge? Would it hurt her ego?

No, Almat must be kept out of this. Let the bad news filter to her from grapevine, it makes the burden of recall easier.

Why did her children take an eternity to change to simple clothes for a simple visit? Vatima wondered.

She did her dress routine almost in a flash, wearing a provocative, body-hugging black gown with red sleeves rimmed in black at the wrist and collar. It gave her tawny skin, a cool, unassuming radiance, inflated somewhat by the slight rouge on her high cheekbones. A thin line of dark eye pencil flared her lashes and animated her eyes with simplicity and beauty, almost childlike. The magic of her oval face derived its power from the pointed low ridge of her nose, trim brow-line, darkened semi-thin lips, and flawless dentition which men found hard to ignore whenever she smiled. She reckoned from the way Hansi Snr melted often when she smiled it must have been the reason he married her in spite of her other qualities.

She turned and caught her reflection on the tint of the window glass torn between self-mock and joy, the former won. She thought she looked beautiful in the yellow and red speckled hat. She realized, however, the preposterousness of self-praise differed not from self-pity. Anyhow, Vatima believed, though not too regal in her looks, her black handbag of yellow stripes, silver buckled half-shoe of black and red suede leather, matched her tall build and attire. She had no one to impress after all beside Hansi Snr who had not yet returned from his official trip. Besides, Almat would not disapprove as a friend.

Hansi Jnr caught his mother admiring herself by the balcony window.

"Mama, you are ever so beautiful!" he teased.

Vatima blushed.

"You know Mama, your beauty amazes me like the beauty of a fairy I always see in my dreams," he bantered.

"And how's she like?" Vatima managed to say, trying not to look flustered by a little child's admiration.

Hansi Jnr pondered. "Can't say. But she is so beautiful that she makes you drool!" he cackled at last.

"Come on Jnr! How did you know such a thing? Here you go sounding like your father, full of flattery," Vatima said. The boy's mind worked like a machine. She could hardly fathom the depth of his imagination. "Thanks all the same for your compliment. If you are set for the visit, call your siblings and let us be on our way. Time is far spent."

Vatima and her three children came out of the porch a minute later and headed towards the garage on the right flank of the mansion.

In white polyester short-sleeve shirt tucked in light-green flannel trouser and held at the waist by a thick black belt of smooth leather, Hansi Jnr looked smart and handsome with his boyish look and ever-curious bright eyes. He walked with a springy poise and exuded the kind of confidence that bellied his four feet five inches build.

Manta suppressed the urge to laugh at Hansi Jnr who danced forward and toyed with the Hansa's sleek rear with his fingers. He often thought Junior too tall for his age, but considering his own height, well over five feet six inches at fifteen calendars, he knew they inherited it from their tall parents.

While Manta did not look garish in appearance and seldom viewed life from Junior or Pram's perspectives, his neatness could not be faulted by any member of the family. Taking after the feline magnetism of his mother, he nurtured trim dark hair on his fairly big head and had an extreme obsession for cream attire. Now dressed in blazing cream sandals and white lace dungaree, his eyes sparkled with unknown inspiration.

A chubby-faced beauty, Pram was a unique blend between Hansi Snr's macho physique and Vatima's gracious elegance. Nevertheless, Manta could see at a glance she had more of their mother's genes than their father's. She was not only a fashion freak but oscillated in same frequency in swagger and thought as their mother.

As Vatima entered the Hansa, she folded the roof with its sensor and revved the engine. Manta noticed Pram pirouette around the lawn hedging the garage as if he had no care in the whole world. Her purple gown spotting ribbons of purple on white silk sleeves was freer at the waist unlike her mother's dress. Pram pounded her cream colored shoes here and there on the hard asphalt of the driveway and danced to a song no one else heard. Her theatrical exuberance soon caused the rest to laugh.

"Laugh if you will," Pram said, not at all discouraged by their leer. "If you want to have real fun..." she touched her head, "it starts up here, in your head." Her hat, a blend of purple and white, almost fell in the gesture.

Manta and Junior found it hilarious and had another

round of protracted laugh.

"Get off my back both of you," Pram cried.

Vatima had pulled the Hansa out to the driveway by now. "Are you coming along or not?"

Pram stopped her dance and rushed toward the Hansa. Junior opened the passenger seat in front and hopped in. Manta and Pram took up the rear. Vatima engaged the acceleration control switch on the dashboard and the Hansa glided smoothly out. She maneuvred the computerized aerophibian on to the glimmering broad road. And in a steep detour to the foot of the knoll, they were soon lost in the gentle traffic of Dawn City's highways. The sweet wind whistling past teased their happy faces as the Hansa sped.

# # #

"Blackhole to all departments. Five micro-swirls before Solar Dispenser's second maneuvre. Countdown begins. Five. Four. Three. Two. One. Zero. Dissipate!" Numa boomed on the Command Module console.

The Solar Dispenser, hovering at thirty thousand feet, began to dissipate Blackhole emissions stored in the receptors through the radiator cones at the baseline. Beams of radiant crimson light pierced the core of Atlantis.

Djenemi watched his monitors with a fixed gaze, absorbing the tension of the moment as he led the intricacies of the maneuvre in the Solar Dispenser flanked by his co-pilots. He reckoned with what they were doing as passing air currents to the centre of an egg through a tiny tube. He knew the pressure of the air would cause the eggshell to explode any moment. He envisioned the shape of Atlantis should it explode as would a disintegrating egg and squirmed on the inside at the flicker of harrowing images criss-crossing his mind.

Djenemi put his emotions on check and perceived the operation instead as a rescue mission and not a careless, whimsical dissolution of an egg by revered Guardians of the Universe. They had gauged the right flow of energy capable of causing Atlantis to bloat. The molten state would be cast in new molds by expert hands thereafter. In the end, everything would remain the way it was at the beginning, except for some measure of displacement. A scion of the Blackhole, Djenemi, found himself always at the center of these operations even when he desired to be exempted from the reforms of their playhouses.

Amid the tensions and soaring anxieties caused by the delicate operation, Djenemi stole a moment to inspire his colleagues in the Lightship's cockpit, all in the attempt to clear the vague, dreary cloud haunting his thoughts.

"I bet those beings down there won't know what hit them," Djenemi quipped, grinning and glancing at his co-pilots in turn. "I can't imagine what the feeling is like to be so ensnared without the slightest chance of escape."

Meni sat next to Djenemi on the right grunted. "What a thing to ponder at an auspicious moment like this?" he said, disapproving of Djenemi's joke. "You are right though, but I think it's safer if we get over with the dissipation. Later, we will have all the time to reminisce."

"Scared of failure, not so?" Djenemi joked.

"Not exactly. I think Meni's just being cautious. The Guardians will be mad if this mission is thwarted on account of negligence of duty on our part," Pema said.

Djenemi cackled. "You are only poking Meni's flame in a different way. Let me tell you Guardians, the tension I see around here would be our first undoing," he sneered. "If you don't loosen up, feel jolly and see the operation in casual terms, you would quiver and fumble through it all."

Meni, snorting, pointed out the last streak of the Solar Dispenser's dissipation on the cockpit's monitor. "Just as we would fumble if you don't shut the control and alert Blackhole," he leered.

"And you thought I didn't see the radiation fizzle out?" Djenemi replied, smiling after what seemed a faint jolt. He shut the control in same breath. "This is not my debut operation you know," he chuckled. He then became attentive as he got Blackhole on the console.

"Solar Dispenser to Blackhole. Dissipation over. We await further instruction. Over."

"Well-done Solar Dispenser, the maneuvre was perfect!" Numa's voice rang out on the Solar Dispenser's console and in all the vessels above Atlantis. "The saucers from the Lightship should descend now to Atlantis. They have just one swirl to rescue the chosen few, and thereafter, the pull-out of the blocs. Our engineers please take note. The gardeners, biologists, architects assigned to the chosen spots for the Rehabilitation phase should proceed as planned. Action, now!"

Numa watched the Lightship stationed sandwiched at thirty-two thousand feet between the Solar Dispenser and the other vessels. He often liked the swiftness of this gigantic wingless vessel. Similar to the Solar Dispenser in its side protrusions - made of layers of rectangular progressions. These now metamorphosed into a sturdy, trapezium-like main body of infinite alloy with an egg-head top and a looming front at the base.

In line with Numa's Command Module, the Lightship belched forth eight glazing saucers in quick succession. Each saucer swooped down in different direction toward Atlantis, two towards Songhai, signalling the beginning of the rescue mission.

Numa laughed. Atlanteans in their gross material forms, even with their spiritual prowess, would never reckon with the invasion of Atlantis by alien saucers with their eyes. This is our swirl of victory!

Aware of the Guardians' scheme, Tonka Manu, however, anticipated their moves within the warm atmosphere of his sanctuary.

# # #

As Tonka Manu started to drift out of his body in readiness for the change he had put in place, a call came through in his ears.

"Finia, your attention is needed in the Disk Center by Guardian Numa. You should be there in less than two swirls. It's urgent," the voice said and disconnected.

Tonka drew a lungful of air and focused inwards after the distraction. Micro-swirls later, his soul floated through the sturdy walls of the mansion and out into the open space above Manu Square.

For a moment, he glanced around Songhai and its magnificent buildings longing to be part of the splendor forever like a chick of half-wit needing a form of cheer from an accursed environment.

He banished the weighty impulses of life in Atlantis and gazed skyward, reeling his soul toward the Blackhole.

He spread his wings and moved through space with speed. He noticed the harmless descent of the eight saucers from the Lightship, which continued their hurried whir towards various destinations in Atlantis.

The saucers' structure often amazed Tonka. He preferred their smaller sizes to the gigantic spaceships. A typical saucer's base resembled a dish with slight curvature. The top looked like a hat with a quaint dome stretched out to the dish's curvature. The saucers were steered by Guardians. Tonka knew their mission to Atlantis just as he knew what his soul's flight to the Blackhole meant. They sped past him as he soared on till the other spaceships reared in his view. Still he went farther into space leaving Atlantis and its turmoil behind.

Soon the sun, a radiant mass of ebullient energy, appeared in the distance, devoid of the scorching bite he had experienced in Atlantis in his body. Wooed by its warmth, his soul flew close to the effervescence and plunged into its core, the Blackhole, veering into the Disk Center.

"You made it just in time, Finia," Numa acknowledged as Tonka Manu swirled into the Disc Centre.

Numa's focus remained unwavered from the screens.

He waved Tonka to a free seat next to Ramune. "Why did you decide to drag us all so early into this confusion we see in Atlantis? Couldn't you have waited a little longer to take proper bearing from the Blackhole?" he asked.

Finia stood stunned for a moment. He had expected the kind of reception he got in the Disk Center. He bowed and took the seat offered him. Finia felt ill-at-ease that Numa thought he carried on with his role as the Manu in Atlantis in a cavalier sense by virtue of his unilateral action.

"I should say I was rather surprised myself that the Guardians refused to intervene for so long, thereby, allowing the birth of a degenerate culture in Atlantis," Finia began, worried over Numa's indictment. "Since the Guardians kept foot-dragging and the Atlanteans were getting out of control, the only logical thing to do was to wrap up the civilization. And if my action appeared unilateral and premature, I guess the Guardians would've to absolve me of the lone step. Under the circumstances I found myself, I think it's the best of so many options."

Numa growled. "The best sometimes is not good enough, Finia, and you know this. Why do you think we sent you to steer that playhouse? Was it not to instil some sanity in the civilization? I remind you again of this fact if you forgot so soon. Here you go apportioning blame on the Blackhole - telling us the blunt point of your flounder or so-called lone step. Or is it ours? You say they got out of hand? Don't try to infer you were ostracized from the Blackhole because you were part of all our meetings. I'm sure we agreed on a line of action, didn't we?"

"Yes, we did," Finia admitted. "It appears I owe the

Guardians deserved apology from all indications. I'll do that in the next meeting."

Numa brightened up, though his stare did not stray beyond the screens. "I didn't call you up here to talk about guilt and penitence – you've sounded the gong already so we have to waltz along. We excommunicated you in the last Blackhole meeting because we sensed this confusion off-shore and tried to surprise you as much as you'd surprise us here. Take a good look at the images of your invocation on the screens and you would know we are not without concern for you or the Atlantis. Go on, look."

Finia glossed through the scenes on the screens and saw again the flotilla of spaceships hovering above Atlantis.

"We called you for one reason," Numa went on, "we still need your presence in the renaissance we've engendered. This means you would have to return as fast as possible to your body in Atlantis after this briefing. You are to start the new civilization along with the survivors from the milieu there."

Fini blanched.

Numa ignored his reaction from a side-glance. "Our records here have shown those that listened to your teaching - for sure you know who they are - and the other arrangements are still in place. We've added something new in the last meeting. We are retaining a small portion of Atlantis, a redesigned speck so to say. There, you and the load of new civilization will find great pastures, abundant food and water, undefiled environment for the next phase of our experiment."

Numa turned in full for the first time since Finia got to the Disk Center to stare at the Guardian. "You are pioneering our experiment till we find another Guardian to replace you," he entreated in a genial manner, pouting at the same time. "That won't be long after the new civilization kicks off. Thereafter, you have all the respite you need in the Blackhole."

Finia's face creased with the news. No Guardian relished in pioneering a civilization even if it were to be in a high sphere of existence. The news that he had to stay longer than necessary in Atlantis, one of the grossest of all the playhouses, with all its dreary prospects, made it even worse to contemplate. All the Guardians were part of the cause and effects of the universe. By implication, he could not renege from a primary responsibility - the safety of all universal forms. He tried to protest, but the words would not just come.

Numa interjected with urgent orders. "Finia, you had better be gone now or else you'd lose your body in Atlantis in the shift of its tectonic plates. I reckon you have enough micro-swirls left to pick up your body and scamper into any of the saucers on the rescue mission. They have been instructed to wait for your return before they leave Atlantis' back to the Lightship. I presume you saw them on your way here?"

"I did."

"Half a swirl, that's just how much time you've got left. Your body in Atlantis is as important as the experiment, without it your soul here can't relate properly down there. So be gone now," Numa said, dismissing Finia with a wave of his hand.

Finia bowed, swivelled on his heels and floated out of the Disk Center. Then he twirled through the Blackhole and vacuous space till he re-entered his body on the foamy seat in his sanctuary in Songhai, Atlantis.

When Finia opened his eyes less than two swirls later, he saw an alien standing close to his body staring down at him. He knew a Guardian had come from the saucers to fetch him.

"Welcome back!" the Guardian said in a deep and soothing voice. "The saucer is waiting outside," he added and walked out of the room through the wall.

# # #

The day dragged on at snail's speed for Daya and his fellow inner circle members meditating in the Divine Theatre's sanctuary. No instruction had come from Tonka Manu in relation to the onslaught of the hurricane. Neither was there any hint that their meditation would be over soon.

The commotion and destruction caused by the hurricane in the neighborhood hampered their attempts at concentration. Despite this, they continued with their meditation, the reason being Daya's awe-inspiring recount of Tonka's order.

Daya tried thrice to soul-travel, and thrice within several swirls, the commotion from outside jolted him back to his body. By the fourth attempt, he sensed the gentle flight of his soul and controlled its exit. Now above the litter of bodies in the Divine Theatre's sanctuary, Daya's soul all at once glimpsed the chaos in the vicinity and beyond.

He recognized amongst the bodies his statue-like form seated in the sanctuary, denied of action. The dismal sight made him swear under his breath.

I don't think I'm the one that flew out of this dense shell, he thought, levitating out of the sanctuary.

Two saucers came to a stop at the verge of the garden in Manu Square at that moment stirring Daya's curiosity. He descended to ground level outside the sanctuary, his heart palpating as he walked towards the saucers.

Daya edged close to the ash-colored saucers a step at a time, cursing self why he had not gone his way and left them alone. As his thoughts raced, the lids of the saucers flipped open to reveal palatial interiors.

Daya gaped, bewitched by the alien wonder of these plate-like flying objects. Four times the size of an average Atlantean, the designs of the saucers perplexed him. A semi-circle of glassy compartments, seats and gadgets lined the base. The pilot's compartment was at the centre of the semi-circle. Daya made out apparent knobs and little mounds of devices on the slab as the mechanism of flight. He could see six aliens in each saucer.

A short, taut chain ladder cringed loose from an indiscernible crack or metal flip near one of the saucers' base and two stocky men with wings, adorned in white garbs, giant boots, thick gloves and helmets, came down the chain ladder.

Daya felt like fleeing from the aliens, but his quivering feet did not quite respond to his impulse of thought.

The Guardians stepped down from the saucer, waved and beckoned at him.

They sensed his timid hesitation and fear. "Come with us," one of them called out to him.

Daya hesitated. They walked, rather glided, past him in long strides. Caught in the spell of their mystique, Daya did not know when he followed the Guardians back to the Divine Theatre. Before then, Daya saw the other saucer discharge two of its occupants who rushed in the direction of Tonka Manu's spatial mansion.

# # #

Set apart at the right segment of the third floor of the Divine Theatre, the sanctuary for inner circle members remained a specter of meditating bodies when the Guardians and Daya walked in.

The Guardians looked around the hall, evaluating the aura of each body. They searched for a blipping radiance from each of them.

Daya noticed this aura emanating from just three from over a hundred bodies. His body at the middle of the hall near a window blipped too, and the other two blips came from the far left near the entrance. He acknowledged his friend and colleague Tullami as the body on the far left while the one by the entrance belonged to Pullama, the young, obsequious inner circle member in charge of the altars at the Manu's mansion.

Daya did not know what the blips or radiant auras meant, yet it gladdened his heart that the aliens came for him and others.

Having spotted the few humans they came to fetch,

one of the stockier Guardians pointed at Daya and said, "Young man, do reclaim your body over there, please." His right forefinger pointed at Daya's shiny aura blip.

Daya's eyes flared suspiciously. Why the imposition? I don't want to go back to that clay now, not just yet. Why don't you - aliens or whatever you are - give me the pleasure of spying on your strange antics? That body there is so gross, dense, paralyzing....I'm sure you alien hulks will never understand how it feels like to be trapped in this cage called body.

"Hey, do as he says," bellowed the second Guardian. Even as Guardians he called us aliens, the Guardian thought.

"We've got no time to waste," the stocky Guardian warned in exasperated gasp. "If you love your soul here then you have to reclaim that body fast, else you stand to lose both forever."

"And when you enter your body, don't open your eyes and let them remain shut until you receive further instructions," the second Guardian added in a hurry. "Understand? We will ensure you capture every scene with your Third-eye as we go along, and you'll remember every detail when you wake up after a brief stupor much later. What did I say?"

"No opening of eyes as I enter my body," Daya replied.

"Correct. Now jump into your body," the stocky Guardian said.

Daya meandered through the litter of bodies in the sanctuary and came to a halt close to his body. He willed himself to hover above it and gradually merged with it.

271

Daya sensed his heart's quick pounding. His Third-eye perceived the aliens and other bodies in the hall just as if his eyes were open.

The stocky Guardian held Daya's left hand and pulled him to his feet. The second Guardian hurried away and came back with Pullama and Tullami's bodies in tow with their eyes closed.

A brisk maneuvring through the litter of bodies and the Guardians steered the three Atlanteans out of the hall through the wall.

They came to a gasping halt beside the waiting saucers. Few swirls later, Daya saw the aliens aiding each of the inner circle members to clamber up the saucers' chain ladders with their eyes still shut.

The lid of the yawning saucer in which he sat recoiled shortly afterwards. Daya then sensed the nausea of sudden drift in the saucer's launch into space. Prior to this, he was certain he recognized the frail profile of Tonka Manu, looking rather puzzled, if not agitated, bustle from the adjoining lawns towards the ladder of the second saucer.

The glimpse troubled Daya's thoughts till the giddy drift of the saucer began. He could not resolve the mystery whether the aliens also abducted Tonka Manu or he worked in tandem with them.

Unknown to Daya, four similar rescue operations took place at the same time at Dhusa, Tulla, Sondibo and Ditara, bringing the tally of rescued Atlanteans to eight - Tonka inclusive. Also, Guardian engineers toiled to erect a new abode for the rescued Atlanteans.

# # #

Titan Race

Vatima Hansi careened the light-brown Hansa through the sharp bend of Knoll Way - the last stretch of the broad express of Dawn City's western fringe. Knoll Way stretched out to the venerated expanse of Dove Grove, which had at its center the sparkling sapphires of Manu Square. Vatima knew the traffic on Dove Grove could be daunting most times. So she sped on in the face of light traffic, trying to make it to Almat's home in good time.

Hansi Jnr and Pram guffawed at their mother's excessive speed and how she had swerved the aerophibian through the sharp bend of Knoll Way.

Hansi Jnr gasped. "Mama, you must be daring to negotiate the bend that way without the Hansa's roof on."

Pram had suppressed a yell as she held on to her seat for support at the rear. "Ma, that was dicey! A great stunt, eh?" she spluttered, searching for her estranged seat belt.

Manta made no comment. He did not mind the speed of the Hansa. It was fun to him.

Vatima glanced sideways at Hansi Jnr who sat stiffly next to her at the front. She chuckled at his expression of fear. A glimpse at the front viewfinder showed the furrows of tension on Pram's dazed stare.

"All right, I'll cut down the flow of compressed air to the cylinders and we will have it going easy," she assuaged.

As promised, the Hansa eased its propulsion to a slow run. The children brightened again, enjoying the scenic beauty as the trip went on.

"We'll be in Manu Square in less than six phantoms. Another half a phantom from there, we'll take a right turn that leads to Waadua Park. Straw Avenue is a little down Waadua Park," Vatima announced.

"It's still a long drive from here," Hansi Jnr said.

"But it's fun all the same," Vatima argued.

Pram theorised, "Dusk dulls every good intention."

"Dusk and intention did you say?" Vatima laughed. "Not with all these flaring streetlights and wholly amazing panorama. It feels like an elixir sometimes when it gets into your blood-stream. It rules your senses. No, it can't be boring in Songhai unless you want it so. Too many bright aspects here that outshines the gloom of life."

Look who is ranting about bright aspects of life or its elixir? The guffawing voice echoed in her head. Can't you just tell them some simple stories of childhood and not confound the interpretation of life that you don't seem to feel yourself?

"What bright points?" Manta asked towards the end of own revelry.

"The glitzy atmosphere of Waadua Park, or the razzle-dazzle of Manu Square for instance," Vatima said. "Think about the other places we've visited before - the cool, exotic view of the waterfront, our mansion's knoll in Dawn City, everything about the city. So much mystique and elegance...." she trailed off, overtaking an egg-shaped red sports Tanyan in low run. She then went on with her argument, "Everything is just there for you to reach out to and make the most of it."

Titan Race

They got to Manu Square in silence and veered off to Waadua Park half a mile down the road. Sixty swirls in the second phase of the day, Vatima's time check showed.

Up in the sky, the golden glow of the yellow-ringed sun had dimmed in the clouds of early evening. Wistful, Vatima beckoned on the hazel light of the fast setting sun to tarry much longer so she could indulge the searing flames of her mind and the eager spirits of her children in Almat Bou's hospitality. Of course, she knew the sun's dive over the horizon was irreversible and their visit will be short-lived.

She turned to the right, a slight distance down Waadua Park, and careened the Hansa on the flawless bitumen towards Straw Avenue.

"Fifteen poles down the road and we are at Almat's," Vatima announced, heedless of the portentous rhythms in the evening sky.

Chapter Ten

Numa's enthusiasm had not waned even after four swirls of intense activities. This began with the swap of position between the Solar Dispenser and the fleet of space vessels leading to the safe rescue of the select humans. The fragile frame of the operation did not affect his psyche. He had started, however, to feel a surge of adrenalin with the gravity of the next move: the most dangerous phase of the operation. He became more attentive, reckoning with the two things important in any operation: clarity of vision and action. Numa cleared his head of any haze and saw to it the Guardians did their job well.

"All Guardians ensure absolute preparedness, give no room for slips. We are entering a precarious phase - the reshaping of Atlantis - and this demands that you're alert and confident." Numa's caution on the Command Module console echoed in all receiving consoles across the Universe.

"Situation report. The bowels of Atlantis are in rapid swell due to Solar Dispenser's dissipation. Seven humans and our Atlantis Guardian, Finia, are safe in the Lightship," Numa elucidated. "All vessels to disengage from present anchor and find safer zones beyond the stratosphere.

"The axis of Atlantis has been programmed to tilt thirty micro-swirls from now, and we are not taking any chances. Also check the magnetic flux of your vessels since you are in the direct field of polarity and realign as the need arise. Blackhole will ensure overall harmony in the flux. Twenty-eight micro swirls to go. Begin countdown."

Atlantis loomed large on the Disk Center's monitors as a giant globe rotating around its axis. Ramune reckoned they would engage the globe in a high magnitude of toss in a couple of micro-swirls. Gripped by the rising tension, yet eager, he quietly followed the speed of the counter on the Command Module as other Guardians did. When it got to six, his lips started to move. Five. Four. Three. Two. One. Zero!

"Tilt!" Numa bellowed at the last count, rotating a control knob on the Command Module mains anti-clockwise.

He observed the uncommon event. It seemed as if they had jerked vague strings tied to the revolving globe at the northern hemisphere, causing Atlantis to tilt a bit over the southern pole.

Grave silence lingered in the Disk Center as the Guardians continued with their fixed stares at the screens.

Numa's excitement drew Hemse's attention. Numa's eyes were trained on the Command Module mains as he rotated the control knob further.

"It is fixed!' Numa declared with delight when he

saw the lift of the northern hemisphere on the screen increase. He gazed away from the Command Module mains and faced his companions. "The energy we've pumped into the globe will take care of the recasting within a blink. When the chaos is over, we'll lift the southern hemisphere to tally with the northern pole. Meanwhile, let's relish in this beautiful moment. We are potters of this delicate globe now spinning before our hands covered in the cosmic clay."

The Guardians observed unusual crack-like signatures rear on the tilted globe in diverse meandering trails, deepening. These soon merged in six loops around Atlantis.

"See, the landmass known as Atlantis is cracking already like a hatching egg," Hemse spluttered.

Numa grunted with relief. "The very first molds of our recast!"

Under the watchful eyes of the Guardians, the six craggy loops continued to broaden in outlook and depth as Atlantis reshaped its landmass.

# # #

The check at the gate was brief. The courteous security man had been expecting them. He signalled to his team at the guard post and clicked the minute remote trigger of the huge grilles of the gate and the wheels complied, reeling inwards.

The Hansi family looked ahead gleefully, admiring the well-trimmed bed of azoras on both sides of the driveway. Incredible fountains rose and fell with great rhythm before their eyes. Beautiful statues dotted the stretch of marvellous lawns which sprawled about a hundred metres from the gate. Almat Bou's magnificent mansion of Gothic pillars and porch sparkled at the end of the driveway.

Vatima waved to the security man's salute and drove up the distance, sniffing the strong scent of roses, daisies and a mélange of flowers in the evening gush of fresh air. The crescent moon streamed down its light, enhancing the rare neon lightings and security lamps around the vast yard.

Halfway up the driveway, the aerophibian Hansa shuddered and coughed in violent bouts to the right. It skidded off the driveway, bruising the bed of azoras as it was hit of a sudden by a tremor. Vatima almost swore as she struggled to put the Hansa under control.

"Good heavens!" she gasped. "It's like Atlantis just sunk by a swirl."

A lump in Hansi Jnr's throat choked a scream. The rude shock petrified him just as it dazed Pram and Manta. They gaped at their mother.

"What do you think that was?" Manta managed to ask as Vatima got the Hansa convertible off the bed of azoras, revving the engine. "Is it the Hansa or Atlantis that quaked?"

Stunned, Vatima hands shuddered. "Atlantis no doubt," she answered, her eyes hooded with fear. "I had the Hansa in control – there's no way it could have galloped like that," she explained further, struggling to calm her nerves.

Hansi Jnr mustered some courage to speak after he had overcome the shock. "Does this happen often?"

Vatima shook her head, reassuring him. "I can't recall any."

"Creepy, isn't it?" Pram squirmed. "Very uncanny this quake or whatever it is."

"Let's forget the incident," Vatima entreated. "I don't think that little freak of nature will reoccur. Is anyone hurt?"

"No one is hurt," Manta said. "Just the jolt, that's all."

"All right children, we'll get along with our fun trip. We can't allow a slight tremor from God knows where to scare us silly, right? Almat Bou will be waiting - they must have seen us through the short-circuit cameras," Vatima cooed in a bid to cheer her kids' stunned minds.

Vatima revved the engine one more time and engaged the Hansa on the glide. Another sinking shudder, graver than the first, rocked the Hansa at that moment and made it careen in a zigzag on the driveway. The shrill screams of the children in the combined impact of the swerve of the Hansa and the sinking motion of Atlantis rent the air. They held on fast to their seats in sharp reflexes and escaped being flung off the Hansa's open roof.

The Hansis could hear the loud crash of cars plying the avenue close to the security post, which caused complete disarray there as the guards fled towards the mansion for safety. They could also hear the crash of more cars into various gates or the giant palm trees that lined the avenue. This made the Hansis squirm with fear.

Ahead of the Hansis, Almat and husband had rushed out to the porch of their mansion to ascertain what caused the wanton noise in the neighborhood. A thundering, unnerving crash nearby, about four hundred phantoms north of their residence, shattered their calm.

Just as they got to the porch, the couple saw the crash of one of the wonderful towers of Straw Avenue by the quake, devastating a number of buildings around it. In the large yard, beautiful fountains and statues had fallen too. Pandemonium took over as their nerves wracked without end.

Not until Almat's shout pierced Vatima's stunned mind, she sat behind the Hansa's controls wide-eyed like a petrified goddess of an unknown time.

"Vatima, get the kids out of the car and run up here fast!" she heard Almat howl in from the front porch.

"Hurry! Hurry!" Bou, Almat's husband, shrieked close to his wife. In a state of panic of their own, they felt more concerned about their guests now caught in the swirling storm outside.

Vatima shoved the door of the Hansa on her side open and jumped out ordering her children, "Come. Jump."

Hansi Jnr sprang out of the front seat and sprinted toward Bou and his wife as nimble as a cat. Pram followed next in a frog-like leap. Manta delayed by half a swirl. He observed briefly the fleeing security team and the general commotion in the yard. The snarl of his mother who had begun to run ahead got him chasing after the rest of the family. The horror, however, had taken full shape.

Titan Race

A third jolt flung Hansi Jnr prostrate on the bed of azoras on the left. Pram's large gown caught and tripped her over. She screamed in agony as she landed on her back. Manta slipped and fell, landing with his buttocks on the driveway, writhing from the pain. Vatima staggered, then crashed headlong but managed to land on her right side, bruising her ribs, spraining an ankle. Pain seared through her like wild flames.

The third jolt on Atlantis swept the running security team off their feet too. They collided with one another and fell to the ground on both sides of the driveway screaming and cursing. The solid foundation of Almat and Bou's marble mansion fluttered like bird's feathers lost in a storm.

Bou Tarama, a square-shouldered, tall man with round crystal eyes which reddened now in hysteria, broke into a run down the porch in pink slacks, light brown sport jacket and snickers, towards Vatima and her kids. A rumbling sound from the eastern horizon stung his ears in deafening resonance and caused him to freeze a few steps away from Hansi Jnr now struggling to get out of the grip of the clump of azoras.

In the faint light of dusk, everyone in the vast yard in different expressions of pain, looked in the direction of the rumble but could not make out what it was. A flash of lightning accompanied by a strident clap of thunder struck across the evening sky.

The horizon brightened up for a moment and they saw the cascade of a truly huge splash of water, a deluge from the Deemen Sea, roaring and rolling across the city. It headed their way, burying every object in its course.

Seconds elapsed before Bou, Almat, and Vatima got over their initial fears and mustered courage to run for their lives. Several other sinking quakes of Atlantis flung them in different directions. The deluge had now encroached onto the easternmost lawns of the Bous' mansion.

Fear held Vatima like a vice. She could not grapple with it in spite of her attempts to be free. She sensed death closing in on her and her children. She ran with the last ounce of energy left in her towards Hansi Jnr who limped along the driveway. She began to scream, "PRAM, MANTA, RUN! DON'T GIVE UP!"

After a few limps, Hansi Jnr stopped. The pain in his legs paralyzed him. He crouched close to the clump of azoras, frightened and deafened by the sound of roaring around him. His lungs burned for lack of air.

Vatima made it to his side despite the seething pressure of the run caused by her failing breath and the tight gown she wore. She dragged him toward the house.

Manta had somehow regained strength. He defied the inertia of the quakes and searched for Pram ahead of him. He found Pram in pain amidst some fallen statues, writhing and confused, unable to run.

Manta shoved Pram on, unmindful of her agony. Together they ran helter-skelter towards the mansion yet to collapse.

The sight of the rumbling water few phantoms ahead cut short Bou's intent of giving a helping hand to Hansi Jnr. He retreated as fast as he could back to the porch along with Almat who had come after him. At the porch now they gasped and rooted for the rest to make it to the mansion. The devious roll of water splashed against the scampering humans and those on the porch, scattering them like herds of sheep without shepherd as it rolled violently westward.

Vatima lost hold of Hansi Jnr in the dangerous splash of water - mother and son flying in different directions. She cried out and tried to swim toward him, but he rode the crest of another tide away from her, choking, coughing, and thrashing out in the flood enfeebled by its force.

"JUNIOR!" Vatima shrieked as she made frantic effort to keep her body afloat, searching as well for Pram and Manta in her choking glance. Tears streamed down her eyes, washed off again by another splash. This must be a nightmare, soon it'll be over, she thought, consoling herself.

When Vatima saw Pram's drowning throes few strokes away from her, almost to the end of the western edge of the flooded yard, she felt the nostalgia of death in the girl's stifled screams and could not bear the pain of irredeemable loss.

She kicked, clutched and thrashed out in hysteria, shrieking "Pram, no!" whenever her head rose above water, but the successive waves denied her every opportunity to save her daughter. Another higher wave rolled over all of them as Atlantis sank further.

Buried in the crushing wave, she almost could see the fangs of death beckon on her. She began to struggle for her life instead, her loving children - two sons and a daughter - momentarily erased from her memory. One last thought flashed in her drowning mind as she sank - perhaps this is the penance for my debauchery in Manu Square.

A swirl later, Songhai and its glamor existed nowhere else but beneath a virile sea. Atlantis, indeed, was never the same again.

# # #

From the point of view of the Guardians, Atlantis was a boiled egg with shell cracking into six parts. Thin sheaths at the crack points like some reliable cell membrane held it from total disintegration.

Despite the relentless widening of the cracks', the imperceptible sheaths bridged the gaps and held Atlantis in place. Occasioned by random shifts of tectonic plates within Atlantis' crust, the downward trend at times affected the poles.

While some parts caved in, other areas bulged out to keep the balance in check. The tilt of the northern pole perhaps, or the emergence of new blocs, reversed the current of the Deemen Sea in the opposite direction - southward. The reversed current raged and surged onto a massive landmass which sank.

Emptying turbulent content into the new hollow, the place where the sea once occupied, drained itself. It rose as a wet bloc of undulating landmass with streams of water linking the wider expanse. The bloc that sank bore the seeds of humanity.

The Guardians could not help but feel sympathy for

the ill-fate of Atlanteans as they watched them fight the bounds of despair and fear and fail to outsmart the besieging water.

Their lack of options of escape touched Tonka Manu's heart too. It stirred in him a tinge of emotion over their wrestle with fate till the spasms of inevitable death lulled their efforts. Their listless surrender to overwhelming water haunted his thought.

Tonka recalled a moment in the Lightship when the feeble struggle of a young boy of three, torn from the hands of a man of sixty calendars in the deluge of water in the city of Tulla, Atlantis' main commercial artery, came under focus on the monitors. The dreary scene of the boy's helplessness in the face of the calamity remained enshrined in his mind even after the horror ended and other less spine chilling scenes appeared.

The little boy's weary effort in the towering waves of water was as ineffectual as the senile attempts of the old man to keep his hold on the child. Tonka could still see in his mind's eye how the boy, separated from his guide by the huge splash, hit the side of a fast reversing car. His piercing scream and the guileless glaze of his eyes before he disappeared in the shroud of water still troubled him.

The scene evoked lots of empathic reactions amongst Guardians in the Lightship. Not even Ganua's euphemism "Death must be a garb of many shades, else there's little cheer in the glare of its single color" could inspire them to see the operation in a different light.

If Tonka had a way of rewinding and recasting the entire operation omitting the scene of the boy and the old man, he would have done it with joy and be exorcised of the prick of conscience. He was well aware, however, that in the subtle game of creation, only one rule mattered - Forward March. The procession had to continue to infinitum no matter how colossal the results, for the one law of the universe - cyclicity - demanded an end must come to every effort, human or divine.

Tonka found solace in such thought. It healed his conscience of guilt. It also inspired him to see the implications of his cause in the soothing euphemism of Ganua. He could not admit anything less than reckon with death as "a garb of many shades." To think otherwise would be a slight to the Guardians and their reconstruction processes. Atlanteans were not dead. If anything, their forms were being redefined.

Tonka heaved a sigh of relief. He could feel the Guardian in him take over from the Tonka who had wriggled at the borders of guilt. He rid himself of conscience's clutches. He now had the will to face the screens with the attention required.

Rescued from Atlantis before the quake and the surge of water, Tonka remembered being flown with seven other survivors in the saucers back to the Lightship. While some Guardians debriefed six out of the seven survivors with the exception of Daya in another section of the Lightship, Ganua and his aides hosted Tonka in the control chambers of the space vessel. So he had seen the initial cracks of Atlantis and how these deepened and pulled out to permit the deluge.

Aside the risen bloc that replaced the Deemen Sea, a riot of continental blocs had emerged from the loops of the cracks. Runoff waters on the risen blocs had formed lakes, rivers, oceans and seas along depressions on Atlantis. Some of the new rivers and lakes did not retain the salty taste of the runoff waters.

Tonka counted on the screens six major blocs and a tiny berg on the southern horn from the differing perspectives of the scenes. Vast fields of sand spread on two of those blocs. Dust stirred and then settled down on the barren fields. Elsewhere, pillars of rocks reared from the recesses of rising continents and deep waters to tower over most part of hosting blocs.

Layered with the grim growths of aquatic vegetation on rugged surfaces, some of the new blocs were not habitable in Atlantean terms, at least, for some time. Yet other blocs had all the chemical prerequisites and vegetation necessary for habitation. Tonka could not discern where the Guardians earmarked as the site of the next civilization. He looked frequently in Ganua's direction hoping the Guardian would read his mind as reflected in the consistent shuffle of his hands and feet. Ganua took no notice until Tonka voiced out his worry.

"Which one of these continents will host the new Atlantis?"

"A little chip off the old bloc," Ganua, the chocolate colored, broad shouldered Guardian with disarming smiles and naive looking eyes, replied. "Over there..." He highlighted the emergent continent on the screen. "Here's the new Atlantis, a chunk of the old Atlantis that survived the deluge. It retains all the minerals and verdure of Atlantis. Not a bad home for the new breed of Atlanteans I would say from the look of things. The engineers have done a marvelous job. Can't you see that for yourself in the few structures they've erected so far?"

"Structures?" Tonka asked, screwing an eyelid.

"Infrastructures," Ganua said. "Houses, roads, clean water, light...an environment that is conducive for the civilization. I suppose you know you don't have to start from the scratch after knowing much luxury. Atlantis' continuity has been considered by Guardians. It has to be a solid base for further launch of civilization."

"Of course, I'm not unaware of that. What infrastructures were you talking about?"

"Just over there," Ganua said, zooming into focus on the screen the landmass bordering the northern shores of the displaced Deemen Sea.

Tonka could not cheer. From his observation of the nucleated community proposed for the select Atlanteans and the stock of extraterrestrials, he did not see anything fantastic to warrant such emotion. Except for the network of not too sleek roads, verdure lawns and gardens, abundant water and food, a warm climate and the other basic conditions for human life, new Atlantis lacked the typical luster and magnificence he had seen in the drowned Atlantis.

He saw instead a glaring erosion of the scientific and technological values of the lost civilization. No means of transportation of any sort, no telecommunication systems, and no blazing street lights - just a speckle of houses at the edge of vast vegetation.

The neighboring forest stirred with a sense of hapless life. A variety of animals jostled in peace despite their distinct characteristics in the rippling pond of life as if cheering at the inevitable return of a more tamed clan of humans.

Species of elegant birds too fawned around the yet inhabited community and capered off and on, chirping, anticipating the birth of a community of Atlanteans and extraterrestrials.

Tonka's mind began to reel afar. Other accessories of civilization were not part of the experiment. The Guardians in their meticulousness would not have overlooked anything. He knew even the tiniest of specks in the operation would not have gone unchecked. He reasoned they might have chosen to equip the new stock of humans with higher psychic potential to enable them perform most of the functions automated gadgets would have done in a normal Atlantean setting.

He felt the Guardians had adopted the option of telepathic communication as a unique replacement for cumbersome monitors and telephones. There seemed to be a unifying factor in mutual sharing of thought forms. An easy way of verifying evil intent amongst the humans. The absence of any defined mode of travel meant the time and space collapsible technique had been introduced to the Atlanteans in the Lightship. They could on return to new Atlantis simply travel around great distances physically and spiritually by an increase in their awareness. This could be done through collapsing time and space barriers as they had done before the end of Atlantis.

"So we are ascribing to the options of telepathy and the time and space collapsible," Tonka mumbled almost to himself. "Atlanteans never in any way lacked these faculties," he argued self-unconsciously. "Why didn't we just allow them to continue in those molds? Why did we have to strain ourselves to reenact what had been part of them if that is all there is to it?"

Having said the words, Tonka regretted his self-indictment for the Guardians were only aiding him to launder his dirty linens soiled by Atlanteans' inexorable aspirations. "Maybe I shouldn't have said this after all the eons of changes like this one. But it gets on the nerves sometimes, you know," he said as an afterthought.

Ganua noticed the hint of remorse in Tonka's last statement. He patted the mercurial Guardian on the side and said, "I do understand how you feel - everyone does - we are all in it. You know we have an ultimate goal and you are just the vital anchor. I admit telepathic communication was part of Atlantis. I also admit the time and space collapsible technique had been in use in the outgoing era, but not in the sense it will be applied from now onwards. In old Atlantis they had options of travel. We had the aerophibian Hansas, hovercrafts, cars and all kinds of ships. In new Atlantis they will only have the option of the time and space collapsible. It will engender creativity and awaken all the knowledge we are storing inside of them at the end. In no time the civilization would be back full swing, much wondrous than her old self. I don't think a Guardian of your status needs any explanation. Perhaps you are just being reluctant about going through the storm of civilization again."

Tonka gave a queer grin. "Perhaps," he conceded, feeling the dread of going back to new Atlantis as its Manu.

Titan Race

#

Dust begun to settle down on the turf of new Atlantis. The still smoldering heat from the grave restructure coupled with swirling dust enveloped the landmass in a very thin layer. With the tilt on the northern hemisphere still in place, the Guardians had put two communities together. Smaller than the new Atlantis waiting to be inhabited, the landmasses on the two other continental blocs were not similar to the chip from old Atlantis in terms of verdure, mineral constituents and climate.

Numa puffed with an air of satisfaction and broke the silence in the Disk Center when the last space vessel bearing the engineers flew out of the continental bloc nearest in comparison in contour and vegetation to new Atlantis.

"Blackhole to all departments. All operations accomplished so far. Keep the spirit high. We are about to lift the southern hemisphere in the best possible way to tally with the northern slant. Consider this maneuvre as vital as any other maneuvre we have done. It will check the landmass from further belch or hiccup. We already have the number of requisite blocs. After the southern tilt, the Atlanteans in the Lightship at the moment can return to their new abode. But not all the extraterrestrials are returning with them. Just few of each stock of extraterrestrials will do. The rest would be blended later in two groups to inhabit the other two blocs where the engineers have done some work.

"The new Atlantis remains the cradle of the whole mixed stock of beings because it'll be the base of our Guardian or Manu. Much later the other inhabited blocs will provide the needed challenge, engendering a new course of civilization. The question of language will be resolved in the telepathic impulses they will relay amongst themselves. Each new Atlantean will soon identify with a particular variant of the languages of displaced Atlantis through telepathy. It'll be the basis of the groupings we envisage in the nearest future.

"Guardian Ganua of the Lightship, please take note. Eight ladies from Venus, three men from Jupiter, five men and two ladies from Mars, five ladies and a man from the Moon, and four men from Uranus are enough to cohabitate new Atlantis. The remaining beings from the Moon and Venus are to inhabit the eastern bloc on your screens. The Martians and Uranutians will occupy the other bloc across the Deemen Sea. The Jupiterians are to be shared between the two blocs. Make sure the debriefing is thorough and get back to me as soon as you can. Over."

"Lightship to Blackhole. Guardian Ganua speaking. Instructions acknowledged. Debriefing underway. Over."

"All right, Lightship. All departments get ready for tilt. Count down from seven. Begin."

Seven. Six. Five. Four. Three. Two. One. Zero!

Numa turned the Command Module mains' knob clockwise an inch at a time and the landmass started a gradual lift on the southern hemisphere. It tallied soon with the angle of projection of the northern hemisphere on the screens.

"Blackhole calling on all departments. Tilt effected. New Atlantis is stable within orbit now. No problem envisaged. Lightship, prepare to send the stock of beings to their abodes within the next two swirls. Congratulations, all departments!" Numa's voice echoed on the console. Now to fellow Guardians in the Disk Center, he enthused, "The drill was quite easy. A mission accomplished. Thanks for your support!"

The Guardians nodded even though they knew the operation was not completed. But the greatest hurdle had been scaled.

# # #

Daya sat crouched at a corner of the debriefing cabin in the Lightship. He stared with glazed brown eyes as if in a stupor, his hair dishevelled. Six other Atlanteans shared the large cabin with him. None of them free from the spell of incomprehension, all staring like marionettes in a high-brow boutique.

Daya soon remembered being flown off Atlantis earlier in a saucer-like spacecraft alongside Pullama and Tullami. He remembered too how they had arrived at the base of a giant spaceship which carried the saucer in its holding and how they were led out of the saucer into a cabin - the cabin in which he sat now. He also remembered they went through a process he did not understand.

He realized his awareness of how they got there dimmed soon after they had passed through a small cubicle, which beamed down purple rays from a huge machine. His memory became foggy and blanked out with nothing to remind him of the past. A giddy space of time and a new awareness took over - the awareness of the cabin to which the aliens had taken them.

Seated now in the large cabin, no alien crossed the range of his vision. The number of people in the cabin had increased too. Five others had joined Tullami and Pullama. On stool-like projections from the metallic walls of the cabin sat four others - two ladies, a man and a boy. His colleagues Pullama and Tullami occupied similar seats. By his reckoning, the young ladies looked twenty-two at most. Beautiful, voluptuous, and full of warmth and guileless stares. Their physiques and modest outlooks gave them away as people from Ditara, Tulla or Sondibo, but certainly, not the flashy and much taller kind from Songhai.

The boy, about fifteen calendars, starry-eyed and lithe in built, came across as a typical Dhusaean. Even then Daya knew he could only hazard a guess. He had nothing to confirm his hunch, when these places belong to a civilization his imagination could only conjure in a faint sense. The more he tried to remember the nature of the civilization flickering in his imagination, the more distant it became. Something still told him the other man in his early fifties could have come from just about anywhere in Atlantis.

Atlantis!

Where had he heard the name Atlantis before? He dug hard into the crevices of memory but found no clue to time's hidden vault. You are imagining strange things, he told himself. He looked at the others. They must be under a spell or trance, he thought. They were all silent, eyes open and distant, not like people who had seen anything stir in a whole lifetime. This cabin of purple rays, to what realm did it belong?

He trained his ears to decipher the ranting outside the cabin, but nothing there droned to him with meaning. The door swung open of a sudden. Three huge Guardians with fluffing wings walked in ushering twenty-eight beings of distinct physiques and skin tones into the cabin. The Atlanteans stiffened on sighting the newcomers but made no attempt to move.

The Guardians led the extraterrestrials in haste through the purple-rayed cubicle one after the other. Daya could not place them as belonging to the Atlantis of his imagination, nor along with the rest in the cabin. These beings from across oceans of time were quite alien to his faculties of reason despite their human physiques. Some were very tall as compared to Atlanteans while some were petit and short. Their skin tones were as varied as their build - chocolate brown, peach ebony, and tawny complexions.

Most of the women had dark fleecy hair, while others appeared blondish. Blends of close-cropped dark and wavy dark-brown were the colors of the men's hair. Both sexes of the newcomers looked exceptional, young and vibrant with supple skins.

Daya watched them blanche from the force of the purple rays on their senses as each went through the debriefing drill in the cubicle. They came out on the other side looking much dapper and calmer, finding space to stand near the Atlanteans.

One of the three Guardians addressed everyone in the cabin as the drill ended.

"Listen, all of you are coming with us back to the saucers. We are going on an excursion to Atlantis," he said. "Your very home. Follow me now."

He led them through an adjoining door. All the twenty-eight extraterrestrials and eight Atlanteans filed out after him to an unknown fate.

Moments later, four saucers crinkled out of the Lightship towards new Atlantis. Another four swirled out - two aimed at the eastern continental bloc and the last two toward the bloc across the Deemen Sea.

A couple of micro-swirls to the bargain and new Atlantis once again knew the presence of human species - few privileged Atlanteans and beings from sister planets. The Guardians' experiment of mixed species had taken due course, giving birth to a new civilization.

Part Three

NEWLAND, RIAGENA

MODERN DAY

Chapter Eleven

Newland, Riagena. January 16, 1996.

Arooster's loud crow serenaded the neighborhood before the first light of dawn and woke Netu Deo from sleep. He blinked his eyes over and over adjusting his focus round the bed in the darkness. Another round of petulant crow weaned his sleep-laden consciousness to the call of a new day. Then the rooster paused without warning.

Netu strained his ears one more time towards the window to catch the early morning crooning of the happy rooster. The indefinite pause of the bird disappointed him for he had begun to love its pleasant herald of dawn each new day. He looked forward to hearing the kind of natural rhythm it provided whenever he stirred from bed for it signified the overcoming of the fear of night and its play houses of evil.

Every time the rooster crowed, he realized it meant the beginning of great change - the change each dawn brings, which could be good or bad. Each time the last traces of night phased away over the edge of civilization enthroning daylight, it seemed to him the rooster reckoned with the need to perfect yet another step in the dance of life. So the rooster's crow this dawn urged him to confront the day with heroism; by honing his mind and then his tired body. He had no excuse to feel weak or slow-witted if even a rooster could acknowledge the day's challenge and flaunt its preparedness in its proud crow.

He felt reluctant displaying a sense of spiritedness even though he had made up his mind to do so lest he rue the only protection he had in an unfriendly world. The name of the game: caution.

He made it a habit to evaluate every morning the steps he had to take the rest of the day. This enabled him to ascertain the number of gambits open to him on life's chessboard; how he would toss his own pawns and kings while eluding stalemates. These ritualistic reflections each dawn were the fertile grounds on which his love for the ways of the rooster grew. Besides waking him from bed, it gave him time to reassess the previous day's anxieties and successes. It also gave him the opportunity to peer into the faint blur of the future.

By virtue of many life trials Netu Deo had developed a shrewd approach to life owing to one belief – the actions of the moment determined the outcomes of tomorrow. Sadly, he thrived daily in a cycle plagued by intrigues. These webs, spun by his adversaries, aimed at disproving his guts. He knew he had to be wary at all times to survive their onslaught.

He stirred in his bed in the brightening hue of morning and his eyes began to take in the outlines of pieces of décor placed in the bedroom. A medium size Thermocool refrigerator took up a corner of the room while two armchairs and a table were placed at the centre. Next to the bed, a cassette tape recorder and a standing mirror were present. His gaze swept through the remaining décor - two palm trees in giant vases on each side of the walls, a shoe rack next to the wardrobe, photos of his earlier days around the room, half drawn pink and cream striped drapes on the window, and a red linoleum carpet on the floor.

All these he could conjecture with some clarity as the light of day filtered through and the minutes ticked on. After a while, the flare of the light sensations overwhelmed the room. Day had out-phased night.

Netu's memory went back four days before this dawn as he glanced around. He recalled in utter relief the prying little game he had with Anne Ofino. He recalled too his prime motivation for doing what he had done with Anne Ofino in Lina Phillip Uwa's dream. He had acted in self-protection, suspicious of Anne's ulterior motives. Yet he did not feel any guilt pangs after the act.

Lina Uwa's proof of her love had been her warning of the danger he would expose himself to should he become reckless in dealing with Anne or any other woman with vengeance on their mind. He had pondered over Lina's advice and used it to guide his stead.

On the part of Anne, she had vowed to hold on to the greatest joy of her life, Netu, the most beautiful discovery of her exuberant spirit. In this regard, Anne had done away with pride and fierce ambition and had in the strange ways of love signed a pact with him to treat him kindly as would a mother. She had done this in the hope he would let go of his suspicions and trust on their feelings for each other. Nevertheless, Netu knew she was also aware he could see through her antics as the glare of a midday sun.

He doubted no one's loyalty or affection. Lina and Anne both had strings wound around his heart as essential parts of his life's growth process. Only a fool failed to learn in the arms of providence, he thought.

After all, he had come to acknowledge life as an endless process of learning. Anne Ofino and Lina Phillip Uwa represented his sublime teachers. He needed to learn the lessons they had to teach him in order to achieve all he had set out to accomplish within the framework of his transit in Newland, Riagena.

He had long admitted he had a mission to fulfil in spite of his chequered life. Yet one thing worried him; knowing other people knew his mission better than he did. This made him vulnerable.

This much he knew, but he had already acknowledged Lina and Anne as predestined actresses from different camps traversing the fields of his mission. Their pretence he could easily discern. In spite of it, he would not forget to be cautious in his walk along ponds patronized by cruel headhunters.

Disembark Netu from your vindictive train. The worst adversary you think you have is the best teacher you will ever have if you bring your head from the clouds to learn, he urged himself as he got up from bed. He yawned mightily and grinned at his philosophical posturing, then began to indulge in gentle exercise of mind and body.

Titan Race

The sun, a faint yellowish disk he had noticed earlier in the eastern cleft of Newland, had sailed high now in the sky. It emitted purple ribbons of light at first and then waves of bluish cloud transformed it into a peculiar phase of luminous orange-gold. Now it flared like pure crystals with yellowish tint, the beams of which overwhelmed the city with brilliance.

Netu relished in the warm sensations of the sun in the mid-morning sky. Its streaking ribbons stole into the room even with the lace overlay and thick half-drawn drapes on the window and got his mind in sweet flight. The fresh gush of wind through the window from outside helped him to start the day on a beautiful note. The day was long born and buzzing noise from the other apartments of the one-story building reminded him of the speed of time.

Neither the busiest nor the most exotic of the cosmopolitan districts of Newland, the neighborhood of OldHill often stirred quite early. He presumed from the din of his friends' chat that they were in the living room. He reckoned Vivian, their cousin, would have been out for work at that hour of day.

Cars honked along the street and children from a private school a little down the slope had begun to chatter on the assembly ground. Close to the window, a stray weaver bird perched high up on the yard's hedge, cajoled and sang nonstop.

Netu halted his exercise to peer out of the window. The weaverbird, not too visible from the angle of view, with its singsong, made him return to his exercise which ended moments later.

Netu bathed in a rush. He had an appointment with an old colleague during his hay days in the Brotherhood of Father Manu. This colleague, Joan Price, had hosted him at home earlier in the week without reservation. They had met by chance at Boye Steve's office in Vintage Brewery. Joan had been hospitable enough to invite him over. Smarting from the reunion he had promised Joan to return at the weekend, Friday, so they could reminisce over the past. And Friday had come in a flash.

Since he had made a promise, it had to be fulfilled somehow even if he found it inconvenient. He looked forward to the visit with so much enthusiasm. They had broached on a number of issues including those days in the Brotherhood of Father Manu. They had recreated every piece of gossip or information there was, curried and given it flesh in the joy of reunion. He wished to repeat this thrilling encounter and this visit to Joan Price's home provided once more the right opportunity to recount.

Netu walked into the bedroom from the bathroom with a yellow towel wrapped around his trim waist. His skin damp from the shower, hair in quaint curls due to remnant droplets of water, and his eyes dazzled with unknown inspiration. A thin moustache complemented his trimmed eyebrow.

Netu looked fresh, youthful, and confident. Though signs of emaciation showed around his eyes and chin, his eyeballs never ceased to glow with vigor, illuminating the corners of his astute mind.

He inclined his head forward and daubed his damp hair with the loose end of the towel denying the droplets of water foothold. Then he rubbed into his skin a moisturizer sensing a chill wind outside, and quickened the care of his hair with a natural herb cream, combing through neatly.

He spent split seconds deciding between a gray blazer of woolen fabric and light green slacks, but he went for the blazer instead. He would be seeing his friend Boye Steve in Vintage Brewery at Bago district, the major industrial layout of Newland later in the day. He needed to look smart knowing they would be visiting another friend of theirs, an upstart millionaire, in connection with their late pal Tom.

The blazer over a black turtleneck shirt, gold neck chain and black shoes, gave his tall build a gentlemanly appeal. He applied his favorite designer talcum powder The Breeze on his face. He loved the lingering fragrance of the perfumed powder more than his expensive cologne. He then strapped his Citizen wristwatch on his left wrist, ready to sail out like magnificent moon over night clouds.

He exchanged brief pleasantries with Lata and John in the living room and excused himself from their patented flattery.

"You guys never stop giving a man false air, do you?" he joked and walked out as their burst of raucous cheer filled the room.

He noticed a very clement weather outside, unthreatened by pockets of dark clouds. The effervescent sun in its sail lit up the sky. The gradual build-up of its warmth had little impact on the rather chill wind, which eased by and caressed his spirit.

He walked up the crest of OldHill with the inspiration to scale all impediments on his way in same manner the chill wind held sway in spite of the sun's incursion. If the wind could dare to show its relevance as an indispensable force of nature, he too would survive whatever the challenge ahead. Every step he took then came light and determined.

Few cars plied the streets for him to worry about. The pedestrians he came across in his walk he hardly noticed. His being flew on the wind of sudden inspiration like a blown balloon in flight. Joy bobbed in his heart, deadening the aches of time.

At OldHill's park Netu boarded a bus to Pen Station. The trip lasted about ten minutes, and then he strolled down a few yards from Pen Station and got another bus to Bago District. Five minutes later, he alighted from the bus and hopped into another one in the heart of Bago District which headed westward.

Joan lived at the western end of Bago District, an area regarded as a vast slum but upgraded in the facelift accorded it by the creative ingenuity of real estate moguls. The area had witnessed an upsurge of posh residential layouts, corporate bodies and small-scale industries just as other medium income residential areas of Newland.

A few miles down the road on this westward strip led to Netu's destination. He boarded the new bus as the last commuter. The brawny driver got behind the wheel and drove out of the park. At the first traffic light along the road, the driver slowed and then braked due to a stop sign. As the light showed green, he engaged gear and sped on.

Lost in thought, an incident before the traffic light evoked childhood memories in Netu. An old woman, probably a grandmother, had lumbered across the road a little distance ahead of their bus in a daredevil stunt with a slim young lad trailing beside her. She had exhibited some sort of motherly bravado that reminded him of his mother's care when he was much younger and headier.

The wary woman had dashed across the road some steps faster than the boy, old enough to cross on his own. Somehow, she had looked back and saw the boy's timid hesitation at the center while a fast moving car overtook the bus and approached him. Where her strength came from Netu could not say, but the old woman leapt back in a flash to the center of the road and whisked the boy off the path of the car. The woman's stunt surprised those in the bus. Everyone thought it daring, but she had just one consideration in mind, the boy's safety even if it meant sacrificing her own life. Netu reckoned with her spontaneous reaction as typical of his mother in a similar situation.

Netu wished he could reverse the hand of time twenty-five years back to his seventh year. Life then had been a unique fantasy; a soaring bubble which would never explode no matter what came upon it, unlike the starkest reality he had grown to know as an adult. His whims had been undeniable commands to his mother who assuaged his needs the best way she could. He did not have to worry then about the rigors of life. The problems of the world did not matter in his happy visions of society. He had ample love everywhere - to give and to receive. He never knew or heard the chants of rancor and abject poverty, and never the stranger he had become with the passage of time in a world he thought he had come to proper terms with.

Time, however, had led him step-by-step, year-by-year, thought-by-thought, from his childhood world of wanton peace to a world ridden with anxiety and so much strife. He did not quite understand why his bubble had burst so soon. He did not understand why time compelled him now to pay rather gravely for his childhood misinterpretation of life's game.

He hated thinking about the present. He knew life's tranquil pond only in his childhood revel. He would recall only that part of him because the pebble of destiny had since rippled the serene pond of his thoughts and spread its sad causes all around him. His one wish: to escape this reality.

His mother had recalled so often the circumstances of his birth. Netu believed without a shred of doubt he could give an exact account of the period, including his mother's travails, as if he witnessed those times himself.

Memories she had recounted too often to him like a great raconteur before a rapt crowd. Before he even had the first chance at recognizing his own existence and those around him, he had learned over and over the whole story of his mother's travails. Quite naturally he recognised in those stories the storm apparent in the life of an orphan.

Fate had dealt his mother an ugly hand at a tender age. Her peasant parents died in mysterious circustances almost in quick succession. The tender little girl child, Dienloko, who had not even the faintest glimpse of life, became an orphan and encountered the awful hills of survival and the inherent problems of a polygamous home. She had numerous brothers and sisters from the other wives of her father Nabibia though. There were a horde of extended family members too. Her mother's sister Mokuni it was who shouldered the burden of her welfare and that of her only sibling, Derpow.

Dienloko's father Nabibia hailed from Brize village about five miles from Baloko village, her mother Eremeni's place; a Waji peasant settlement in mid-west Riagena. Her parent's death came as the turning point in her life. She lacked parental care and love as a result. In the harsh years to follow, she never would have the chance to know such desired affection.

Dienloko lived with her aunt Mokuni in Baloko village after leaving Brize village her maternal home. A rapid exposure to the thawing process of peasant life took the fun out of childhood pamper and turned her overnight into a woman. The ill-timed death of her parents challenged her infant will to survive - and survive she did.

So impressed by Dienloko's prowess in handling chores at home and in the turbulent streams of life, Mokuni spared no lesson in preparing this ravishing beauty for womanhood. Not as smart, her sibling Derpow did not have the magnetism Dienloko had. Despite this, Derpow too had begun to catch up on life and her physique had flared with a peculiar attraction.

At barely fifteen years, Dienloko's poise and tawny beauty, stuck on the lips of eligible bachelors of Baloko, neighboring towns and villages. Pressure mounted on Mokuni as a result to accede to one of Dienloko's many suitors who thronged her home daily. Mokuni considered it wise to save Dienloko from the hands of lusty admirers. Dienloko then became a young bride during the dry season of her seventeenth year to a vibrant, handsome young man from Brize village.

The course of Dienloko's life did not veer in the direction Mokuni had envisaged. Dienloko became fate's sad victim. Her marriage broke up thirteen years later from a rosy beginning, not due to a love lost, but owing to an unsown seed in her womb. Her family upheld the notion of children as the pride of womanhood. Her sterile clinging to love meant nothing but a negligible emotion to them.

When they could not prevail upon Dienloko, they resorted to the use of force to spare her the anguish of a self-imposed barren life. They arranged for her to remarry to have children before she reached menopause. They believed luck would smile on her not with Nabibia but elsewhere.

Guided by her family's careful selection of eligible bachelors, Dienloko got married to Deo Baanu, Netu's father – a young, tall, handsome, pragmatic and renowned peasant of Baloko. Her family's prophesy came to pass. Luck did smile on her three years later. Amid speculations regarding her presumed barren womb, Dienloko gave birth to her first child, a beautiful and tender girl who passed away while the euphoria garnered momentum. Then the intervening three years before Netu's birth - years of fervent prayers and wistful thoughts.

At last, Dienloko fulfilled the purpose of her living with the birth of Netu. In Netu she had a father and mother she hardly knew rolled in one. The love she never felt ooze from her parents due to their early exit she showered unend on Netu and did almost anything within her powers to comfort him and ensure his safety. She had three other brilliant daughters in later years, but Netu remained the fulcrum of her life. Wherever he turned, her life also turned along with it.

Netu remembered too his early school days and the triumphant facade his mother exhibited whenever he bustled home from school hungry and tired. She would hold him by the hand or shoulder with affection and inquire about proceedings at school. She would ask if anything was the matter with the gruff way he looked at times - soiled uniform and unkempt hair. After he had given her all the right answers, she would urge him to change to his casual wears and then there would be plenty food to eat. And in those moments of scrutiny or cathartic maneuvres of hers, Netu would observe her affection and fawning in every gesture and it became quite clear to him that he meant so much to her.

Netu later found out Dienloko was not as soft as she had always portrayed to him. While she spared nothing to comfort him, she also spared nothing to discipline him. He recalled incurring her ire once - the harshest of all her reprimands ever.

In elementary school at the time, about nine years or thereabout, he had pilfered a fifty Rinai bill his younger sister Neretou found near their house. He had used the money to propitiate the rage of a much older member of his play group whose bicycle he had damaged while on lease to him. He knew where Neretou stashed the fifty Rinai bill on his mother's order. So he helped himself with it to save his face amongst peers. His childish extravagance in school drew the attention of a senior pupil - a young mass servant in the Holy Cathedral, where his family worshiped.

The senior pupil had interrogated him over the fifty Rinai bill, disconcerting his inexperienced mind. When his answers became incoherent, the senior pupil knew he had stolen the money. A little boy of about nine could not afford a fifty Rinai bill in the early nineteen seventies. No sensible parent would have given his or her child of nine a fifty Rinai bill either. The senior pupil informed Netu's mother and also returned the balance of the money he impounded from Netu while the latter relished as a spendthrift.

After school hours Netu had rushed home nursing a battered conscience. He changed into a short and shirt in a hurry and disappeared like swift breeze before anyone noticed his presence. His mother had sent for him where he had gone to play with his peers. He came gasping to answer her call, presumptuous of her motive. She had smiled and cajoled until he was within her grasp. She then pounced on him and demanded with a stern voice, "Where's your younger sister's fifty Rinai bill, the one you took?"

Netu almost called her bluff but sighting her fiery eyes, he told her the truth. "I spoilt somebody's bicycle and was forced to repair it…" he had stammered while in her firm grip.

"Is that why you took the money?" she fumed.

"Yes."

She held his two ears and pulled him up as if to

increase his height and said, "Then I'll teach you how not to steal next time! I was brought up clean - not a rogue, you get that? You must learn to be like me."

She raised Netu up a little higher by the shoulders and smacked him real hard eliciting a shrill cry from him. He tried to escape from her clutch but to no avail. Until one of his elder brothers intervened, she continued with her smacking and did not let go.

Netu learnt the lesson of that unfortunate step and the cause of itchy hands. It nipped his rearing bud for pilfering. Although his peer group influenced him in other harmless ways, which he concealed so well from his family, as long as he did not take part in any sinister game plan or implicated himself in theft of any kind, his mother gave him the freedom to soar as high as he could.

His daily escapades or financial drives bordered on raising funds through menial jobs for some lazy married folks. This enabled him assuage his desire to see his heroes and heroines in the movies or the cinema houses. None of these had any adverse effect on his academic life. His intelligence made the family look up to him to hoist the bright lamp of intellectual power in the dimly lit tunnel of their aspirations.

When at twelve Netu broke the jinx in Deo Baanu's household to enter secondary school, the joy of his mother and the rest members of the family were boundless. They called him the "Jinx-breaker!" For over two decades it had seemed an impossible tangent to climb for the earlier generations of the Baanu household, most of whom had dropped out of school at the elementary level and taken to other vocations with lesser prospects of carrying the family's torch onwards.

The news of his admission then reached them like a well-orchestrated ruse, but they had cause to celebrate when the facts became clear. Happy her son had blazed the trail in the Baanu lineage, Dienloko knew Netu's mark would take a length of time before any other family member eclipsed it.

Years later, after Netu had experienced the luminous heights of secondary education through dint of hard work, Dienloko Deo would not begrudge her son much for throwing everything he had ever worked for down the drain in one of the most disconcerting decisions of his young life. He refocused his zeal and dogged pursuit of the Golden Fleece to the reality of the transcendental in the Brotherhood of Father Manu.

Netu never would forget how she had encouraged him to stick to his vision and desire, ascetic lifestyle or not.

"Son, don't let anybody push you around or tell you otherwise, it's your life, just go ahead and make the most of it," she had said and he had thanked her wholeheartedly for understanding. He felt overjoyed she never thought like other family members he had become an eccentric who had wasted his prospects in vain spiritual pursuits.

Now he had put behind him the experiences of the bigoted years with the Brotherhood of Father Manu, now he had begun to reintegrate himself into the mainstream of society. Now no longer the "despicable" pox infesting his healthy family, they had forgiven his spurious decision. Their remarkable change of attitude towards Netu surprised him.

Ten long years it had been, all wrapped up in a minuscule time bag as if it were yesterday. Flakes of memory once again sparked in his mind's eye. He looked back now, into the nudging heart of his mother during those moments of trial. It appeared as if he had lurched himself to a strange land where he had lost his way, surrounded by indeterminate forces toying with him.

No longer in the Brotherhood now, he found it difficult to rationalize if his mother had been justified by her belief in his decision to opt for the Brotherhood. If Dienloko had the slightest doubt regarding his future on his return home, she did not show it in her hearty welcome just as his father, Deo Baanu. He guessed from his father's momentous remarks that he had seen the hand of providence in his son's exit and return.

The bus conductor had called Netu's destination for the third consecutive time before the latter returned from the alluring planes of memory to indicate his intention to alight.

"Were you asleep all this while? I've been shouting Pedumo bus stop all along," snarled the conductor at Netu.

"Pardon me," Netu replied politely. "I was deep in thought."

The conductor calmed down. "All right, you can alight now," he said as the driver braked at the edge of the road.

A warm breeze teased Netu as he alighted from the bus. The sun had risen in glory and the breeze had embraced its light remarkably. He waited by the roadside for a car to pass, crossed to the other side and walked straight on for about forty metres. He then veered to the slope on the left that led to the path to Joan Price's home.

As he had envisaged, Joan Price was still indoors. Clad in maroon short and black T-shirt, Joan looked athletic in his mid-thirties. He exuded a sunny mood, which masked his unpredictable temperament and astounding frankness as they shook hands.

"I almost forgot we had a date. But you're damn lucky I had little doing this morning. Please, do have a seat," Joan said, waving to a couch on the left wing of the compact living room.

Netu could not conceal his surprise. "I would've felt bad if I hadn't met you at home," he said, evaluating Joan's statement. "Perhaps my spirit kept you glued indoors."

Joan shrugged cheerfully and said, "Likely. Most likely."

"I knew you agreed to call back but it just slipped my mind we had it fixed for today," Joan apologized and sat opposite Netu on an armless chair. "My fault though. When a man's thoughts are hinged on how to spin more money, you know what to expect." He grinned.

"That's okay," Netu said. He had no grouse to settle insofar as Joan knew the visit had been mutually scheduled.

"What's your weekend like?" Joan prodded, his curious black eyes piercing through Netu's mind field like the cold, calculated gaze of a ravenous owl at a prey.

Netu shrugged. "Drab. The usual penurious circle of being. I wish it were better."

"Same sad story everywhere," John lamented.

In Netu's obvious elegance and sly reference to poverty, contradiction glared. Months ago he would have accepted Netu's inference to the rough side of things because it was rightly so. Not after all the rumors he had heard about Netu benefiting from Father Manu's largesse. Though he was not the envious type, it did hurt his feelings to note some people had all the luck. While their efforts were aided and garnished, spurring them higher and faster, he found himself toiling all alone, thriving only on the account of his guts.

"That's the way it is," he said on a note of self-pity. "You have to be on your toes all the time to beat the crushing impact of living these days. My brother, if anyone ever told you, life is easy, he's the greatest liar that ever lived."

"No doubt about that. We all feel it – it's a tough world meant only for tough people," Netu said. "We ought to learn to toughen our damn hides to survive the hard times."

"You don't even need to learn that, you just get toughened with the unexpected punches you get on your psyche daily - financially, socially and otherwise." Joan laughed.

"That is true, of course." Netu had seen all manner of punches in his lifetime. He had to admit their varied import toughened him. "Yes, with every new punch your hide thickens each day."

"Like a mason's lay of solid bricks - one upon the other," Joan said, laughing. He got up from the armless chair, changed the television channel with the remote control and turned affably toward his guest. "What do I offer you, my brother?"

Netu feigned disinterest. "You want to bother about that?"

"Come off it Netu. You are my guest, remember?" Joan reckoned with Netu's refusal as coy. "I was just going to have my breakfast, there's something I'm preparing for breakfast. I hope you wouldn't mind boiled yam and sauce at this hour of day?"

"Why, no. Anytime, my brother."

"Austere times, austere meals, you know."

"You can say that again!"

"No kidding. We should be talking about something more exotic."

"In good time."

"In good time?" Joan puffed, surprised. "How long are you going to wait for that? For eternity? The good time is now."

"Perch where your guts will take you."

"Cut the damn joke, my brother. Don't let your pretty arse be a non-mover. You get it?" Joan cockeyed and made to leave. "Let me see what's going on in the kitchen."

"Soothe yourself," Netu said.

Joan hurtled off to the kitchen, whistled and crinkled pot covers there. Above the television's din, the strident clatter of utensils from Joan's rather late breakfast preparations, made Netu's entrails churn with hunger. Netu knew he needed Joan's food in spite of his earlier pretence. His fast wheeling mind tried to understand the past events, which had led him to the present predicament. The more he tried to piece the facts together, the more confusing it became. This continued until Joan returned from the kitchen.

"Butter fried milk cakes in fine sauce and boiled yam - not a bad combination, won't you say?" Joan declared, playing the caring host. "It'll be ready in a second," he exaggerated further.

"Really?"

"Yes."

"I haven't tasted those delicacies in a long while. You bring back Brotherhood memories in Soloj city. Their kinds of milk cakes are unbeatable."

"I remember well. How can I forget their sumptuous treat?"

"Uhmn, my mouth is watering already. I just want to savor those sweet little things again."

"You will, in a few minutes." Joan lowered his bulk onto the armless chair; it creaked a bit. He fixed his gaze at the glass top of the center table, a brooding frown knotting his face. Something seemed to rile his mind. "Have you been to the Brotherhood of Father Manu lately?" he asked with a clinical undertone, disconcerting Netu for a moment.

There had been a desperate, impatient attitude Netu had observed about Joan's non-stop fidgeting. He had no iota of doubt Joan would, regardless of the bond of friendship, attempt to clear the air surrounding the gossip that he had benefited from Father Manu's patronage. About time he put Joan's prying little tricks to rest.

"Yes, not long ago," Netu said. Nobody's business if I bask in the largesse of Father Manu.

So the rumors were true after all, Joan acknowledged. He had become quite cynical about friends who still maintained strong links with the Brotherhood despite his fanatic leaning to the course in the past. He would rather forget that part of him. He saw it now only in the light of a fine beginning, an inescapable school where he had learned some lessons as part of a fundamental spiritual journey. It registered in his conscience now as doctrinal germs that did not fit any more into his new belief pattern. He needed to be rid of the tendency amongst his Brotherhood friends, the idea of trying to drag him close to a shadow he wanted to elude. In spite of it, he respected Netu as an individual and would need to handle him with the greatest diplomacy.

"And how are they?" Joan responded, trying not to be antagonistic from the onset.

Netu hesitated, chewing a corner of his lip, and then shrugged. "Well, I guess they are doing well. The usual people we left behind and few new entrants. Same old structures, new buildings here and there. Not the magnificent splash you so often imagine. You know how it was like," he said furtively, avoiding the core of the matter. He added as an afterthought, "Well, Father Manu sent for me through Dini - and I went to answer his call reluctantly. But there were other people I wanted to see and the opportunity availed itself."

"Father Manu sent for you?" Joan edged forward on his seat. He saw a new angle to the rumors, which interested him.

"He did."

"What for?"

"Nothing much really. He said he wanted to see me because he missed me. You know, he said I'd created a vacuum no one else could fill, and such cajoling stuff."

Joan huffed in disbelief. "He missed you?" he asked with contempt. "Missed you indeed! I suppose you didn't abscond from the Brotherhood like many others?"

"No. I left on his instructions," Netu said with hinted nostalgia. These issues they had talked about before. He would be too glad to banish them forever. "Why should I abscond when I entered the Brotherhood legally? You know I'm not cut out for rash decisions. My exit was legal and timely too." Netu said in a cold voice, his manner somewhat despondent.

It gave Joan the clue he looked for. "Since your exit was legal as you said, there's just one way of looking at it. I suppose he wanted to compensate your efforts while there. He had done this for others before, and you happen to be lucky. And since you were so indispensable, I presume your pay-off was fat!" he said, laughing.

Netu squirmed, embarrassed by Joan's unabashed joke. "How can you say a thing like that?" he chided. His lips pouted in fleeting thought.

"Ah, we heard all those who backpedalled came back with bags of money," Joan went on leering.

"He took care of my transport fare back if that's the way you see it," Netu said frankly. "But I don't buy that stuff."

Joan sniggered. "And how much was it?"

Damn Joan and his leer. What a blunt way to be envious, Netu thought. Joan's artlessness annoyed him.

He flailed his hands in an impatient gesture. "Transport fare."

Joan cackled like the tongues of excited fire. "Of course, transport fare. But why so little? If he's got so much dough to fling around, he should give me the call and I'll be glad to invest some of it," he said with a lingering smile. "Some people have all the luck. I wish I was that lucky!"

Supercilious bastard, Netu cursed under his breath. He had never thought Joan could be so derisive. Netu could feel an air of revulsion about it all as he looked at Joan and his mocking gestures. Why would anyone think time had softened him to the point of compromising? And what compromise in a system he had not by any means dissociated himself from? Would I ever understand these cross-carpeting faggots, he thought.

"Dini you said came to fetch you?" Joan asked as a diversionary move.

"Yes, it was Dini," Netu said coldly.

"And how's she?"

"Doing well, I guess."

"I can't imagine how she persuaded you to get along."

"I went because I had nothing to hide."

Joan laughed, the insinuation backfired. "Sure you have nothing to hide - like everybody. Tell me about Dini."

"Dini Nuke?"

"Yes."

"What's there to tell?"

"I still can't reconcile the fact that someone like Dini would continue to hang on there without thinking of what she would do with her life. It's a strange kind of complacence. It bothers me."

"Are you that miffed?"

"You're damn wrong. How can I be miffed? Perhaps you don't bloody well see it the way I see it. Tell me, what future have any of those cranks got there? What?" A hint of anger was evident in Joan's voice.

Netu thought there were better ways to unravelling things than casting aspersions. "You had your own reasons for going there I suppose?"

With his cynicism blazing like fire that refused to be doused, Joan gazed suspiciously at Netu. "I went there because I had a conviction I was doing the right thing. I had all kinds of perceptions about the future of the Brotherhood. While I was there, I felt it was the ultimate dream. I don't feel the same pulse anymore. Now my energy is dissipated in a different direction. I think I'm a lot more circumspect, cynical even about my own beliefs then," he said.

Netu purred to the remark about conviction ignoring the bitterness perceptible in Joan's dark emotion which tried to shroud his objectivity.

"Don't you see it is the same hypnotic emotion? Conviction! What keeps the likes of Dini there is conviction. They never see anything wrong with the Brotherhood just as you never saw anything wrong with the enclave while you were there. For them, we are the prodigal sons and daughters. We are the ones the pity is on. We appear to them as people who have lost track and must get back before we get mired in our own filth."

"But Father Manu is toying with them - the ladies - and that's the most worrisome part of the whole story," Joan remonstrated.

"How do you mean?" Netu countered, loathing being disrespectful.

Joan's gaze drooped. "Well, there are stories...."

"Stories?"

"Stories. Incredible stories of foul-play."

"Mere speculations. Frivolous at best."

"Don't tell me you are that dumb."

"Well, no one has been able to prove a damn thing. So I take it as campaigns of calumny from envious courts."

"Campaigns of calumny indeed."

"Prove your point if you will."

"I will as long you'll listen." Joan had begun to lose his nerves. He pictured Netu as a damn crank, a blind fanatic who did not recognize a cul–de-sac if he saw one. "That Tanpi lady for instance..."

Netu snorted. "What about Tanpi?"

In Joan's grim cast eyes flashed a hint of triump. "Tanpi was a cobra he shouldn't have woken."

"Woken?" demanded Netu. In every game of wits, a fool always reared whose naive jokes uncovered the wise man's storeroom of inordinate ego. Netu knew if he probed a bit, Joan would reveal his fears.

Joan waved off Netu's seeming protest. "You know we were close - Tanpi and I. She told me ugly things I can't repeat here - lewd things."

Netu feigned astonishment. "And you believed her?"

"I don't believe Father Manu's infallibility either."

"That Tanpi girl was a lousy bitch that kept flaunting her body to whoever cared to see."

"Bait enough to catch even the eyes of a saint!" Joan laughed at Netu's innocence.

"She caught your eyes I'm sure."

"Well, I won't deny that - and so are others - highbrow saints!"

"Do you know something I don't know?" Netu rebuffed.

"Don't push me further than you've done," Joan said curtly. "Of course, you know these things. You're only too weak to acknowledge the scum beneath the supposedly clean river of your faith."

"Our faith."

"Not anymore. That was in the past. I have a new faith now. I like to see myself now as a new person."

"All right, what's your grouse?"

"My grouse?" Joan felt embarrassed. He puckered

his thick lips in a fit of rising anger, swept his low cut hair back and then forth with his left hand and said, "My grouse is that he should allow them to go home - every single lady in the Brotherhood lest they get defiled."

Netu straightened up on the couch and studied Joan shrewdly.

"You are exaggerating," Netu said, desperate to bring Joan back to his senses. "If a vagrant fish doesn't go nibbling at pretty bait, there's no way it would be caught. They stir up the mud themselves with their lusty winks and wiggles and swaggers, and they are the ones that cry wolf."

Joan looked dumbfounded. He gaped at Netu as if he had been struck with a sledgehammer on the head. He recoiled into his erstwhile antagonistic shell.

"And I suppose the revered saint doesn't have any blame for baiting the swimming fish?"

"No one asked the fish to acknowledge the bait."

Joan had one of his raucous laughs knowing Netu had unwittingly boxed himself into a corner. "Someone owns the aquarium in which the unlucky fish swims - same person owns the bait - more or less an inevitable imposition which the vagrant fish can't help but acknowledge. Do you still think the fish was the one that stirred mud?"

Netu sought a more scathing diversion. "Well, as someone who was once caught by Tanpi's irresistible bug, would you be frank enough to tell me if you were the owner of the pretty aquarium in which Tanpi laid her nets?"

"You cunning idiot!" Joan teased. He stood up and breathed down on Netu. "Talking with you is like talking to some of those old-fashioned religionists, they never learn."

He pulled the armless chair backward as Netu burst into a prolonged laugh. He then swivelled in the direction of the kitchen. "I'm hungry. People like you make me hungrier. Perhaps after food I can size you up again on our debate. Meanwhile enjoy your fanaticism."

Netu kept laughing till Joan left the room to the kitchen. Their last meeting had been no less a rhetorical joke of the Brotherhood's ideals. To Netu's amazement, it had ended in a truce like now. Differing on principle neither of them had treaded the line of total submission, but the end seemed a mutual meeting point of their various arguments. Netu conceded Joan wanted to ostracize self from the Brotherhood, a band of men and women he could not denounce in spite of his new faith.

Joan returned from the kitchen with his butter fried milk cakes in steaming sauce and boiled yam punctuating Netu's wandering thought. Netu helped to clear the tabletop of some old newspapers and magazines as Joan lowered the large stainless steel tray. A wispy steam drafted the sauce's sweet aroma from the tray. Blending with the familiar pungency of boiled yam, Netu could not resist its aroma.

"I hope you like it," Joan asked, pointing to the meal. "You go ahead, there's plenty left for me in the kitchen."

"All of this for me? A damn big feast I must say!"

"Savour the milk cakes first and put me on the scale."

"You toasted them just fine!" announced Netu between bites of the milk cakes. "Not bad, not bad at all! Eighty percent!"

On hearing Netu's praise song Joan went to the kitchen to fetch his meal. He returned in a moment and they ate in silence. Until they finished their rations and drank large quantities of cold water, only the drone of the television and its intermittent flick of vivid scenes broke the silence.

Once he had cleared the dishes to the right racks in the kitchen, Joan Price became his gregarious self again. He delved without restraint, as Netu had anticipated, into the rippling lake of his mind to stir to the fore whatever imperfection he perceived as tainting the Brotherhood in spite of its greatness as a spiritual enclave.

"Netu, it's not that I despise the Brotherhood as much as you imagine. No, I still love the place. The memory is fresh and rare. My conscience is at war though with the infection evident in a strict society of puritans," he said like a pontificating saint.

Netu kept silent and listened. Over the years, he had been able to discern truth from the most banal of jokes by listening patiently.

Joan wondered for a moment if Netu's ever-countering spirit had suffered a sudden death by virtue of the food he had eaten. Netu's silence amazed him.

"There's decent pride in the ambition of a man who acknowledges the right moment to quit," Joan said.

Why does a man floored in the ring of anxieties, feel he can roll the dice of life on his palm and turn up secret winning numbers even when the mandatory count is over? Why does he still conjure time's long drawn strength, joggling his wit in a bid to disprove the full echo of his groaning? Joan thought, and then asked, "When the lethal blows of time enfeeble a man's attempts to fight at the forefront of war, what exactly would he be proving by being obstinate in not throwing in the towel? Is it what you call greed, or the enlarged fear of failure? I surely want to know!"

Netu laughed inwardly at his friend's cold rage, believing Joan's impulses had given birth to a potential mathematician. New theories on faith, or the Brotherhood experiences, had taken roots too in Joan's tempered mood. Staring stone-faced at his friend, Netu allowed Joan vast fertile plains to sow his theories.

Joan knew he loved to argue for the sake of it. He loved to flaunt the seeds of his wisdom like the petals of a sunflower awakening at sunrise. Netu's deliberate silence, however, killed his need for argument. Therefore, he must bare his mind with or without Netu's response.

"Father Manu's time is over," he murmured in a deepset voice, thumbing the remote sensor, selecting a new channel on the television just so he would not have to see the flustered look on Netu's face.

"That's a weighty thing to say, Joan," Netu cautioned, but it glared as the nicest of baits.

"Damn! You think I don't know that?" Joan growled, irritated. "His time's long up. Just sniff around, look at what's happening and you'll get the full picture of things."

He straightened up nimbly, pacing in the compact

living around the thin space between the couches, centre table and the wooden cabinet which held the cache of electronics. Joan's invectives continued after a loud huff and shrug of iron-cast shoulders.

"Netu let me be honest with you, the grace had since left. Don't ask me where the grace left to because I don't know. I'll stake the life of my mother, Father Manu is just walking along like an empty shell with no real substance to command his prior mystique. Catch my drift?"

"How did you come to this strange conclusion?" Netu asked.

Joan sighed impatiently and lunged onto a free couch next to the armless chair on his right, casting a curious and unwavering gaze at Netu. He distrusted naive fellows.

"I knew this since my Brotherhood days," Joan said with great conviction. "Before I left the scene, in one of those improbable levels of being, I met The Realized One on whose errand Father Manu came. He said he is aware of obvious lapses in the handling of the reins of the Brotherhood, well-structured as it were to soothe all human adventures and spiritual needs. He said he had taken note of all the complaints from interacting souls. Looking through the vast spectrum of human thoughts - through their unpredictably hostile emotions - he found no one competent enough to entrust such a huge task. So in spite of my contention against Father Manu's continuity, he said we should still give Father Manu time to steer the divine ship till the one being groomed was psychologically ready to mount the saddle and pick up the reins."

"You are not joking, are you?" Netu demanded, realizing the lesson in Joan's revelation.

Joan affirmed with a nod. "That was then - many years gone now," he said, frowning. "What followed afterwards showed me the successor had reached the stage of maturity, and perhaps the envisioned switch had taken place unknown to mortals. Lo and behold, a new Manu and a retinue of seasoned ex-Manus. In their midst was Father Manu pleading for an extension of his tenure. Although he gave his respect as expected of an incumbent to the younger Manu enthroned, his plea was unanswered till the vistas of that level of being faded away. I can't recall if the league of Manus gave credence - even the least - to his plea."

This was no longer news to Netu who reckoned similar hints had come from several quarters in the past. Some ex-adherents had talked about this as a way of settling whatever grouse they had about the enclave. The second types of hints came from those on the neutral line whose decency of language mirrored their character traits in the Brotherhood.

Netu knew a lot about the venerable ways of the Manus to bother pestering Joan about details. His fear anchored instead on the depth of Joan's knowledge. Did Joan acknowledge Netu as the person The Realized One referred to? Did he recognize Netu as the newly enthroned Manu in those "improbable levels of being" as he had called it? He would find out anyhow.

"From the picture I get of it in my head, it's like you guys had a celebration of some sort?" Netu prompted.

"I guess you're right, a ceremony of some sort," Joan said.

"You saw the new Manu, I suppose?"

"From where I was? Sure."

"His physique and adornments must still be as fresh as morning roses in your head."

"I remembered the exact impressions while in trance-flight but I lost the details as I woke," Joan prevaricated. "I guess he was young, somewhat tall – can't remember the rest."

"That presupposes he couldn't have been someone you've met before physically?" Netu urged on.

Joan shook his head. His excitement waned fast like setting sun.

Netu reckoned Joan was being evasive. So he changed tactics, baiting Joan. "I've had similar insights as well."

A new radiance subsumed Joan's mood. "Are you sure about that?"

Netu nodded in agreement. "I want to believe there's a more prosaic dispensation emerging out of the old order - I'd seen that kind of switch-over personally." He wanted to shout aloud that he was the one they talked about but he just could not urge himself to do it.

Joan's response seemed cynical. "Do I take it to mean an entirely new thing, or is it a gilded feather from the old peacock?"

"A lot of factors will determine that," Netu said, "but there's the likelihood it would anchor elsewhere. Even if it doesn't work as we expect due to some permutations that we may not fully understand, it matters not in as much as there's a fulfilling grace to it."

"Ah, well, it better be as fulfilling as you say. A repeat of what we have on ground will be awful - you know, disastrous."

"No, incensing!"

"Whatever the expletives," Joan said, grinning.

On that note of concession, their chatter changed from reminiscences of their stints in the Brotherhood to more pertinent personal issues.

"Joan, I need a job," Netu said. "Would you know about a job opportunity anywhere? I feel like I'm being stifled in a strait jacket without a steady source of income."

"A job you say? What a moment to seek assistance! I have no idea the kind of job you seek, but there's none I know of at the moment. I don't have an enlarged pool of friends who've got the right clout to fetch you a good job..."

"I'm not asking for anything specialized, Joan. Just any damn job would do for now. I've no choice. I'll be okay with whatever is offered. Or even supplies of any sort to companies will fill the lonely hours of inaction. Joan, I'm serious."

"Any job is no job at all," argued Joan. "Supplies have become exclusive preserves of some cliques in companies. Unless you belong to those cartels it's not easy to penetrate."

"I know the situation well enough, but even as a physicist by training, I still have to start from somewhere at least, no matter how lowly placed it is."

"Of course, Netu. I'll think about it." A thought crept into his mind just then. "Supplies? Of course, there's a chance we might work on something together - two good heads are better than one they say. You know Sebio Tony, don't you?"

Netu acknowledged with a nod.

"He offered to assist if I could get some rich guys to supply iron billets for his company which is the foremost dealer in the rod industry. The returns are high on both sides but I've not made the right contacts. You think you can make any progress in that regards? If you handle it well you might shelve the damn idea of working for stipends," Joan enthused.

Netu could not believe his luck. His eagerness showed in his gaze. "Is the offer still open?"

"As open as the sky. Why don't you reach out to Sebio Tony? Talk it over with him if you think you have a good lead. He'd be glad to assist. But let me warn you that he might want to engage you in a little sermon. I'm sure you won't mind."

"Why should I mind his sermon? Because he'll think I'm still on the enemy's camp? Come on, Joan!"

"I just thought I should let you know."

"Well, thanks. You'd give me his address then?"

Netu had long wanted to see Sebio Tony a well-placed ex-Brotherhood member in Newland. Everything is working in my favour, Netu thought.

"The LIWIN at Bago district. It's before the paint manufacturing house - you won't miss it even in a dream. Tell him I gave you the hint and you'd like to be briefed on the technical details of the deal."

"It won't be hard to trace."

"Get on with it and keep me posted on your discussions, will you?"

"You can count on that. I've one or two people who might be interested in the deal. They are well-connected. We'll sell the idea to them and see if they'll buy it wholesale."

"Good. Just make it stick."

"I'll do my best."

The prospect of a big deal inspired Netu. He fixed his mind on it and refused to reckon with Joan's petty gossip about Father Manu or the Brotherhood. He thought of the big picture of things instead, a time in the future when he would not have to crawl in search of a job, when he would be seen as an indispensable stream in the arid terrain of society. He left with this new mental picture, like a triumphant butterfly answering the sweet call of nectar, to Vintage Brewery to see Boye Steve.

# # #

The visit to Vintage Brewery turned out to be a short one. They could not visit their friend the upstart millionaire in Diosh District due to Boye Steve's unexpected work load in his office. Joan insisted on a new date and Netu rescheduled for noon the following Thursday.

The timepiece in the reception lounge showed a quarter past two o'clock in the afternoon; the vigor of day still evident in the full scorch of the not yet waning sun. Netu stepped out of the visitors' lounge at Vintage Brewery a happy man. He waved a passionate goodbye to Boye Steve, but almost recoiled in the spanking hot wind back to the lounge for shelter. The intense sun's heat warmed him up like frozen food through a microwave.

He recovered from the rude burst of humid air in time to channel his thoughts coherently. He had time on hand to while away. Home culled a lonely prospect he loathed. His mind searched for a form of inspiration. His strides lengthened on the aisle of the street with his mind undecided where he would shore his aches and excitement on next.

The Brotherhood!

Oh, well, it would be enough medicine to apply on the longing in my heart. This, however, seemed a damnable, whimsical need to dare the odds. Nonetheless, he had not been to the Brotherhood at Newland's Vidya Valley or the headquarters at Danabi City for two weeks at the stretch.

All that while, Netu Deo had ignored Father Manu's call for him to join a guild of editors for the layout of the Brotherhood's tabloid - the twentieth edition. His fugitive Waji spirit, however, hungered now for some fun, and the Brotherhood seemed to be the place to visit. After all, the first phase of his spiritual honing had begun at the Brotherhood where he came to terms with the call of destiny as the next in the line of Manus.

Netu chose the Brotherhood at Vidya Valley, less than five miles away, instead of the over two hundred miles journey to Danabi City from Newland.

Full of expectations, he plodded through the maze of streets from Vintage Brewery and made it to Pen Station in twenty minutes regardless of the force of the midday sun.

Few paces down Pen Station led him to the motor park. He scrambled into a big bus milling with Vidya Valley bound commuters and managed to find a free seat in the middle. The engine set off in high pitch as the driver engaged it, and in the usual jaunt, jerking movements of overused vehicles, the bus coughed and cringed out to the main road to Vidya Valley. Few minutes later, he had alighted at Ashi Park.

Great expectation tempered his hurried walk from Ashi Park, Vidya Valley's apex bus stop, to the Brotherhood on the crest of the eastern slope of the fast growing suburb. Thoughts ran wild in his mind. Who were those on retention at the Brotherhood? Would he be as welcome as he had always been? Had time altered the alchemy of his significance in the Brotherhood?

Netu's visit to the headquarters of the Brotherhood in Danabi City fourteen days prior had tested his popularity as yet unequalled. But the red carpet reception he toyed with in his head would not be as expected if newbreed inmates had taken over affairs now in the Brotherhood at Vidya Valley. These newbreed may not be aware of his sterling record there.

Of course, his joy would soar if providence availed the sort of people he had dreamt of seeing again, especially Pa Nyto Smand. From Smand's point of view, Netu glared as a promising, indispensable spiritual protégé: the anointed one, soon to bear the weight of the human tree as the next Manu. He seldom made this point clear, but Netu knew the direction of Pa Smand's Waji conscience and proverbial chatter. Would Pa Nyto Smand, his spiritual adviser, be there?

Their meeting during his visit to the Brotherhood in Danabi City had been brief. There were ample tidings to tell the old man now, and wisdom to glean from the sage too.

The climb up the steep road to the eastern apex of Vidya Valley on foot with the sun high up in the sky bored Netu. Nonetheless, he made it to the crest of Vidya Valley aided by the force of deep inspiration.

By now, the residents at the main guard post of the Brotherhood had identified his gangling form heading up the steep. He could tell the creasing semblance of warm smiles on their faces even in the slight distance. Doubts that assailed his mind vanished. He realized their grimaces and amiable dispositions meant they still welcomed him.

Tifan Fiko, the stout, dark-skinned, apple-faced man in his early thirties, extended a crushing handshake, grinning in the self-aggrandizing fashion of his Baruyo pedigrees. Netu had to apply as much pressure to save his hand under the impact of Tifan's sinews.

"Howdy!" exclaimed Tifan, admiring his ex-colleague like a well-dressed mannequin in a highbrow boutique.

"Fine. And how are you?" responded Netu slapping Tifan affably on the chest.

"Ah, well, we are okay." Tifan said.

"Look who's here!" beamed Rebono Bulem, the temperamental electrician, an indigene of Barlaca from the southeast of Riagena. He pushed past the swing door of the guard post and came to gasp next to Netu smiling and encircling his huge arms around Netu's frail body in a bear hug. "I knew I'll see you soon after the last time at Danabi City."

Netu winced from the import of the hug on his spine. "Of course, but I got tied up somehow," he replied, extricating himself from the Rebono's strong arms.

"Boy, glad to see you!" quipped Tifan the debonair resident from the Baruyo extraction.

"I'm glad you are still around keeping the old flame alive!" Netu said.

"We want to see more of you - you are a source of inspiration you know!" Rebono said.

Netu smiled. "Well, I'll remember that!"

"I hope this isn't one of your disappearing acts?" humored Tifan, gesturing like a comedian in a circus.

"Would you rather I was tied down to some immobile pole?" countered Netu, winking and flashing his neat set of teeth.

"I didn't mean that," argued Tifan, sensing Netu's guffaw.

"And I didn't think you would," replied Netu. "By the

way, who are the residents posted here? Is Pa Smand around?"

"Yes, he is," Rebono said. "You'll find him on his haunches at the usual place inside. The old man is having a swell time."

"I can imagine."

Tifan smiled. "And there's Dullab too. He is in charge here."

"Dullab? By God! Where is he?"

"Inside - in his office. The one before Father Manu's."

"All right, I'll get along pals. I have to do a little catch up with Dullab and Pa Smand."

"You're welcome!" Rebono said.

From behind the high walls of the Brotherhood, cheerful voices pitched against the gentle rustle of the evening breeze. Netu flinched in recognition. He thought the lilting voice from the din with the highest note sounded familiar - a young lady's voice. The sweet tone of the voice lingered in his head as he swirled free of the guard post towards the entrance.

The wrought-iron gate cringed ajar at that moment and a swarthy guy of about twenty-five, a resident in the Brotherhood who Netu had known as a rough diamond of character, huddled out of the gate, almost bumping into Netu. Startled by the familiar gait of Netu, he stepped aside at the gate's edge and looked at the visitor.

"Mine, oh mine!" Timoni gasped as his vagrant mind returned from a long flight to acknowledge his comrade standing by the door. "Netu! Netu! I'll be damned! You've changed quite a bit," he quipped extending his large palm for a handshake. "Where the damn hell did you go to all this while?"

Netu placated in a friendly undertone. "Nowhere in particular, Timoni. I've been around. Perhaps I should be asking you the same question. My dear Timoni, where have you been all this while?"

Timoni grimaced undecidedly. His beady eyes found anchor skyward. "Here and there - you know the damn routines here. This moment you are busy there, the next moment you are here. The lengthiest respite one ever gets is the brief moments between meals and the long boring trips of routine postings."

Timoni lapsed into a sustained laugh after which he glanced behind him and called out to someone in the outer sections of the reception. "Hey, Fiara, see who we've got here, Netu Deo! He'd changed so much in so short a time."

Netu craned his head and saw the lady Timoni referred to as Fiara. She looked frail but had a shiny dark complexion capable of stirring a man's heart. Her eyes twinkled like beads, accentuated by a sweet face, which like the lens of a powerful electronic microscope, revealed the deepest of a man's heart. She rose from her seat in the outer reception and peered at the man Timoni conducted toward her.

"Ah, Netu!" Fiara exploded, jumping happily around her desk like a cooing dove. The ponytail of her dark brown hair swished about her shoulders coloring her sensuality in innumerable shades over pink silk organza blouse and black gabardine skirt.

Netu had never seen excitement as wanton as Fiara's or anyone so happy for his sake. It made his heart explode with joy too.

Fiara had smiled and jumped a dozen times before Netu got to the large glass encasement, the lodgment arm of the reception where visitors' valuable items were kept on their way to the amphitheatre. Fiara held out her arms through the open window and admired him, trembling with elation.

"Good to see you. Netu, you're looking brighter and finer each day!" she said, her slim hand straying to tease the stubble on his chin.

Netu winced, astonished. Emotions of this kind were not allowed in the Brotherhood, yet Fiara had put old-fashioned notions in their right rungs of history, daring to show some degree of affection without the inhibitions her resident status had induced on her human nature.

"Uhmn, you look cool just as ever!" Netu said. "Fiara you are the one that amazes me with such radiance."

Fiara grinned and held onto his hand tenderly, sending sensual messages through his being. She remembered something of a sudden.

"Now, don't you dare move, I have a surprise for you! Hold on now," she said and rushed off to the far edge of the glass encasement on the right, turning there to the right and into an inner chamber. She came out blushing seconds afterward with another lady of a lithe build in tow.

Fiara tried shielding the lady behind her with widespread arms. "Netu, guess who is behind me."

Netu looked beyond Fiara anticipating her surprise package and saw Pere, one of his closest female colleagues in the Brotherhood. Pere smiled, waved and bustled past Fiara to the lodging area. She took Netu's hand with the delicate care an egg deserves as she reached him from behind the wooden desk-like divide of the glass encasement.

"It seems like ages you know," she said in a soft, impassioned voice. "Missed you greatly."

"Pere, I miss you too. Every one of you good friends," Netu said, his heart pumping faster.

Pere Mejeli had aged beyond her thirties from Netu's reckoning. Gaunt looking now, her once full cheeks had shrunk like smoked bull's hide etching visible lines of stress around her eyes. Her once sexy dark eyeballs, which always wrenched his control and ensnared his emotion in a slavish sense, were now dull and seemed to be fed with a fast waning ardor. Her beauty had suffered from the transformation on her face. She seemed like a woman of fifty, though there was nothing to suggest the kind of senile posture peculiar to those within that age range in the agile way she held his arms, and in the brusque way she had rushed pass Fiara to the wooden desk-like divide of the encasement. Her trademark grins were still evident, her veins livid with Shani blood and her gaped teeth were impeccably white.

Netu still recognized her as the Pere Mejeli of those good old days of his in the Brotherhood. Yet, he reckoned she had not learnt to adjust to the changing times. Netu admitted also that if she had changed with the times as expected, perhaps time itself had exhorted its pound of flesh from the way she looked, pale and dejected.

"Hey, what went wrong with those plump cheeks and good looks of yours? You look pale and forlorn. Were you sick?" Netu asked in a lowered voice. "Or you've abandoned thoughts of beauty care and...?"

Netu acknowledged the flustered look on Pere Mejeli. His words stung her like a thrashing whip. The impact on her skin appeared gentle but it left tremendous pain searing through her being. He noticed her eyes drooped for a moment and he pitied her feeble struggle with self-pity.

A sad grin reared on Pere's face. "I was sick all right," she said lamely, "but I guess I'm fine now." She then gazed at him in a bold, determined pose.

"I thought as much," Netu consoled. "It'll be nice to have you back in your usual bloom though - a stunner that shape is any day!"

"Don't flatter me, Netu."

"Ok, if you won't accept a deserved compliment."

"Some other time perhaps. Obviously a blind man could tell the ghost in human apparel standing before you."

"Don't be ridiculous Pere. By God, you're still a marvel! Lots of rest and a little food will fill out all the deep hollows."

"You need to see Pere eat - man it's like a feast of a thousand famished elephants," Fiara intruded.

"Don't mind Fiara and her robust humor. I eat moderately," Pere argued with pride.

The ensuing peal of laughter washed off the inflections of health and the suggested remedies.

"Timi is here as well. Have you seen her?" Pere chipped in.

"No, I just arrived," Netu said. "It's a whole family then?"

Pere nodded affirmation. "Log in your items while I help spread the news to her and others. She'll join you in a minute," she said and bounced out of the encasement. She came out to the terrace through an annex of the reception, grinned and swaddled her frail body towards the residential quarters of the Brotherhood out of bound to non-residents.

Fiara lodged in Netu's big brown envelope in euphoria noting the sparse contents. "You'll collect the envelope on on your way out."

"That's fine by me, Fiara."

Just when Netu turned away from Fiara to begin to explore deeper into the confines of the Brotherhood, Pere returned stealthily with Timi.

From another section of the Brotherhood emerged three young ladies and two young men, residents of the Brotherhood who were close to Netu at various times. On sighting Netu they cooed and twirled like drunken wild Newlanders with joy and gratitude to the purveyor of all known and unknown human actions for the return of the prodigal son.

The whole of Netu's being ruptured; an infinite lifting of spirit to profound realms in his nervous stead as they hugged, touched and looked him over.

The claws of his doubts still lurked in the realm of his thoughts despite this beautiful feeling he felt in the presence of the female residents of the Brotherhood. Nothing they did seemed to erase his fear or his whiff of suspicion bordering on Pere and the other sisters. He sensed they were at Vidya Valley, probably, to induce pressure on his psychic space and haul him straight back to the Brotherhood with the subtlety spiritual warfare demands.

The fact that Pa Smand, Dullab, Tifan, Rebono and the sisters were at the same place at the same time was enough reason for him to suspect foul-play. The curious nature of his Waji spirit spelt intrigue.

Of course, his fears soon found vindication in the words of Timi his presumed spiritual mother when they had a moment of privacy.

"When are you coming back, son?" she whispered, gazing down at her feet, nibbling with the fingers of his hands in hers.

Netu observed a foreboding gleam in her drooped gaze. It made him uncomfortable. "I can't say when - perhaps it'll never happen. Perhaps it is best I don't come back at all. I don't have the courage anymore to..." he murmured and broke-off.

"To come back? To face all the pains of the Brotherhood you mean?" Timi interjected with a frown. "Are you going to leave me here all alone to fight this war? Your brother is gone to the beyond, you're the only one left, and you still insist I go alone?" Her voice trembled and her hands against his were a nervous wreck.

"Your other son - my spiritual brother - is gone I know. It hurts even to acknowledge the fact that he's no longer here with us, but you see it is difficult for me now. The situations are not the same as they used to be. I'd like to be back like everybody says but I just can't help forgetting the trauma of the times I've seen in and outside the Brotherhood. I've got to get my bearings straight, be responsible for whatever actions I take about my life."

Netu every so often felt disadvantaged when Jare Nom's name came up in his discussions with members of the Brotherhood. Such recollections were akin to a reversal of the clock of his life to the sad moment when he wrestled ineffectually with death in defense of his friend Jare Nom. How he wished death had spared his friend's life.

Netu had watched helplessly the torment of the young man, a little older than him. The groaning and rather fierce remonstrations Jare Nom had with sneaky death, the last emboldened yet laborious battle to dispel the grotesque hands of the illness that snatched his life, were memories that still haunted Netu. The name Jare Nom, threw up now the stark reality of his own fate and made him surrender like a coward. He would not let Timi, the human bridge between him and Jare Nom use their perceived spiritual filial bond to blackmail him into undue submission.

Timi had the quizzical, despairing look on her face again. "Can't you see the evidence of the trauma we are all passing through? I'm worst hit. Take a good look, son. The war as you see it is still at its infant stage – I'm as traumatized as you are. I heard all the gory stuff, which stole you away from us - but your father, the Manu, loves you so much. He wants you back. He wouldn't just stop saying it. He too has had it rough with the forces of the dark but he had to continue to lead us. If he should relent in his effort and retire, who will champion the cause we've fought so hard for all these years? Son, please, I need you. We need you," she pleaded at the verge of tears.

Timi Liati's supple chocolate brown skin had stretched unevenly in the harsh bouts of anxiety in the Brotherhood. Perhaps from the attacks of the vile spiritual elements she hinted of. Netu imagined it along the lines of cindered earth. Though she still retained the luster of her dark gray eyes and fullness of lips, her bust had shrunk. She seemed a caricature of her former voluptuous self. Netu wondered what had eaten her up and made her so fragile and yet so ardent in terms of her faith?

"The epidemic has hit you no doubt," Netu admitted without deep emotion, "but you are still on the inside, that makes the difference. It's a world apart."

"What's the meaning of that?"

"It's better, safer, not to leave the Brotherhood in the first place. Once you're out, you're simply out. You hear a new rhythm, a different song, different dancers and audience. And here you are in the thick of it all trying to make meaning out of the nonsense you perceive all around. And you begin to see things you never would have seen, and you hear baubles of all kinds that you never dreamt of, and you wonder what it all boils down to. Timi,

I really want to do as you wish but the rhythm doesn't seem to strike twice with me. Please, do understand. I know you will."

That much he could let himself say. He would allow none to plunder the treasure of his heart no matter the bond between them. His fate and the things already agreed upon between him and his mentor Father Manu were secrets better kept sealed.

Timi retrieved her hands from his and gestured in a cold, ominous way with them. Her down swept gaze rose now to level with his stubborn, unyielding stare.

"I won't bother you anymore if you carry on with this headiness. But don't be too far away from us while you contemplate your return. My heart would be gladdened if I know you are within reach. Think about it son. Here is home. Our home. Your father is waiting anxiously," she entreated, putting back some warmth into her pale look.

Netu forced himself into a meaningless, dry and raucous laugh as if it were his last. Affected in a grand way by his wiles, Timi did not know when she joined in laughing her deep-seated fears away. Her first real laughter in a long while.

They met Pa Nyto Smand lounging alone with a light heart by the indoor swimming pool of the stucco for residents when Timi Liati guided Netu to the poolside. The stucco had several adjoining apartments, bordering the sweeping lawns of the farthest western spread of the Brotherhood.

Pa Smand stared at the beautiful grounds ahead - florid rising and splashing fountains, radiant flowers and fine trees - with the deep vagueness of an ageing mind that he did not notice the approach of the duo from behind him.

When Netu and Timi came to stand next to Pa Smand, however, in a florish of instinct peculiar with the aged with sight on the decline, the perfume of human presence assailed his senses. Apprehensive of a sudden, he turned and saw in the blur of his failing sight two figures towering by his side.

"Who is sneaking up on me? And what is it?" Pa Smand queried.

"Pa Smand, it is Timi Liati. You have an august visitor here," she said, brightening up.

"Oh," Pa Smand drawled. "Timi, I didn't notice your entrance." His gaunt features leaped with a sudden glow like the merry bursts of a flame in cavort. "Did I hear you right? A visitor? And who could it be?"

"Netu Deo!" Netu said without waiting for Timi's introduction. "Pa Smand, it's your son, Netu Deo." He took up a position perpendicular to Pa Smand's gaze.

"Ah, ah, Netu! Forgive the poor sight and weak memory of an old man. What a pity I couldn't recall your face and your sweet voice. Come, come son, come sit by my side!" Smand fawned.

"Excuse me Netu. I guess I'll drift along till you're through with your daddy here. I'll be in the reception area by the gate. Pa Smand, please, take care of your son," Timi Liati said retreating.

Pa Smand dismissed Timi with a waved his hand. He

wanted more than anything to be alone with his spiritual protégé at this moment of reunion. "He's in good hands surely. He'll join you much later. You can go my dear daughter."

"I'll be with you shortly," Netu told Timi. She left them in a hurry.

"Son, quite some time you've been off the scene," Pa Smand began. In his rheumy eyes were glints of trepidation. "I was going to call you for a long chat at Danabi City the last time you were there but the next thing I knew - you were gone," he snapped his fingers, "to oblivion. But I'm glad you came to see me here."

"Pa, my visit to the headquarters of the Brotherhood was a short one. I tried to contact you while there but protocol worked against my schedule so I had to leave. I'm sorry we couldn't see till now."

"It's no longer an old man's pain since you are here son, and I believe you are in good mental and spiritual shape."

"Everybody thinks so, Pa."

"And what do you think?"

"I don't think what I think matters."

"Well, if you want my opinion, I think they are right son. I can sense from your aura that all is well with you."

"I believe you Pa if you think so yourself."

"I can feel it so. It's in the air. And we've discussed about you a lot - Father Manu and I. I'll let you into our little gossip, but it can't be right here. Son, I think we better move inside. They gave me this cosy little apartment bordering the poolside over there." He pointed towards the swimming pool. "We'll go inside and get it all spilled and sorted. Help me with my staff and shirt and I'll lead the way."

Pa Smand lumbered to his feet. Netu went to fetch the shirt and staff on the edge of the lounging chair.

On return, Netu observed Pa Nyto Smand. Sixty-five years of real thawing, plus fifteen years of reclusive life in search of esoteric meaning and the last ten that winded up at the Brotherhood, never in a way robed Pa Nyto Smand of his huge build, nor his spiritual ardor. Sixty-five years in rewound time, the now stooping Pa Smand would have easily loomed amidst his Waji clansmen or the various societies of his spiritual sojourn as the most likeable of the brawny, brash, macho men around.

His great height and size perhaps were the measure of the degree of his abundant compassion and the roots of a glaring father figure Netu treasured. What would have looked like a large skull with a thick shock of black hair had been shaven clean with a gleam like polished eggshell. Wrinkles had also made gutters on his otherwise handsome face and formed ringlets around his sky blue eyes, and the inevitable sagging of his nose-line, lower and upper jaw turned his speech to a jawing, guttural treat. But the old man still had livid strength that surprised Netu as they went round the pool to his apartment. And Pa Smand's cheery attitude seemed as if he was a child all over and time reset to the dawn of his youth.

The Brotherhood had been kind, indeed generous

to Pa Smand from Netu's on the spot assessment inside the apartment. An old man's welfare was as sensitive as that of a sulking toddler and this factor accounted for the unsparing care given his apartment. His needs in relation to his wiles were extravagantly catered for in the choice of décor and other accessories by a team of residents under the supervision of the head of Vidya Valley's Brotherhood of Father Manu.

A courteous attendant assigned to Pa Smand appeared as they entered the living room. He gave a solemn salute and asked, "Would you need anything so urgently, Pa Smand?"

"Bless your soul Niima," Pa Smand responded. "I was about buzzing the pager to draw your attention to our visitor here. Netu is back and that means you'll prepare an early dinner for two or three. He'll be having dinner with me, and let it be real sumptuous like the one you prepared the other day. We have to give my son an unforgettable treat. I'm sure he doesn't even remember how food in the Brotherhood tastes like anymore." He puffed brightly. "If I need anything else I'll let you know."

Niima who wore loose red slacks and yellow apron turned to Netu. "You're welcome, Netu!" He bounced out of the room thereafter.

"Now son, have a sandwich or two and a cup of warm milk before Niima prepares dinner," Pa Smand said offering Netu from a side pier table of cross-banded mahogany a tortoise shell commode, which held some fruit sandwiches.

Netu accepted the commode with gratitude. Pa Smand poured a glassful of warm milk from a polychrome teapot on the pier table with swiftness that belied his age, and placed it on a dumbwaiter by Netu. Only then did Pa Smand retire to his favorite walnut sofa, a patriarchal glint of satisfaction inundating his pale blue eyes.

While Netu ate the fruit sandwiches, every slight twitch of muscle of his or faint fidget from the ageing man, seemed an interminable pulse of expectation between them. Their minds reeled with secrets they were willing to share with no other than themselves.

Pa Smand waited patiently for the right moment. He allowed Netu finish the last of the two huge sandwiches he had made by himself, which was all to boost his ego as a once high ranked chef and let the young man also gulp the last drop of milk in the medium glass before unburdening his mind.

"Netu, I think it's high time you made a U-turn," Pa Smand said impassively. "We can't have you running around out there to our detriment. Son, there's no gainsaying that you belong here. There have been great upheavals ever since you left us. The whole place is never the same again - it appears charged with radiations that are burning everyone up. They are all confused - the residents. They lack everything you had; your kind of humility, leadership traits - good Brotherhood relation went extinct with your days. The Manu knows this and confided in me so many times. After you left, everyone started seeing the gem in you, sadly not before. That is a bad precedent but we must learn to forgive the past. Son, there's so much ahead of us to worry about, so much to hold on to. Endeavor to see Father Manu as soon as you can and tell him you are back for good. Do that for me, son. This time you'd be held with high esteem. Of course, people have always had regards for you, especially people like me who know who you are."

Pa Smand trembled as his gnarled hand searched for a handkerchief in his side pocket with which he wiped off cascading teardrops. His impassiveness all the while had only been a cover for an emotive thrust.

Netu knew the old man was just as vulnerable as any other he had known despite efforts to maintain a calm posture. The tears he saw streaking down Smand's face roused Netu's emotion too. He stood up and lent a soothing hand, touching Pa Smand affectionately on the shoulder.

"You've always been nice to me in words and in deed and I wouldn't now pay you back with defiance, but Pa Smand there's much to consider," Netu said and wandered off to the right corner of the room to observe a blown poster of Father Manu on the cream papered wall.

The grizzled look on Pa Smand lit up with no foreboding traces when he saw the possibility of a mellowed heart from Netu's remark. He almost smiled now.

"You'd come right away then?" he demanded.

Netu backed away from the poster, ignoring Pa Smand's bloated optimism, nodding without great commitment. "Come I will, but it can't be right away."

"Why delay when you know you can ride the storm as it is?"

"I can't back out of some important business commitments, fast yielding deals, so abruptly. It won't tell well of me."

"When will you be through with these deals of yours?"

"Say a couple of days, weeks, perhaps a few months."

Netu might as well have knifed Pa Smand at the temple with his evasive answers for the light on the old man's face dimmed fast.

"You are not too keen on coming back, are you?" Pa Smand quizzed in a manner that looked almost like a plea.

Netu went back to his seat worried. "I've always belonged here Pa, so I don't fret over a return match. It only requires my being on the gutsy side. I've cause not to be hasty in my decision to return though. My mother - she needs all the help she can get from me, lest she thinks I've abandoned her as fate abandoned her when she became an orphan so early in life. I'll come once I've seen to her urgent needs, and then she'll have no excuse to hold me back from whatever I want to do."

Pa Smand sat, brooding on what Netu had said; caustic though the meanings of it, undeniable were the facts. Soon he gave oblique assent.

"Mothers are a precious lot and we need more than perfection in handling them if one must gain their respect and necessary blessing," Pa Smand said. "At the same time a man's independence of mind and spirit is non-negotiable."

"True," Netu concurred despite the ambiguity of Pa Smand's words. "Right as ever. The line of tow between the two options is thin - and wisdom is the determinant, right?"

"Take your time and balance the simple equation my son," Pa Smand urged in cryptic undertones. "The world isn't going to end today or tomorrow. You have a lot to gain or lose on your side. For me, time has been friendly, fair."

Pa Nyto Smand unfurled the secrets he wanted to share with Netu after this attitudinal display of wisdom.

"Son, you've never failed, never ever through all your incarnations. This one is no exception. You've always fought bravely till the end. And this is authoritative. Take it from me or leave it. See, it was you and I who toiled to lift Father Manu up the podium of world acclaim. We did all we could to get him there – son, you were marvelous with your brave, selfless efforts - but there was a sudden brazen intrusion that got us gasping at the eleventh hour. Kinsha, that retrogressive son of a seven-humped bitch, stole in on us and extinguished the sea of light and the props we'd put to enhance the lift of the Manu on the world stage. There came an eerie darkness as a result and stampede ensued. People screamed, howled, shouted and the cursed name of Kinsha rang out everywhere as the culprit. The perfidious, good for nothing brat escaped in the stampede, but we knew it was him. Our vigilance paid off somehow. Else, that idiot would've mired us all silly, though it caused us a hell of pain to rectify the damage. That's the kind of hatred you've been up against. I know it son. It isn't easy but you have the right courage and resilience to overcome the most brazen of adversaries," Pa Smand said in restrained rage, the target of which was Kinsha.

"When was this," Netu asked, bewildered.

"Few months back," replied Pa Smand. "Father Manu confirmed the revelation. He was sure it was no fluke experience."

"I see," Netu's mind reeled on a puzzle-piecing shuttle and many isolated events began to glue back in poignant whole. All the battles he had fought with the Sectwean cult, the Locci, and other spiritual power blocs, all boiled down to this – Kinsha and the horde of avengers of his role in the end of Atlantis.

They rambled on for another hour, which included early dinner before Netu managed to escape Pa Smand's chatter to see Dullab in his galleried office adjoining Father Manu's near the row of stucco buildings.

The Vidya Valley's Brotherhood of Father Manu spanned seventeen and half acres of sweeping lawns broken in an ingenious fashion in the interspersion of vibrant trees, lofty fountains, superbly contrived row of four stucco buildings, a five thousand capacity auditorium, a hard tennis court, part Lemurian style refectory and dressing rooms for non-residents, and the Manu's magnificent duplex with a galleried entrance hall.

The overall view of the Brotherhood's expanse either from the keen eyes of an insider or from its prominence on the crest of Vidya Valley was as fresh in aesthetics as it had been for Netu at the dawn of its birth. It stood now eight years later even grander in quick appraisal on his way to Dullab's office.

The whole place still remained un-deflowered; voluptuous and intrinsic in its wooing of Netu's mind like a pretty lady, yet untouched her vaginal beauty.

Netu met Dullab, "the pragmatic governor" as peers often called him, and his aides in the galleried entrance hall of Father Manu's, which doubled as temporary office for the head of Vidya Valley's Brotherhood. Netu had easy access to the office on the ticket of his status as a respected ex-resident of the Brotherhood despite normal time wasting protocol.

Most of the present drafts of residents were far beneath Netu's station during his time. But he had taken time in his clamber up the hierarchy of the Brotherhood to cultivate friendship with other residents through deep-seated care and wisdom. His genial disposition had endearing qualities too that they had often turned to as parameters for divine growth. Their obsequies and express clearance for him to see Dullab and his retinue of assistants this day therefore hinged on his actions of the past.

The centre point of Dullab's plea - a blunt repetition of what the others had hammered in vain - hinged on the grand effect Netu's return would have on the entire band of adherents. Netu stood his ground; as inscrutable as ever. He was not going back to the Brotherhood no matter what.

"I don't think I want to come back, Dullab," Netu said frankly. "But I'm happy seeing you guys."

The excitement he felt surging now, if he would ever call it that - even as he was rumored as the head that bore the crown next – centred on the great physical condition of Dullab and ninety percent of the other male residents. They were charming, healthy and sturdy in spirit quite unlike half the females whose physiques and spirits had known the sledgehammer of a present yet improbable monster. Their motherly natures perhaps made them more prone to dreary influences, Netu thought with slight discomfort.

"Should you be in need of funds or some physical assistance, we would be here to give you a hand," Dullab said while stashing few Rinai bills into Netu's side pockets as he escorted him half way to the gate much later. "You deserve a better treatment than this Netu, but do bear with us. We'll make necessary amends next time. Call my attention any time and be assured of our cooperation whatever the matter is."

"I won't forget the offer," replied Netu, shy as usual.

"See me before the week runs out. If there's a streak of luck and unexpected cash flow, you can be sure of something coming your way too," harped Dullab.

"Thanks for your concern."

"Hey, forget it. What's more to living if not this caring and sharing that we champion daily? Nice thing you called here - others won't even bother about what goes on here once they are out. And if not for the bureaucratic bottlenecks we often encounter here, people like you shouldn't be left alone to jostle out there. There should've been adequate plans for the future, the welfare of your kind..." Dullab paused in his lamentation. "Gosh! It's sad! Let's just forget it. Before the weekend, right? Be here. Okay, catch you then."

"So long Dullab," Netu said with a handshake.

Netu dashed back to see Pa Smand to thank him for his hospitality as Dullab retreated because his attention was needed at the auditorium.

Netu retrieved the brown envelope he had lodged on arrival with Fiara at the reception. Pa Smand's words, "We're waiting for you to come help put the house in order" echoed and trailed his thought. Much like the shadow of his profile cast on the stone terrace in the awning of early night by the lights around the reception area. The old man's words haunted him a great deal. Yet, he had made up his mind about the choice he would make.

As Netu Deo made to leave the confines of the Brotherhood after Fiara had crosschecked and certified the contents as he had left them on his arrival, word of his exit spilled around. Timi, Pere, Manda, Fiara and others came to see him off. They were not allowed beyond the gate because it contravened the rules and regulations of the Brotherhood for residents. A resident could go outside the gate if on an important assignment but leisure walk was forbidden beyond the gate.

Pere Mejeli earned Netu's admiration by breaking the Brotherhood's tradition in a bold, audacious manner. She smiled her way through the security team of Rebono, Tifan and Timoni at the gate, rallying as if about to retreat but instead walked past them to Netu's side on the driveway. Although she had gone beyond the gate, no one raised an eyebrow.

To Netu's surprise, they let her have her way with him as one of those they had admired while in the Brotherhood. Besides, the Brotherhood was neither a slave camp nor a torture chamber where only the master's will prevailed in spite of the necessity for spiritual and mental discipline. Freedom at any pedestal seemed untenable if the individual will was bond by the strange fetters of human caprice. Netu thought the young men at the guard post must have viewed it from this perspective and might have been sick and tired of some of the Brotherhood's out-dated traditions by this gesture of theirs.

"Are you not defying tradition coming this far?" Netu whispered as Pere tugged side by side with him down the slope of Vidya Valley.

"Who cares anymore about what anybody thinks?"

"You're attempting to hold a tiger by the tail, Pere."

"Let it bare its fangs," Pere declared. "I know its fixtures too well to be scared."

"It pays to be cautious though."

"I've long thrown caution to the wind. You can't stand on both sides of the divide and hope to win a war," she said with a dark grin. "I've been doing it the sublime way for God knows how long and have got the hell for it. It's about time I do it my own way. I want to please no one but me."

"What if your way turns out rough and injurious to self?"

"Well, my luck."

"Ill-luck perhaps."

"Not after all these years of hard-line training. I don't have to lecture you on this, do I? Our conditioning in the Brotherhood has been to endure great travails, a humbling of the mind and spirit, accepting every trial on the path as an act of providence. Do you expect me to ride the horse of fate and accept unnecessary jolts at this point of my spiritual growth? Swallow ample 'don't do this, don't do that' and you simply lose your sense of direction."

"Well," Netu said laughing. "I've never known you to be so witty, full of nerve and conceptions."

Pere Mejeii gestured shyly. "Ah, well, the Brotherhood gets one wizened each and every day." She brightened and gazed at Netu in an accusatory manner. "You are a lot wiser I should think with your vacation and all that?"

Netu raised a mischievous eye. "Don't go sounding that vacation crap like everybody's been telling me, Pere. You just talked about riding the horse of your fate, and you believe I'm naive not to see the wisdom in it?"

The subtle force of Netu's words jolted Pere to a sharp halt. "Wait a second Netu!" she said frisking him on the shoulder, halting his pace. "I hope you're not thinking what I'm thinking in my head?"

Netu affirmed with a lizard-like nod. "That's why I've been kind of stubborn about coming back," he said walking ahead of Pere.

Pere caught up quickly with him. "Don't do that Netu," she gasped.

"I shouldn't? Why?"

She fidgeted. "There's a reason."

"What's the reason?" Netu demanded, halting.

"The Brotherhood sisters are here for a reason." Pere

Mejeli's gaze drifted to a posh villa on the lower bed of the slope of Vidya Valley.

A cold realization crept into Netu Deo's head and rendered it temporally numb. A hint he had tried to downplay when Pere, Fiara, Timi, Manda and others appeared at the same time and place to welcome him, came succinct now with meaning. They were at Vidya Valley to fetch him with their spiritual dragnets.

"I believe the reason why we are here has a lot to do with you," Pere broke in. "Two days before we came here, I saw something I intend to divulge here."

Netu's pace slackened, and his marked quizzical stare took over. "And I reckon," he mumbled kindly, "it's crucial, not so?"

"Yes," admitted Pere. "It's important. There was this huge lamp, a golden antique lantern with an astounding glow, entrusted to Timi for cleaning and safekeeping in my trance-flight. Half way through the cleaning, she broke the fragile lantern bulb. Perhaps due to her recklessness in handling it. Darkness descended and overwhelmed the whole arena where Timi did the clean-up. Then I saw this bright light, a bright hue on the other side, off our area. Father Manu was furious and everyone he sighted including Timi got his ire over the broken golden lantern bulb. He asked me to take over the lantern from Timi, mend it quickly, do a diligent clean up and let it glow again. But he said we should go and fetch you right away or he won't ever step back to our side of the pervading darkness. He would only return on the condition that we mend the lantern and fetch you. In the revelation, Father Manu released a list of would-be scouts, ladies predominantly. The second day after this spiritual drama, the actual manifestation of the revelation took place. All the ladies short-listed as scouts for the mission were whisked from Danabi City to Vidya Valley. That's how we came here."

Pere Mejeli paused to reel home the import of the narration. "The motive of our coming from what I've told you is obvious. We are here to bring you back whatever way we can," she went on anticipating his assent or defiance.

Netu stood there speechless for a moment. The sheer intrigue of their complex scheming bewildered him. I've never ever had a wrong hunch. I've just proven this again with Pere's revelation, he thought. Some wild fantasy they must be up to if they think they can bring me back to the Brotherhood so easily. And they think I'm the shattered lantern that invoked darkness on their psyche? Or is my absence in this bigoted society of puritans the cause of darkness they seek fiercely to redress? Dreamers they all are!

He whistled, concealing his racing thought with a passive grin. "I recognized this fact from the minute I set my eyes on you, Timi, Fiara, Manda, Pa Smand and Dullab. It's too compact a team of brotherhood veterans for a sensitive person like me not to notice. And knowing this - I mean what your mission is all about - how do you hope to accomplish your objective?"

Pere could not help but laugh. "Psshaaw!" she exhaled, stomping ahead graciously. "Why do you think I'm divulging all this to you? I thought if you knew our position relative to yours it would make it easier for us to handle."

"And you are sure I'll concede?"

"Not by a long shot. I was gambling on how close we were in the past. I had to take the risk to alert you and to plead with you to understand our standpoint."

Netu circled his long arm around her shoulder in a dispassionate way and said, "Of course, I understand."

Pere flinched but allowed his arm to linger on her shoulder. Night had swept over the spawn and the residents at the guard post would not see the comforting arm on her shoulder despite the sea of filtering dim light points around the neighborhood.

They walked in close contact in silence for a few metres. Netu perceived her jumpy stead and replaced his stray hand to his side. Luckily they did not encounter any late arrivals to the Brotherhood as it often was on the street. Only two cars had sped past since they left the gate and there had been no other encounters with Brotherhood adherents.

Every so often they cackled without care and bumped into each other along the street and each time a strong electric charge whirred between them. Upon the Brotherhood's hardline teachings both of them had gleaned some rare lessons, enough to dissuade their minds of the kind of emotion they felt being close to each other.

Netu wrestled with his own kind of sentimental mind games. Walking next to Pere Mejeli in the early night had its pleasures akin to the imagination of heaven's splendor. Yet a dreadful thumping troubled his heart, mixing and grading his emotion into two distinct levels: joy borne on the fragile wings of fear.

The pleasures her solicitous presence wrought in his heart enchanted him like the colors of a butterfly - beautiful and thrilling in the refined points on the canvass, but dark and grotesque in the other parts. This picture of Pere prevailed upon his swift thought - one tender frame with two different realities.

His momentary fear soared on fragile wings owing to the darker tint of her personality. He trusted her and would risk even an oath regarding her sincerity. Yet she had a dreary past that threatened his onward peace and their present chat along the street. Predestined or not, she had begun to assume a role now in his life that frightened him. And this went far back as Atlantis.

A splurge of memory overwhelmed him as they walked. Three years sped backwards in Netu's mind to the Brotherhood's headquarters in Danabi City and a secret rendezvous he had had with Pere Mejeli flipped back into perspective.

Persuaded by Netu's determination to find a plausible link to all of the Brotherhood's staunch adherents and their past incarnations into a book of enduring history, Pere had agreed to a rendezvous with him in the Brotherhood's press gallery keeping faith with his promise of absolute secrecy. Her bid to court what he termed "New history." He had assured her of Father Manu's consent with his pet project and that the outcome of the meeting would be confidential.

Coming on the heels of a sour, platonic relationship with Pere, it seemed a great gain on Netu's part to have convinced her to the project. The harvest was even greater than he had envisaged. Pere's undeniable weakness for his idealism and charisma earned for him a harvest of never heard of secrets.

"In the Nibi kingdom of pristine Riagena, I was a queen who was deified later," ventured Pere Mejeli as Netu began to take notes while recording her voice on tape.

"I'm still being worshipped until date by the Nibi progenies. Back then I was a revered queen. Powerful and awed even by rival kingdoms, my people the Shanis rallied around me for their spiritual and material well-being. We never had a sour moment during my reign. We expanded our kingdom as often as our whims allowed and devoid of the great tribal upheavals and insurgence that plagued the era. Perhaps my deification after my transition was simply to immortalize their pragmatic queen. They often consulted my spirit for guidance or protection and the results were profound. It has ever remained so."

"Are there relics to this effect?" Netu goaded. "Can you adduce from your present contact with the Shanis if this Nibi deity does actually exist? Is it not just one of their myths?"

Pere nodded. "Relics abound all right. I'm the renowned Natum of Nibi Kingdom - the deity is the relic of my queenship. Check it out if you will."

"I'm only checking facts - the book has to be factual, well-researched, you know, well-articulated."

"Okay."

"What would you place the time of your reign as - the century?"

Pere's eyes which glazed with enviable pride now were fixed on the floor in thought. She pouted with a vague recollection of an untrained historian's mind.

"I'm afraid I can't be as exact as you expect, but it's likely about fourteen centuries ago - the tradition has endured to date though," she said, refocusing her gaze on Netu.

"I'm aware the Nibi Kingdom florished long before the invasion by the offsprings from our sister continents. That much I know," Netu said. "But this Natum factor in the notoriety of that prosperous and chivalrous kingdom is certainly new knowledge. Not history's fault, I must admit. I think I hadn't delved real deep into the root of that epoch before."

Pere made no comment.

"Where do we wheel to next?"

"Uhmn," Pere murmured. "Wheel on to Mars."

"Mars?" Netu asked in wonderment.

"Sure, Mars."

"Ah, yes, I remember, the Martian war! Let's hear it from the lady. I heard you talk about it some time ago. I'd be glad if you'd tell me everything you know about Mars."

Pere leaned forward on the conference table in the quiet press gallery. Her thick lips parted in a valiant smile, intimidating in spite of its pleasant need.

"I'm a Martian incarnate," she said without inhibitions, "and as a matter of fact, the lady commander of their fleet of warships."

An admiring, but quizzical look spanned Netu's face. "You don't mean...?"

"A woman can be the commander of a planet's fleet?" responded Pere.

Nodding Netu said, "I was imagining the thrill of it. Isn't it rather too wanton for a...?"

"Now, see who is sounding so out of tune," Pere cackled in her sleek leering way. Her ambience was momentary. She became a mask of seriousness the next moment. "As I realized not long ago, that is how it was. In Mars, I'm not the passive girl you know here. I'm mean, ruthless, astute and, a damn good commander of the Martian forces."

"Come on, Pere! You are the limit."

"For being frank? Cut the humor Netu."

They laughed, argued, joked and cheered again about the might of a planet commanded by a woman of great candor, foresight, and will of steel. Pere it seemed had an edge over Netu's apparent male chauvinism.

"I wait for the next anchor," cued Netu.

"Atlantis!" Pere proffered.

Netu flinched. Atlantis. The name bore a sharp needlepoint through his memory, routing flickers of distant guilt. At the same time he perceived sensations overwhelming the instinct of guilt in him rooted in the mysteries of Atlantis.

He saw in this suggested excursion of Pere a great chance to unravel his remarkable place in the history of

Atlantis. He had a rather faint glimpse of that dispensation as the Tonka Manu whose rage ended it all. But he knew little or nothing about the antecedents that provoked his rage. He wanted to unravel the varied participants on Atlantis' stage and who they were in the Brotherhood of Father Manu or in present incarnations. If Pere was willing to disclose her role in the end of Atlantis, then he was willing too to draw up a pattern from her tale. He would add her facts to what he knew and construct a permanent link between the denizens of Atlantis now incarnated as residents in the Brotherhood.

"Atlantis?" he gasped.

"Why, you look surprised?" Pere quizzed, perceptive of his eagerness. "I can tell when you are excited. What's Atlantis to you?"

"Atlantis means many things to many people, I'm not an exception. You are the one on focus, remember? For the purpose of your curiosity, take this hint. I was a denizen of the civilization and, I've discovered I played a unique role in it. But let's leave it at that till we are through with the missing pieces of your part."

"Shy, not so? I suppose you expect me to tell you all I know about Atlantis, so why hold back what you know from me?"

"Cue me in later."

"No. Let me hear you spill now, even a little of it will be a great spur," replied Pere.

"Ever stubborn, won't take no for an answer," Netu joked. "All right, I had something to do with the end times of the Atlantis civilization. That's all I know."

"I can't figure a damn thing out of the smokescreen you've pulled on so smartly."

"Your role in Atlantis, Pere."

"Evasive son of a gun!" Pere said, laughing. "I guess you won't budge." She paused for effect. "I'd say I was responsible for the demise of Atlantis," she resumed, her countenance and tone reflecting a modicum of remorse. "I'm confused as to why I was picked for the sordid role, but it was my fault Tonka blew up the civilization the way he did," she trailed-off.

Netu adjusted his sitting position, inclining now on the conference table. A feeling of conquest welled on the inside of him. His vision of Pere glared as fate's reluctant porter molding the myths surrounding the yet known facets of Atlantis into a singular picture of reality. Self-unconsciously, she had begun to posit a link between herself and the other denizens still unravelled in the tragic drama of that great epoch. He wondered what level of shock she would have if he told her he was Tonka Manu. He allowed her to reveal more and take him to the shores of his past.

"I'm listening," he urged, staring raptly. "How did you cause the Manu to blow up Atlantis?"

Pere hesitated, trying to recollect vague outlines of bitter times, impulsive actions and reactions.

"What I did," she said with deep emotion, brushing the polished top of the long conference table with a forefinger, "could be likened to what Miss Gehu did to Father Manu some time ago at Danabi City. I'm sure you heard about Miss Gehu's antics?"

"Right, I heard the sad story," said Netu. He had heard of Miss Beauty Gehu's vexed notion of defiance in Father Manu's office during a session of reprimand witnessed by numerous residents and non-residents at the Brotherhood's headquarters. Accused of an unholy plot in the Brotherhood along with few others, Miss Gehu - he heard - had tried to redeem her image by employing strange aggression. Like a wounded bull, she had torn her blouse to pieces and an inconsequential fraction of her skirt in the process. Half-naked before stunned Brotherhood members, she had wept pleading her innocence. In the act an unprecedented taboo had been committed. Later as the rumor went, Father Manu pardoned Miss Gehu because she sent a team of elders to assuage his anger.

"It's absurd to find one such state of confusion and with vengeance on mind, but there are times in life you just want to prove your innocence in some inexplicable ways. I doubt what my intent really was but when the allegations refused to abate from all sides, I felt I had to kick back where it hurts most. Enraged beyond measure I tore my clothes before Tonka and the other Atlanteans in the reception lounge of his spatial mansion - weird sort of dementia you'd say. This you would agree was a sacrilege of grave consequence. I did not realize the wrath I had incurred for the entire civilization at the time. When I got home, many strange occurrences - natural phenomena though they were - began to take place on an alarming scale beginning with a violent hurricane. Well, I never thought I had anything to do with the havoc or the hurricane or the danger signals in the bleak sky. As a result, I was least prepared for the shock that came towards dusk."

Pere Mejeli paused and looked at Netu Deo with pained calm, like an animal denied of skin, slowly recovering from an agonizing bruise in the softest corner of the heart, at lost for words or sound.

"It must have been harrowing," Netu prompted.

She shrugged off the agony of recall and came alive again. "Harrowing is understating the facts, Netu. It was hell! The way this whole damn past was revealed to me - I see it all so clearly even as I talk with you - my three children and I, two vibrant boys and a beautiful girl, were in an aerophibian, driving towards another section of Songhai the capital city of Atlantis to visit a close friend. There was calm in the hitherto thunderous, murderous sky and the beautiful neighborhood was peaceful as we approached my friend's house. We went through routine check at the gate and drove into the vast grounds of the property anticipating happy moments ahead. But by a certain quirk of our predestination, an unseen time bomb of wholesome terror was unleashed on us at the nick of time. In hindsight, I see it all as the most bizarre of fate ever to grace any era of human existence because it tampered with life itself." Pere paused on a forlorn note.

A look of shock and excitement knitted Netu's facial muscles as he stared intensely. "In my mind's eye I see a highly dangerous scenario before me," Netu nudged.

"Cataclysmic havoc," Pere boomed in response. "Atlantis quaked, belched and sank like scenes from an awful nightmare and we were flung apart, forward and backward, on the hard driveway. After several quakes that seemed to sink Atlantis, we jumped out of the Hansa - the aerophibian car - as advised by our guests who were at the porch of the mansion, but nothing worked in our favor from that point onward. Next we heard a strident rumbling in the near horizon, just beyond the easternmost hedge of the vast yard. When we looked at the source of the frightenig rumble, we knew death was near."

"What made the frightening rumble?" Netu asked, sensing the ghoulish nature of what Pere hinted at.

"A huge tower of cascading wave, which splashed and threw us apart. Separated from my three children, the huge wave swallowed us, and soon enfeebled our maneuvres aimed at safety. We couldn't even swim to in subsequent splashes. We were just minor specks in the colossal destruction that became the lot of Songhai, and I believe the entire Atlantis.

"I can still hear the shrill cry of my children - before they were drowned. I can also see the struggle and agony of a weary mother who had lost not just her three lovely children but on the verge of losing her own life under the roaring current of titanic waves. The fear engraved on my mind and face as I sank at that moment was chilling."

Pere shrivelled from the images of her momentary conjuration. "Netu, it was gory. I tell you this. And I admit that at that point when I recognized the ghost of my dear life as death knocked, my sacrilege before Tonka Manu came to haunt me. It was the final blow that led me into the beyond. I suppose Atlantis met its end in that manner."

Netu observed her put on a smile now as if unaffected in the least way by the dreary picture she had called forth on her own easel.

Netu drew a heavy breath and stirred, stupefied. He did not pretend he understood the irony of their present dispositions viewed rationally in the context of their parallel interests in Atlantis. He came short of appreciating why fate had tricked him to hobnob now with Pere, someone he would rather see as an adversary in his other incarnation. Why he felt emboldened in the ongoing act as a spy prying into Pere's guided past he could not really say. In spite of it, he took fate's unusual zest with its ironical twists as he had always taken the many intrigues of his life.

"Oh, boy!" he gasped at last. "It seems quite a halo of dread! The swiftness of the waves as you recounted must have crippled any attempts at escape. It was the mother of all surprises for Atlanteans."

"No one escaped the onslaught. The splendor went down with the waves," Pere said. "Can we now get to your own roles in Atlantis?"

Pere's eyes sparkled with sentimental interest. She had often used this with great effect to soften him. "The key to my past is right in your hands. Let's even up scores a bit. Would you now open the door to your past for me?" she cajoled, grinning.

Their eyes locked for a brief spell. Netu's pan stare gave way to a discerning smile, and then he laughed. Her eagerness to discover his past bewildered him. But she seemed to be in order.

"I was a denizen of Atlantis too," Netu said.

"But," Pere interrupted, "what was your role?"

"I have no answer to that question right away without due consultation elsewhere."

"Meaning?"

"I'll get back to you some other time with what I know. I need to validate the piecemeal information I have of my past role in Atlantis. I don't want it to be a fruitless conjecture."

"How are you going to do that?"

"I'll have to ask Father Manu about it and see what he'll come up with," Netu said.

Pere puffed, disappointed by Netu's refusal to talk in-depth about his role in Atlantis, believing he did not trust her enough to disclose his secrets. Nonetheless, she had no regrets sharing hers with him. She reckoned he would one day walk out of the thin smokescreen he had put on to confide in her. She could put a bet on that.

"I give up the chase," she said. "Whenever the validations are over, you can trust me to keep your secrets."

"Settled."

"Yes, settled."

At the end of the rendezvous with Pere, Netu felt twice as wise as when it began. After reviewing the turbulence of the past and the intrigues of the moment, his resolution found onward strength. He would walk on the path of life with all the wariness it deserved.

Now, shelving the sad memory of Atlantis, they walked side by side in the early night as he observed the scenes of Vidya Valley.

He broke the lingering silence. "You have any idea how long you'd be staying here, Pere?"

"No," she said, glad he spoke at last. "No one knows these things. A week or two perhaps. It depends on how long we take to make you see reason."

"You don't give up do you?" Netu laughed and went on, "It means we still have time to see each other before your party zooms off in another direction."

Pere grimaced happily. "We'll be waiting hopefully for you - the sooner the better."

At the western apex of the up-flung, bow-shaped street, Pere signified her intention to retreat. "I better get back before they start screaming kidnap or blue murder," she bantered.

"Right. You've done a wonderful job with your sweet company, Pere. What would you have me bring along for you when next I call?"

"I'll leave that to your discretion."

"Alright. I'll think of something nice and portable."

"Stay out of trouble, remain cool!" Pere advised and stomped down the steep hill whistling like a happy child.

"That goes for you too!" Netu called after her. He watched Pere swagger down the slope till her figure blended perfectly with the invading darkness of night, and then he turned and cracked one of those lingering smiles of his and walked off toward Ashi Park.

The next moment, another component of his life that drew his attention daily, magnified in his inner eye

- Lina Phillip Uwa. He would have to inform her of the Brotherhood's plans to bring him back. A trusted goblin in times of trouble, he needed her now more than ever before.

Chapter Twelve

Save for the five people who stood in solemn ritual taking in the consistency of the night's illusion on the water surface and the gentle toss of the glimmering yacht in moor, the shoreline was empty.

Also, save for the recurrent lapping of low surf and the resounding hiss of salt sprays on the shoreline that thrilled these adventurers on the private jetty which extended toward the endless mist of sea at the tip of the beach ridden Landai peninsula, it could have passed as an eternal monument created in nature's most tranquil and exotic setting. They watched the full moon depart unhurriedly, donating soft petals of its ambience on successive rolling surf with poetry of wondrous motion.

On the sandy shore, the shimmering points of the moon's reflections on it or on the jetty's embankments, danced back to the troughs of subsequent surf. These were re-flung in an enchanting bob and flare. And the array of stars above, aiding the tingling illusion, made the surface of sea a marvellous constellar dance in the eyes of the crew.

"Friends, we're getting on board the yacht. We're hitting the low tide, a non-stop sail," said one of the men, rubbing his two hands to keep warm. His thick raincoat and gloves could not insulate him from the stirring cold wind and its bite. He pulled on his face cap and clambered down the ramp to the yacht's stern.

"I'm on your heels, Netu!" a lady called out, dragging a traveling bag on the jetty's platform toward the yacht. "The wind is murderously cold but it's not a deterrent to our mission. If we set sail now, we'll make it before dawn."

"Need any help with the bag, Lina?" Netu called back.

"No, thanks. I can manage. Just get on with the yacht's lights and get the engine going. We shouldn't be procrastinating."

"Are the others ready?"

"They are right behind me," Lina said.

"We've got to hasten up getting on board. We're sailing behind time," Netu said, disappearing into the yacht's lounge. "The wind is just right for our sail. We won't encounter much high tide before dawn. By then we are safely berthed at our destination."

Three others, two men and a prim lady joined Netu and Lina in the yacht's luxurious lounge. Netu climbed back to the jetty to undo the mooring chains while the others scurried in search of packing space for their light gear.

The next moment Netu Deo heaved himself to a seat in the captain's cabin. He engaged the engine and the yacht roared to life as Lina Uwa joined him, clinging on to her raincoat.

"Netu, I'll be at the stern, you handle the rest."

"Why stay at the stern when we can both steer her from here?"

"I want to hold the forte while you do the steering."

"No, you're staying right here with me, Lina!"

"Don't argue it, Netu. You can steer the yacht whichever way you want and be confident all will go well with my psychic support."

"Your proposition is high fallutin. I suppose you know what you're doing?"

"Fear not - there's absolute control."

"In that case you have a blip caller by your side so we can keep a tab on each other. There's the lounge on the top deck if you need to ease off tension. And enjoy the wind slap and whistle past you by the swimming pool."

"I won't need all that at the moment. I just want to hold the forte for you, honey. Now, gun the damn engine!" Lina said and made for the stern, picking up the blip caller.

"Good luck at your venture, Lina!"

"Good luck, Netu!"

The custom made luxurious yacht eased out of the jetty and garnered up steam in the opposite direction, toward the realm of endless mist, a scar of broiling water and counter surf trailing on both sides of its wake.

Poised at the stern, Lina Phillip Uwa watched the receding glitzy panorama of the waterfront and Landai as a whole. Their mansion by the upper fringe of the jetty seemed in the fast motion of the yacht to have an embellished grandeur. The various neon fittings in and around the grounds under the glare of the moon and stars were like a confluence of briliant laser rays producing astounding illusions. The waterfront was even a lovelier illusion. In her mind, however, there were other priorities.

The other members of the team walked up to her side on the stern's railings and made her turn cursorily.

"We intend to lounge by the pool up there," pointed the youngest of the men - a brash, queer character of a man.

Lina thought she recognized a devious gleam in his pale eyes even with the hazy lighting at the stern.

"I'm content here," she said, devoid of warmth.

"Say you want to be out here alone?" demanded the other lady, climbing up the upper deck with animal vitality. "Hey, why don't you come up with us? Four is more than company you know," she added glancing at Lina on the stairs.

"I like it here," argued Lina. Their patronizing gestures offended her somewhat. An unexplained loathing for the trio took over her senses. She knew intuitively they were a bag of trouble. Or perhaps, it was the product of her warped imagination.

The second hefty man nodded with indifference and hastened after the others. Lina spied them with spiteful curiosity and riveted her attention to her self-assigned task of keeping vigil at the stern.

Far into their sail, far across the sea, numerous ships and yachts sailing toward Landai came so close to their line of compass. The fear of collision with the other yachts was palpable in the hearts of the five adventurers.

Netu, as captain, showed his mastery of the sea and the controls of the yacht. He veered to a new compass point each time a collision with an oncoming yacht seemed inevitable. Yet if not for Lina's reliable holding of the psychic forte and her strong advice to remain on course each time he panicked, he would not have had the nerves to pull through. She stood at the stern like an unmovable rock, inspiring Netu with sweet words through the howling windy.

The moment of anxiety went after they crossed the sea. Now they were cruising smoothly in a canal. The dawn sky had commenced its usher of warmth and brilliance. Though the sun was yet to rise in full, a warmer burst of wind replaced the earlier chill of the night around the mangrove lined swampy bank of the canal. It also had a sweet whining appeal in their ears.

Netu noticed Lina enter the captain's cabin. Her face appeared ashen-gray with hate or anger or despair. He just could not say which.

"Are you alright?" Netu demanded, worried by her sour state. She nodded an answer but he was not satisfied with the response. "I'm not so sure you're okay, Lina."

"I want these fellows to alight somewhere nearby, Netu," she replied taciturnly.

"Alight? What do you mean?"

"Let your friends on the top deck get off at the nearest

harbor. This is vital."

"Why propose such a crazy thing?"

"Just let them disembark I say. Don't be heady," Lina warned.

"But why," grumbled Netu. Her bags of tricks were inexhaustible and often helped in harnessing his roughened ride, but this obtuse decision was not one of her usual tricks. It left him as numbed as a dead mind.

Lina gestured to a distant outline of a harbor along the canal through the cabin glass.

"Look, over there. Less than two leagues ahead, there's a harbor on the right. Let them alight there, then we can proceed with our journey." She ignored his astonished, gaping pose. "Make sure you do as I say." She left him at that moment.

"What excuse would I give for such an impulsive action?" he shouted in anger. "It's foolhardy."

Lina did not respond. She went back to the stern. Fortunately the others had eavesdropped on their rather loud exchange so it became quite easy on Netu's part to convey the sad message at the harbor. They were ready to disembark even before he had the courage to tell them.

"You don't need to say any thing. We are disembarking at the harbor. We heard her orders and we'll comply to save you the torment of passing on the message. We know it's not your wish," the prim lady said on behalf of the two men.

Titan Race

Netu Deo pulled in the yacht at the harbour unhappy about the developmen. Their three companions carted their gears and left the yacht without rancor. After their exit, Netu tried to engage the yacht out of harbor but the engine remained as dead as a rock. None of the control mechanisms responded to his touch.

Stuck at the strange harbor, the canal's currents, treacherous to their aspirations, swirled the yacht off anchor and steered her toward midstream. Netu tried within his powers to fix the fault, if any, but he found none.

Lina's indifference at the moment of trial confounded his rage. He could not understand why the engine had to give up at that point, and why Lina felt so indifferent. He sat pounding angrily at the combinations on the ignition board as if by such fury he could get at the fault and rekindle the spirit of his obvious imbecility.

His tensed gestures no less indicted Lina as the cause of the malfunction of the yacht's engine. The accursed idea of sending their comrades packing at the harbor was hers. Look where that decision landed them both, he cursed between breaths. And the heck, she did not even care about their predicament - as indifferent as she was by the stern.

He remembered the cabin had its own blip caller and reached for it, but found it equally dead like the engine. This rendered his idea of calling for assistance from the harbor a waste of time. In the alternative, he thought the blip caller with Lina would serve the purpose. Therefore, he scampered out of the captain's cabin in search of her at the stern.

No trace of Lina at the stern either. Surprise glared in his eyes. He ran up the stairs to the top deck but the same windy emptiness welcomed him. His pulsing veins now bordered on panic. Where had she gone?

Netu hurtled back to the bedroom on the deck below and found it empty as well. His intestines began to knot. In his spine tinkled the eerie chill of deep fear. The luxurious yacht, the harbor and even the brightening horizon of the canal, assumed a spooky tint. Were they doomed? Had he been lured to a voodoo land where he had been trapped witlessly?

"Lina. Liiinnnaaa!" he cried out, but the swift wind swept off his voice's resonance as ineffectually as his strive to maintain calm, or start the dead engine.

He climbed down to the captain's cabin, worried. It dawned on him a trap door had shut so against him and nothing aside his will would get him out of trouble.

He began another check on the controls, this time a lot more calmer. He knew without doubt he would win. He had always won his battles in the past.

The dream reel reached its terminal at that juncture. Netu woke from slumber perspiring, nestled in the warm arms of Lina Phillip Uwa still sound asleep on her small bed. He noticed his face close to hers on the pillow and could smell the strong odor of their profuse lovemaking hours earlier pervading the air of the room.

He extricated himself from her embrace and sat up in bed, apprehensive. What a dream, he mused. He regarded Lina in the dim light of the clustered room appraising how benign she looked in sleep. This contrasted sharply with the iron lady of his dream whose uncompromising whims he had appeased like a goddess, and to his detriment.

Denied of a sudden of Netu's bodily warmth and comfort, Lina stirred, still dreamy, clasping him back to her bosom.

"Where do you think you're running to now? It's not yet dawn," she yawned, snuggling into his outspread arms.

"I'm not running away, Lina. Had a dream, that's all. Now go back to sleep," he said, laying his head back on the pillow.

"Tell me all about it later, ehn?" she whispered and drifted off to sleep.

"Sure," Netu mumbled as Lina resumed her faint snoring.

Netu could not sleep for a length of time. He rummaged unend through his mind for answers to his dream. The dream had an ominous quality. It bellied any superficial interpretation he could give it. He could easily deduce from the delicate ending of their cruise in the yacht the dream's ominous quality. Without a shred of doubt, a stark revelation of Lina's near future role in the wondrous cruise of his ship of destiny. This he believed for the facts were clear. She had pledged to hold the forte for him while he fought at strange frontiers. This she did without blemish through their sail across the sea. But in the canal, she had acted differently with her insistence on sending the other members of the team home at the first harbor in sight. And his assent to her demand resulted in the engine's malfunction, which lulled and almost killed the spirit of the sail. This duplicity of purpose puzzled him about Lina.

Why Lina insisted he should stop at the harbour and discharge their comrades with the impassiveness one would accord only a drift log, he could never fathom. Were they vermin of some kind out for his flesh, whose pretence he was dumb enough not to see? Who exactly were they? What meaning would he ascribe to Lina's motive? He stared restlessly without focus. He gave the dream due analysis until he exhausted all angles to the metaphor and respite came in sleep.

When they woke two hours later, Lina reminded him of his promise during the night. "What sort of dream did you say you had in the night?"

"We'll talk about it later," Netu placated needing time to think it over.

"If that's what you want, I'll wait," she replied.

Ensconced on Lina's bed after breakfast, Netu reminisced on the delicate aspects of the dream.

"Certain aspects of the dream I can understand but not why you said the others should disembark. It's absurd," Netu said, wanting to understand Lina's motive through the discourse.

"No, it wasn't absurd," Lina retorted.

"I don't get it."

"How could it be absurd? If those fellows were not meant to hop off at the harbor, I wouldn't have insisted the least."

"And how did you know they were bound for that strange harbor?"

"I only gave my interpretation based on your revelation. It is clearly suggested by the tone of the instruction I gave you in the yacht - they were not part of the otherwise smooth sail towards a treasure-laden terrain. That's my guess."

"But that's the sad part. The instruction you gave seemed our bane, for the yacht's engine stopped functioning with the exit of the others."

Lina smiled wanly, she disliked Netu's insinuation. "So you think I was responsible for the yacht's treachery?" she asked, snorting. "Rubbish! You did say I repeated several times 'our way is free!' Does that sound like mischief to you? I'm of the opinion you wanted to fix it all alone. Probably self-conceit had a hand in the crisis."

"I don't buy that crap," snapped Netu. "Even if self-conceit had anything to do with it as you rationalize, I should think you're as guilty as I am. When I needed you most at the forte you were nowhere to be found – you simply vanished into nothingness. Isn't that the gravest portrait of self-conceit?"

"Boiling so hot over what is crystal clear? Don't you have the eyes to see what those fellows stood for? I say this emphatically, their leaving was an advantage we had."

Netu's puff was strident and mocking. He considered Lina, annoyed that she kept buck passing the blame to him.

"Haven't I warned you enough in the past about your associations? Have you forgotten of the revelation in

393

which two fierce ladies came after you to my residence to reclaim something you took from them, and one of them said she wants promotion by sacrificing your neck?"

Netu nodded affirmatively. "You did."

"Didn't I warn you of a certain devious black lady who came to dump your battered, bleeding body by my door and hurried to fetch some hooligans to complete the blood game she'd started? Did you also not remember how in the revelation I had to carry you to a spiritual haven around Ashi Park? And how we prayed and your broken bones and ribs mended miraculously and the black lady and her collaborators ran away for fear of our reprimand? You also remember, I suppose, the revelation about the white envelope? I presume some lump sum of money, given to you by someone to aid you financially and which you in turn gave out under hynopsis to the black lady? When I questioned you about it, you told me nothing like that ever took place. All these and more perhaps represent the fellows I drove from the yacht, so stop casting blames on me."

"Don't consider this a spree for aspersions, Lina. I only said what I said the way I understood it, so don't fume," Netu said. "I gave all your warnings the utmost importance they deserved. Needless to say I'm still inspired by their meanings. You may have your tantrums and weaknesses like normal human beings do, which is commonplace. But I'm yet to disprove as senseless your judgment on fundamental issues of life. Your analytical, discerning mind is not given to frivolous excuses and bland resignation. I've been amazed at the rate at which some of your revelations have come to pass, which makes it even more inspiring for me to keep listening to your advice."

"Skip the rhetoric, my dear. You've said enough as it is. Flowery language won't get you anywhere except you see the danger in an unwary step and take decisive actions to avert it. As for the yacht and all that, I see the decision at the harbor a necessity. That brings us back to the present. How do you intend to spend the day?"

Lina's charms were in display again, and Netu sensed his heart yielding.

"I won't be going out early," she urged with cryptic uundertone, winking.

Nothing so unsettled Netu as Lina's self-assuredness, much like an incandescent sun that never sets, ever inspired by its relevant streak in the abyss of human groping. And a man's greatest hurdle, it occurred to him, lay in the uncontrollable huffing of the heart, especially when its sweet tinkle comes from a woman's subtle charms and self-assuredness. As he regarded Lina, he felt a longing in his heart. If she reared as the hurdle he had to cross, he might as well do it with the finesse it required.

"How about a kiss?" Netu cajoled. "That's how I want to start the day."

"You're not getting any," Lina replied with cheer.

"I'm going for it anyhow."

"Do not touch me. Don't you dare."

Netu stood up sprightly, reached out to her and lifted her beaming face to his. "Of course, I'm not going to touch you! I'm just a doctor out to feel your heart pulse," he joked. "Now let's see what it is like."

Their lips met, soft and warm, hers parting in haste to take his tongue and the next moment they reciprocated each other's caresses.

As Netu pulled Lina up and swirled her to the bed, she realized he occupied a space in her heart as the only man in the world she could not resist. The feelings she had for him went beyond lust; she adored him crazily. And he seemed to recognize the power she had vested on him in the way he domineered over her emotion. Lina knew her own desire and ambition enslaved her to Netu as her wise master. And she was proud nonetheless being a slave to no other person than Netu Deo, the Manu in the making.

Part Four

BLACKHOLE

PAST

Chapter Thirteen

Disk Center, Blackhole. 2023.

When Numa entered the Wisdom Hall from the aisle, all Guardians in the Blackhole meeting rose and bowed their heads in reverence of their patron. Their magnificent wings – huge and diaphanous feather-like structures – complemented their immaculate attires. The beautiful Hall still looked impressive after innumerable eons of Blackhole's existence. Evident too was the usual draft of gas on the floor. It embellished the ethereal qualities of the Guardians in its illusion against the array of light.

An air of urgency pervaded the tranquil atmosphere of the Wisdom Hall. It registered with the Guardians as the last meeting in the series of experiments they may undergo before new Atlantis and its breed of humans reached the envisioned point of stability.

Numa, Blackhole's enigma, had addressed this same crop of Guardians some twenty-five thousand calendars ago in Atlantis. The focus of the meeting had been the degenerate culture of the human stock, which rolled irrevocably towards the brink of collapse eliciting the Guardians' line of intervention. They had worked in concert with the Manu in Atlantis, installing as it were a new dispensation of grafted intelligence in new Atlantis. Intellectual resource from some of the PlayToy's sister planets were pooled to this effect.

The new human experiment had grown from that point. Its roots steeped in wisdom and intellectual prowess. Out of the civilization came many distinct fruits and heavy burdens too. And in all of its phases of nurture, throughout the infantile stages up to its spawning glory, vast human civilizations florished and formed the bedrock of other civilizations. And in all the gloried heights of various civilizations and their eventual end, there had always been at the helm of each epoch, the essential function of a presiding Manu.

Many Manus, therefore, featured in the unstable motion of the human experiment. And Numa had seen the beauteous rhythms of the good mixed with the insidious thunder of the bad on new Atlantis with the kind of resignation typical of Blackhole's patron.

Numa stood now without the aid of his golden scepter before the Guardians in the Wisdom Hall. He admitted the Guardians had done much to enhance human creativity and inclination toward the positive expression of own will in the last twenty-five thousand Atlantis' calendars. He also reckoned out of the innumerable eons of existence of the PlayToy, the free reins nature of the human will itself had, no sooner than the divine statutes were laid, gone to stretch the volition on the negative. The Guardians were back as a result to the drawing table they had left long ago with the aim of cleansing their PlayToy.

"Well, Guardians, I welcome you to this meeting. It has become vital from time to time for the sustained existence of the cosmic system," Numa began with some steam after croaking clear his vocal chords. "Please, take your seats."

The Guardians bowed and sat back on their seats.

"It's over twenty-five thousand calendars since we had a major gathering of this kind," Numa went on, "and our preoccupation then was to help midwife the efforts of Finia in closing the chapter of Atlantis on a tidy note. Thereafter, we threw our weight behind the experiment of cross-breeding of the human stock and beings from neighboring planets in that solar system. The same Finia was given the mandate to pioneer the experiment. The results from the new Atlantis as experimented were indeed in order from the initial phase. Several splendors were delivered of the inscrutable womb of new Atlantis. Several Guardians were prepared by us too to take up the mantle of power after Finia to engender our programming down there - in new Atlantis.

"But with the advent of new splendors and new leadership and perceptions, the intellectual capacity which allows for rational action began its perverse incursion into the statutes of the divine put in place at the beginning. What we witnessed was recurrent anti-climax in every climax of civilization. The most worrisome of all the blunders of the period in review is the near futility of a cross-section of Guardians sent to reinstate Blackhole's statutes in the various civilizations that thrived at one time or the other.

"Some of the Guardians sold out lustily to the seductive instincts of the women of new Atlantis. Some were only too lucky not to be trapped by the insidious influence of materialism. This group became complacent and numb to our promptings. We had another set of strict and disciplined Manus in Atlantis that carried out Blackhole's mandate, at least, to a great degree. This group, I'm glad to say, scored above average where others failed."

Numa paused. His handsome face furrowed. He toyed with his grey stubble, softly plodding through gas clouds on the floor towards the tip of the crescent of Guardians on the left. He paced in deep thought around Guardian Sujes' seat at the tip of the row of seats.

"All of us have gone to new Atlantis in different bodies to test run our plan - from Sujes here to Hemmas there," he reminisced, pointing across the row of seats. "Individually we've all done our best. We've given everything we have to empower humans and their understanding of their nature. But as we look back and focus on the prevalent chaos on new Atlantis, we are surely haunted by the sad aspects of our experiment." Sighing he added, "Fellow Guardians, we are yet to adorn the coveted crown of accomplishment. In spite of all we've done, the situation of new Atlantis is even more precarious than before."

Numa plodded back to his seat at the center. "Twenty-five thousand calendars in relation to Atlantis' is quite a long time for humans. For us, it is just a moment," he continued. "The damage that has befallen our playhouse is much within that length of time. The events soon to pass on new Atlantis will even rock us harder than the past. There's complete reliance on the intellectual capacity on the part of humans, and they are conquering the material planes as fast as we intended. We consider this Blackhole's ache. The human surely will prevail if we don't pre-empt what we clearly see as eminent danger without checks and balances. The point is we must start a new design for our broiling playhouse."

Another brief moment of silence. Numa balanced his pinto golden cap on his head. The fiery glaze of his eyeballs curried an unflinching intensity. "Perhaps, the time screens will explain it much better."

Numa's thoughts aligned with the blurry screens above the Command Module console and they came alive with vivid images.

The splendor referred to by the new Atlanteans as the Piscean Age glared now on the main screen. The Guardians observed the flickering scenes with great attention. They reckoned with it as the original fragment carved out of new Atlantis at the time of their last major redesign of the PlayToy during Tonka's tenure. They saw marvelous architectural designs. Gems of divinity had spread their roots in all facets of the epoch through the teachings of the Manu of the era. This glared in the actions and interactions of the human stock and in the structures that panned out on the time screen.

The screen blurred again for a moment and then lightened up to reveal two other distinct blocks inhabited on the continent. The level of maturity of its humanity seemed greater here than in new Atlantis. A blend of the intellectual and spiritual occasioned by the presence of the extraterrestrials from the sister PlayToys referred to as planets by humans was perceptible to the Guardians.

"As you can see," Numa went on, "the first splendor that came after the deluge replaced Tonka Manu's new Atlantis. There was a challenge to that cradle though. The continental blocs with the extraterrestrials were in psychic contact with the new Atlanteans. The next civilization came as an offshoot of the first and it was the anchor point of several Manus after the cradle lost its divine mandate. We witnessed the florish of our third human experiment, indeed the entire gamut of human experiments leading to the modern experience.

"In the calculations of the human calendar, we are in the year 2023, which count began presumably after the purported death of one of us here, Guardian Sujes, whom they've said so many false things about. Going by their calendar we've got barely two hundred and twenty three calendars years before the year 2023 - our projected commencement date - for the next round of total cleansing of our stables, the human family and related strands. Two hundred twenty three calendars on that globe may take generations of humans to experience in full. But looking ahead of time as we've done, the future scenario of our Playhouse is as nauseating as the events of Tonka's Atlantis. I'm a bit mild in my assessment of new Atlantis' future as it shows in time's distant bubble.

"Life on our PlayToy has degenerated beyond what we can tolerate. We might call the various influences on that Playhouse a deadly shaft of hatred, anger, jealousy, deception, covetousness, inhumanity and every damnable vice thinkable. This shaft is boring straight unimpeded into the heart of new Atlantis, gurgling and desecrating its once unblemished values. The future of the PlayToy is doomed unless..." Numa trailed-off, worried as he sat on his seat.

"Of course, we are going to be swift in our intervention," he continued, "but we can't wait till the last hour. We are adopting a bandwagon mentality this time. We will checkmate their silly caprices step after step, gambit after gambit. A massive invasion of our PlayToy's terrain by Guardian decoys it would be. We will bring our plan to climax in absolute secrecy; then comes our last laugh. We will clean the slate of new Atlantis once and for all and usher in a super psychic human race, which will be called the TITAN RACE."

Isolated murmurs of agreement amongst the Guardians greeted Numa's pronouncement. In haste to elucidate on his proposition and the choice of name for the new human race, Numa rose and walked towards the screen at the backdrop. He waved his right hand in an arc and the Wisdom Hall began to spin, as if falling into a warp.

A thick mist enveloped the Guardians in their giddy downward fall. The descent through time's void continued for some swirls. When it stopped at last, the mist had gone, and they were now giants in the palace of the Vral in an ancient civilization in one of their PlayToys.

"Now watch the drama of the past," Numa said through their thought-waves. "We're back in Lemuria! Six million calendars ago."

# # #

Zyla edged close to the golden throne of the Wise One in the heart of the palace. His beady blue eyes questioned the Vral.

The Vral observed the gangling boy of seven seasons with amusement. "Son, you're bored. You need some action," he communicated in thought-form.

Zyla nodded. "Yes."

"Sit by my side for a moment. A life changing adventure awaits you, little god of Lemuria."

Zyla sat on the seat next to the throne as bidden. He threw a shrewd gaze. "Vral, did you say little god of Lemuria?"

"We are all gods. Capable of many things."

"What are we capable of?"

"You'll soon find out."

Zyla noticed the Vral's dark blue eyes dart from one corner of the courtyard to the other. His huge built of almost eight phantoms and dazzling robe on the mountain-like throne amazed the young man. A tall Lemurian himself, Zyla thought the Vral cut an extraordinary portrait with his height and mystique.

"Summon the stone-wings," the Vral said to his chief counselor watching the scene at the edge of the steps to the throne.

"As it pleases the Wise One," replied the chief counselor, departing towards the outer sections of the courtyard.

"To what purpose do we owe this breath?" Zyla's

thoughts broke into Vral's with the departure of the chief counselor. "We appear so blessed and gifted. It must be towards an end."

The Vral fixed his gaze on his son of near six phantoms. Zyla's curiosity reminded him of so many things he'd like to explain to the fast growing boy. "Nothing happens by chance," he said. "We're not a cosmic ruse either."

"What's that?"

"We're not a game of chance, that's what."

"So?"

"Come with me, little god of Lemuria. Time to sate your quest." The Vral rose with agility from the throne.

"To where?" Zyla demanded, trepidation choking his voice.

"We're exploring Lemuria. To find purpose to your existence."

Zyla scurried after the Vral. They made a detour to the open space beyond the courtyard with the palace courtiers trailing behind.

"Go back to your duties," the Vral ordered the courtiers. "Zyla and I want to be alone for a moment."

The Vral looked towards his right and saw the stone-wings berthed at the entrance of the palace.

"It's ready for use," the chief counselor said, noticing the Vral's approval.

"Good," the Wise One said. "We're boarding right away."

Zyla gaped at the giant boulder his father referred to as the "stone-wings." His young mind played tricks with him, but he kept silent.

The Vral swooshed his right hand and graduated steps appeared at a corner of the stone-wings. He walked up the boulder to the top. "Come on, Zyla," he called after his awe-struck son. "This is one of the magic of the age."

"What's it for?" Zyla asked, climbing up the steps, following the example of the Vral. Once on top of the boulder next to his father, he sat and looked down in awe. "What next?"

"Patience, young man," cautioned the Wise One. "Patience."

The stone-wings began to buzz on its own accord, and the next minute it lifted off the ground and sped skywards with semblance of wings at its sides, almost unsettling Zyla who had not ridden on such a device before.

"Woohoo!" Zyla gasped. "This is scary."

"Easy," the Vral said, glancing sideways at Zyla. "Brace yourself." The wind swept across their faces with its cadences as they flew higher and higher until the entire horizon came into view.

"How do you direct this stone?"

"Your mind. Everything is subject to the mind's control."

"How?" Zyla did not grasp his father's allusions.

The stone-wings continued to soar, seamless, with their robes flailing in the gentle wind.

"The stone-wings is an extension of light. And what bigger light is there than man?"

"Light. Lemurian god. Too many concepts, Vral," argued Zyla.

The wise One gave a shrill laugh. "This is the reason I want you to take this flight on the stone-wings. Have first-hand knowledge of the immense powers at your disposal as a Titan."

Zyla cast his gaze into the far horizon. He saw several stone-wings cover the skyline like a flock of birds. He swung his hand in glee in their direction.

"Vral, look over there, stone-wings," he exclaimed.

"Those things don't exist in the true sense of it. We conjure them each time we have need for them."

"You confuse me," Zyla remonstrated in the whistling wind.

"We create our circumstances as we choose." The Vral sat now on the boulder looking over the fields and sprawling splendor below.

"Tell me more."

"Soon."

The stone-wings began to detour. The Vral swiped his hand and a fog parted like a veil before the flying duo. Zyla could make out giant beings going about their everyday businesses beyond the parted fog.

"These are the Titans," the Vral said. "Giant beings that once walked these terrains. They were genies of some sort. The Guardians' idea of masquerading amid human consciousness. . ."

"The Guardians?"

"Yes, the Guardians?"

"Who are they?"

"We are, little god of Lemuria! You're a Guardian."

"I'm a Guardian?"

"We all are."

"What does a Guardian do?"

The Vral grinned. "A Guardian is a higher being assigned with the task of taking care of one form of human existence or the other. Like the one we just left. A god in human form."

"That's it? Nothing else?"

"There's more to it. We're here to express the gift of life. Be in tune with the Light. Retrace our steps back to the Source."

"I see."

"No, you don't. You're a god! Nothing is impossible before a god."

Zyla's nod was more out of stupefaction rather than an assent to the Vral's line of reasoning.

The stone-wings now touched down on a field populated with a horde of giants. Zyla had never seen this band of humans before. He could hear their thoughts as if they emanated from the depths of his heart.

"I can hear them speak. Their future opens up like

flower petals or microfilms before my eyes," he quipped with an air of fascination.

"It's part of the adventure I wanted you to experience," his father said. "We don't need to speak to hear each other. It's inherent in us. And we can travel too by any means. Now you know why I said we're gods?"

The Wise One outstretched a hand and a large blackbird flew down and perched on his palm. "Go tell the clan, the Vral is coming," he said to the bird, which squawked and flew away to deliver the message.

"You speak with birds too?" queried Zyla stunned by what he had seen.

"We're wired to speak with all creatures. They are condensations of Light just as we're Light too. We only need to tune into their frequency to understand them."

Stepping down the stone-wings, the Vral strode leisurely on a moist bed of grass toward the community in sight. He beckoned on Zyla to follow suit.

At the edge of the field, the Vral touched a blade of grass and spoke to it in his heart. "May I know your significance to our existence?"

Zyla stopped in his track, confused about the Vral's theatrics without the grass.

The sharp edged grass wheezed and then a small, still voice echoed in the Vral's heart. "I'm a healer. Use me for the treatment of ailments."

The words filtered into Zyla's stream of thought. "So plants talk too?" he asked, astonished.

The Vral ignored him and focused intently at the spire of grass. "What sort of ailment do you cure?"

"The kind that numbs the heart."

"Wow! Medicine for the heart," Zyla bellowed.

"Shhhh, be quiet," the Vral said with a finger across his lips. Turning to the grass, he asked, "How do we apply you?"

"My fluid is sufficient."

Enthralled, the Vral probed further. "That's it?"

"Sure."

"What else can you offer our kind?"

A raucous laughter from the grass rent the Vral's heart. "The gods always want it all. But I'll tell you. Magic!"

"How?"

"Speak to me in your hands. Make a wish and see it happen."

Nodding his head, the Vral plucked the blade of grass and placed it on his left palm.

"Easy, man. That hurts," the grass lamented, squirming.

"Sorry about that, friend," the Vral apologized. "Never meant to hurt you, but I was eager to test your potency."

"Go ahead then."

"Take me to the pristine beginning of things."

"That's a tall order. Doable though. Hold your son's left hand with your right hand."

The Vral did as bidden.

"Repeat these words after me," the grass said. "I'm an energy form, free and boundless, pulsing through creation. Let my essence unfold like it was in the beginning, for I desire unity of purpose."

The Vral's feet tingled as he recited, "I'm an energy form, free and boundless, pulsing through creation. Let my essence unfold like it was in the beginning, for I desire unity of purpose."

Zyla and the Wise One could feel an instant tremor course their bodies as an energy field swirled around them, lifting the mist in the green field, and with it, the duo's souls into a portal in the hazel sky.

The portal parted the space between Lemuria and the outer worlds. Zyla and the Wise One hurtled through it, still holding hands, gazing upon the infinity of stars, feeling ligher and lighter in their ascent, shedding their ethereal bodies one at a time.

The longer their upward drift lasted, the more they lost touch with the consciousness of Lemuria and its load of problems or worries. The more bodies of ether they shed, like freight trains dislodging their cargoes at various terminals, the more they became conscious of the hollowness of their existence, which was nothing but condensations of Light.

Zyla became aware for the first time that the magnificent blue sky held other secrets other than its awe or vastness. It was not all about clouds or stars or rotating planetary bodies, it certainly led to the Source, the beginning of life itself in its pristine state. He realized their bodies were gone, yet their consciousness remained in another dimension as specks of Light.

As they reeled further into the unknown, Zyla heard the voice of the Wise One saying, "Man's sojourn to Lemuria and many other Playhouses from the Source was as a speck of Light from the Blackhole. Now, we are back there, swimming in the ocean of Light?"

Bewildered, Zyla tried to appraise the Vral's words, but noticed instead a swift shift of consciousness.

They were back in Lemuria with their bodies intact in the field where the stone-wings had landed moments ago.

#

"Those were the Titans," Numa said, still standing at the palace of the Vral. "We had to shrink the height of those men and women to appreciable sizes in subsequent epochs because of the apparent disadvantages of size in furtherance of our goals in later splendors."

Numa snapped his fingers and a whirring ascent began. In a few swirls, the Guardians were back in the Wisdom Hall, Blackhole. The screen at the Hall's backdrop brightened up with full slides of pristine beings, hulky but human in every way.

"The Titans," Numa said. "Great beings they were. We want to construct the next millennium of uninterrupted harmony, bliss and enhanced psychic and creative intelligence on the planet along Titanic lines. Not in size though, but in their psychic abilities. The TITAN

Titan Race

RACE billed for year 2023 and beyond will be non-compare. Guardians are going to inhabit the PlayToy in transmigrated bodies to teach the humans how to love and why peaceful co-existence is imperative. The Blackhole will have its replica on new Atlantis for as long as a thousand calendars, and then we will hands-off and watch human affairs as we have always done. So we came here to talk about the TITAN RACE and the moves that demand urgent attention before we enter the super-psychic age proper.

Part Five

NEWLAND, RIAGENA

MODERN DAY

Chapter Fourteen

At the sight of her kitchen bound mother, Anne Ofino bustled out of the half-shut ladies' room where she had been peeping. She gave a slight twirl and then posed like a model on the walkway in front of her mother, in the kitchen.

"How do I look, Mama?" Anne inquired, flaunting the result of a meticulous dress routine she had just done.

"Honey, you look like Remwill District's Cinderella in that dress!" responded Mrs Rewa Ofino. "And what's my little girl doing dancing in that exotic dress this morning?"

"Visiting someone."

"Who?"

"You already know him."

"That Netu of yours?"

"Yes, of course."

Mrs Ofino regarded her ravishing daughter with a clinical mind, shifting the quaint bundle in her hand to the left.

Anne wore a lace bustier dress of re-embroidered floral, complemented with a double organza coat, flowered at the neck with a large bow. The ensemble made her look like a princess, who had just stepped out of the pages of a fairy-tale. The dress accentuated her lithe physique and gave an emphasis on her provocative curves. Her hair, which was neatly combed to the back, had few strands of hair bobbed in front and swished close to her right eye. Anne's brown eyes sparked of innocence in spite of the inflections of the dress. Mrs Ofino thought she had never seen her twenty-five-year old daughter look so young and tempting.

Mrs Ofino's brow arched. "You really must be dancing fast. Netu is all I hear every day around here."

Anne spurred to the remark. "There is song in my heart that has overwhelmed my thoughts."

"Don't tell me you are in love, honey."

"Well, I'm not sure what love means. But I do know that I feel something stirring within me."

Mrs Ofino considered her daughter's words for a couple of seconds. "Love is like a rare bird. You can try to tame it and analyze its complexity. But this bird could be elusive, disappointing, with strings of nightmares to its credit."

"You've always told me that."

"Come here, my daughter." Mrs Rewa Ofino drew Anne to herself. She placed a tender hand on her shoulder and asked in a whisper, "Does he also feel for you as much as you feel for him?"

Anne blushed. "You mean Netu? I suppose he does."

"You are not sure, yet he has written a symphony on your heart?"

"I have no doubts concerning Netu's love for me. But the issue of the baby with Mike-"

"What now, honey?"

"Mama, I'm just so damn scared of losing him," Anne confessed. She diverted her gaze, hoping that her mother would not see the anxiety evident in her eyes.

"The feelings that Netu and I have are real. Still, I fear that something may sever this bond between us."

"No, honey. You must put these negative thoughts out of your mind," Mrs Ofino said, tightening her grip around her daughter's shoulder. "I have no doubts that his feelings for you are true. Never allow fear to guide your emotions. As your mother, my advice is, always learn to have a clear head in your dealings with men. If you expect too much from this relationship, then you are bound to be disappointed. Every man has got his weakness, these you can exploit for good or for bad. And always learn to be on the good side of things. So let your dance be slow and steady, honey. Now don't let me stop you from going to see him. Your happiness is what counts. Go my sweet little girl!"

"Mama, I don't have the words to express my gratitude. You always understand my thoughts."

Anne knew her mother as a mercurial character who was soft and hard depending on the mood. But at almost forty-five, Anne felt her mother looked much younger after giving birth to seven children. She still had a stunning physique with an angelic face. A paragon of beauty she could not match.

"What are mothers for?" Mrs Ofino intoned with motherly pride, interrupting Anne's flight of mind.

"Thank you all the same!"

"Oh, don't mention, Anne," Mrs Ofino said, and began to reminisce. "It may be hard to believe but I was in your shoes, once. I know what it's like to feel one's heartstrings struck for the first time as a young lady. The way you feel for Netu is how I felt about your father. You're bound to have sleepless nights because your thoughts revolve around the man harping upon the strings of your heart."

Mrs Ofino retrieved her hand from Anne's shoulder. Steering Anne by the waist, she gazed into Anne's eyes.

"I was overwhelmed by such passion when your dad asked me to marry him. I accepted wholeheartedly. Though there were other admirers, your father's care and understanding was unmatched. Those other men were pretenders."

Mrs. Ofino sighed, as a shadow of grief crossed her face.

Anne could see the moisture welling up behind her mother's eyes.

"I will never understand why God took him away from me so soon."

"I feel for you, Mama. I know how it hurts to lose someone so dear," Anne said with great sympathy. "We all miss him."

Sensing that her mood was putting a damper on the situation, Mrs. Ofino's lips curled into a weary smile.

"It's all right, honey. You should go have some fun. I've come to terms with you fathers death. Your happiness is my priority and if I must find solace, let it be through the profound joy that Netu has brought into your life." Mrs Ofino motioned to the baked goods that lay on the table. "You can carry some fried milk cakes for Netu. I think he may need them. Off you go now. And don't stay too long," Mrs Ofino said, focusing on her kitchen chores.

For a brief spell, Anne regarded her mother affectionately. She thought about motherhood and wondered if she could ever emulate her mother's kind of care and replicate same with her own children.

Anne's energy often went in other insignificant directions. She either dotted around Netu Deo in faraway OldHill or searched for a job or a party to attend. Her mind was always on the move. Even when she found time to be at home and there were no social distractions as such, she would endure her son's whimper and pestering not more than a few hours. Her mother always came to the rescue.

Anne often dreaded the possibility of handling her own family affairs after marriage without her mother's assistance. As a single parent, she could handle a lot of things knowing her mother was always there, a dependable pillar. But all that would change once she got married. Would she be courageous enough to scale that hill with the required patience and finesse?

The idea of marriage appealed the least to Anne despite the insistence of Mike, her son's father, and her parents. She never loved Mike beyond his money's worth anyway. What happened between them, she considered a mistake - a damn trick of circumstance, which resulted in the birth of a son. Never would she allow a repeat of their episode of heady adventure for it would amount to a willing endorsement of own slavery.

She had been a resident in the Brotherhood of Father Manu for four years. During this period, a chronic cancer was healed of her. Anne often referred to the illness and subsequent healing as the reason for her long stay in the Brotherhood. Before her final conversion into the spiritual movement, she had met Netu Deo at a Brotherhood seminar in Gunu City in eastern Riagena.

The opportunity to chat with him at the seminar did not avail itself due to the regimented lifestyle of residents in the Brotherhood. But Anne saw in Netu Deo everything she desired in a man – a quiet disposition, gentle, approachable, charming, tall, light-complexioned, plus a sweet and soft-spoken voice. One look at the glaze of his sexy eyes and neat dentition as he smiled and talked with great humility with the other officials of the seminar, made her rupture pleasantly.

She could infer he was in a position of authority in the Brotherhood judging by the manner he conducted things within the scope of the seminar. She knew at once she would love to love him without reservation. Although it was their first encounter, he seemed an old friend straight out of different time setting and space.

As fate would have it, when she later became an adherent of the Brotherhood and opted to be a resident, she could not renege from a predetermined course. They fell in love almost at once as if they were only rekindling an old flame long smoldering. But their love had its peculiar constraints. Sensual relationships were forbidden by Brotherhood regulations. Love, by whatever definition, could only be expressed outside the ambit of sex for all residents. So she had taken it easy, nursing hope that the future would unite them in an unrestrained, permissive environment.

Things happened rather fast to her detriment and she found herself out of the Brotherhood in four years without Netu around to cushion the effects. In the interim, she had searched for a reliable shoulder to lean on at moments of anguish and hopelessness. Still ensconced in the Brotherhood, Netu was so sheltered from reality to know or feel the financial and emotional pains she went through daily.

She remembered Mike came into her life at this point just after her stint with the Brotherhood. Mike's shoulders seemed comforting at the time for he paid most of the bills that accrued in her renewed bid to continue her education at the tertiary level. Like a patient angel Mike reared whenever she needed him. Her mother and the other members of the family encouraged the affair because it was convenient for their needs, but Anne knew her heart belonged to Netu. It ached for him and him alone.

In the second year after her exit from the Brotherhood, news of Netu's exit reached her. She could not believe her luck. She thought of flying through the sky to experience his tender arms in whatever probable nook and cranny he hid himself. Yet she owed Mike an emotional debt for his efforts at rescuing her out of financial constraints. In

425

spite of it, she could not resist the temptation to fantasize about her and Netu.

She succeeded in contacting him by chance through the assistance of a close friend of his. Her heart leaped with rare joy when she realized he was as curious about her whereabouts as she was about his. Their love flowered from the re-union and with strong wings, capered over diverse emotion fields.

Mike's financial assistance in her life increased, especially when she discovered she was pregnant with his child despite all the precautions she had taken. This threatened her romance with Netu. Afraid she would lose Netu as a result, Anne had told him the bitter truth about her pregnancy. Netu did not flare at her as she had thought. Rather calm and understanding, he had said he would not stop loving her even with the baby from another man. She was swept off her feet by this unselfish clinging of Netu to the gift of love.

A year of inaction reared in their romance while she weaned her baby - partly due to the demands of the newly born child and partly due to the prominence of Mike in her life as the proud father of her son. Netu, however, kept to his words and accepted her situation as love's inexplicable test and continued with the relationship with as much verve against advice. Mike and Anne began to drift apart, but it did not stop her chances of gaining favor from him at dire times. That favor Mike would not deny the mother of his son. And Anne had the better of two worlds with the sneaky arrangement.

In Mike's dutiful magnanimity, which she called the prize for lust, she had financial solace. In Netu she knew genuine love and spiritual power. She needed both influences to keep her sanity in the turbulence of the world. She strove to maintain both at the expense of Netu and Mike's welling passions. Only in respect of Netu the barbed idea of marriage was ever acknowledged as worthwhile. And portraits of her as Netu's wife commanded her wistful revelries. Anything, anyone who stood in the way of her ambition meant something which invoked the monster in her to crush with all the strength and venom she could muster.

Now, Anne became restless with longing knowing she had missed Netu's warm cuddles and lusty stares for almost a week. She wanted so much to hold and touch him all over again, feel Netu's tender lips tickle her nipples and his soft hands dart over the undulations of her supple body evoking dream-like pleasures.

Smiling over her recollections of how she became entangled with Netu in a web of love, Anne swaddled after her mother to the dining table to fetch the milk cakes she would take along to Netu's place. And she had put on the bustier dress with the double organza coat to impress him. He often disliked heavy make-up so she had applied faint mascara, lipstick, face illuminator and sweet perfume to stir his romantic sense. She figured he would be pleased with her enchanting poise.

The other members of the rather large Ofino family were chatting in the boy's room. It made it easier for her to sneak out of the house. Their guffawing remarks often spoilt her romantic dreams. She deemed it safer to avoid them than cede to their incessant jokes which painted her as a double-timing faggot incapable of holding her own in love's swift currents. Netu's place in her heart, of course, had her family's approval, but her relentless resort to Mike for financial aid worried them despite its convenience. Toying with the emotions of her two lovers' at the same time felt out of place with her family members. There had to be a clear limit in everything, and her family reckoned she had exceeded hers.

Anne did not think so. To win in any game, the element of smartness was as important as the element of luck. She managed her double-timing well in being smart. And in being lucky, she had men she could easily manipulate. A simple story with a simple ending - she saw her chances and exploited them to the fullest.

Anne Ofino left the house in a hurry to the bus park. Saturdays in Remwill District - the sprawling suburb on a patch of land bordering Newland's harbor on the southern end - seemed to Anne a mild echo of the hustle and bustle of weekdays as she walked. Even so early as eight o'clock in the morning crowds had begun to mill around the interwoven, dirt ridden streets. Unlike most weekdays the streets were filled with people, petit traders and food vendors who called out to pedestrians and commuters on top of their voices to sell their goods, the throng of men and women on the streets this day looked a lot more urbane in regal wears and patient strides. A rare sight in an environment such as this with dense population, Anne thought. Most of the houses were derelict or cramped up in the style of unplanned cemeteries, devoid of the luxury of playgrounds and marvelous lawns.

Puddles, murky alleys and oozing sewage pipes, pungent dirt and gutters were routine spectacles for residents of Remwill District. Anne had seen these scenes most of her life. But in this core of filth, a paradox about Remwill District amazed her. Anne could only place its contradictions within the context that it exemplified a lotus flower which beauty and fragrance comes from the murk of human society. A lotus flower would never be seen in the choicest of places, always its roots are found firmed onto the dirtiest of lands or ponds or lakes. Its magnificence or beauty almost always sprouts through the specter of that filth. To her, Remwill District symbolized this contradiction.

It surprised her somewhat that in these derelict houses of Remwill District, stars had been born. On the puddle and dirt ridden streets, little children had played their little games and frolicked through the squalid conditions of their birth to stardom in and outside Newland in several fields of life. So many geniuses of Riagena had been born in this suburb and in a variety of ways it had stunned the human intellect as a highly improbable breeding nest for achievers in society.

Anne thought perhaps the harshness of the very conditions the people were born into toughened and drove them to overcome the sociological impediments they confronted daily going by their successes. She took this bearing from her own harsh childhood. She conceded if she and her siblings could face the odds so well with all the enormous problems they had had to surmount growing up in a family of ten with her dad as the sole bread winner, then it was possible for others to excel where the burdens were lesser or the zeal to survive stronger.

Anne pondered over this while meandering through the throng of pedestrians on the street and made it to

Remwill District's second major motor park half a mile down 9 Hope Street where her family lived. She took a cab from there to Diosh Park.

She also pondered while in the cab about the intimacy between her and Netu. He occupied her mind as the epitome of all she never had in other men: compassionate, benevolent, brave and loyal. Anne likened Netu's knack for revealing the soft-center of his robust heart to the compulsiveness or earnestness of a religious convert. And he had his undeniable constituency in the broad plains of love. His impassioned spirit to selflessly give of his own time, money and energy often to cushion her plight and those of others around him left her gasping every moment spent with him about his intense personality, which had no parallel in the whole of her love life.

I have never loved any other man as much as I love Netu, she thought. But here is the flux of ironies in which I swim. I'm at a crossroad with the rearing conflict. How could two opposite seeds of reality, given life in the strange mercies of one womb, be so engaged in a brutal conflict of existence? How practicable is it for me to feel love and loyalty and in the same vein seek vengeance? I must be going out of my mind. No, it is the clique that has a warped mentality. They want me to destroy my lone source of peace and joy. I won't. To hell with them!

Anne's thoughts ran wild. How inexplicable and upsetting could her unwitting endorsement of the clique's manifesto be? How did she get herself enlisted into this cult of renegades and their brazen schemes? In hindsight, her enlistment came close to twenty-five thousand years. Atlantis had been the grim stage of the clique's unholy game, and the Locci put in place the weird props.

How senseless the motive of the Locci's sad script of brutal drama? Anne cursed. Frustrated in no small measure, working in perpetual shadow of the Manu, a minority of Atlanteans had met with the desire to overthrow the Manu. Members of the Locci, conscripted in secret, were drawn according to their ambition and love for rebellion. The less willing and daring candidates were coerced through mysterious circumstances. But the Manu nipped their ego in-flight.

An unwilling candidate at first, Anne's leverage in the Locci came via her flair for rebellion. This was good enough reason for her to be coerced and initiated into the Locci with fanfare. The rites of initiation took a more spiritual than physical dimension. Anne did not regret her wild engagement for obvious reasons. Her budding desire for intrigue was one, and the enormous diabolic grip the Locci had on the system through clandestine manipulations was the other. The Locci became the sweet answer to her inner crave. She embraced it without reservations.

The Locci's nemesis, however, came in the person of Tonka Manu – their sworn adversary. The Locci and entire Atlantis vanished in a deluge caused by the rage of Tonka thereafter.

The memory of the end of the Locci and the entire gamut of Atlantis would still linger thousands of years later in the minds of former Atlanteans. And the likes of Anne Ofino would reconvene and re-hoist the Locci's flag, vowing to avenge the misdeed of Tonka Manu by tracking down any Manu that walked the surface of the PlayToy.

Anne shuddered in the cab. A paralysing kind of fear gnawed at her sense of calm. Her nervous gaze swept across the far side of the expressway, staring without seeing.

Damn the clique, she reflected in silent outrage. Why are they doing this to me? Why are they trying to deny me love in its unblemished form? Must they always purvey my future on a dreary platter? Why did they at all allow me to reckon with the sweet pulse of the heart? Now I'm stuck with cupid's own son, and to revoke my feeling is nigh impossible. Yet I must swing by the immutable laws of the clique. How do I deliver their prize without endangering my heart and turning it into shards? No. I will not destroy Netu as ordered for the fact that I love him. I'll protect him instead for he has taught me to love. The very reason I promised to treat him as my son, brother, friend, and lover. Damn the clique! Damn the consequence!

With this resolution, Anne felt a sensation of dare, and saw only the bright images of tomorrow's dawn, one she would experience with Netu. A cool, self-comforting grin now smothered her melancholic posturing. Her glistening eyes riveted from the watch of the road's far side and focused ahead with a hint of determination and foreshadowed joy. The cab approached Diosh Park. In matter of minutes she would be in Netu's arms; the only place that meant something to her.

Chapter Fifteen

Anne Ofino walked into the living room of the three-bedroom apartment Netu Deo shared with Lata and John in OldHill an hour and half later, grinning like a bride waiting for her groom's kiss.

Netu's excitement over her elegance overshadowed his jokes about her choice of skimpy designer wears cut to flaunt her sexuality. Torn between pleasant surprise and the knowledge she had done this probably in his honour, Netu squelched a sweet whistling sound wide-eyed as she flung herself at him on the couch with hands outspread like a soaring eagle.

"This dress must have cost someone a fortune," he said breathlessly, balancing their combined weight on the couch.

"You like it?" she gasped, her hands forming a tender loop around his neck, her body pressing against his.

"Marvellous!" he cried, disengaging his hold on her waistline, studying her.

Anne's face brightened with indescribable joy. She held his face with both hands, gazed into his enchanting eyes and kissed him, smearing his lips with her red lip gloss.

After she let go, Anne sat next to him, huffing and glowering. She rolled out a neat Kleenex from her handbag and wiped away the red lip gloss on Netu's lips she had transferred via her kiss.

"I'm sorry about the lip gloss," Anne said. "I was too excited to take notice."

"Never mind," Netu replied, entranced by the round, fleshy highlights of the bustier dress on her chest. "How did you get this?"

"What?"

"This flamboyant dress."

"How did I get it?" Anne growled in mock displeasure. "I bought it for sure!"

Netu laughed in comical abandonment. "I never said you stole it. Probably robbed someone to get it. Ehn?"

"I robbed you perhaps to get it," she bantered, and then an instinctive reckoning with reality. "Where are your friends, Lata and John?"

"Gone to buy some food stuff from the market at the crest of OldHill."

"Oh, that reminds me - I brought some milk cakes along. Mama had extra for the week and obliged me some. She said you might need them."

"What a sweet mother! She was right, you know. I sure do need them. How's she – your mother I mean?"

"She's fine."

"And your siblings?"

"They're fine too."

"And my pretty baby here is fine as well I suppose?"

Anne giggled. "You bet I am!" She briskly pulled out a bundle of toasted milk cakes from her handbag, her mother's gift for Netu, and raised it for his appraisal. "Your milk cakes," she announced. "Want them right away or later?"

Anne rose and thrust the foil bundle into Netu's hands. "Hold this for me while I get a bowl from the kitchen." She paced few steps away from him and then halted, sensing she could still induce some humor out of the situation.

A shrewd smile lighted Anne's face. "And Netu, keep your itchy fingers off the milk cakes till I get back with the bowl. Did you hear that?"

"Cross my heart," Netu said with dramatic effect, but grumbled afterwards, "Why the veto? I thought you said your mother sent the milk cakes to me to eat? How come you dictate to me on what to do with what's rightly mine?"

"You're wrong sweetheart. If I didn't sanction you, there'll be no leftovers for me – you'd swallow everything in a second. See?" she joked and swaddled off.

Her veto did little to put Netu's appetite in check. When she reappeared, he had already munched a piece of the milk cakes.

"Didn't I say you shouldn't meddle with those milk cakes?" Anne began to laugh. "You heady mule!"

"Well, in case you're not aware, there's mutiny in the house. Sanctions no longer work anymore. You're out of government – sacked in a new coup," Netu mocked between mouthfuls of the milk cakes. "How about crossing over to my party? You know you never win on the other side of government."

Anne stood with the ceramic plate in hand and regarded Netu. She saw a cryptic possibility in Netu's remark, which gave it the quality of a joke with deeper meaning. Though wary she also felt a kind of rare amusement.

These ever flickering sparks of their bonding, the work of chemistry so hard to understand, enslaved her in the beautiful labyrinths of passion. And it was foolhardy for her to imagine she would ever have enough of Netu - his time, care and love.

"I decamp," she declared, whisking the unwrapped foil bundle from him and emptying the content on the plate. "But don't imagine I won't have my veto back someday. Governments are transient experiences, aren't they?"

"That'll be the day," Netu challenged airily.

Prior to Anne's visit, Netu had engaged himself in a grand reconstruction of the isolated events of distant times in which he had been a participant leading to the schemes of the historic present. As the information trickled in from different quarters, limited still by the facts yet known, he had seen recurring parterns and had begun to collapse the vast time denominators into a component of meaningful history.

His reconstruction, almost filled with facts, was now

replete regarding his roles. Two essential bits were still missing in the history of his past. These tiny bits were Anne and Lina. Who were they in the treacherous games of Atlantis? And whom do they represent in the on-going reality?

The facts had emerged from his reconstruction: he was Tonka Manu in Atlantis. In the words of Pere Mejeli, she acted the part of the unfortunate Atlantean whose sacrilege led to the end of Atlantis and flung its huge landmass to its sad place at the bottom of the Deemen Sea. Implied somewhat in Pa Smand's eulogies, even in Netu's own personal experiences, or in Father Manu's nudging, and the random ranting of numerous residents of the Brotherhood, his aura towered as the next in the line of Manus after the incumbent.

And by the strength of his calculations, if all the key participants in Atlantis twenty-five thousand years ago were now part of the new humanity in Riagena and marching on with Father Manu as he had noticed, Anne Ofino and Lina Phillip Uwa were as entwined with the past as they were with the present. Yet he was only aware of their past and present roles in his life in a vague sense.

A voice screamed on the inside of him, reckoning with their guile and pretensions. He would not compromise a half-picture of history. He would strive to complete history's emerging picture or nothing at all. And Anne would provide the clue he needed.

Just as the moon began to illuminate the hideous shadows of OldHill's alleys in the cool evening and its orange light cast its essence on the tapestry of tenement buildings and quaint high-rise facilities, Anne and Netu retired to his bedroom from the living room.

Sprawled on his bed, fussing in his mind the best way to unravel the mystery, Netu soon dozed off.

Anne sat next to him, her back inclined on the wall in yogi lotus, reading a paperback. The lingering silence perhaps caused Anne to stir, showing concern. She stared at his slumbering face and noticed a part frozen smile. She thought he might have been smiling for her before he drifted off in sleep. Her own dreams assailed her happy mood as she looked at him with affection in her eyes. Then she continued with her reading, banishing the effect of the dreams on her thought impulses.

He gasped awake about fifteen minutes later and spoke as if in deep stupor. "Wow! What a dream this was!" he intoned, eyes half open.

Anne lowered her paperback and peered with a hint of apprehension at him. "Speaking in your dreams again, ehn?"

"I'm quite awake," he said, yawning. "I wasn't speaking in any dream. I spoke after the dream."

"Oh." Anne felt reassured. She dropped the paperback on the bed and asked, "Was it an interesting dream?"

"It's interesting," Netu affirmed, nodding. He rolled to his right side and used his right palm as pillar for his raised head. He reckoned with the glint in her eyes, curious instead of being apprehensive. "It's quite unique, stands out as one of the best dreams I've had in recent times."

Anne's eyes glowed with anticipation. "Yes?"

Netu told her some aspects of the dream he had a moment earlier but not the real issues at stake in his chat with Father Manu.

The main slant of the dream he said was more of a routine camaraderie between two Manus - the younger one playing a prominent role in the enthronement of the older one who in turn was to prepare the grounds for the repeat performance of the younger one.

"I think I deserve to be congratulated," Netu bragged after his story.

"It's incredible. A rare one absolutely," Anne acquiesced. "But don't blow your trumpet asking for accolades."

"What makes you say that?" Netu said, stunned by her evasive non-reckoning of the obvious.

"The stuff you just mentioned - your part in the plot and humanity's destiny - are stale news for those who know."

"Do you know?"

Anne got up from the bed feeling unduly intimidated. Once her feet touched the floor she gave him a taunting, derisive glance. "Who doesn't know who you are, Netu?"

"I....I....I'm at sea, Anne," he stammered. "You're getting me confused." Vistas of distant past replayed in his mind's eye, reconciling all the hints about Atlantis.

Anne said with a contemptuous disposition, "You must be given to the belief that you are sacrosanct in this Manu business, don't you? Let's face it Netu, this soul saving venture wasn't exclusively an affair of the Manus, there were other participants at the backstage."

"And I suppose you are bent on reasserting your place in the dispensation in question?"

Netu's bland self-effacing took Anne to the edge of exasperation. She sat back on the bed by his feet with derision in her eyes.

"I was there in the era before Father Manu's just as you were there. Well, you were the Manu, but don't forget I was even closer to you then than I am now."

"Hmnnn, I don't contend that."

"It wasn't our first meeting either."

"I'm confused over your assertion."

Bewildered by Netu's lack of knowledge of their other incarnation in spite of several hints she had given him prior, she knelt down on the bed slack-jawed, disbelieving.

"Do I infer that you don't know much about the other times we've met in this great journey of life? If you admit this, then I'll be really stunned thinking you're the next in the line of Manus."

"Sometimes I have nothing but hints. I come to absolute conclusions only when I act on those hints."

"Then let's see how your hints work out. Tell me wise one just who I was in the dispensation before Father Manu's?"

"My wife," Netu said in a shy tone. "And we had four kids."

"Hey, you got that right!" Anne echoed, renting the

quiet night with an artful laugh. "But I dare say you wouldn't know about the other three incarnations."

"No, I don't recall any," he admitted frankly. "If I'm to proffer a guess, I'll say Atlantis. I was the Manu then, you know."

Anne snorted and pushed him out of her way in mock contempt. She climbed back to bed and snuggled beside him.

"Don't always talk of Atlantis as you would talk of your bedroom schemes," she said, staring into his eyes like a mischievous brat. "You weren't the only one there mark you. As a matter of fact, our little scheming, you and I, started then and it has gone four incarnations so far."

Netu pulled himself to his haunches, happy that his probe into the past was almost over with this revelation. The components of his reconstruction were almost complete.

"Tell me sweet little one about the three other incarnations!" he cajoled.

"Did I set a fly free under your pant?" Anne asked. "Why the sudden interest about the past? No, I'm not telling."

"I know you will," Netu said, cuddling her prostrate form.

"Alright, alright, I'll tell you but in a nutshell. It's a long story. But I'll make it snappy."

"Whichever way you want to tell it, I'm ready."

Anne evaded Netu's probing stare and rolled onto her

back, fixing her gaze on the lifeless expanse of the ceiling boards. She reached into the vaults of time, prodding, recalling and reanimating events long buried.

"It all began in Atlantis," she said with a nostalgic tremor in her voice. "We were supposed to be the active participants in Tonka Manu's ship of divinity. That includes all Atlanteans besides Tonka. And we lived our lives that way for a long time. But attitudes are prone to change when people experience the rigorous daily processes of living coupled with all forms of ego trips. It would be proper to admit that it was these weird ego trips, which Atlanteans embraced that engendered the kind of spiritual balance prevalent then.

"Different spiritual groups, with their secret modes of operation, started to work against the divine process. Their aim was to have some degree of credibility and to have the right to power brokering. The Locci to which I belonged was the most notorious of these subversive groups. The group itself wasn't new in the era. It had survived the era of Manu Waadua and Tonka Manu inherited it so to say.

"But we never had as much peace as we had in Waadua's period. Tonka saw the antecedents of our actions and worked against our schemes. And as you know by now, you as Tonka ended that era in a violent fashion and everybody went down with it. Whether there were survivors is one thing I don't really know. Maybe you ought to tell me what it was like then," she smiled, prevaricating. "But as far as I know, none survived the terror and reign of lofty water over Atlantis. All the stalking, and all the ongoing schemes, rose out of the anger and loathing of that unfortunate end. The Locciens and the other groups, though washed off Atlantis, vowed in their varied levels of hibernation to hunt the Manus reincarnated from Atlantis and stifle their growth as painfully as our loss in Atlantis.

"I was among those pardoned after the deluge, and you and I met again in different bodies." She trailed off warily.

The glimmer of excitement flickered out of Anne's eyes as a sordid scene loomed in her mind's eye.

"I came into your life in a particular incarcantion and we got married. But the hatred in me for your role in Atlantis was a sensation that consumed me with one notion - vengeance," she went on.

Guilt spasms ran through Anne, jolting her away from her evasive upward gaze. She gazed forlornly at Netu. "I died in that incarnation because I wanted to hurt you so much – it boomeranged."

Shocked glared in Netu's dark brown eyes. "You did what?" he demanded in a stammer.

"I died because I was a grudging soul whereas you were all loving and caring."

"Sad, isn't it?"

"Really sad."

"How did you recognize me even in that encounter when I wasn't the Manu?"

Anne gave a throaty laugh. "You like cracking silly jokes at serious moments, Netu. I recognized you then the way I recognize you now. You brokers of divine power always manifest along with signs we can easily see and acknowledge. Your stars dazzle the sky each night we look up to the heavens. What we do next is to trace where the manifestation of the stars are. Simple."

"Is that how you traced me?"

"I'm not obliged to answer the question."

"Well, that was the initial incarnation in which you said you died. What happened in the second encounter?"

"I avenged my death in the first incarnation," Anne laughed chivalrously.

"How was that?" Netu, ill-at-ease with Anne's revelation, deduced in those few words of hers the rationale for their third and fourth meeting. Vengeance.

"We met the second time and it looked real good between us. We hit it off on an inspiring note, but another woman lured you away from me. You succumbed to her whims and married her. So, both of you had to pay for your perfidy."

"Perfidy?"

"Yes. You strung my heart and threw it to the hounds. So the lady who masterminded that callous action of yours and yourself had to go."

"Where?"

"Both of you went to blazes."

"We died you mean?"

"Died - like death."

"Oh, my God! You had the heart, the audacity to do

that to me? To someone you said you loved?" Anger took over Netu's presence of mind.

"It was provocation," Anne argued. "I had no choice - it just happened as a matter of natural consequence."

Netu distrusted her lame, unconvincing argument. The fragile wings of his longing heart were employed of a sudden in a swift intuitive caper away from an emergent ogress in the field of his vision. Anne Ofino.

Fear lept into the core of Netu's heart and shaded the brilliance of his eyes with a dismal tint. "And the third incarnation witnessed a truce?" he prodded earnestly, wanting a reason not to feel intimidated by Anne's pronouncements.

"Something close to that."

"Nothing bizarre presumably?"

"We were happily married in spite of side flings you had every so often. You always returned to me a penitent lover."

"So what is it going to be like this time?" It was the vital puzzle he wanted resolved. Whether it was true he died in another incarnation due to a woman's anger did not worry him as much as the issue of her ongoing games.

"We have each other, not so?"

"Yes, but in what capacity? As an adversary or a lover?"

"Your cynicism is appalling, Netu. Don't you ever think of anything else?"

"Our trail has been strewn with your own vengeful emotions yet you point fingers at..."

"Netu, stop," she cautioned impatiently, cutting short his wind of aspersions. "Being damn vindictive isn't the issue here. The feelings we share now would determine the next trail of events. Period!"

"Just supposing this relationship hits the rocks - you can't ignore that factor in any relationship - what would be your reaction? Won't you attempt to pick up your old hatchet of vengeance and attempt to complete the age long ritual of the Locci?"

Anne frowned, rage upwelling within her. "Don't insult my intelligence," she snapped. "My religion is love, and I'm vowed to it. I pay for love with love and..."

"And for hatred with hatred?"

"Anyone's guess. I don't have a choice than to attack if, and only if, I'm offended. Remember - only if I'm offended. But don't get lily-livered because of my frankness. I'm not thinking of hurting you or anyone, not someone as dear as you anyway."

In truth Netu disbelieved her. He had learned over the years never to trust anyone no matter their intentions towards him. Though Lina Phillip Uwa's hints bordering on Anne had been proven in Anne's theory of vengeance, he knew Lina was not without her own schemes.

Now, he plunged back deep into the oceans of memory. Beyond good intentions, Lina and Anne flickered on his mind's screen as products of the Locci. Without any haze of vision, he could see the Locci assembly now as he had seen in his trance flight before his exit from the Brotherhood at Danabi City.

He could recall seeing a crowd of men and women sitting under an expansive canopy in a splendor that defied his comprehension. Someone addressed the large crowd, and the person was himself. As the incensed orator, the brave and boisterous nature of his speech mellowed the crowd:

"I know you all – every one of you here," he recalled asserting to the crowd. "When I came as Tonka Manu, all of you here were there trying hard to ensnare me. Now you are back in this dispensation with the old crazy mentality that you can enact the evil drama of Atlantis. You'll surely fail like trampled flies just as you failed in Atlantis. If you think being smart is the key to your quest, I'll tell you the Guardians of the Universe are the smartest of all beings and the Universe is our play."

Two unforgettable faces he remembered in that fretful crowd were Anne and Lina. He did not forget either the faces of a mélange of other colleagues, mostly men in the Brotherhood. But at the moment, Anne and Lina stood out as sore thumbs belonging to distinct hands of a cursed body. They were the indisputable avengers of the Atlantis drama where he had held sway.

Again, he could not explain in whole Lina's conflict of motives. Her actions and utterances at protecting him seem to negate her avenging consciousness. Why would she agree to protect him when she had the right tool and opportunity to ruin him forever?

She might have been in a rival group of the Locci. He thought that Lina's war with the woman referred to as Anne in her revelations, implied this. But there was a catch here too. She could not have meddled with the

Guardians' plans if she thought he would by his sleekness of character deny her the savoring of the meal on the table. And he knew her mentality - she often bragged like Anne that she had a firm hold on him - reasoning he needed her support to feel safe at all times.

Netu laughed at himself, startling Anne. Fools they all are to think they've got me where they wanted as their pawn.

"Anything the matter?" Anne pried.

A cunning smile glared on Netu's face. "It's personal."

For three years he had been with Anne. Yet in those three years she had never known the pleasures of uninhibited love making with him due to the depth of what he knew about her. He felt now the right time had come for him to gain Anne's confidence and win the subtle war they had long embarked on. Of course, he had a clear mental picture that the only viable option he would use to win the war remained the weapon of passion.

He reckoned with Anne as a freak for spiritual energy. Anyone who would give it reined on her heartstrings as its master. He had plenty to give. In spite of her claim that she loved him, the basic thing she needed was his spiritual energy. With it she had access to infinite power. She craved for it. The same weakness, which Lina and other decoys of nefarious spiritual cliques had. And he needed a friend in the enemy's camp, an asset of inestimable value in the schemes of subtle war. Without wasting time, he exploited the window of opportunity.

"Anne, I want you to make love to me," he said, drawing her close.

"What was that again?" she demanded, disbelieving. The man she wanted most in her life and whom she could not have for three years offering himself wholesale without any cajoling. Cynicism crept into her head.

"I want you to take me as you please," he stressed. "Make love to me."

"Don't tease me, Netu. I know you don't mean it. You never would."

"Anne, I mean it. Just do it."

Anne wrestled with her conscience. "I don't want to be the one to spoil your aspirations, Netu. I like it the way we are. I'm used to your idea of playing safe. Let it be that way, please."

"I asked for it. You didn't force me, did you?"

She huffed, confused, hesitating, and then stirred with the instinctive energy of long suppressed passion. "Okay, I give in," she said, flailing her arms in submission. "But don't cast blame on me if anything should go wrong with you."

"Nothing would go wrong."

"Are you sure?"

"Of course, I'm sure," Netu assured her.

"That puts me in the clear!" Anne sighed heavily and began to undress in frenzy.

Netu watched Anne until she was done, and then with languid gentleness took off his own slacks and undies.

The next moment they were one sweet rhythm of blended forms. But the spurious concession would haunt Netu later with its inexplicabilities.

End of Book One